For Jem in appre effoats ... more comfortable

We Came From Königsberg

Max Overton (signature)

By Max Overton

Writers Exchange E-Publishing
http://www.writers-exchange.com

We Came From Königsberg
Copyright 2013 Max Overton
Writers Exchange E-Publishing
PO Box 372
ATHERTON QLD 4883

Cover Art by: Julie Napier

Published by Writers Exchange E-Publishing
http://www.writers-exchange.com

ISBN ebook: 978-1-922233-10-3
Print: 978-1-922233-10-3

Foreword

Elisabet Daeker and her family exist, though their names have been altered at the request of the surviving family members. They want the tale of their remarkable 'Mutti' told, for the benefit of their own families, so that her sacrifice and determination should live on, but they also wish to preserve their privacy. Their harrowing journey from Königsberg in East Prussia to Schöppenstedt in West Germany (and beyond) is a matter of record, and the events of that terrible time were extracted from the memories of her children many years later. Joachim, Werner and Kurt were especially helpful, showing me documents, suggesting reading material, and regaling me with anecdotes dredged from their memories. Some of these half-remembered events conflicted with known history, so I have massaged their tales into what I believe is a coherent account of a very brave and loving woman in a chaotic period of German history.

Names have been changed throughout this book, and any coincidence with real persons is just that – coincidence. I have put speech into silent mouths, given movement to still limbs and ascribed motives as I saw fit. If I have offended anyone, I apologise in advance. This is a story where fleshly fiction is wrapped around the bare bones of truth.

As a point of interest, I lived in Düsseldorf for a few years in the late 1950s, and visited many of the places in which the Daeker family lived at that time. I used, as an eight or nine year old boy, to cycle in the flat land bordering the Rhein, and it is entirely possible that, in the farmland around Lohausen, my path actually crossed with that of a teenage Joachim.

--Max Overton

Reference books consulted in the writing of this story:

The Fall of Hitler's Fortress City: The Battle for Königsberg, 1945
Isabel Denny, 2007, Casemate Publishers.

Nazi Germany and the Jews: Volume 1. The Years of Persecution, 1933-1939
Saul Friedlander, 1997, HarperCollins Publishers.

Germany 1945: From War to Peace
Richard Bessel, 2009, Simon & Schuster UK Ltd.

Gotterdammerung 1945: Germany's Last Stand in the East
Russ Schneider, 1998, Eastern Front/Warfield Books Inc.

The Essential Hitler: Speeches and Commentary
Max Domarus, Edited by Patrick Romane, 2007, Bolchazy-Carducci Publishers Inc.

Red Storm on the Reich: The Soviet March on Germany, 1945
Christopher Duffy, 1991, De Capo Press

After the Reich: The Brutal History of the Allied Occupation
Giles MacDonogh, 2007, Basic Books

The Atlas of World War II
Dr. John Pimlott, 2006, Courage Books

Blue Division Soldier 1941-45: Spanish Volunteer
on the Eastern Front
C. Caballero Jurado, 2009, Osprey Publishing Limited

Kapitel Eins (1)

The navigator sat bent over his charts, the bone-shaking roar and vibration of four Rolls-Royce Merlin engines almost ignored as he plotted the course of the Lancaster bomber. He checked his figures once more and thumbed the intercom.

"Five minutes out from Bornholm Island, Skipper. Ahead and slightly to port."

"Roger, Dickie. I see it."

Dickie counted down the five minutes and spoke again. "Correct course to 090 degrees, Skipper."

"Roger."

Dickie felt the Avro Lancaster bank slightly to starboard.

"Coming up on 090 degrees...mark."

"Forty-two minutes until we turn onto our bombing run, Skipper. Then nine minutes to target."

"Roger, Dickie."

The navigator went over his calculations, noted the time and checked it against sunset times for their position. Night would be blanketing the earth beneath them, but at twenty thousand feet they still experienced a glimmer of rapidly fading daylight. He checked his figures once more, then flicked off his desk light and drew the heavy curtain back. Forward, in the darkness, he could make out the hunched shapes of the Skipper and the co-pilot, the faint glow of their instruments, and beyond them only the blackness of the eastern sky. He knew, though, that in front, behind, and on either side were other Lancasters, all moving along parallel courses that would, within the hour, bring them over the East Prussian city of Königsberg. The bomb load dropped on the city would be devastating.

"You could almost feel sorry for the poor buggers," he murmured.

*   *   *

The sun set through a bank of low cloud that evening at the end of August 1944, flooding the smoke-tainted air with ominous shades of red and orange. Families walked the tree-lined streets and parks of old Königsberg, enjoying a brief promenade in the warm evening air. Workers laboured to remove the rubble from bomb-ravaged sites or quench the fires that still smouldered in the eastern quarter of the old city. From time to time, families and workers alike looked up into the darkening skies with varying degrees of apprehension or fear. The waxing moon, washed out and pale in the western sky and just over three-quarter full, was still several hours from setting, and would later cast its pallid glow over a darkened city. Moonlight, and the scattered glow of embers from burnt-out buildings would, that night, aid any cold and hungry eyes looking down through bomb-sights on the city from twenty thousand feet.

The air war had largely passed by Königsberg, the city being too far distant from the main theatres of conflict for bombers to reach easily. However, German military reverses on the Eastern Front were changing this: Soviet aircraft were increasingly raiding the area, but so far had inflicted little damage. Then three nights previously, a large force of British Lancaster bombers had suddenly appeared out of the western darkness and rained down a deadly storm of explosives on the unsuspecting eastern suburbs. The fires still burned, and though casualties had been light, few people had slept each night since until the approach of daylight had removed the likelihood of renewed attack.

Darkness fell, shrouding the old city, and its citizens hurried about their business, praying that the enemy would leave their home alone. The men of the Luftschutzpolizei – air raid wardens – made their rounds, searching out unnecessary lights and checking on bomb shelters. Motor traffic died away and silence descended, broken only by the distant sounds of the rail yard, and the murmur of roosting sparrows in the trees that lined the streets. Stars emerged, fading and brightening as skeins of smoke sifted across the sky. The moonlight strengthened, casting a silver glow over the waiting city.

Elisabet Daeker, a young woman of Königsberg, was too busy to wait for enemy bombs to fall. She had a large family to feed, and no man to help her. The bombs of three nights ago had fallen far from her home and had not fallen since, so she put all thoughts of the war from her mind, and concentrated on the needs of her family. Her mother had died the previous year but her seventy-five year old father still lived in a small apartment – fiercely independent and resisting any attempts by his children to take care of him. Her mother had left Elisabet her share of the proceeds from the sale of the farm years before, so she still had Reich marks in the bank.

Although food rationing limited the diet of the citizens, Elisabet had managed to provide for her family by judicious use of official rations, augmented by fresh produce from her uncle Erich's farm near Elbing, south of the city. These occasional shipments of eggs, milk, butter and vegetables – sometimes even a little meat – almost fell under the category of black marketeering and might have attracted severe penalties – incarceration or worse – if the local officials had known and chosen to act. However, her late husband

3

had been a Party member, and if the officials knew of any wrongdoing, they turned a blind eye, looking after their own. Elisabet disregarded such dangers for her family's sake, though she was cautious in her breaking of the law. Nothing was to be gained by overt resistance to punitive laws, but she was not above a little subtle subterfuge if it benefited her family.

Elisabet lifted the lid of the iron pot on the stove, releasing a gust of scented steam. She stirred the stew and tasted the simmering liquid, nodding with satisfaction.

"Helmut," she called, wiping her hands on her apron. "Come and set the table. Kurt, make sure your brothers have washed their hands."

A small dark-haired boy ran into the kitchen and stopped abruptly, lifting his face and sniffing, a smile breaking out across his face. "It smells nice, Mutti."

Behind him, a larger tow-headed boy bumped into the smaller child and shoved him to one side. "You're in the way again, Kurt."

"Mutti called us both."

"But she told you to get the children's' hands washed, dummkopf. So what are you doing in here?"

"Helmut, be kind to your brother," Elisabet reproved. "Kurt, go and do as I said."

"Yes Mutti," Kurt said, and ducked out of the room. Helmut shrugged and crossed to the sideboard, where he took out six large plates and six small ones. He carried them across to the kitchen table and set them out, adding cutlery, cups and glasses.

Elisabet carried over a wooden cutting board and knife, together with a loaf of fresh-baked bread still warm from the oven and a small dish of butter. She sliced the bread and lightly buttered it, setting out one slice on each small plate. The deep yellow butter melted into the warm bread, pooling like liquid gold, the aroma of the bread augmenting the rich smell of the stew.

Two small boys and a toddler came tumbling and laughing into the kitchen, ushered in by Kurt. The dark-haired boy pulled them into a rough line near the sink for inspection, though the toddler ran straight to his mother.

"Hands all washed?" Elisabet asked. "Let me see." She bent to examine the upraised hands, lifting them gently to her face to imbibe the fresh scents of soap and the unique smell of each of her children. "Very good, Werner...you too Günter." The toddler tugged at her skirts and she turned her attention to him with a smile. "Hmm, what's this, Joachim, you seem to have missed a spot. Here..." She rubbed at the offending smudge of dirt with the corner of her apron before turning her attention to the older boys. "Good, Kurt...and you, Helmut." Elisabet nodded her satisfaction and gestured toward the table. "Take your places, children."

Elisabet served the meal, ladling out generous portions of the vegetable stew onto the plates, and pouring half glasses of milk for the three youngest children. The older boys and she enjoyed cups of weak ersatz coffee. They set to with a will, and for several minutes the only sound was of the clatter of cutlery against china and polite requests for another slice of bread.

As the first pangs of hunger were assuaged, murmurings of conversation arose. The two younger boys, Werner and Günter, chattered away in low tones about some private subject, sometimes including Joachim, while the older boys talked of things that had occupied their day. Elisabet listened, and only interjected if the conversation was in danger of straying from the paths of wholesomeness.

"Konrad Schultz showed me his dagger today," Helmut remarked. "It's a beauty. His father gave it to him because he's being sworn in as Hitlerjugend on Saturday."

"Did he let you hold it?" Kurt asked.

Helmut hesitated, struggling with his desire to appear more important. "No, but he held it close so I could see it properly. I'm going to have one when I join, aren't I, Mutti?"

"We'll see, but that's a long way off. You can't join until you're fourteen."

"But I can join the Deutsches Jungvolk when I'm ten."

"That's a year away yet. Besides, I need you to help me at home, Helmut. You must be the man of the house."

Pride warred with disappointment in the young boy's face, but he shrugged and changed the topic of conversation. "Anton says there are dead people in the ruins of Kirchen Strasse."

"We will hope not," Elisabet said. "However, that is not a suitable thing to talk about at the dinner table," she added.

"Afterward?" Kurt asked.

"No. How was school today?"

"All right. Two boys got into a fight in the playground."

"I saw that," Helmut said. "Victor started it. He said Rudi's mother was a...a Pole."

"What's a Pole?" Werner asked.

"Someone who comes from Poland, dummkopf," Helmut jeered.

6

"Enough, Helmut," Elisabet said. "Apologise to your brother."

"Yes, Mutti. Sorry Kleine Junge."

"Why is somebody from Poland bad?" Günter asked.

"Herr Vogler says they are untermenschen, not real people. He says..."

"That is enough, Helmut. You should not be listening to Herr Vogler. He is a troublemaker."

"He's our teacher and a Party member..."

"Yes, and you are too young to tell the difference between propaganda and truth. Do not believe everything that man says."

"Papa was a Party member too," Günter said.

"Where did you hear that?" Elisabet asked. "You were too young when he left."

Günter glanced at Helmut, who shrugged. "I told him," the older boy admitted.

"Your father was a good man. Nothing like Herr Vogler. You shouldn't compare them just because they were both National Socialists. Lots of people belong to the Party and many of them are decent, honest people who are just trying to..." Elisabet broke off and took a deep breath, calming herself. "All I'm saying is, you shouldn't judge people by who they happen to be, only by what they do. Do you understand?"

"Yes, Mutti," Helmut muttered. The other boys nodded, though the younger ones looked doubtful. Joachim just giggled and beat the table with his spoon.

"Now, help me clear away the dishes and I'll read you a story."

For several minutes, the only sound in the kitchen was that of plates being gathered up and placed by the sink. Elisabet ran water and added a little soap, scrubbing them clean and handing them to the older boys to dry. Werner and Günter put them away in the sideboard, while Joachim sat at his mother's feet and dabbled his fingers in splashes of water that spilled onto the hardwood floor. As she reached the last dish, Elisabet stopped and cocked her head, listening.

Helmut looked at his mother. "What's wrong, Mutti?"

"Shh, listen."

The other boys put down the plates in their hands and turned towards their mother, apprehension starting to show on their faces. Distantly, a siren climbed in pitch, winding up laboriously and holding its desolate, wailing cry for half a minute before descending to a growl. It rose again, and now another, nearer, started up, like wolves baying at a bomber's moon.

Elisabet dried her hands on her apron and turned to face her children. "Go and put on your shoes and coats immediately. Use the toilet if you need to and wait for me in the hall."

Günter started to cry. "What is it, Mutti? What's happening?"

"Just another air raid. Nothing to worry about, but we need to go to the shelter, just like we did three nights ago. Nothing happened to us then, did it? Now get ready, quickly."

"It's those British bombers again, isn't it?" Helmut asked.

"Very likely, now go and get ready – hurry."

"I hate them," Helmut declared. He ran to get his coat and the other children followed.

Elisabet set about collecting what they would need for the evening. Since the last air raid three nights before, she had prepared a bag containing blankets and

8

cushions, some cork-stoppered bottles of water which she had renewed daily, a tin cup, and a box of home-made biscuits. She quickly checked the contents before lacing up her sturdy shoes and shrugging into a heavy coat. The evening was warm, but she knew it was better to have too much in the way of clothing than too little.

"Is everyone ready?" she called out.

Elisabet went out into the hall and checked over each child, making sure their coats were buttoned and shoelaces tied. Werner had his shoes on the wrong feet so she knelt and quickly changed them over.

"Can we take our toys?" Günter asked.

"Only if you can fit them in your pockets. Now hurry, the planes are getting closer."

The children scurried to find a favourite toy and thrust it into a pocket, and within two minutes were back in the hall, though Joachim dragged a small stuffed horse behind him. Elisabet added it to her bag and took her youngest son by the hand.

"All right, stay close together. Helmut looks after Werner, Kurt looks after Günter, and Joachim stays by me." Elisabet picked up the heavy bag and switched out the light so it would not contravene the black-out laws when she opened the door.

The sound of the sirens rising and falling was much louder out in the street, and the western sky was lit by moving pillars of light showing up in the smoke and dust-filled air. Yellow flashes and the distant crump of explosions told of the inexorable approach of the falling bombs and of the anti-aircraft fire directed by the city's defenders. Every now and then, a ghostly cross would hang in the columns of light for a few moments and flashes of light would march across the sky to meet it. The howl of the sirens now had a counterpoint of sharp explosions and the darkened streets were lit as though from a summer lightning storm.

"Hurry." Elisabet led her family down the street and round the corner to a small beer hall whose cellar had been turned into a bomb shelter for surrounding streets. The beer hall itself was a burnt-out shell, having succumbed to a fire unrelated to enemy action earlier in the year. A Luftschutzpolizei guard ushered them down the steps as the first explosions sounded off to the west.

"Hurry, Frau Daeker," the guard urged. "Those verdamten British bombs are coming closer."

The cellar was lit by electric bulbs strung on wires from the ceiling and already contained forty or fifty people – mostly women and children. Elisabet guided her children to a vacant section near the bottom of the stairs and sat them down in a small circle on the dusty floor. A woman sitting nearby with her two sons and young daughter smiled and made room for them. The occupants of the shelter looked toward the newest arrivals, some nodding a greeting or saying something, others just looking away after a few moments.

The guard closed the cellar doors and the sound of the sirens and explosions became muted, though a faint vibration could still be detected through the walls and floor of the shelter. Every now and then the floor would shudder as a bomb fell somewhere close, and a deep 'crump' would make people look up in alarm. The electric lighting flickered and a few people readied candles in preparation for a power failure.

Elisabet sat her children around her, huddling close, with Joachim in her arms and told them stories – some bedtime ones from the big book of Grimm fairy tales they had at home, and when the subject matter seemed a bit dark for their present situation, she switched to tales of her childhood and stories of her parents, the boys' Opa and Oma. They laughed at her recollections, for she tried to talk only of good memories – sleigh rides in the winter, picking apples in the autumn orchards, or running along country lanes in the spring when all the trees were in new leaf and bluebells carpeted the forest glades. As she talked, the woman and her children drew close to listen, and Elisabet made room for them.

"That is lovely," the woman said, after an anecdote about escaped chickens and rounding them up. "You were so fortunate to grow up in the country." She blushed. "I'm sorry, my name is Marlene Theiss. These are my children – Jan, Ernst and Lotte."

A fair-haired boy of about twelve looked up, his expression intense and serious. "Guten abend, Frau." His brother, slightly darker and half his age, nodded his head shyly, but his sister, a beautiful blonde child of ten smiled and said 'hello'. Elisabet responded with introductions of herself and all her children. The boys greeted the Theiss family politely, though Joachim said nothing and Helmut eyed Jan with wary hostility.

"You did not grow up in the country?" Elisabet asked.

Marlene shook her head. "I was born in Berlin, and grew up there. A big city is not such a great place for children."

"Königsberg is a lovely place though."

"Oh yes, I came here to be closer to my husband Dolf. He was given the post of Stationmaster on the trains until...until he volunteered. He could not bear to see other men marching off to glory and him being

11

left behind. He..." Tears gleamed in Marlene's eyes and she looked away.

Elisabet reached over and squeezed the other woman's hand. "He volunteered for the Front?" She sighed. "Mine did too and..."

A roar and crash of timbers cut her off as the cellar shuddered and shook. The lights flickered and went out, plunging the room into darkness. Women and children screamed and men shouted out in alarm. Elisabet clutched her children close and in the darkness held little Lotte along with Joachim. The lights flared, dimmed and steadied, and a fine rain of plaster fell from the cracked ceiling. People looked at one another, fear slowly being replaced on most faces by relief, though some now displayed anger. Crying children were comforted by their mothers and conversation started up again, though the tenor was now very different.

"Those verdamten British swine," swore an old man. "Who wages war on the innocent, eh? If they were down here instead of in their cowardly airplanes, I'd show them."

"Sure you would old man," jeered a youth in the far corner of the cellar. "It's quite a different thing when you have to face a man with a weapon in his hands. You wouldn't be so brave then."

"What makes you think I haven't, you junger Spund? I'll have you know I was in the Great War, when our victorious army showed those damn British and French how to fight."

The young man laughed. "Yet you lost."

"We were stabbed in the back by the Bolsheviks and Jews at home."

"That's right," another man exclaimed. "But not this time. Our Führer is leading us to victory."

12

"That's not what I've heard," muttered a one-legged man seated on a bench along one wall. "The Russians are coming."

"That is defeatist talk," snapped a thin old man with a small smudge of moustache just like his revered leader.

"Can you deny it? Listen to the stories of soldiers invalided home from Russia. Things are not going well for us in the East."

"You dare to say we are defeated?" spluttered the thin old man. "My son is SS Unterscharführer Brandt in the Auschwitz Konzentrationslager, and if he heard you say that, he'd drag you out and arrest you. You'd probably be shot, and good riddance, I say."

There were murmurs of agreement from several other people and One-leg hunched head down on his bench and tried not to meet anyone's eyes.

"Does anyone else agree with this traitor?" Old Man Brandt asked. "The Führer has promised us victory, and how indeed can we lose when our enemies are sub-human? I mean, Jews and Slavs and Russians – one good German soldier is worth a hundred of them."

"I don't doubt it, but what of the British and Americans in the West?" asked another man. "I've heard that they are good fighters and have invaded France and Italy."

"They will be thrown back into the sea. Our Führer has promised it."

"Well, that's all right then," the man said with a smile.

"Your comments sound defeatist too," Brandt said. "I should report you."

The man shrugged. "I only say what many people think." The cellar shuddered again, the lights flickering but remaining on, and more dust fell from the ceiling. "They promised us that no bombs would fall on German soil, yet here we are."

Brandt snarled and glared around him. "The only reason our enemies succeed in anything they do is because we have traitors in our midst, people who give less than full commitment to our eventual victory."

"Many of us here have made sacrifices for the Fatherland, old man. I look around and I see fatherless children, widows, other fine German women whose husbands, brothers or sons are facing death on a daily basis, while you sit here in relative safety boasting of a son whose only risk is in guarding helpless men locked behind barbed wire, far from the Front."

Brandt flushed and his voice quivered. "How dare you, you traitor. I demand to know your identity. I intend to report you to the authorities."

The man stood, a tall man with a lined face and haunted eyes, grey haired though still young. He stood to attention in his rumpled Volkssturm uniform and faced his accuser. "I'd salute, old man, but I lost my right arm fighting the Russians at Kharkov eighteen months ago. Eleventh Panzer division. I also lost a brother and nearly a hundred of my comrades in the same battle. I returned home to find my house destroyed, my family dead, and everything I knew in ruins. Do not talk to me of sacrifice and commitment." He started to sit down again and stopped. "Oh yes, you need my name to report me – I am <u>Zugführer</u> Ernst Hirsch of the Königsberg Volkssturm."

He sat down and slowly people started clapping. A woman passed him a biscuit, and another, a cup of ersatz coffee. Old Man Brandt visibly shrivelled though he still scribbled the man's name down on a piece of paper.

Despite the continued rain of bombs and the wail of sirens heard mutedly through the shelter doors, few of the explosions came near enough to shake the nerves or precipitate more dust, and the children fell asleep, curled up in blankets near their mothers. Elisabet and Marlene stayed close, sharing resources and taking comfort in a common experience.

"Do you think he is right?" Marlene whispered.

"Who? The old man?"

"No, the one he accused of defeatism, the man with the missing leg. The one who said the Russians are coming."

Elisabet was silent for a time. She debated the risk of saying what she thought and weighed it against her feeling for another woman struggling to bring up children alone. In the end, she decided to trust Marlene, though she cast a wary eye toward the thin old man who still glared angrily at the young Zugführer.

"I think it very likely the Russians are coming," she whispered.

"But the Army will protect us, won't it? The radio broadcasts say we are winning victory after victory."

"To say otherwise is defeatist," Elisabet observed. "Yet our victories edge ever closer to home. I think there is something they are not telling us."

Marlene shivered. "What are the Russians like? You hear stories."

"I think they are men like other men."

"That bad?"

Elisabet smiled. "There are some good ones, as I'm sure you know. What I meant was that Russians are not monsters, merely men who are no doubt angry that their homes have been destroyed and their fami-

15

lies killed. They may want to take revenge on Germans if they get the chance."

Marlene thought about this. "But we are innocent. I've never hurt a Russian."

Elisabet checked that her children were asleep. Joachim shifted and opened his eyes briefly before falling asleep again. "We may be innocent ourselves, but terrible things have been done in the name of the German people," she said. "When my husband was home on leave, he would tell me of things he saw in Russia and Poland. Men and women killed indiscriminately, even children. Villages burnt and cattle slaughtered. My husband said that if ever the Russians were in a position to invade Germany, they would exact a terrible vengeance. He said if that ever happened, I was to flee to the West as fast as I could."

"How? There are restrictions on people leaving the city, and even if you could get permission, where would you go?"

"I don't know. My grandparents owned a farm near Elbing. My uncle owns it now. I could probably go there."

"If the Russians come to Königsberg, they'll come to Elbing too," Marlene pointed out. "I think I just want to get as far away from Russia as possible."

"I have relatives in Dresden," Elisabet said. "That should be safe enough."

"Providing you can get permission to go there." Marlene yawned and shook her head. "How much longer do you think this air raid will go on for?"

"Who knows? Get some sleep if you want to. I'll keep an eye on the children."

Elisabet got up and went round the children, drawing up the blankets and adjusting cushions in an attempt to make them comfortable. Werner woke while she knelt beside him.

"Is it over, Mutti?"

"Not yet. Go back to sleep."

The young girl, Lotte, was fast asleep beside her mother, and Elisabet settled herself with her back to the wall where she could see all eight children and Marlene. She smiled as she looked at each of her sons in turn, and then at the blonde curls of little Lotte.

"What is her life going to be like, living in such a terrible time?" she whispered to herself. "I, at least, enjoyed a happy and peaceful childhood..."

*   *   *

Memories are strange things. I have very few from an early age, most being little more than half-remembered incidents that seemed to happen to someone else. Most of my early memories are about nothing – or almost nothing. For instance, I can remember sitting in my mother's lap near a warm wood fire on a winter's evening, and watching my brother Hans playing on the floor with his toys. My father sat opposite us, reading a newspaper and smoking his pipe. The scent of the tobacco smoke was quite distinctive and smelling it again always brings this scene to mind. Nothing else happened – there was nothing to imprint it on my memory, yet there it is, my earliest memory. I must have been no more than three or four years old.

Other early memories are jumbled and it is hard to put them in order. I can remember helping my mother in the kitchen and being covered in flour. I can dimly recall being afraid of something that I thought lived under my bed until father showed me I could chase it away by standing up to it and refusing to be afraid. I remember school and a playground bully

17

who made me cry. Hans came to my aid and dried my tears, picking a wildflower from beside the road to bring a smile to my face once more. I enjoyed some lessons – ones on the geography of distant lands, or being read poetry, or painting. I remember those quite clearly, and can even call up images of some of my teachers, but though I must have learnt arithmetic and history, I cannot recall a single thing from those classes.

The different seasons figure prominently in my early memories – hot summer days where we would picnic in the shade of leafy trees, or swim in the sea, and warm still evenings when father would take us outside to look at the stars. He could name many of them and Hans learnt them off, reciting them back to him to earn a word of praise, but I just wove stories around their names. I would tell these to my mother and she would laugh and clap her hands at my inventiveness.

Autumn brought the ripening of crops and we would all go to my grandparents' farm near Elbing to pick apples. I would help with the milking and watch as my Oma churned the milk in an old wooden churn, bringing out globs of fresh gold butter. We would go down to the seashore too, making a day trip of it, letting the chill wind off the Frisches Haff bring a glow to our cheeks, the salt spray lifting from the crashing waves and matting our hair, sand grains stinging our bare legs. Our feet would sink in the white sand or crunch on the drifts of broken shell as we collected shiny stones, and once – the incident stands out in my memory – father found a small sea-polished piece of amber, gold and translucent, looking like a drop of liquid sunlight. He had it set in silver as a brooch for my mother.

Winter is a hard season, but can bring joy to children. I used to play in the snow and make snowmen with my brother's help. Sometimes my father would pull us through the snowy country lanes on a sled, or we would race down a hill, laughing and screaming with exhilaration as the icy air burnt our cheeks. I remember hot milk drinks in front of the fire, and the deliciously safe feeling of sitting in our little parlour of an evening while a storm raged impotently outside. Father would turn the radio on and through the crackle we would hear strains of operatic music or news broadcasts of people talking about things that made no sense to me.

Spring brought a release and the burgeoning new life in the countryside lifted our spirits once more. The sun shone warmly, the trees put out fresh new leaves, and flowers pushed up through the thawing soil – bluebells covering the wooded ground like a blanket of smoke, daffodils thrusting up through the fresh green grass. Birds built nests and Hans would risk life and limb, climbing high to secure an egg which would be blown carefully and added to his collection. I was discouraged from climbing, and in truth had little desire to do so, but we would compete to see the first schmetterling of the year. Hans was more active than I, and roamed further across the countryside, so was often the first to see one. It was usually a lemon-yellow butterfly fluttering in the buckthorn hedgerows, while in the fields between the buckthorn hedges, calves bawled for their mothers and lambs leapt and raced over fresh new turf under fair skies.

As I said, I can remember all these things from my childhood, but fail utterly if I try to put them in order. The only events I can date with any certainty were in the summer of 1924 when my grandfather died and my parents moved to a new farm in Metgethen, and 1930 when we moved to Königsberg. We still made forays into the countryside to visit my grandparents' farm near Elbing, though it was then owned by my father's elder brother Erich. For the rest, I became a city girl and swapped the freedom of the countryside for the fascination of an old and historical city...

* * *

Another explosion jolted Elisabet back into full wakefulness. The cellar was plunged into darkness and dust and plaster rained down on the huddled inhabitants. Children awoke and many started screaming again. The electric light did not come back on, and several men lit candles or flicked on cigarette lighters, casting little flickering pools of light among the shadows of the cellar. After a few minutes, the Luftschutzpolizei guard produced a battered kerosene lantern and lit it, illuminating the frightened faces of the people nearest the doors.

"That was a close one," the guard said, "But we mustn't worry. We're quite safe down here."

The guard grimaced a few minutes later when another bomb cracked the ceiling of the shelter, showering debris over the refugees. He moved everyone back from the centre of the floor, though the cellar was so crowded the open space was no more than a few paces across.

"We should leave," said a woman.

"Nonsense," replied the guard. "We're safer here than in the streets with bombs falling."

"Unless the ceiling collapses."

The cellar shuddered again and they heard a huge crash above them and the sound of rubble falling on the cellar doors.

"We'll be buried alive," a man yelled. "Let us out."

Several people moved toward the cellar doors and the guard moved across to bar the way. "I'm in charge," he said. "And I say we remain."

"Mutti," Günter whispered. "I'm frightened."

"There's nothing to be worried about. Stand close to me and hold the blankets over your heads – that's it."

Through the cellar doors they could hear a cacophony of wailing sirens, the whistle of falling bombs and the dull crash and thump of explosions and the rumble of falling masonry. Smoke seeped under the cellar doors and mingled with the dust in the air to start people coughing.

"Fire!" a woman screamed. "We'll be burned alive."

People surged toward the doors, pushing the protesting guard to one side and pulled the doors open. Broken bricks and rubble tumbled inward as the doors opened and a blast of hot air made several people cry out in alarm. In the street beyond, the night had been banished by the glow of fires, and smoke and dust filled the air.

Elisabet waited until most of the other refugees had left the shelter before venturing out, her children clinging to her in terror. She stumbled over the rubble and edged out into the partial shelter of a building next door to the burnt out beer hall. The remaining walls had collapsed inward and the pile of rubble groaned as it shifted, threatening to descend into the cellar below.

The sirens still wailed, but the crash of exploding bombs slowly moved away toward the city boundaries, leaving relative calm in their wake. Elisabet looked around, judging the safest place for her family and led her children back around the corner to their street and their home. They had to step over rubble and once had to skirt a smoking crater in the street. There were many people about but all were busy with their own business and nobody bothered a young woman and her five children. As they reached their house, the sirens wound down and the All-Clear sounded.

Their house was unscathed, though other homes along their street had suffered superficial damage. The electric power was off, apparently for several streets around them, so the houses were all in darkness. Elisabet let them in and lit candles, leaving the children sitting around the table in the kitchen while she made a quick check of the rooms to make sure there was no real damage. She heated a little milk on the wood stove, and the boys sat and drank it, eating a plate of biscuits between them before being led off to bed. The younger boys were still frightened by their experiences and insisted on sleeping with their mother, so Elisabet tucked them all in her bed, leaving only the two older boys, Helmut and Kurt, to sleep in their own bedroom. They boasted that they were not frightened, but after an hour, crept into their mother's room with blankets and pillows and lay down between the bed and the wall.

Elisabet stretched out an arm to her eldest sons, careful not to disturb the youngsters already asleep beside her, and smiled. "Sleep well, meine lieben kleinen."

Kapitel Zwei (2)

Life continued, but the attitudes of people changed after the bombing raids. Whereas before, people willingly believed the propaganda churned out by newspapers and radio that the gallant Wehrmacht was pushing the Russian forces back and that victory was imminent, now people opened their eyes and saw the damage that the war had wrought on their beloved city. Much of the city was in ruins, particularly the central area where many old buildings had been damaged and fire had gutted many more. The death toll was horrific, and more bodies were being discovered daily as workers slowly sifted through the rubble. This ability of the enemy to inflict such damage spoke not of a foe being hurled back by the forces of Aryan Righteousness, but rather of an enemy rampant and dangerous.

The bombers had not returned after that second terrible raid, yet the damage had been done, both to the physical city and the spirit of its inhabitants. Fear gripped the populace and many fled the city for the relative safety of the countryside before Erich Koch, Gauleiter of Königsberg, called a halt. Those leaving the city were defeatists and cowards, he said. He hauled a few able-bodied men before Party courts and had them publicly hanged to deter further desertion. It worked, and though unrest was evident in the city, few now tried to flee.

Then, within less than a month, the Gauleiter changed his mind. Perhaps it was because he had a genuine change of heart, but more likely he envisaged thousands of useless mouths to feed when the Russian Army arrived and Königsberg devolved into a fortress city, holding out until the last man and the last round of ammunition. Koch declared that women with young children were to be evacuated to small towns in the surrounding countryside until such time as the fearless German forces under the inspired leadership of the Führer freed the city from the threat of the Bolshevik horde.

Elisabet applied to be evacuated to her uncle's farm near Elbing, but the administrators were having none of it. The town of Mohrungen in the southwest was her designated destination and she would not be permitted out of the town except by special permit. Evacuation centres had already been assigned and Frau Daeker was to present herself with her children to the temporary passenger railway station at the Güterbahnhof on the south side of Königsberg on the twenty-seventh of September for evacuation. Miraculously, this freight yard and a single line had escaped damage during the air raid that had destroyed so much of the city.

The problem of what to take was perplexing. The evacuation notice made no mention of allowances beyond saying that transport would be by train and that space was limited. Nobody could say how long they would be away from the city, making it harder to judge what they would need. The most anyone would say is that they could return when the danger had passed. If Party broadcasts were to be believed, that meant a few weeks at most; if you listened to the hints dropped by returning soldiers, it might be months or years before they could return home – or never. Elisabet decided on a compromise of six months.

The next day, after the older children went to school, and the younger ones played together in the front room, Elisabet drew up a list of everything her family could possibly need for a six-month period. It was a very long list, and after reading it through, she started to whittle down quantities and eliminate some items altogether.

Rations were to be supplied, but Elisabet put aside her own tiny stocks of flour, salt and sugar, biscuits, and an assortment of tinned food – whatever she had in her pantry. She added pots and pans, crockery, cutlery, and cleaning supplies, before moving on to bedding and clothing. After a few hours she sighed and made herself a cup of ersatz coffee, sipping it and studying the voluminous list. Then she started crossing out items.

"If we take all this, we'll need a truck to move it."

Elisabet laid out the remaining items on the floor of the kitchen and bedrooms and dug out some battered suitcases and a few open-topped bags. She started packing, but quickly found she still had too much. More was put aside, but by the time the older children arrived home from school, Elisabet was no nearer being able to cram everything she wanted to take into the cases.

"What are you doing, Mutti?" Kurt asked.

"We have to leave the city for a while, and I'm packing what we need."

"Why do we have to leave?" Helmut asked. "I like it here."

"So do I, but the Gauleiter says all the families must leave. We are being sent south to Mohrungen, near the lakes. I'm sure it'll be lovely there and we'll all enjoy ourselves."

"Like a holiday?" Kurt asked.

"Yes, that's right. A holiday."

Helmut looked around at the bulging suitcases and the mounds of clothing and other things as yet unpacked. "We have to take all this? How long are we going for?"

"I don't know how long, but we should be prepared. Are you hungry?"

Elisabet took the older boys through into the kitchen, where she prepared some tinned meat sandwiches and a drink prepared from carrot and beet juice. The younger children came in, chattering about the games they had been playing, though Joachim sought his mother's arms and sat contentedly sucking on a crust and watching his brothers.

"What about Joachim's pram?" Kurt asked.

"What about it?"

"You could pile that up with clothes and stuff. It would be easy to push."

"We'll need it for Joachim. He can't walk far at his age."

"You could stuff things around him. He wouldn't mind."

"Is everyone going?" Helmut asked.

"Going where?" Werner asked.

"Are we going somewhere?" Günter chipped in. "When?"

Elisabet smiled. "Yes, we're going to stay somewhere out of the city for a while. The day after tomorrow. And yes, Helmut, we're all going. We're a family."

Helmut frowned. "What I meant was; is every family going? All our friends?"

"I'm not sure, but I think only those families without a father and with many children. Like us."

"So Anton Naumann won't be going? His father works on the trams and he has no brothers or sisters."

"Probably not. Why?"

"Well, I just thought, he has a big cart he made with old bicycle wheels. He might let me use it. We could pack a lot of stuff in it."

The next day, the twenty-sixth, was spent visiting relatives and friends in Königsberg. Elisabet had a single brother – Hans – who had lost a leg earlier in the war and now held down an office job. His wife and children had moved down to Dresden for safety, but Hans remained behind, unwilling to desert his post. Elisabet also had several aunts, uncles and cousins, together with their families, to visit and bid farewell. Many tears were shed and fervent assurances given that the separation would only be temporary. She then called on Hans.

"Come with us to Mohrungen," she said. "You've done your bit for the Fatherland."

"I'm surprised at you sister," he replied, though his smile took away the sting of his words. "The Russians are coming and I can still hold a rifle."

She thought she might be able to persuade her father. Her mother had died a year before and the old man – seventy-six next birthday – missed his wife terribly.

"Come with us, Vati, please. It is going to get very dangerous around here."

"Nonsense," the old man said. He looked around to make sure they were not overheard. "I regard the Russians as liberators. They will do away with Hitler once and for all."

"But Vati, they are killing our people everywhere."

"Only fascists, I'm sure. I'm a communist – I have been all my life. The Russians are my comrades and I will welcome them."

27

Elisabet bowed to the inevitable. "Well, it's not as if we are going across the world. We'll be in Mohrungen, and we can always write to each other."

Early on the morning of the twenty-seventh, Elisabet attempted to bring some order to the chaos within their house. She fed the children early and then, with the children handing her things, packed each bag and suitcase and strapped them onto Anton's cart, adding more items such as blankets to the top of the load and tying them on. Joachim's pram was also loaded up and each child dressed warmly, for the day was chilly with a hint of rain in the air.

Elisabet had, the day before, withdrawn part of her money from the bank. They had not allowed her to withdraw it all and had given her a receipt for the balance. She could only hope that her remaining funds would be available if and when they returned to the city. Elisabet took a last look around their home, switching off the lights and shutting and bolting the windows and doors. They all stood on the street outside for several minutes, looking at their home – the only one the children had known – and then silently turned and started down the street. Neighbours who were staying looked enviously at them, but wished them well anyway. Others – strangers – just stared. The streets were busy with people, a feeling of restlessness gripping the populace as women and children started gathering, moving toward the railway station. Helmut and Kurt pulled on the cart, while Werner and Günter pushed. Elisabet pushed the pram with one hand, and carried a bag in the other, while Joachim alternately toddled beside her or rode in the pram atop the luggage.

Street by street they moved south, and other fractured families joined them, swelling into a column of refugees moving through the stricken city toward the Pregel River, then over the Krämer Brücke onto the Kniephof, and by the Lange Gasse across the Grüne Brücke onto the south side and the freight yards. They passed many ruined buildings, but at least the rubble had been cleared from the streets, allowing easy passage. People lined the streets, watching the procession of refugees. Most stood in silence, expressions alternating between envy at their fellow citizens being allowed out of the doomed city, and pity at the hardships forced upon them. A few called out in sympathy or wished them good luck, but in general, the only sound was the shuffling of feet and the creak and thump of wooden-wheeled carts as they negotiated the pot-holed roads.

The freight yards were a tangled mess of craters and twisted metal, but a single track ran south and waiting by a makeshift station was an engine and a long train of carriages. Officials and soldiers stood waiting for the refugees and as they arrived, started pushing them into lines and grabbing baggage, throwing it aside. Voices lifted in protest, only to be overridden by the officials.

"Hand luggage only," called the freight agents. "You can only take what you can carry on board. There is no room for surplus baggage. Hand luggage only."

A woman had wrestled a hand cart close to the train before a guard stopped her.

"Not allowed. Leave it here."

"But this is a family heirloom – my grandmother's china cabinet. I cannot leave it behind."

The guard shrugged. "I have my orders. Women and children are to be evacuated, not china cabinets. Leave it here."

"No, I will not. Where is your Inspektor?"

The guard called over his superior officer, who listened to the woman's pleas. Then he called over two other guards and pointed to a nearby crater.

"Throw it in there."

The woman screamed a protest but the guards obeyed and the antique china cabinet shattered and broke in the rubble-strewn crater.

"This is not a game, citizens," the Inspektor said. "You are allowed hand luggage only. We do not have the room for anything more."

"But I have brought all these cases," said an old woman, pointing at a nearby cart. "I can't carry them all on. Please let me bring them all."

The Inspektor shook his head. "Choose what you want to take, or my men will choose for you." He lifted his voice to speak to the column of women and children. "You cannot take everything. There is no room. One bag per person. Choose now. After all," he added with a smirk, "There are plenty of craters that can be filled with the rest."

"I have a large family," Elisabet said. "If I am not allowed to bring everything I need for them, how am I to support myself and my family?"

"You will be issued with rations."

"I have a toddler, a young boy who cannot walk far. If I am forced to carry him I cannot carry a bag. How is this fair? Let me at least bring his pram."

"If I allowed you I would have to allow everyone..."

"And where is the harm in that? I am a good German housewife with five fine young sons. Are we to be treated badly just because we are being forced from our homes? Shame, Herr Inspektor, shame."

Several other women nearby likewise raised a clamour, uttering cries of 'Shame' and the Inspektor flushed and rapidly retreated to consult his own superiors. He returned a few minutes later.

"You are allowed one wheeled cart per family, but it must travel in the freight wagons, not the passenger wagons."

"Thank you, Herr Inspektor," Elisabet said. "Your kindness is noted."

The Inspektor refused to meet her gaze. "Just get aboard please."

Elisabet took out what she thought they might need on the journey and then tied the pram on top of the cart. She wheeled the whole thing to where other carts and prams were being loaded onto the freight wagons and waited as the carts before her were lifted aboard and secured in place. When it came to her turn, the soldiers shook their heads at the pram tied on top of the cart.

"One cart only. You heard the Inspektor."

"I have only one cart," Elisabet pointed out. "The Inspektor did not say what we could have in the cart. I choose to include a pram, which my youngest child will need wherever we are."

One soldier scratched his head and looked for the Inspektor, but the other one grinned. "She's got a point, Max. One cart, and who cares what's in it."

Max nodded. "All right. Unless we get specific orders to exclude such things, it's done. Hermann, help me stick it in the back. Aus den augen, aus dem sinn, and if the Inspektor comes along, we haven't seen it."

Elisabet gathered her children to her and, laden down with suitcases and bags, boarded one of the passenger wagons. The wagon was already crowded and many children were crying and complaining of

31

the heat and stuffiness. Despite the chill in the air, the lack of ventilation was rapidly turning the air foul.

"What are we to be packed in like this?" asked one woman. "Cattle?"

"Nein," another said with a bitter laugh. "Juden."

"The air will be better when we start to move," Elisabet reassured her boys.

They found a short bench seat and a patch of floor and camped on it, using the cases as a territory demarcation. Loading continued and the carriage filled, yet still the train stood in the station.

"When are we leaving?" Kurt asked.

"Soon."

"I want to go pinkeln," Günter said.

Elisabet looked around her and asked her neighbours if there were any facilities, but nobody knew of any. A few people said they could use one too if she found it. She stood, and with Günter holding her hand, started edging her way through the throng to the door. A guard turned her back as she sought to alight though.

"Please stay on board, Frau. We will be leaving soon."

"My son needs to use the toilet. There are no facilities."

The guard grimaced. "Let him climb down here. He can pinkeln on the wheel."

"What about myself? And other ladies? We need somewhere private."

"I don't know. Wait here, I will go and ask."

While the guard was absent, Elisabet let Günter use the wheel, and then sent him back to tell the other boys they could come, two at a time, to relieve themselves. Word swept through the carriage and many boys availed themselves of the opportunity. When the guard returned, with the Inspektor, it was to find a group of boys lined along the outside of the carriage, relieving themselves on the gravel of the train yards.

"Here, we can't have this," the Inspektor cried. "It's unsanitary and improper."

"What do you suggest we do then, Herr Inspektor?" Elisabet asked. "There are no toilets on the train."

The Inspektor looked up at her and frowned. "You again? You must use the...the freight yard facilities." He consulted his pocket watch and groaned. "We should have left an hour ago. Well, hurry up then, Frau. As soon as you've done, we can leave."

A number of other women climbed down and were led across the ruined freight yard toward some shattered buildings. As soon as the women in other carriages saw them, they clamoured for similar privileges, and it was another hour and a half before the last of the passengers had been hurried aboard the train.

Despite the urgings of the Inspektor and guards, however, it was another hour still before the carriages shuddered and the engine blew off a blast of steam, creaking and squealing into motion. The train crept through the train yards and onto the line south, passing slowly through ruined freight yards and past bombed out buildings. The train lurched and rattled but, by slow degrees, it moved out into the countryside.

The children were excited, crowding as close to the windows as they could, pointing and exclaiming as quite ordinary things slipped by, seen from an unusual viewpoint. Then the train ground to a halt. Steam blew back past the carriages and everybody wondered what had caused the delay. Someone asked a guard running past, but he just waved them away. After a few minutes, the train started up again in a series of jerks and continued on its laborious way.

Throughout the afternoon, the train rattled on at scarcely more than walking pace, stopping often for a few minutes at a time for no discernible reason. Once, they were shunted onto a branch line and waited for over an hour until a train passed slowly in the opposite direction, its flat freight cars laden with military hardware and its carriages full of soldiers. The children waved, and the soldiers raised a cheer, especially when they caught sight of the women on board. Then they were past, and their own train was backed out onto the main line and resumed its journey west of south.

The monotonous scenery – farms and forest – and the slow pace of travel, lulled the children and only the older ones stayed close by the windows. The younger ones fell asleep in their mothers' arms or clamoured for food and drink. There was a feeling of comradeship amongst the adult travellers, a feeling of shared hardship, and ones with an extra blanket or piece of food shared it willingly with their neighbours. Every few hours, usually close to a patch of forest or wooded area, the train would halt and the guards instructed everyone to stretch their legs and seek the shelter of the trees if they sought physical relief. They warned though, that they were to board the train again immediately the whistle blew, or else they would be left behind.

The same routine carried through the night, leading to disturbed sleep and fractious children by the next morning when the train steamed slowly into the Mohrungen station. Chaos ensued as the small town station was overwhelmed with refugees and their baggage. The freight wagons disgorged their loads, piled up on the platform, and women with crying children picked through the carts and suitcases for their belongings. Eventually, order was restored and the queues started, where families waited to be let through the barriers into the town.

Each woman gave her name and was handed a scrap of paper bearing the address of the rooms assigned to her, and a cursory set of directions. Also included were tokens for the first week's rations, to be collected daily from the town hall. Elisabet took her papers and walked through into the town with her five children. The older boys pulled the cart once more and Elisabet pushed the pram with Joachim in it while the younger boys each carried bags.

"Where are we going, Mutti?" Helmut asked.

Elisabet looked at the piece of paper in her hand. "Kampf Strasse."

"Why is it called that, Mutti?" Werner asked.

"I don't know. Perhaps there was a battle around here."

"I bet it was the Wehrmacht driving the Russians out," Kurt said.

"Don't be a dummkopf," Helmut said. "This is Ostpreussen. The Russians have never been here." He thought about it for a few seconds. "Nor will they ever be," he added.

"Will our house have a garden?" Günter asked.

"I don't know, liebes kind. Let's wait and see – and Helmut, don't call your brother names."

"Yes Mutti," Helmut said, but stuck out his tongue at Kurt when his mother looked away.

They found the house, but not until they had pushed and pulled their carts through the main part of the town and onto a road that led down to a little

35

stream. The house itself was large and had at some point obviously been a boarding house as there was a little foyer and stairs disappearing into shadows pervaded by the aroma of cooking cabbage. An old man came out to greet them. He leaned on a walking stick and regarded the little group with a sour expression.

"You'll be Frau Daeker," he stated. "You're late. We expected you last night."

"The train only arrived in Mohrungen this morning."

The old man looked at Elisabet's five children with a grimace. "Five? We were told two. You're going to be crowded. We have you billeted in Apartment Six on the second floor. Three rooms, a small kitchen, and you share a bathroom with everyone else on that floor. Sign here." He thrust a register book at Elisabet.

She sighed. "You see, boys, it won't be so bad. We have three rooms and..."

A bark of laughter from the old man stopped her. "You share those three rooms with another family, Frau Daeker. What do you think this is? A holiday home? We are making nothing out of you refugees, you know. We could be renting these rooms to paying guests instead of getting a pittance from the State." He shook his head and ambled back into the building. "Well, come along then. You can leave your cart round the side of the building when you've unloaded it. It'll be quite safe; nobody will steal it..." he cocked his head on one side as if a thought had struck him. "...unless another one of you refugees takes it." He cackled and started up the stairs.

"We are not refugees," Elisabet called after him. "We are evacuees, and not by choice."

The hall on the second floor was dim and reeked of cooking and overcrowding, but as they shuffled along under the weight of their burdens, they heard a shriek of delight from the end of the corridor.

"They're here, mama!"

A moment later, little Lotte Theiss ran out and threw her arms around Elisabet.

"Lotte? What are you doing here?'

The girl's mother appeared in the doorway behind her, and her brothers peered out from behind her. "Welcome, Elisabet. We've been expecting you."

"Marlene. You have? How did you know we were coming? And when did you get here?"

"Come in, come in. I have water on and a pot of tea waiting. You must be tired after your journey."

Elisabet and her boys crowded into the little apartment, whereupon the boys immediately dropped their bundles and started chattering with Jan and Ernst, while Lotte accompanied the women into the little kitchen. Marlene poured boiling water into a teapot and soon the perfumed scents of raspberry leaf tea filled the room. She poured a cup for each of them, and a half cup for Lotte, topping it off with cold water.

"There's some for your boys too, if they want it."

Elisabet listened to the excited conversation from the next room and smiled. "Maybe later. Now, tell me how you knew we were coming. It seems like a huge coincidence that we are assigned to the same apartment."

"Well, we weren't originally. We arrived the day before yesterday and shared the apartment with two old ladies." Marlene laughed. "My boys are well-behaved, but it was all a bit too much for them, so the next day I talked to Herr Eisen – he's the old man in charge –

37

and he moved them in with another old couple on the first floor. You were to have been billeted with them, but we all agreed you'd be better off up here with us – especially after I saw your name and recognised it." She suddenly looked worried. "I was right, wasn't I? You would prefer it here? I know it'll be a bit of a squeeze but at least we know each other and the children can play together."

"Will ten people fit in three rooms?"

Marlene smiled. "It'll be tight, but I think we can manage. I thought perhaps you could take the larger front room, we'll take the smaller back one, and we'll share the one next to the kitchen."

Elisabet nodded slowly. "And the bathroom?"

"It's down the hall. We have to share with apartment Five, so we'll have to make some rules about using it."

"Sounds like you have it all worked out."

"Please don't think I'm controlling, but I thought I'd better do something. You can change the arrangements if you like."

Elisabet shook her head. "No, it sounds fine. Thank you, Marlene. You have made our evacuation a lot easier to bear."

Kapitel Drei (3)

Autumn slid into winter in Mohrungen, and life assumed a new and different level of normality. The evacuated children were assigned places in the local schools, and though there was a measure of enmity displayed by the local children, there were enough evacuees to prevent wholesale bullying. Jan and Helmut provided a bulwark against aggression and many times came home battered and bloodied from their efforts protecting their younger siblings. Elisabet had no fixed employment; she did not want to use up her savings and managed to augment the basic rations dispensed daily at the town hall with a small amount of money earned by cleaning for some of the local dignitaries. She bought extra food and invested some of the money in buying wool, which Marlene knitted into warm clothing for the children – jerseys, scarves, gloves and hats – and then into surplus scarves and gloves which they sold in the weekend markets. The extra income came in useful when winter chills brought on sickness, or a new pair of shoes was required by growing boys.

For a while, the Königsberg evacuees lived in the daily hope that news of a German victory would arrive and they would be allowed back home. It did not come, and they reluctantly started to look toward a longer exile. The news in the papers and on the radio continued to raise expectations, but people had become used to reading between the lines or sifting the few grains of truth from the chaff of propaganda. Battles took place and were counted as victories, yet the Russians still advanced.

Marlene had brought a radio from home, and though reception was not good, and the voices faded in and out amidst a continuous crackle, they still got enjoyment from it. After dinner, they would all gather in the shared room and listen to opera or dance music, sometimes even shuffling and leaping to favourite tunes, or listening to news broadcasts.

Since the horrendous air raids in August, Ostpreussen had settled into an uneasy peace. Returning soldiers told of Russian troops massing, or hinted at reversals, but as yet, no one seemed interested in their little bit of Germany. They breathed sighs of relief and looked forward to their favourite holiday – Christmas. The Party frowned on the religious aspects of the holiday, even to the extent of trying to change the name to Julfest, but many of the citizens of the Reich quietly got on with their own celebrations, clinging to their own beliefs.

"Can we have a fir tree, Mutti?" Kurt asked.

"We'll see. They might sell them in the markets closer to the holiday."

"There are forests near here, Tante Elisabet," Jan said. "We could just go and cut one down."

"I'm sure all these forests belong to someone," Marlene warned. "Don't take anything without asking permission."

Jan shrugged and leaned back, whispering to Helmut. "I'm damned if I'm going to let some rich landowner prevent us from having a tree for Christmas. Are you with me?"

"Yes!"

"Even if we can't get a tree, we can still make decorations," Elisabet said. "If we all keep a look out for coloured paper and things, we can hang those up around the apartment."

"And stockings?" Werner asked.

"Will Weihnachtsmann come?" Günter asked excitedly. "Does he know where we are?"

"I'm sure if you are a very good boy between now and then, he will bring you something," Elisabet said with a smile.

Snow fell early that year, a harbinger of winter, and very pretty it looked too, large flakes swirling through the air, but it only added to people's misery. The days became cold and grey; the snow melted to slush and refroze to ice overnight. Fuel was in short supply, as was electric power, and people bundled up in coats and woollens even in their own homes. Elisabet and Marlene came to see one of the advantages of their domestic arrangement with the advent of the cold weather. So many bodies in three small rooms meant the temperature remained bearable for long periods of time. Trips to the unheated communal bathroom became a trial however, and visits were hurried, especially in the dead of night.

Christmas approached, and everyone redoubled their efforts to find things to make the occasion festive. School ended and the children hung around the shops looking for anything colourful. Bottle caps and scraps of paper were strung together on cotton threads and hung about the house, joined by threads of coloured wool. Jan and Helmut returned cold and wet one day from the forest with sprigs of holly. Marlene took these and dipped them in a solution of Epsom salts obtained from a pharmacy. When the liquid dried it left the surface of the dark green leaves sprinkled with tiny crystals that looked like a scattering of snow.

Elisabet bought beetroot and carrots – there was no fruit to be had – and with some calf's foot jelly made red and orange concoctions that even if they

41

did not taste like fruit jellies, at least looked festive. Traditionally, Christmas dinner included a goose, but poultry was out of reach of the evacuees, and, in fact, most of the townspeople of Mohrungen. There were chickens in the town, egg-layers, but they were jealously guarded, and not for sale. Yet despite this, two nights before Christmas, Helmut and Jan returned from one of their foraging expeditions with a still warm chicken tucked inside the older boy's coat.

Elisabet was horrified. "You didn't steal it?"

"Steal what?" Marlene asked as she came in from the hallway. She saw the chicken dangling from Jan's hand. "Oh, Jan, no."

"What?" Jan asked truculently. "Why do you assume I stole it? We found it."

"You just found a chicken?" Elisabet asked. "Where?"

"By the side of the road..." Jan said.

"...in the country," Helmut added.

"It was nearly dead so we..."

"...so we picked it up."

"We were going to look for its owner, but then we thought he might accuse us of stealing it."

"But you did steal it," Elisabet said.

"No, Mutti," Helmut said. "We...we..."

"We liberated it," Jan said with a grin. "Besides, it was almost dead, but we wrung its neck to be sure. You don't want it?"

A downy feather drifted to the floor and Joachim toddled over to it and picked it up, while his brothers peered at the carcass with fascination.

"Well," Marlene said, looking at the plump chicken. "If the boys hadn't rescued it, a fox would probably have got it."

42

"And it's dead now," Elisabet added. "We can't just take it back to its owner."

"It's Christmas..."

"And the children need something to brighten up the festivities."

"We have some herbs and bread to make a stuffing."

"And I'll roast the chicken," Elisabet concluded. "Give me the bird, it needs plucking and gutting. I'll have to do it outside."

Jan handed it over. "Er, don't let anyone see you..."

"Was I born yesterday?"

Jan and Helmut's light-fingered exploits did not end there. The night before Christmas, they dragged a small fir tree up the stairs to the apartment and propped it triumphantly in a corner of the shared room. Elisabet and Marlene stared at their eldest sons and at the excited younger children, and refrained from making any accusations.

"Did anyone see you?" Marlene asked.

"No, mama," Jan said. "We were as quiet as mice."

"Very cold mice," Helmut added.

He was visibly shivering, so Elisabet made them both a cup of hot ersatz coffee, and added a spoon of their precious sugar. While Jan organised the smaller children in decorating the tree, she drew Helmut to one side and whispered to him.

"Stealing is wrong, Helmut."

"I know, Mutti, but this isn't really stealing."

"What do you mean?"

"The owner of the forest has millions of trees. He won't miss a little one and it makes us happy."

Elisabet watched the children from both families laughing and chattering as they stuck little bits of coloured paper or strands of wool to the branches and saw the joy in their expressions.

"What about the chicken?" she asked. "That was stolen too, wasn't it?"

Helmut grinned. "Liberated, Mutti." He saw his mother's frown and became serious. "I know it was wrong, but we're hungry and away from our homes. Will one chicken really be missed? One that was lost already?"

Later that evening, the night before Christmas Day, they opened their presents, though this year that involved no more than rummaging in a sock pinned to the mantelpiece and extracting tiny objects slipped there over the last few days by parents and children alike.

Marlene had baked sweet biscuits, using whatever she could find in the markets to eke out the rations which were barely enough to keep growing children fed. Elisabet had tracked down a dozen small apples from the last harvest, adding one to each stocking and slicing the remainder thinly to add as a topping to light pastry, sprinkled with sugar and cinnamon and baked. Extra sugar was hoarded and bartered, and the two women fashioned a sugar mouse for every child. Small toys topped off the meagre stockings, wooden animals, and a jigsaw puzzle (unfortunately with a piece missing). Both Elisabet and Marlene refused to buy the toys often offered to children of the Reich – toy tanks, planes and guns.

The children had banded together and managed to buy mothers and 'aunts' small luxuries – a cake of scented soap, a tiny bottle of rose water, a hairbrush (used but in good condition), and a yellow-painted enamel schmetterling brooch. The money for these things had come from shovelling snow, or running errands for old folk, or collecting pine cones for fuel. Each task brought a few precious pfennige, and gradually they amassed enough money to buy presents.

Elisabet clapped her hands with joy over the brooch and kissed every child, and Marlene. "It is lovely. I remember beautiful yellow butterflies from my childhood and this brings it all back to me. Thank you."

The next day, they sat down to a dinner more festive than most dinners the evacuees enjoyed. One chicken did not go far between ten people, but they all had some juicy herb-enhanced meat and made up for it with ample roasted vegetables – potatoes, carrots, swedes, and parsnips. Cabbage added a bit of pale green to the dishes, and was followed by brightly coloured vegetable juice jellies and sweet apple pastries and biscuits.

After dinner, they followed a family tradition and each told a story, either recounting something they had experienced or making something up. Elisabet told them of a trip to the seaside and finding a wonderfully sea-eroded shell with gleaming colours, and Marlene told of a visit she had made to the Museum in Berlin and a hall full of expertly stuffed animals in lifelike poses. Jan passed on a story he had heard from a returning soldier of conditions in the east, but Marlene quickly moved him on.

"It's Christmas, Jan, we want positive, uplifting stories."

Helmut told a story from school, and Kurt recited a poem he had heard. Ernst invented a story that involved people falling over and looking foolish. The story brought gales of laughter from the other children and smiles from the adults. Building on the good humour in the group, Günter told a joke, and Werner

45

made up a long and involved story about the people in Mohrungen. The tale petered away inconclusively, and in the silence that followed, Elisabet led a round of applause.

With a lot of encouragement, they even coaxed a story out of little Joachim, though the plot bore a strong resemblance to his mother's story about finding a shell on the beach. Lotte was now the only one who had not told a story, and she ran to her bed and brought back a notebook.

"I've been writing a story. May I read it out loud?"

The story was quite short and reflected a little girl's love of beautiful things and her hopes for the future. It was set around a girl called Anna who lived on a farm near a lovely forest. She had a pony of her own, and a dog, and chickens that she knew by name, and a duck that would fetch a stick if you threw it. The boys all laughed at this and it was a few minutes before she could continue.

Bad men came to the farm and took Anna's father away, but she prayed very hard and one day her father returned, bearing lots of presents for her and her brothers, and they all lived happily on the farm and nobody came to bother them ever again.

"Oh, that is a beautiful story, Lotte," Elisabet said. "I hope very much it comes true for you."

"It's only a story," Jan grumbled, still upset that his mother had upbraided him for his war story.

"Yes, but a very uplifting one. We all want peace, don't we? Maybe one day soon it will come and we can all live happily in our homes again."

They sang. The Daeker family had a tradition of singing, though the last few years had produced few occasions worthy of song. Christmas was different though, and Elisabet led her sons in singing carols, and the Theiss family joined in. *Stille Nacht, Heilige Nacht* was a favourite, and Elisabet's pure voice filled the apartment with glorious tones that made little Lotte cry with the joy of it. *Weihnachtsglockenspiel* followed, *O'Tannenbaum*, and many others. The Party had forced changes to some popular carols, doing away with references to Jesus and inserting appropriate ideological substitutes, but Elisabet changed the words back to the originals whenever they sang them.

Christmas passed and the New Year approached. The scraps of chicken and the bones were boiled down to flavour pots of soup, and the sugary biscuits were consumed, licked fingers picking up the last crumbs. Snow fell heavily, but the women still had to trudge through the drifts to the Town Hall to pick up their daily rations. That only occupied an hour or so each day, so most of the time was spent curled up with their families telling stories or playing games.

The weather eased slightly on New Year's Day itself, and the older boys took the youngsters out to play in the snow. Elisabet and Marlene knitted and listened to the radio, especially to the Führer's New Year's Proclamation. They listened more from habit than from a desire to hear the message, though Marlene still worshipped the man, having actually met him many years before.

"He was so imposing, Elisabet. Everyone was lined up along the sides of the street, and he came strolling past, shaking hands and receiving the adulation of the crowds. I slipped between the guards and offered him a flower, and he took it, thanking me, and kissing me on the cheek." Marlene sighed, her hand straying to her face. "I'll never forget it."

Elisabet nodded, having heard the story before. "That was, what, fifteen years ago? He's changed,

Marlene." She lowered her voice to a whisper. "Look where Germany is now, following that man."

"Oh, he'll save us yet, just you...shh, he's starting..."

"Deutsche Volk! Nationale Sozialisten! Mein Volksgenossen! Only the turn of the year causes me to speak to you today, Mein Deutsche Volksgenossen. The times demand more than speeches from me..."

"He doesn't sound well," Elisabet observed. "His voice is shaky and..."

"Shh."

"...the fateful struggle of Mein Volk. Although our enemies have proclaimed our collapse every New Year, they placed particular hopes on this past year. Never before did victory seem so close to them, when one catastrophe followed another..."

"He's admitting it?" Elisabet asked in wonder.

"No, he's not," Marlene declared. "He can't be. You'll see, he'll announce some major setback for our enemies. Now listen."

"...spirit of a statement that I made at the memorable Reichstag session of September 1, 1939, declaring that Germany would never be defeated by the force of arms or time, and that a day like November 9 would never repeat itself in the German Reich."

"I can't believe it," Elisabet muttered. "Have they even told him what the Russians are doing?"

"Shh," Marlene repeated, leaning closer to the crackling radio.

Elisabet leaned back in her chair, shutting out the broadcast, the stuffy room in Mohrungen and the chill of winter, remembering happier times.

* * *

I live in exciting times, even if Königsberg is far removed from the centre of the world. By the centre I mean Berlin, the capital of our beloved Germany.

48

Great things have been happening these past few years, even if I have been too young or too insulated to appreciate them. Since I turned sixteen, my Vati has explained current events to me, though of course, I also heard the same things, though from a different point of view, from my school teachers.

I learned German history, of course, and how the Germanic race has always been envied by the lesser races that surround it. Throughout our long and fractured history, we have always sought leaders who could inspire us and lead us to the glory that is ours by right. My teachers told us of Charlemagne, of Frederick the Great, of von Bismarck, of Metternich, and of the Kaiser – great military leaders held in high regard within Germany. This past year, my old history teacher, Herr Avram Ziegmann, has been dismissed, and a new one set in his place. It was whispered that Herr Ziegmann was dismissed for being a Jew, though why that should be so terrible escapes me.

Herr Otto Wetters, the new teacher, lost no time in letting us know that he belonged to the Nationalsozialistische Deutsche Arbeiterpartei, sometimes abbreviated to the Nationalsozialist or Nazi party. He informed us that Herr Ziegmann was dismissed for belonging to something called 'International Jewry' and had been working to overthrow the German State. I found it hard to believe that such a quiet intelligent man as Herr Ziegmann could be so evil, but my knowledge of affairs even within Königsberg was so small, I had to accept the words of my teacher. We never spoke of Herr Ziegmann again, and I don't know what became of him.

Herr Wetters now spoke of a new leader, Herr Adolf Hitler who, he said, although not yet a national leader, would soon thrust himself upon the world stage and lead Germany back to greatness. Others spoke of him too, not always in praiseworthy terms, so I asked my father about him, telling him what my teacher had said.

"Your teacher is a fascist," he told me. "Do you know what that is?"

"No, Vati."

He considered for a few moments, no doubt wondering what I could understand at my age – I had only just turned sixteen and had enjoyed a sheltered upbringing.

"Fascists are people who are nationalistic and authoritarian, believing that the State should control all aspects of your life, and that one man – a dictator – should rule them. This Herr Wetters believes Adolf Hitler is the natural leader of Germany."

"But you don't, Vati?"

"Heavens, no." He thought for a few moments more and asked, "Have you heard of Communism?"

"Isn't that what Russia has?"

"They like to think so, but Russian Communism is as totalitarian as fascism. True communism is where the people rule and there are no classes – nobody to rule over us, no servants. Wealth is shared so nobody goes hungry nor lacks any of the necessities of life."

"It sounds wonderful. Much better than fascism."

"I've always thought so, Elisabet. That is why I am a communist, as is your Opa."

"Can I be one too?"

"It is a serious matter, but I'll consider it."

A month later, we received the startling news that Herr Hitler was to visit Königsberg and give a speech before the Federal Elections on March 5. All school children were to be given two days off; there were to be parades, flags and decorations, after which Herr Hitler would address the nation through the wonder of radio from in front of the hotel near the railway station.

I begged to be allowed to go. My Vati was not at all happy with the idea, but my dear Mutti said there was no better way for me to see the error of fascism than to see it in action. So we all attended the celebrations as a family.

We had moved to Königsberg by then, so it took no great effort to make it into the city centre. People swarmed everywhere, smiling citizens and large numbers of uniformed Sturmabteilung – brown-shirted Stormtroopers of the Nazi Party. These Brownshirts strutted everywhere as if they owned the city. They smiled at everyone, obviously being in a jovial mood, and greeted each other with that peculiar stiff-armed salute of theirs.

The Nazi party was just one of many political parties contesting the election the next day, but you would think they were the ruling party from the appearance of the city. Large red flags with the white circle and black hakenkreuz or swastika hung from every lamppost and many public buildings. Even private homes displayed these flags, sometimes alongside the flag of Ostpreussen, but usually alone. Brownshirts handed out little swastika flags on sticks to passers-by, but their smiles quickly disappeared if anyone had the temerity to refuse their gift. My Vati took four of the flags when offered, but slipped them into his coat pocket, only bringing them out when another group of Brownshirts hove into view.

On one street corner, a group of students displaying armbands that identified them as members of the Social Democratic Party were busy tearing down a Nazi flag from a lamppost when a group of Brownshirts happened upon them. The Stormtroop-Stormtroopers raced forward and a melee ensued. I did not see the outcome as Vati hurried us away, but a street farther over we saw a large number of Brownshirts hurrying in support of their comrades.

"What will happen to them?" my brother Hans asked. "They weren't breaking the law."

"No, but their foolishness will cost them a beating at the very least. You do not tweak the lion's whiskers in its den."

The parades started. Brownshirts gathered in huge columns and marched through the streets, their long black boots crashing to the pavement in unison, their smart uniforms gleaming and fresh young faces beaming with nationalistic fervour. Despite them being fascists, I was stirred by the sight and I felt my heart beat in time to the martial music. The Stormtroopers burst into song, the Horst-Wessel-Lied, and I felt another surge of admiration.

The flag is high! The ranks are firmly closed!
The SA march with quiet, steady step.
Comrades shot by the Red Front and reactionaries
March in spirit within our ranks.
Clear the streets for the brown battalions,
Clear the streets for the storm trooper!
Millions are inspired when they see the swastika,
The day of freedom and of bread dawns!

My father saw my face and his expression darkened. He drew me aside and bent to look in my face.

"Do not be taken in by this nationalistic fervour, Elisabet. The Brownshirts are a bunch of thugs and unless Germany votes sensibly tomorrow, we may end up with them on our streets permanently. Then God help us."

Hans overheard my father's words. "But Vati, isn't it too late for that? Herr Hitler is already Chancellor."

"Yes he is, but his party is still in a minority. He cannot govern successfully without the support of the Reichstag. Every right-minded person must strive to prevent that."

Herr Hitler gave his speech that day, and his words were sent by radio all over the country. It was accounted a great day for Königsberg, and many people felt that this man would bring Ostpreussen back into the fold of Grossdeutschland, doing away with the shameful Polish Corridor imposed on Germany after the Great War.

He called it the Day of the Awakening Nation and spoke for a long time, haranguing the audience, throwing his arms about in jerky motions, slamming his fist into his hand to emphasise his arguments. I cannot remember what he said in most of his speech, but I can remember a bit toward the end, when he was winding up to a crescendo.

"In the end," he said, "we do not live for ourselves alone; rather, we are responsible for everything that those who lived before us have left behind, and we are responsible for that which we shall one day leave behind to those that must come after us. For Germany must not end with us."

I always remembered his avowed intention that Germany should not end with him, especially almost twelve years later, when Germany and the German people were being ground into the mud by foreign armies, all as a result of Herr Hitler and his Nazi policies.

*   *   *

"Elisabet. Elisabet?"

Elisabet looked up to see Marlene staring at her. "Sorry, has the speech finished? I was remembering better days."

"They'll come again. You heard him."

"I doubt it. He promised us glory when he first came to power, but has delivered only horror."

"What horror? We're a bit uncomfortable, but as soon as the Russians are driven back, we'll be able to return home. I don't expect it'll take long now."

Kapitel Vier (4)

They had news of the Russians less than two weeks later. Jan burst into the apartment, breathless after running all the way from the Town Hall.

"They're coming! The Russians are coming."

Marlene paled, her hand rising to her throat. "What are you saying? And why aren't you in school?"

"I was at the Town Hall, talking with my friends, and I overheard one of the officials on the telephone. He said..." Jan thought for a moment, remembering. "There has been a great battle. The Russian Army has crossed the Vistula River and is sweeping westward with the Wehrmacht falling back before it. He said the Russians will be here within a week."

"What nonsense," his mother said. "Our army is advancing, not retreating. All the news broadcasts say so. You shouldn't be listening to scaremongers and defeatists, my son."

Elisabet frowned. She got up and put her coat and shoes on. "Keep an eye on my children for me. I won't be long."

"Where are you going?"

"I just feel like a walk."

"But it's snowing."

Elisabet left the apartment building and took the road into town, moving carefully on the slippery surface. There was a small crowd of people in the Town Square, milling about and discussing the latest news. She recognised a woman she had stood in line with when collecting her daily rations, and tugged gently on her sleeve.

"Magda. What's happening?"

Excitement warred with concern in the old woman's lined face. "The Russians have crossed the

55

Vistula River and our forces are...are..." She looked around and lowered her voice. "...retreating."

"When did this happen?"

"The news just arrived, but it happened about five days ago, so...the twelfth."

"The news is official?"

"Yes. The mayor says there is nothing to worry about, that there is no evidence the Russians attacked in force. It may all be over by now."

Elisabet did not think so, but she said nothing, just excusing herself and walking off. She listened to the conversations around her but they told her nothing new, so she returned home.

"Jan is right," she told Marlene. "The Russians have attacked, five days ago, but nobody knows if they were thrown back or not."

"Of course they were," Marlene said. "The Wehrmacht is strong."

"It was a lot stronger two years ago, and look what happened at Stalingrad. That's where my Rudolph died."

Marlene reached out and squeezed Elisabet's arm. "I'm sorry, my dear. I didn't mean to dredge up old memories."

"It's all right. I only meant that Germany is being bled dry while the Russians grow stronger. What if their attack is not stopped?"

Marlene stared at her friend. "You think the Russians could come here? This far?"

"I don't know, but I don't think I want to be here if they do."

The other children came home from school, and the news of the Russian advance was the main topic of conversation, spiced up with unsubstantiated rumours and wild speculation. The adults put a stop to it, saying that discussion was premature as the only news they had was several days old already, and that no doubt the army would stop them.

Privately, Elisabet was worried. Her husband had told her about the Russians on his last leave before he went to Stalingrad.

"Don't ever get caught by the Russians," he had said. "They are absolutely merciless." Rudolph had shrugged his shoulders. "One can scarcely blame them, I suppose, after what we did to the Russian people. Just make sure you're far away if they ever get to Königsberg."

Their situation changed the next day. The children were at school and the women had finished the housework and were settling down to a cup of coffee before collecting their rations, when a loud roar set the windows rattling in their frames. They rushed to the window and stared open-mouthed as two aeroplanes roared low over the town, circled and raced back.

"What is the Luftwaffe doing here?" Marlene asked. "Don't they know where the Front is?"

"They've got red stars on them, not crosses," Elisabet said. "They're Russians."

As if in response to her words, they heard the juddering thump of cannon fire and part of the town clock erupted in a shower of masonry and glass. An air raid siren started up, and on the streets, people screamed and ran for the dubious shelter of their homes. The aeroplanes made another pass before heading back east, and a truck on the road out of town ran off the tarmac and burst into flames.

"Oh, you cowards," Marlene screamed. "Wait until our boys get here, then we'll see how good you are."

"They're going, and so are we," Elisabet said. "It's not safe here anymore."

"Go? Go where? Königsberg? How can we? We were sent to Mohrungen."

"The authorities are scarcely going to want women and children caught up in the fighting. I'm going into town to see if I can find out what's happening, and I'll bring the children back from school. You start packing."

"We can't leave. Not without permission."

Elisabet sighed with exasperation. "They'll give it. Will you start packing?"

Marlene wavered, and then nodded.

Elisabet was back in less than two hours, all the children in tow. She shook the snow off her boots and fixed them all something to eat, while Marlene prepared a hot drink. The children were full of questions and bubbling over with excitement, chattering about the fighter planes and being taken out of school so abruptly. Elisabet let them talk as they ate, but deflected any questions as to what was happening until they had all finished.

"All right. You have a right to know what is happening, and I'm going to tell you just what the officials in town told me. You may not fully understand, but I need you all to do as I say, without argument. Marlene, your children will, of course, do as you say."

"What is it, Mutti?" Helmut asked. "Is it about the planes?"

"In a way. The Mayor and Councillors have issued a statement that the Russians are heading this way. All men over the age of sixteen are forbidden to leave, but women and children are encouraged to do so. I have decided that we, as a family, will leave

Mohrungen and seek safety. The Mayor says there are boats leaving from the port of Gotenhafen around the end of January, so we must make our way there."

"How?" Marlene asked. "Do we go by train again?"

Elisabet shook her head. "There is no available transport, he said. If we want to go to safety, we must make our own way to the port – on foot."

"But that's...hundreds of kilometres," Marlene cried. "And look at it out there. How can we possibly walk that distance? With small children too."

"It's either that or wait for the Russians to get here," Elisabet pointed out. "Besides, it's only about a hundred kilometres. I looked on a map they have at the Town Hall. If we leave now, we can easily make it by the end of the month."

The smaller children chattered excitedly about what a big adventure it would be, but Jan, Helmut and Kurt looked serious. They had been out in the icy and snow-covered roads and knew this was no easy venture.

"Where do we sleep at night?" Jan asked.

"I don't know," Elisabet confessed. "I suppose if we're near a town we might be able to find a room for the night."

"What about food?" Kurt asked. "Will we still be given rations?"

"If we're careful, we have enough food to last to Gotenhafen, and maybe even a bit for the boat ride. Come now, children, gather your things. We must leave quickly."

"Today?" Helmut asked. "Shouldn't we wait until tomorrow morning?"

"And how much closer will the Russians be tomorrow? We could be ten kilometres closer to Gotenhafen by then."

Marlene looked out the window. "It's snowing again. It might be better to wait for better weather. We're a hundred kilometres from the Front here. It'll take them weeks to get this far – if they ever do."

Elisabet frowned. "I'm leaving with my children – today. If you want to wait and see, I can't stop you, but I wish you'd come with us. There's strength in numbers." When Marlene said nothing, Elisabet looked at her children and clapped her hands. "Quickly now. Dress warmly and pack your clothes up. We are leaving immediately."

Marlene and her children watched their friends packing. Lotte was crying and Ernst looked as if he wanted to.

Jan whispered to his mother. "We should stick together."

"All right. We're coming too. Quickly, children, pack your things."

The cart they had when they first arrived – the one that belonged to Helmut's friend Anton in Königsberg – was still stored behind the building, but had filled with snow and dead leaves. They emptied it out and used rags to scrape it as clean as possible. Then they loaded it with as much warm clothing as possible, adding blankets, all the food and bottles of water, and such personal possessions they could not be parted from. The whole thing was covered with an oil-skin to keep out the falling snow. They each carried a bag of some sort, though they used packs strapped to their backs where possible. Werner was very proud of his little rucksack, stuffed with food, some clothing and his favourite toy. He paraded in front of the others, laughing with delight.

At last they were all ready and waited in the gently falling snow for the signal to start. Elisabet looked at her children, and at Marlene's family, noting that they already looked tired and apprehensive. She wondered for a moment if she had not made a dreadful mistake, but she saw the smoke still rising from the town where the fighter planes had wrought destruction, and knew they could not stay.

She smiled encouragingly. "We'll take it in turns to pull the cart. Jan and Helmut, would you start please? Kurt and Ernst, you can push."

Elisabet wheeled the pram, which Joachim refused to ride in at first, wanting to march along beside his brothers. A hundred metres of trudging through the snow dispelled the excitement, however, and he then clamoured to be picked up. The little procession wound its way into the town centre and through it, onto the road leading northwest toward the coast. Roads and fields were almost indistinguishable beneath the thick cover of snow blanketing the countryside, except that roads had a double line of fence posts sometimes piercing the whiteness and the tracks of feet and wheeled vehicles marred their pristine state. Sunlight glinted off the wintery scene, making it look like a Christmas postcard, but the chill ate into their bones and quickly dispelled any festive feeling.

They were not alone on the road, old men, hundreds of women and children – Königsberg evacuees and citizens of Mohrungen – plodded along in front, behind or beside them, having decided that flight was preferable to an uncertain future as the battle lines crept closer. Some pushed carts, others wheeled prams or dragged sleds, while others trudged with sparse possessions in bulging suitcases gripped by hands encased in woollen gloves, their backs

61

bowed beneath the weight and the shame of being driven from their homes.

The day was grey and cold, a north wind picking up the fallen snow and driving it into their faces as they wrestled the cart along the icy roads. Hands became numb and exposed faces reddened and dried under the relentless frigid blast. Their pace slowed, and the women handed over bags and pram to their older boys, taking their places on the handles. Evening fell, early in that season, and despite the spires of Mohrungen still visible behind them, they knew they had to stop for the night and try and get some warmth and food into them.

"We have to stop," Elisabet gasped.

"Where?" Marlene asked. "There's nowhere to shelter."

Elisabet looked up and down the road. Some of their fellow travellers had fallen by the wayside, and others had forged ahead, determined to put more kilometres behind them. A few had camped in the snow, propping blankets above them and huddling to keep out the cold. Gaunt, skeletal trees lined the road on one side and bare snow-covered fields on the other. Here and there, hummocks rose, pristine white, hinting at structure beneath the frozen covering, but offering no protection. Certainly, there was no shelter by the road, and Elisabet feared setting up camp in such an exposed place as others were doing. She eyed the open fields once more, then the hummocks...perhaps in the lee of one, she wondered. One of them, fifty metres away in a snow-covered field, looked slightly angular, possibly a trick of the fading light, but perhaps not.

"Wait here," she said. She looked at her children, almost crying at their slumped, exhausted postures and shivering bodies. "I won't be long."

Elisabet trudged through the drifts beside the road and clambered awkwardly over a fence before setting out over unmarked snow toward the angular hummock. As she approached, she felt a surge of excitement because she thought she could see dark timbers outlining the edges, a less than perfect covering of snow.

"Thank God," she murmured, and dropped to her knees, pushing aside the snow to reveal a tiny, half-collapsed sheep byre. The floor of the shelter was bare with only a light dusting of snow over a pebbled bed of frozen faecal pellets. The broken slats of the back and sides partially supported a timber roof, but the gaps between the wood were firmly plugged with hard-packed snow.

She got to her feet and waved. "Come across!"

Elisabet struggled back to the road to help the children across the snow-clogged field and into the shelter. They could not take the cart with them, so pushed it as far off the road as possible and removed blankets and the oilskin, and a selection of food and pans. The pram, holding a few clothes and a bit of food, was pushed into the sparse shelter of a leafless bush.

Inside the sheep byre, they spread the oilskin and piled blankets onto it, getting the children wrapped up and as warm as possible. The heart wrenching sobs of the younger children lessened to muffled whimpering as they snuggled up to each other, their little limbs shivering uncontrollably.

Jan and Helmut gathered dry fragments of the wood fallen from the roof and walls of the shelter,

63

constructing an open pyramid of sticks. The older boy found a scrap of paper and crumpled it into the base, adding some wisps of straw. He struck a match and cupped it in his hands until it burnt strongly, then stuck it into the base of the pile. The paper flared up, the straw caught and crackled, and then, just as the first flames died down, the first fine wood slivers ignited. A few minutes more, under Jan's gentle guidance, and the fire took hold, throwing back the gathering dusk and flooding the byre with warmth.

"That was great," Helmut said, with admiration and envy tingeing his voice. "Where did you learn to do that?"

"Hitlerjugend."

"I thought you had to be fourteen."

Jan shrugged. "Deutsches Jungvolk then. I would have moved up if we'd stayed in Königsberg."

"I'm going to join next year," Helmut said. "I'm nearly ten."

When the fire had taken hold properly, Marlene wedged a pan full of snow to one side, and Elisabet pushed ten potatoes deep into the embers, using a stick to prod and turn them every few minutes. They opened two cans of sausage and cut thick slices of bread, smearing them with a little butter. Marlene added dried raspberry leaves to the boiling water and stirred it, releasing a cloud of fragrance into the tiny shelter. She poured the liquid into mugs and added a spoon of sugar to each one.

They ate their bread and sausage and drank hot raspberry leaf tea, as their bodies slowly warmed and the shivering stopped. Elisabet hooked the potatoes out of the embers and gingerly broke one open, splitting the charred and ash-covered skin to release a puff of steam. She passed it to Jan and broke open another one. They all ate one – carefully – the young-younger children waiting until they had cooled completely – and then crunching the burnt skin, determined to consume every scrap.

They slept huddled together for warmth, bathed in the flickering light of the fire. The children fell asleep almost at once, exhausted by the excitement and the cold, arduous trek from Mohrungen, but Marlene and Elisabet remained awake for a while.

"Do you really think we can make it?" Marlene asked. "Maybe we should go back to Mohrungen, or even Königsberg, and trust to the army to keep us safe."

"We have to keep going. Even the authorities in Mohrungen said women and children should leave. The Russians are coming."

"We could go back to Königsberg. At least we'd have our homes there to go to, and the children would be warm."

"You don't think the Russians will come there too? What will happen to the children then? I hate to say it, but I think Germany is beaten."

"I can't believe that. You heard the Führer in his New Year's speech. Germany will win yet. They are gathering a new army to push the Russians back."

Elisabet shook her head wearily. "Maybe Germany itself will hold firm, when the army is fighting on its own land, but I think Ostpruessen and Poland are lost. I'm going to get my children to Germany – to safety – one way or another. I hope you'll come with us, but you must do what you think is right."

Marlene was quiet for a long time, and then, just as Elisabet thought she must have fallen asleep, she murmured, "Everybody else seems to be fleeing, so we'll come too."

Elisabet reached out and squeezed the other woman's hand. "I'm glad."

The fire had died down to embers when the grey dawn light drove back night's dark covering. Elisabet woke first and eased herself out of the shelter and round the back to attend to her personal needs. Marlene and Lotte joined her, and the boys tumbled out of their blankets, curious about their surroundings now that they were rested and fed.

Jan built up the fire again, though he had to prise a few boards out of the byre walls as fuel. Marlene brewed another pot of tea, and they all ate a thick slice of bread before dousing the flames, and gathering up the blankets and oilskin.

The younger boys raced ahead across the field, their long shadows keeping pace. They laughed and threw snow at each other but stopped, staring, when they got close to the road.

"The cart," Werner yelled. "It's gone."

"Somebody stole it," Günter added.

They ran to the road and quickly confirmed the fact. At some time during the night, someone had wheeled the cart away, along with most of their food, spare clothes and personal possessions. The thieves had left the pram, possibly because it was half-hidden by a bare bush, but everything else had gone.

Jan shouted out threats at what he would do if he found the thieves, but Marlene and Elisabet calmed him, pointing out that there was nothing they could do. They had a few tins of food left in the pram and some of Joachim's clothes, so they piled the blankets on top and made a loose bag of the oilskin to carry the rest. Other refugees were passing by this time, and listened sympathetically to Jan's angry complaint.

"What is the world coming to?" asked an old woman. "Fancy stealing from your countrymen."

"Bastarde," added an old man. He dug in the pocket of his great coat and produced two wizened apples, offering them to Jan. "Share them with your brothers and sister."

Jan thanked the man and cut the apples into pieces, handing each child a piece. Elisabet gathered them all around her on the road.

"The loss of the cart is serious, but it need not affect us," she said. "We have lost some food and clothes, but we'll be able to move faster without it. So, best foot forward and let's see how far we can get by tonight."

They did make good time that morning. Whether it was because they were rested and fed, or because the absence of the cart really did make a difference, or indeed whether the presence of so many other refugees filling the road spurred them on to greater efforts, they were many kilometres farther on at the end of the short winter's day.

Marlene spotted a barn some distance off the road and they made for it, seeking shelter for the night, along with close on a hundred other people. They crammed in, and slept on stale straw that night. Mice rustled in the darkness and people cursed, scratching at flea bites. A fire was too risky amid the straw within the barn and too exposed to the weather outside, so they nibbled on raw carrots and turnips stored at the back of the barn, and fell asleep to the murmur of strange voices.

The third day was a continuation of the second, though their energy waned and the children were exhausted and crying long before nightfall. Joachim rode in the pram most of the way, but when he

67

wanted to get out and play in the snow as they walked along, Günter, Ernst or Werner got a chance for a short respite. The adults walked, as did the older children, and everyone had a turn at wrestling the wheels of the pram through snow or over icy ruts in the road. Hands froze in the chill air and the tips of noses went numb, so they rubbed them to restore circulation and stumbled on. They camped that night by the side of the road, sheltering under the spreading branches of a fir tree, and building a small fire from fallen needles and pinecones. Blankets scarcely protected them from plunging temperatures and they donned every stitch of clothing and huddled together for warmth.

The next day they had to make the decision whether to go through the city of Elbing, or bypass it. There were arguments for either route, though Elisabet thought the city might provide some advantages as they were nearly out of food. Then Kurt said something that made Elisabet consider another option.

"Remember grandpa's farm?" Kurt said to Günter. "And Kaiser – how he used to pull us around in that little cart? I wonder if we'll ever see him again."

"Maybe we should go to the farm," Elisabet said.

"What farm is this?" Marlene asked.

"My grandfather Gottfried had a farm east of Elbing. We used to go there sometimes. He had a huge dog, a wolfhound or a mastiff or something, and he used to hitch it to a little cart and give the boys rides." Elisabet laughed. "Happy days."

"I'm sure, but why would we want to go there now? Aren't the Russians coming?"

"A couple of reasons. We could shelter there until we find out what's happening. There'll be food there too, and we'll need food if we head for Gotenhafen."

"Your grandfather's still there?"

"No, he died a few years ago, but he left it to his eldest son Erich, my uncle. He'll make us welcome and help us."

It took them another day and a half, walking along almost deserted country roads in the opposite direction to the flood of refugees. They intersected the rail line and this enabled Elisabet to gather her bearings, leading them first to the little country station and then another hour or so to the entrance to her grandfather's farm. She stopped on the road looking up the long rutted driveway now covered in a blanket of snow. People had passed this way recently, many people judging by the footprints and churned up tracks left by two or more vehicles. The trail led not up the driveway but had cut across the fields, smashing fences along the way.

"What's wrong?" Marlene asked.

"Someone's been here." Elisabet pointed to the tracks. "Somebody who didn't care if they did damage."

"Russians?"

"Or refugees."

"They wouldn't damage property."

"Things are different now."

"You want to go in?"

Elisabet nodded. "I have to. Besides, we've come this far and almost exhausted our food. We've got to get more if we're going to make it to the port."

They walked slowly up the driveway, past the grove of sheltering pines, to where they could see the farmhouse and barn. The house was little more than a burnt out pile of rubble, and the barn was similarly shattered, though the flames had not completed their work on the painted timbers. Elisabet stood and stared for several minutes before wiping away a tear.

"What has happened? Could the Russians have got here so quickly?"

"And are they still here?" Jan asked.

Marlene looked all around at the frigid fields under their blanket of snow. Nothing moved, and the only sound was a soft sighing of the wind in the pine branches and a distant rumble of thunder to the east. "I don't think anyone's here now," she said.

"Perhaps we should look around," Helmut said.

"Where's Kaiser?" Kurt asked. "Is he here still?"

"I don't think so," Elisabet said. "Uncle Erich will have taken him when he left. Boys, have a look in the barn, we'll try what's left of the house."

The boys ran off toward the barn, while the two women, Lotte and Joachim, made for the tumbled down ruins. It had been stripped bare, and what had not disappeared was in fragments – furniture, china, and bedding.

"No...no bodies, thank heaven," Marlene said. "They must have had time to run away."

"I hope so," Elisabet said. "I'd hate to think Uncle Erich and Auntie Therese were...were under that lot." She shuddered and turned away. "There's nothing for us here."

A shout from the direction of the barn sent them stumbling out into the open. Jan and Helmut raced from the ruined barn, screaming with excitement, the object of their attention, a chicken, squawking and fluttering ahead of them. The boys chased it into the snowdrifts where the poor bird floundered and screeched as first Helmut and then Jan pounced on it.

70

The squawking was cut off suddenly and Jan held it up by its feet, the chicken's head dangling lifelessly.

"Chicken for dinner," Helmut crowed. "And there's more in the barn."

The smaller boys had cornered another chicken and were making futile grabs for it as it ducked under fallen timbers, flapping up the walls in an effort to escape. Kurt held another one in his arms and was soothing it, talking to it in a low voice.

"This is Chickie," he said proudly. "She came to me and she's mine."

"Well, she's yours until we eat her," Helmut said.

Kurt scowled and held the chicken close to him. "She's mine," he repeated.

Joachim struggled to get down from his mother's arms, and toddled across to where Kurt sat and stroked the chicken, a big grin on his face. Lotte joined them and they all sat and talked to Chickie, telling her what a beautiful bird she was.

Helmut helped the other boys catch the third chicken and wrung its neck when it fell at last into their eager hands.

"I doubt there'll be eggs as it's winter," Elisabet said, "But it's worth a look anyway." The boys enjoyed a hunt in the straw. They even found three, probably ancient and preserved by the cold weather, and one of these was cracked and empty.

"It's getting late," Marlene said. "We should stay here tonight."

The remnants of the barn provided some shelter from the wind, and the straw gave them soft beds, though the squeaking of mice alarmed Lotte and Werner. Elisabet and Marlene plucked and gutted the chickens, while Jan laid a small fire on a patch of ground swept free of straw. Kurt wept when Chickie

71

was sacrificed for the common good, but Helmut took him to one side and explained matters to him.

"We can't take her with us, so she'd have to stay here all alone."

"We could take her," Kurt objected. "I'd look after her."

"How? What would you feed her? Chickens eat grain and we don't have any."

"But she's my Chickie. She came to me."

"We'll get you another one. I promise."

Reluctantly, Kurt allowed himself to be persuaded and looked away as Helmut went off with Chickie. Later, when all three birds were crackling and spitting over the fire, it was impossible to tell which bird was which and, after a long hesitation, Kurt joined in the feast, telling himself that Chickie was one of the other birds. Every scrap of meat was eaten and the bones sucked to remove every last smear of fat. Jan and Helmut even crunched some of the bones.

"What do we do now?" Marlene asked as the boys settled themselves for sleep, snuggled deep in the straw. "Head for the port?"

"Elbing first, I think," Elisabet said. "I'm sorry we came out of our way to get here, but I honestly thought we might get some supplies."

Marlene smiled and stroked Lotte's blonde curls. "We had a lovely chicken dinner, and we have eggs for breakfast. It wasn't a complete waste."

They opened the eggs over a piece of curved metal that may have been part of a vehicle, and one was rotten. The other was marginally edible, and gave them a taste of egg each to satisfy their hunger. There was one other revelation awaiting them as they prepared to leave, and it was not a pleasant one.

The boys had been playing outside, running and throwing snowballs, when Günter let out a yell. There was a moment's silence, and Helmut called out.

"Mutti, you'd better come see."

The boys were clustered around an object mounded with snow halfway between the ruined house and the barn. Kurt was weeping quietly, and Günter was losing his breakfast in a drift of snow. Elisabet stepped closer and saw the remains of a large dog, lying on its side, its lips drawn back in a snarl. It had been eviscerated and clotted blood had frozen beneath it. Helmut tugged at a leg, but it was frozen to the ground.

"Is it Kaiser?" Kurt asked in a small voice.

"Yes, I think so."

"He was a good dog. He used to pull us around in that little cart, remember?"

"I remember," Werner said.

"Me too," Günter added. He wiped his mouth on his sleeve and wouldn't look at the corpse again.

"We should bury him. Make a cross."

"The ground's too hard to dig in," Helmut said.

"We could cover him with snow," Jan volunteered.

Kurt thought about this. "But it'll melt in the spring."

"Then the ground will be softer and someone will bury him," Helmut said. "Isn't that right, Mutti?"

"Yes. Come along now, let's cover him with snow. We have to be on our way."

They mounded the snow high and patted it down. Helmut found a paling in the barn and scratched the name 'Kaiser' on it with a rusty nail. Kurt asked him to add something else, something nice, so Helmut scratched a few more words – 'Er war ein guter Hund'. He stuck it into the mounded snow. They said

73

their goodbyes and started down the driveway to the road, turning in the direction of Elbing.

The country roads were still almost deserted, but when they came to a main road, they found it thronged with refugees. They joined the stream of silent people, saving their energy for the trials that lay ahead. The road took them south of Elbing, so they turned off toward the city, while many of the other refugees continued westward. They made their weary way along the roads and this time it was odd to see refugees coming toward them, fleeing the city.

"Are we going the wrong direction, Mutti?" Kurt asked.

"No, our immediate needs are different from theirs, but we are all fleeing from the Russians."

They sheltered that night in a farmhouse. The owner came out to the road and offered such hospitality as was hers to give, to any families with children. Elisabet and the boys found themselves bunked down in the parlour along with twenty or thirty other refugees, packed almost wall to wall. The farmer's wife fed them all bowls of soup, corned beef and crisp-crusted loaves fresh from the oven, smeared with real butter. They ate well, and slept well, feeling safe again, but the next morning they filed out of the house and onto the cold road once more. Another half day brought them to Elbing.

Once in the city, she led the little group along streets packed with refugees and the detritus of their passing. Household goods were strewn on road and pavement, abandoned as their owners discovered them too heavy to carry. Harried looking police sought to control the flow of people and once or twice they heard shouts as looters were chased away from broken shop fronts. Elisabet sought out the offices of the Ortsgruppenleiter in the city centre. She climbed the stone steps of the Town Hall and entered the office where she looked around for someone to help her. The officials looked harried. There was a detachment of SS busy hauling documents out of the building and either loading them on trucks or burning them in the centre of the courtyard. The children gathered around the flames, watching with interest as papers curled and blackened, sparks and ash lifting on hot up-currents into the crisp winter air.

Elisabet approached a young SS Unterscharführer and got his attention. She introduced herself, pointing out that she was a war widow with five children, and made mention of the fact that her late husband, Rudolph Daeker, had been a Party member.

"What is it you want, Frau Daeker?" asked the young SS Unterscharführer politely. "As you can see, we are very busy."

"We are obeying a government directive to evacuate to the West," Elisabet said. "On our way, we were robbed, and all our food and most of our clothing were stolen. We need to replenish our supplies."

The Unterscharführer shrugged. "I understand, Frau Daeker, but what can I do about it? We don't have the resources to track down your stolen goods."

"We have a little money, but no ration books for Elbing. If you would issue some to us, we could buy whatever else we need."

"I doubt you could find anything," the young man said with a wry smile. He looked beyond her to Marlene and the children. "Who are they?"

"My children. Also, my neighbour, Frau Theiss. She and her children were robbed too."

"I cannot issue ration books, and even if I could the whole city is in a panic. Everyone is leaving, or looting, or hoarding food, despite being shooting offences." He glanced at the children again and smiled. "Take your tribe through that alleyway there..." he pointed, "...to the kitchens and ask for Rottenführer Hüber. Tell him Unterscharführer Wirth says you can have as much food as you can carry."

"Thank you, Unterscharführer, you are very kind."

"Look after your sons, Frau Daeker. The Fatherland will have need of them very soon. Heil Hitler." He saluted and turned away, back to his duties, and Elisabet went out to the bonfire.

They trooped through the alleyway, following the aromas of cooking food and found an open-air kitchen with several SS men tending cooking pots, tunics off as they laboured to provide food for their comrades. Elisabet asked the nearest man, who hooked a thumb in the direction of a portly older man in an ill-fitting SS uniform.

"Rottenführer Hüber? Unterscharführer Wirth said to ask you for food. He said to tell you we could have as much as we could carry away."

The man frowned and looked at the women and children. "Why on earth would he say that?" He shrugged. "Well, I'm not about to argue with my Unterscharführer." He pointed at vegetable bins dimly seen within the open building behind him. "Help yourself." The Rottenführer watched as they stuffed potatoes, carrots and swedes into pockets, and filled up the spare spaces in the pram.

"Where are you heading?" he asked Elisabet.

"Gotenhafen. We hear there are ships leaving for Germany."

"You'll be hungry and tired by the time you get there." He went over to a trestle table and cut large slices of bread. "Here, start buttering." The Rottenführer uncovered a plate of sliced meat and started slapping pieces onto the bread. Some of his men looked up curiously, but said nothing. "Beef. Good with a bit of sauerkraut, but we don't have any."

When each of the children was munching on a thick sandwich, Hüber thrust the remains of the loaf at Elisabet. "God speed, damen."

"May fortune smile on you for your kindness and generosity, Rottenführer Hüber."

The road from Elbing turned more westerly, converging with the coastline of the Bay of Danzig. Many people from Elbing joined them on the road, and at times there were so many people they were reduced to a shuffling walk. Gradually, the effort of walking in icy conditions made people turn aside or stop altogether, and Elisabet took advantage of people tending to walk on the sides of the road and led her family along the centre. This worked well at first, then other people started to throw off the shackles of conventionality, and the whole road became a pedestrian passageway.

They sheltered that night in the front garden of a small cottage in a tiny village apparently without a name. In the absence of barns or buildings of any kind, or groves of trees in which to shelter, they climbed the low wooden fence and camped in the lee of a hedge, draping blankets to ward off the wind and sitting on the oilskin. Jan started a small fire, and the owner of the cottage came out angrily and told them to move on.

"Please," Elisabet said. "We have small children. Let us camp here tonight and we will leave at first light."

"I will call the police and have you evicted."

"Do what you must, but we shall stay until they arrive."

The man swore at them and stamped back inside, slamming the door. A little later, the man's wife came out, muffled against the cold, and brought them a pan of hot cabbage soup.

"Forgive my husband," the woman said. "He forgets we must stand together against the common enemy. The soup is little enough, but it is all I can do."

Elisabet and Marlene thanked her and fed the warm broth to their children before it cooled off. They cleaned the pan out with snow and left it on the doorstep for the woman to find in the morning, and huddled together for warmth. True to their word, they packed up and moved on, leaving behind only scuffed snow and the ashes of their fire.

Two days later, cold and hungry, they arrived at the banks of the Vistula River, close where it flowed into the Bay of Danzig. Or rather, where it would flow when the weather warmed. Now, the river was a sheet of snow-covered ice, crawling with little figures as people crossed its frozen waste rather than braving the bridges. Elisabet led her family to a bridge first of all, but they were turned back by army guards.

"Convoys only," they said. "Use the river, Frau, it's safe enough."

"But I have small children."

"Sorry. Orders."

They stood back as a convoy of army trucks roared up, their tyres slipping and spinning on the icy roads

78

and crept across the bridge, exhausts pouring out blue smoke. Scarcely had they crossed than eight Panther tanks appeared on the far side and rumbled across one at a time, the bridge groaning and dipping under the weight of the armour.

"They're going to fight the Russians," Kurt yelled. He ran to the side of the road, jumping up and down and waving his arms.

The hatch on the leading tank opened and a young Oberleutnant smiled down at him. Elisabet ran to pull Kurt back from the path of the tank and the officer saluted her silently before ducking down into his turret again.

They slipped down the banks of the river and ventured out on the ice, following trodden paths in the snow that wandered across the expanse. Elisabet hoped that by using proven trails they would avoid thin ice, and despite hearing load groans beneath them that started Ernst and Günter crying, the ice held and they crossed shivering to the far side.

Refugees packed the roads as they neared Danzig, as thousands who had fled from around Königsberg now joined the exodus. An old man and woman, carrying no more than the clothes they wore, told them what had happened in Königsberg. They shared their food with the old couple and listened to the tale of their escape.

The city Gauleiter had delayed the flight of civilians until the twentieth of the month, but many had risked death fleeing the city, and many more had fled from villages nearby. The old couple had crossed the frozen Frisches Haff to the port of Pillau, and thence down the Nehrung, the sandy spit that separated the Frisches Haff from the Baltic Sea. It was a terrible trip, exposed to bitter cold and freezing winds off the Baltic, and then they had trudged across fields covered in drifts a metre deep to reach the rela-relative safety of the Danzig road.

"We have friends in Danzig," the old man said. "We'll be safe there."

Elisabet and Marlene guided their children closer to the presumed safety of the Baltic ports, using roads where they could, and taking to the fields where they could not. They listened to the mumbled rumours that spread through the flow of refugees, sifting sense from wild speculation, desperate to believe that safety was at hand, afraid to set themselves up for disappointment. And through it all, the frigid air blew off the sea, drying and cracking exposed skin, robbing the body of warmth and numbing feet encased in ice-caked shoes.

The road led past Danzig, skirting the city with its streets clogged with military vehicles and personnel, either moving south and east to help stem the Russian advance, or seeking to board ships destined for Kiel, deep inside the Fatherland. Either way, it was no place for refugees, whether on foot or like some lucky ones, riding on horse-drawn carriages and wagons. The tide of people carried them past, heading north along the coast.

Two days later, they drew close to Gotenhafen, moving slowly now as thousands of refugees clogged the roads and ice-slick ways. Troops were out in force, herding the people, watchful for able-bodied men seeking to shirk their duties or for youths deemed worthy of service. Several times, soldiers shouldered their way through the crowd and hauled a man out, yelling at him with hate-filled faces. Their expressions seemed to say, 'I have to serve, so who the hell are you to try and sneak away?' These unfortunates were beaten up and dragged off to some menial service or just shot out of hand by the side of the road.

Jan attracted a few close looks as he was a tall boy, and once or twice soldiers hauled him aside, but on closer inspection it was obvious he was too young. The other boys were not worth even a glance, and the families slowly advanced on the dock area. A great ship could be seen ahead of them across a sea of heads.

"You see, boys," Elisabet murmured. "There is a ship to take us all to safety."

"We should be so lucky," complained an old man beside them. "Haven't you heard? They're only taking submariners and their families."

"But what about all these people? What are they going to do for us?"

"What they've always done," grumbled the old man. "The Party officials get everything, the people get nothing."

"That's treason," hissed a young woman nearby. "You should be shot for saying that." She looked around and spotted two soldiers patrolling nearby. "Over here, soldaten. A man is uttering defeatist statements." She waved to attract their attention.

The old man cursed and slipped away through the crowd. The soldiers tried to follow but were hampered by the crush and gave up. Elisabet and Marlene held onto their children and inched forward as the crowd overflowed the road near the waterfront, eventually coming to a standstill near a great barbed wire gate and fence around the docks. Through the wire, they could see the ship, the *Wilhelm Gustloff*, taking supplies on board, and a trickle of passengers being allowed up the gangplanks.

"We need to be on that ship," Elisabet said.

Kapitel Fünf (5)

Night fell over Gotenhafen, though activity on the docks continued under subdued lighting. The crush of refugees gradually lessened as soldiers and the Naval Women's Auxiliary siphoned off women and children into the great brick warehouses lining the dock area. Soup kitchens had been set up, and thin blankets were issued to people lacking their own supplies.

Elisabet and her boys joined a long line, with Marlene and her family just behind, and after a considerable wait, each person was given a metal bowl with a few spoonfuls of vegetable soup and a hunk of black bread. They carried them to one side and found a place to sit among the throng, where they gratefully consumed their rations. The press of bodies around them and the noise kept them awake and the children active and interested in their surroundings for a long time, but as the temperature rose to comfortable levels in the warehouses, they slept.

In the morning, they were fed again – ersatz coffee and more black bread – and then the news came that the *Gustloff* and the smaller liner *Hansa* were boarding civilians and if they could get aboard, they would be taken to Kiel. Excitement gripped the refugees and they poured out into the streets again and through the barbed wire gates onto the docks. The Daeker and Theiss families, having given up their positions for food and warmth overnight, found themselves separated from the ship by a mass of people. They pressed forward slowly as refugees were shepherded on board, but were still a hundred metres shy of the gates when the ship's horn sounded and the gates started to close.

A great clamour arose from the refugees excluded from the docks, but no more people were allowed to board. An hour later, they watched as the gangplanks were hauled away and the great ship slowly eased away from the dock, guided by tug boats, and out into the harbour. An announcement was made that the *Gustloff* would return in a few days for another load, but in the meantime, other smaller ships would be taking on passengers.

They watched the liners steam out into the Bay of Danzig, before returning to the warehouses for more food and shelter from the bitter winter weather. The mood of the refugees was sombre, filled with fear that the Russians would arrive before the ships could return, and intense disappointment at having missed out on a place in the ships. Toward nightfall, word came that the *Hansa* had docked again, having developed engine trouble in the Bay, leaving the *Wilhelm Gustloff* to steam on alone, with only a single boat as company. Hope rose briefly that more people would be allowed to embark on the *Hansa*.

"What do you think?" Marlene asked. "Will we be able to get aboard?"

"I doubt on board the *Hansa*," Elisabet replied. "It'll be full already, but we were promised other ships. Maybe even the *Gustloff* when it returns. That should only be a few days. In the meantime, we have food and shelter."

The same plain fare was doled out that evening, but the quantities were a little less, as despite nearly nine thousand refugees embarking, thousands more had arrived in the course of the day. Elisabet and Marlene found a new place a little closer to the entrance in the hope that if a further embarkation was announced, they would be closer to the head of the line.

There was an air raid that night, and the wailing sirens struck terror into the hearts of those that had suffered before. Panic arose and people pushed toward the doors, but soldiers barred the way, shouting out that there were no bomb shelters and that people should keep close to the walls. Gradually, a semblance of calm was restored, and the crush of refugees within the brick warehouses waited for the bombs to rain down and the buildings to collapse on top of them. The sirens went on, rising and falling, but there were no explosions, and even the droning sound of the aircraft diminished. The 'All Clear' sounded, and people sighed with relief.

"The swine are passing us by."

"They're heading for Königsberg. I feel sorry for those bastards."

The lights dimmed and everyone settled down to get as much sleep as possible, but in the middle of the night, there was a considerable commotion outside with men shouting and the sound of running feet and trucks roaring away from the docks. Most people tried to ignore it, once they found it was not directly impacting them, but a few spoke together in low tones and the officials looked stunned at the news that came in to them. After a while, a senior naval officer made an announcement.

"A Russian submarine has made a cowardly attack on the unarmed passenger ship *Wilhelm Gustloff* and sunk it. We have no word of the casualties involved, but they are likely to be high. Be assured that the Reich will take steps to avenge our innocent brothers and sisters, cut down so pitilessly by the black-hearted, cowardly enemy, and we will bring righteous destruction on all those involved. Do not be fright-frightened, nor waver in your determination to serve the Fatherland – other ships will be arriving in the next few days to continue the evacuation of refugees, and your safety is our priority. We will not let this happen again. Heil Hitler."

Elisabet and Marlene looked at each other, horror written on their faces. Jan uttered angry comments about what he would do to the submariners, while Helmut and Kurt listened to him attentively. The younger children played or slept through it all.

"I'm not sure I want to board a ship after this," Elisabet said.

"Me either," Marlene said. "But what can we do?"

"Well, they're not forcing us on board, so we can just walk away. They won't try and stop us."

"And go where?"

"Back to Germany – to safety. I'm still determined to get my boys home."

"But how? It's a very long way."

"Walk if we have to. We can head west and try and stay ahead of the Russians. The army will be fighting them and I'm sure will stop them."

"What about going back to Königsberg?" Marlene asked. "They're going to defend the city and I can't imagine the enemy is strong enough to take it if it is defended with determination. We could be safe there until the war ends and we can go back to our former lives."

"I don't think we'll ever see those days again. No, I'm heading west. I have family in Dresden. I'd really like you to come with us."

The port of Gotenhafen was in uproar the next morning, the authorities trying to lay on a rescue for the survivors of the Gustloff, and also bring other, smaller vessels to the dockside for more refugees to embark. Elisabet, though determined to leave the port, insisted they all eat as much food as was on offer.

"We don't know where our next hot meal is coming from, so eat all you're given. Then we'll leave."

Outside, they found it harder to leave Gotenhafen than they thought. Nobody prevented them, nor deliberately put obstacles in their way, but refugees still streamed toward the docks in a great crush of people that filled the road, and the children found it hard to struggle against the human current. Elisabet led, with Joachim in the pram bundled against the cold, and her four older sons strung out behind her, holding hands and keeping as close as possible. Marlene and her smaller children followed, with Jan bringing up the rear. They used the sides of the road, taking advantage of parked vehicles and knots of soldiers to ease their way south, back the way they had come just a day or so before.

The two families spent the night in an alley, still within the port town, shivering in doorways. They could not risk a fire, so gnawed on stale bread and raw cabbage leaves, drinking icy water from a bottle. Spirits sank, and the younger children sobbed from the cold and hunger. Their mothers told stories or sang in a low voice to encourage their children, and hugged them close to share body warmth.

They were up and moving again at first light, shivering violently in the bitter cold until exercise warmed their limbs. A frigid wind from the east sapped their strength, but it veered to the north and blew against their backs, lessening the pain on their exposed faces. Wind sores formed, chapping cheeks and lips, and their eyes watered constantly.

Refugees still streamed northward, but rumours had spread faster. The Russians were forging westward, would be in Berlin in another month, or had been halted by a German offensive. German troops were attacking all along the Front; German troops were retreating all along the Front – nobody could say for sure, but nobody stopped to see the outcome. They all kept fleeing, striving to reach the perceived safety of Gotenhafen, or, like the Daeker and Theiss families, were taking their chances elsewhere.

They reached Danzig, where the road branched. One lay south-eastward – the one they had used when they fled from Elbing. The other ran southward, inland, and here the families stopped.

Marlene pointed east to the coast. "That's the way we came."

"I know," Elisabet said, "But that leads us toward the Russians. We need to go south and then find a road westward."

"Königsberg is also to the east. I've been thinking – we should go there."

"Until the Russians arrive. You don't honestly think the army can successfully defend the city when it's retreating everywhere?"

"That's just rumour," Marlene said sharply. "Germany will win eventually. The Führer promised. We just have to give him a chance to defeat our enemies."

Elisabet sighed. "Marlene, you know that's not going to happen. Germany has lost the war. We just have to survive."

Marlene grimaced, her forehead contracting into an angry frown. "That is just the sort of defeatism that has led to our present situation. I believe in the Führer, and in our gallant army, and I'm going back to wait in Königsberg until the final victory."

"Then what was all this fleeing to Gotenhafen with us? You certainly acted as if you realised the Russians were winning."

"You are very persuasive," Marlene admitted, "But I have come to my senses."

"At least let me take your children to safety."

"They will be far safer with me. In fact, I am willing to look after your children if you are really concerned for their future."

"Never," Elisabet whispered. "The road east leads to death."

"You are dreaming if you think you can walk hundreds of kilometres in the middle of winter and survive."

"Please, Marlene, change your mind and come with us."

"No."

"Then we must part," Elisabet said sadly.

The two families separated, Marlene Theiss taking her three children – Jan, Ernst, and little golden-haired Lotte – back toward the east, and Elisabet Daeker led her five boys – Helmut, Kurt, Günter, Werner, and Joachim – on the road that led south, in the hope of finding a route through Poland that would bring them to safety in Germany.

Elisabet stood and watched the other family leave, knowing that in all probability she would never see them again. Nor would she see Königsberg again – her beloved city would be overrun by the Russian Army and she would be prevented from ever going back. The Theiss family reached a bend in the road and Elisabet lifted a hand in farewell – but only Lotte looked back and waved – and then she was gone.

*   *   *

When I was a girl, I believed the people of Königsberg, and indeed of the whole of Ostpreussen, supported Herr Hitler. No, on consideration, that is a dreadful thing to say and untrue. Let me instead say, most people supported the Nazi Party, and at the time it seemed a very reasonable thing to do. My parents never supported him or his party though, and while there were elections to vote in, always supported those that opposed him. In fact, the March 1933 elections, before which I heard Herr Hitler speak in Königsberg, were the last free elections held in Germany until after the war. The Nazi Party won something like 57% of the votes in Ostpreussen, though nationally they never achieved a majority. After 1933 it did not matter as all other political parties were outlawed.

You might wonder why Ostpreussen was so supportive of the Nazis. I am no political expert, but I believe it had a lot to do with our separation from the rest of Germany. After the Great War, Poland was given German territory, especially a corridor to the Baltic Sea which cut Ostpreussen off from the rest of the country. The Nazi Party promised to restore the old borders and bring us back into the fold of the Fatherland, so naturally many people voted for them.

I have said that the 1933 elections were free elections, though that is not strictly true. The Brownshirts flooded the city and made a point of confronting any opposition, bullying them and preventing some people from exercising their vote. They handed out little badges to people who had voted for them and made it plain that people not wearing the badges could expect rough treatment. Many people claimed to have voted for the Nazis who in fact did not, wanting to avoid trouble, but my parents were not willing to compromise their beliefs. They refused the badges when offered them, and walked back through Königsberg with heads held high. I have never been so proud of them.

Life under the Nazis was, at first, not so very different from our existence under the Weimar Republic. Germans are an orderly race and like to do things properly, so if the authorities present us with good reasons for doing something, we tend to go along with it. Unfortunately, we had not yet learned to distinguish between propaganda and the truth, and by the time we saw through the Nazi message, it was too late. We had lost the means by which to make a meaningful objection, and could now only follow along the path that led to war. Those who still tried to object, disappeared, or were subjected to persecution until they recanted. They continued to be viewed with suspicion, though, so most people quickly learned to keep their opinions to themselves and toe the party line.

You will understand that much of what I was brought up to believe was taught to me by my parents, and my father in particular, who was a member of the Communist Party. The Communists were outlawed after 1933, but my parents continued to inculcate proper values in my young mind at home. I had other influences though, as the Nazi party sought to control young people through education and propaganda. Our school teachers ardently taught us German history coloured by Nazi prejudices, and the organisations we were pressured to join added to our indoctrination. I was brought up with liberal views, but had a veneer of conservatism and fascism laid over me.

Königsberg became a colourful city under Nazi rule, though harshly, brazenly colourful. It has always been a beautiful city with many fine old buildings and beautiful parks, but now flags and banners adorned public buildings – great sheets of blood red with the white circle and black Hakenkreuz – or swastika – of the Nazis. Matching this adornment were men in gleaming new uniforms, black and brown, jackbooted and fanatical, who marched in the streets, mingled with the citizens and filled the theatres and restaurants. Torchlight parades stirred our hearts, and rhetoric turned our heads. Excitement filled the city, and pageantry and spectacle appealed to young and old alike. Neither my older brother Hans nor I were immune to the promise of a New Germany, and despite our parents' disapproval, we celebrated our love of the Fatherland.

My brother Hans is a few years older than me, tall and strong. Along with every boy, he was required to join the Hitlerjugend where he revelled in the physical training afforded these youths. He took up athletics and weight training, developing his muscles to the extent that he became one of the best young weight-lifters in the country. A few years later, when Herr Hitler show-pieced the country and his regime by holding the Olympics in Berlin, my brother represented Germany and performed creditably. He returned to Königsberg and, along with other athletes from the city, was given a rapturous welcome.

I joined the Bund Deutscher Mädel, the girls' equivalent of the Hitlerjugend. We learned all the womanly skills favoured by the Nazi Party – cleaning, cooking, cleanliness, the rearing of children, and were, of course, given many long and boring lectures on Party doctrine. Our bodies were trained as well as our minds and we were taken on long hikes in the country, camping out beside camp fires, singing songs and learning folklore. We were encouraged to spy on our neighbours and indeed to police our families, alert for any word or action that fell short of the Nazi ideal. On one occasion, I can remember, one of the girls tattled on another she thought had faltered in her course. The tattler was rewarded and the culprit punished by public shaming.

We were expected to learn womanly duties, but to remain chaste until marriage. This was not always possible as youths and girls in the flush of health mingled together on state occasions, and made opportunities to meet in private. Pregnancy outside of marriage was frowned upon, however. The Party saw us as wives and homemakers, future mothers of the next generation of National Socialists and were determined that we should demonstrate the high and pure ideals of wholesome German Womanhood.

I have to admit I was not our instructor's favourite pupil. I was too independent of thought and loved my neighbours too much to ever spy on them or report the many small infractions that inevitably occurred. In addition, I enjoyed the attention of Hans' friends, also in the Hitlerjugend, as much as they seemed to enjoy the attention of a blonde pigtailed girl in uniform. I flirted, but naturally I was careful and defended my maidenhood, for we were taught that womanly honour was a distinguishing mark of the German maiden.

When I was seventeen, I had to complete my *Landfrauenjahr*, my year of land service on a farm. This

93

was easy for me as I had been reared on a farm and was at home among livestock and crops. I milked cows, fed chickens, mucked out pigsties, harvested apples and helped bring in the hay. I also helped around the farm house, cooking and cleaning and looking after the Frau's two small children. I also fell in love.

His name was Hermann and had been sent by his parents in Frankfurt an der Oder to learn something of country life. He did not enjoy his stay – except for my presence – but he found something that interested him. Too interested, you will say, but he was a nice young man and we were both healthy young people...

* * *

A hand tugged at her skirts. "Mutti, I'm cold."

Elisabet sighed and looked away from the empty road leading to Königsberg, and picked up Günter, hugging and comforting him. Of course, Joachim then demanded attention, as did Werner, so she embraced all her children before turning them to face the road south.

"Come then, children. The sooner we set off, the quicker we'll get warm."

Elisabet pushed the pram with Joachim inside, together with the last of their food and their blankets and precious oilskin piled on top. The children wore as many clothes as possible, a useful way to carry them as well as keeping them warm. Snow covered the road except for a central rutted strip of packed snow and ice where vehicles had passed by recently. They kept to this strip as the dangers of slipping on the ice were less than the exhaustion of fighting their way through drifted snow on the edges. Every now and then, trucks would pass, loaded with soldiers or supplies, and they would have to stop and wait for

94

them to pass. The soldiers would stare at them list-listlessly, or ignore them totally, their expressions blank between helmets and turned up collars of greatcoats. The children waved at first, but lacking a response, soon just stood and watched, before resuming their laborious passage south. The pram lost a wheel, and now they had to balance the little vehicle to prevent it tipping over, as well as wrestle it through the snow and ice.

It had stopped snowing, but the wind still stood at their backs, sometimes gusting sufficiently hard to unbalance them on the unstable surface. The cold bit at their extremities, despite socks and sturdy shoes, gloves and woollen hats, and soon Werner and Günter were complaining that their feet had gone numb. Elisabet took shelter behind a low stone wall and examined their feet, rubbing their reddened toes and squeezing them to restore the circulation. Then she fitted some dry socks and reluctantly put their wet shoes back on. They cried, but got up again and tottered on.

Elisabet would dearly have liked to talk over her options with another adult, and wished Marlene was still with them. Instead, she talked to Helmut, and though her nine-year-old son could offer few useful opinions, it felt better just to be voicing her thoughts.

"A lot of people will be heading for Berlin," she said. "But if the Russians break through, that's where they'll go too."

"Where then, Mutti?" Helmut asked.

"Dresden. Your uncle Hans' family lives there. They will welcome us."

"Won't the Russians go there too – if they break through, that is?"

Elisabet nodded. "Very likely, but nobody has bombed Dresden as it is an old and beautiful city, so perhaps the Russians will leave it alone too."

"This is the road to Dresden?"

"Yes...or at least one of them. I thought it might be better if we stayed on the main road south for a while, past Graudenz and Thorn, possibly even Posen, before turning west. I think we'd make better time. The problem is that I don't know where the Russians are, and it may be better heading west on the smaller roads immediately."

Helmut could offer no opinion on this, so walked in silence beside his mother. They were not alone on the road as everywhere, people were moving west, away from the threat of the Soviet Army. Carts passed them, travelling either north or south as people interpreted the direction of the danger, and others, on foot, cut across the snow-drifted fields or unused small country roads. Horses trudged head down, hooves slipping on the ice, and people scarcely gave them a glance, wrapped in their own thoughts.

Dusk crept upon them surreptitiously under a leaden sky, and Elisabet took shelter with her family in the partial shelter of a ruined stoned cottage. A fallen wall had allowed drifts of snow into the structure, but a back corner remained intact, and they ensconced themselves, piling some of the fallen stone as another low windbreak. While Elisabet tended to the immediate needs of the younger children, comforting them, Helmut tried to make a fire, having observed Jan make one before. He and Kurt gathered fallen timber and added a sweeping of dry leaves from a protected crevice. It was hard work, and Helmut was almost crying with frustration by the time the tinder caught fire. It built slowly, and finally ate into a great beam that had fallen from the roof of the build-building, heat blossoming out and making them cry with the sheer delight of warmth.

They cooked the last of the root vegetables supplied by the SS cook in Elbing, and brewed up a weak pot of ersatz coffee. It was not a nutritious meal, but it was reasonably filling and the hot drink made them feel better. They slept huddled together, and woke stiff and cold at dawn. The fire had gone out in the night, and the remains of the coffee had frozen solid in the pot. Elisabet decided against relighting the fire, but did add some slivers of charred wood to the diminished supplies in the pram before setting out once again.

The snow held off once more, and as the day progressed, the cloud thinned and weak sunshine lit the white landscape. The light lifted their spirits, even if they derived no heat from it, and the children played beside the road until their strength gave out. A convoy went past, trucks filled with Wehrmacht troops. Kurt waved and ran alongside one of the trucks for a score of paces, calling out.

"Hello, soldaten."

One of the men dug into his pocket and lobbed a small object out into the snow. Kurt leapt to catch it and sprawled headfirst. He got to his feet, grinning, and holding aloft the stick of candy. Other soldiers laughed, and a small shower of candies followed. When the trucks had passed, the children gathered up the sweets and sucked and chewed the delicious sugary treats. For a time, the journey seemed almost enjoyable, but as hunger set in again, their play faltered and the small boys begged to be carried. Joachim was too small to walk far, so spent a lot of time in the pram, but sometimes when he got out stretching his legs, either Werner or Günter could take a turn and ease their weary limbs. The older boys and their mother had no respite though, trudging endlessly on through the snow, wrestling the three-wheeled pram along icy rutted roads.

They passed a small farm and looked wistfully at the smoke pouring from the chimney of the stone cottage, and at the sturdy barn beside it. Elisabet thought about begging some food off the farmer, but he came out with a dog and, in Polish, angrily told them to keep going. He watched them out of sight before returning to his fireside.

After a frugal meal of stale bread and weak coffee that evening, sheltering in the old burnt out frame of a vehicle, Elisabet and the younger children settled down to sleep as best they could. Helmut drew Kurt to one side and whispered to him.

"I'm going back to the farm to see if I can find anything to eat. Are you coming?"

Kurt looked at the faint white landscape beneath the dark night and shivered. "It's a long way back. What if we get lost?"

"We can't. We just stick to the road and it'll lead us there and back. Besides, it's only a few kilometres or so."

"There's a dog," Kurt said desperately.

"It'll be locked up. We're only going to scrounge around for something to eat, not break into his house."

Kurt could not think of any other objection that would not reveal his fear, so he allowed his older brother to lead him away into the darkness.

Both boys felt the loneliness and exposure of the open road, and soon Helmut put out his hand and firmly clasped Kurt's. They walked down the middle of the road, their hearts beating fast in their thin chests. Time passed slowly and they hardly seemed to be moving in a vast snowy plain.

"Where is it?" Kurt quavered. "We should be there by now."

"Soon. See that wall? We passed that just after the farm."

Kurt eyed the low stone wall uneasily, as if he expected something or someone to be lurking in its shadow. He put his brother on that side and almost ran past it, dragging Helmut by the hand.

The farm loomed in the darkness, the only light coming from a chink in an ill-fitted shutter. Helmut and Kurt studied the darkened cottage and barn from the road, building up their courage.

"Wh...where's the dog?" Kurt asked.

"Probably in the cottage," Helmut said. "I'll go and look there, you check the barn."

"Couldn't we go together?"

"It would take twice as long then. Look, nobody will see you. Just sneak inside and see if there's anything we can eat."

"What sort of thing?"

"Anything."

Helmut slipped off into the shadows, leaving Kurt to make his way slowly to the barn, shaking with fright. Minutes passed and nothing leapt out at him, so he got more daring and eased the barn door open with no more than a muffled creak. It was completely dark inside, without even the hint of moon glow from above the clouds. He gulped and looked toward the cottage, hoping to see his brother.

"There's nothing here," he whispered. Nevertheless, he inched his way into the barn, keeping his back to the wall. He stumbled and almost cried out when he bumped into sacks lined against the wall. Kurt's heart slowed and his breathing became more even when nobody reacted to his clumsiness, so he bent down and ran his hands over the sacks, feeling the knobbly outline of its contents. He pulled the top of one sack open and lifted out one of the objects, sniffing it gingerly.

"Potatoes." This was definitely something they could eat, so he put the potato back in the sack and tried dragging the sack toward the door. It was too heavy and it fell on its side, spilling its contents. Kurt tried again and found the sack was lighter, so he emptied out a few more, and then more, until the sack was just light enough to carry. He staggered toward the door, feeling very pleased with himself.

The farmhouse was still in darkness and there was no sign of Helmut. Kurt could feel panic rising in him at the thought of finding his way back to Mutti and telling her he had lost his brother. He did not think a half sack of potatoes would soften the loss.

"Helmut? Where are you? Please answer."

As if in response, a crack of light split the side of the cottage and as the door opened, a boy slipped out into the night. Helmut had only run a few paces before the door was flung wide by a man who shouted in rage and, at his feet, a dog barked and leapt forward.

"Run, Helmut, run!" Kurt screamed.

Helmut raced for the road, the dog after him. For a moment, Kurt wondered what to do, and then realised he had to help somehow. He bent and cast about with his hands in the dark for a stone, but found only snow and straw. The dog was almost upon his brother when he remembered the potatoes. He threw one with no result; a second skittered in front of the dog, almost on Helmut's heels and the dog faltered, startled. A third clipped the dog's flank and it yelped, scrambling back before it stood facing the road and unloosed a volley of barks.

Kurt slipped out of the barn with his sack of potatoes and sidled toward the road. The man in the doorway yelled imprecations in Polish, but the dog had decided it would see the intruders off from where it stood, so Kurt took to his heels and caught Helmut up several metres along the road.

"Sehr gut, Kurt," Helmut said. "That was a good shot with the stone."

"It was a potato. See?" Kurt held the sack open. "Why did you go into the house?"

"If there was any food there, it was going to be inside, wasn't it, dummkopf?"

"So what did you find?"

Helmut grinned, his teeth gleaming faintly. He opened his coat and took out a loaf of bread and two other smaller objects.

"A bit of cheese, and a lump of butter."

Kurt sniffed the cheese appreciatively, and prodded the butter. Despite the cold air, Helmut's body had warmed it and the outside was soft, almost oozing.

Helmut tucked the food away in his coat and licked his fingers. "Come on." He led the way back along the road to where the burnt out vehicle housed the rest of their family.

Elisabet was awake and pacing the icy road, looking one way and then the other. As the two boys hove into view, she gave a sharp cry and ran to them, hugging them to her fiercely.

"Where have you been? Don't ever go off like that again. I was so worried."

101

"Sorry, Mutti," Helmut said. "Look, we found food." He drew the bread out from under his coat, and Kurt held up his part sack of potatoes. "We got them at the farm where that nasty Pole was."

"He might have hurt you," Elisabet said. "Then where would I be? Without my two kleine männer?" She kissed them both and examined their booty. "It is wrong to steal, but it is a greater wrong that children should go hungry. I am not angry, meine lieblingsjungen, but tell me before you think of doing anything like this again."

Kurt hugged his mother, and Helmut grinned. "Yes, Mutti, but can we have some bread and cheese now? I'm very hungry."

Kapitel Sechs (6)

They heard the sound of the approaching battle the next morning, far to the south and east – a rolling thunder that went on and on beneath a sky that looked leaden but gave no hint of storm. Elisabet stopped and cocked her head to one side, listening, and other refugees slowed their flight south to listen with her.

"What is it?" Elisabet asked an old man. "Is it thunder?"

"That's the sound of battle. I heard it a quarter of a century ago in France. It's the sound of big guns pounding some poor bastards."

"The Russians?"

"On the receiving end, no doubt. Our boys will be giving them a pasting," said the old man.

"Are you sure? I heard the Russians had broken through."

"That's defeatist talk. Shame on you, Frau. You are setting a bad example for your children."

"If you're so sure we're winning, why are you fleeing with the rest of us?"

"That's a good point," said an old woman with a grown daughter supporting her.

The old man shrugged. "I have no doubt our boys are winning, but at my time of life I have no desire to get caught up in a battle, so I'm getting out of their way." He started to move away and turned back for one last word. "You can be sure if I see a Russki, I'll give him a good German boot up his backside."

"Of course you will, old man," muttered the woman. She looked at Elisabet and her children. "That's men for you, but it's we women who have to

103

bear the pain of their wars. You get your children far from here is my advice."

"I intend to, Frau," Elisabet said. "Gott, mit uns."

The presence of the battle to the south made Elisabet think again about her plan to first drop down below Berlin and then head for her brother's family in Dresden. Perhaps it would be more sensible to put some westerly distance between them and the ongoing hostilities before veering south again. She racked her brains for knowledge of the roads through Poland. Just ahead was a crossroads where the road from Elbing to Landsberg an der Warthe cut to the southwest. That would be easier going than fighting their way through snowdrifts in the fields.

Elisabet turned right, and joined a stream of refugees fleeing from Elbing. They mostly kept to themselves, heads down, lost in their cold and misery, and after a few attempts at conversation with fellow travellers, Elisabet kept to herself, concentrating on looking after her family. There were convoys on this road too, but the trucks seldom contained soldiers. Instead, men in SS uniform manned heavily laden vehicles moving westward at a steady pace. They stopped for no one, and on the second day, near the town of Preussisch Stargard, one of these trucks skidded on the icy road and demolished a horse and cart laden with furniture. The SS officer in the truck got out to examine the damage, looked briefly at the shattered cart and injured people, and told the truck driver to drive on.

The old couple driving the cart had been thrown off, the woman landing in the snow beside the road, but her husband, equally ancient, fell between the truck and the splintering cart and had his legs and chest crushed. He lay on the bloody ice and snow, screaming weakly, and scrabbling at the snow with his fingers, while his wife, who had escaped with only cuts and bruises, wept and wailed. She comforted her dying husband as best she could, but he had passed beyond all help and his bloodless lips quivered and his sightless eyes stared up at the grey sky. Other refugees gathered, and offered water and clothing, but there was nothing anyone could do. The old man shuddered and died, and the woman's screams redoubled in vigour. People stood around, not knowing what to do, and one or two women drew the grieving widow to her feet, offering condolences. They tried to lead her away, but she would not go. Her husband of fifty years lay dead on the road, and all her worldly possessions lay strewn over the roadside. She sat in the snow and cradled the old man's head in her lap, rocking and crying, and refused to move.

"Come, alte Frau, you must get up. You will die here in the cold."

"Let me be. I cannot leave my sweet Ranulf. He needs me."

"At least come into the town. You can be looked after there."

"No. I will stay with him. Let me die here. There is nothing for me now."

While the women tried to persuade the widow, some of the men were examining the horse and discussing its fate. It stood beside the road, shivering violently, one leg hanging limp and covered in blood.

"Broken leg. It won't survive."

"It would be a mercy to put it down."

"Lots of good meat on it."

"Who's got a gun?"

Other refugees were sorting through the old couple's scattered possessions and Elisabet saw several people walk off with items – a silver jug, cutlery, an iron pot, a tablecloth – and she wondered how people could shed their civilised habits so quickly. She thought about saying something, but a scuffle broke out over some small object and knives were drawn. Her children were more important, so she turned away.

"Are they going to shoot the horse, Mutti?" Helmut asked.

"I expect so. It's badly hurt and it would be a kindness."

Helmut looked at the horse and the men gathered round it. "Can you eat horse?"

"What? No, don't look." Elisabet grabbed at her children, shielding them with her skirts but Helmut twisted away, curiosity etched in his face.

He saw the rifle raised and pointed at the horse's head, heard the muffled report and the abrupt flurry of limbs and spray of blood as the beast fell to the snow. Men quickly gathered round it, wielding knives. Helmut went pale.

The old widow wailed again from where she sat. "That's my horse. How am I going to drive my cart without my horse?"

"What cart?" a youth said. He kicked the splintered remains.

"It was your horse, alte Frau," one of the men corrected. "It's just so much meat now."

"Fair's fair," said another. "It was her horse. Give her some of the meat."

"We should all get some," yelled a woman with two small children. "Why should you have it all?"

A tall man in the middle of the crowd around the carcass stood up, his forearms bloody, and pushed a lock of his hair aside with the back of one hand. It left a red smear across his forehead. "My friend here shot it, and I'm butchering it, Frau. Doesn't that give me rights?"

"Maybe, but we're all hungry," the woman said.

The butcher shrugged. "There's enough for everyone."

Elisabet was torn between hurrying her children away from the bloody scene, and with getting her hands on some of the horse meat. Helmut looked as if he was going to be sick, while Kurt and Werner stared wide-eyed at the horse slowly being dismembered. Günter stared at the dead man, while Joachim slept in his pram which was propped against a fence so it wouldn't tip over. Hunger won out and, leaving the children on the roadside under Helmut's care, Elisabet pressed forward and received a chunk of meat from a fore-leg, bloody and with the hide still attached. She wrapped it in a scrap of cloth and led her children away.

They ate horse that night, huddled in a small lane off the main road. Helmut had had the presence of mind to take a few pieces of the shattered cart and that night used it to start a small fire. There was insufficient fuel to cook all the meat, so Elisabet sliced off a small amount and roasted it impaled on a sliver of wood. The boys looked at it askance, remembering where it had come from, but the smell made their mouths water, and hunger drove them to consume it all with chunks of partly cooked fire-baked potatoes and stale rye bread. They hunched around the embers of the tiny fire, covering themselves with blankets and, shivering, passed into sleep. The next morning they continued on their way, chewing on crusts of bread as they walked.

Refugees choked the roads at times, swarming across the countryside, the crush exacerbated by large numbers of Wehrmacht and SS troops falling back in front of the Russian advance. Guns blazed continuously beyond the horizon now, filling the waking mind with a low rumble of approaching horror and haunting dreams snatched in fitful sleep. At times, pairs of Soviet planes swept overhead, raking the roads with cannon fire, leaving burning trucks and screaming people in their wake. Elisabet always had one ear cocked for the growl of their approach and hurried her children into the fields before they arrived.

"Where is the damn Luftwaffe?" men would scream, shaking their fists impotently at the red-starred aircraft.

"Curse Göring," yelled an old man after one attack, but people edged away from him in case he would be arrested.

Rumours abounded, but nothing could be verified. Some said the Soviet advance had been halted and the enemy thrown back in confusion – but why then were the German soldiers retreating? Others said that cities like Königsberg and Danzig had already fallen and everyone in the city killed. All that was certain was the bone-chilling cold, the hunger, and the palpable fear of thousands of refugees.

The area around Tuchler was a military base and convoys of trucks carted away equipment constantly, roaring away toward the city of Schneidemühl. Explosions erupted from the forests behind them as the soldiers blew up installations to prevent them falling into enemy hands. A howling storm descended

108

on them. Freezing winds swept in from the north-northwest, whipping up loose snow and driving into the faces of the refugees, stinging exposed parts and adding to their misery. Elisabet turned off the main road and hurried to a patch of forest, pushing through the undergrowth to the tall trees and taking shelter beneath a broad-limbed fir. She hung blankets from low limbs and anchored them with fallen limbs, while the boys gathered dry pine needles and cones, bark and twigs, and Helmut lit a fire.

They were two days in their makeshift shelter while the storm blew itself out. Horse meat and potatoes were on the menu for every meal, and they consumed the last of their supplies. Elisabet knew they would have to move on the next day, so fed her boys with every scrap she had. She made them strip off wet clothing and sit huddled in blankets while the fire lifted eddies of steam from their clothes, replacing it with pine-scented smoke. Meanwhile, the sound of battle could now be heard intermittently over the howl of the wind.

"What's going to happen, Mutti?" Kurt asked. "What are the Russians like?"

"I've never met any," Elisabet admitted. She hesitated, torn between warning them with tales of caution and not wanting to frighten them. "They're like other people, I suppose."

"Will they shoot us?" Werner asked.

"Of course not. Why would they? Soldiers don't make war on women and children."

Elisabet wished that was true, but knew it was not.

*   *   *

I met Wilfrieda in the hospital at Königsberg. She came from a farm north and east of Memel, a city on the coast at the northern end of the Kurisches Haff, where she worked hard to keep her family fed and was generous to those less fortunate than her. I don't believe she ever hurt anybody, least of all the Russians, but it didn't save her. In August 1944, just before the bombers destroyed large parts of Königsberg, the Russians advanced on the Baltic lands, overrunning the German troops in the area. No one expected the horror that was to be unleashed on them, but the attack distilled fear into the minds of every Ostpreusse. Wilfrieda survived – at least for a time – there in her hospital bed.

When the refugees were evacuated to Königsberg after our army retook Memel, Wilfrieda was one of them. The city authorities put out the call to families of party members to visit the injured in hospital and remind them of Germany's destiny to ultimately triumph over its enemies. As my husband had been a party member, I was called on and assigned Wilfrieda. She lay in her bed, heavily bandaged and bruised, looking like she had been beaten severely. I introduced myself and for a few minutes prattled on about my life and my children.

"I have never even seen a Russian," I said. "Except a few prisoners on work detail."

"They are animals – nothing but animals that walk upright and carry guns." Wilfrieda closed her eyes, breathing fast. Her tongue moistened her split and bruised lips and her bandaged fingers fluttered on the sheet. "Refugees came to our farm, honest folk from the north, fleeing the soldiers, and because the Wehrmacht was nearby, they thought they were safe. They camped on our farm and we welcomed them, feeding them and giving them pasture for their animals to graze. They were Germans, and our neighbours, nein?"

110

"What happened?" I asked gently.

"The Russians happened." Wilfrieda looked away, tears in her eyes. After a few moments she looked back at me and then away again, to a window where the sounds of the city came to us faint on a summer breeze. "They came swiftly, tanks and men on foot. Our own soldiers were overwhelmed, and then they advanced on the town, rounding up men, women and children and driving them before them, whipping them and clubbing them, so that any German soldiers still fighting had to fire on their own folk."

I said nothing, for my mind had frozen at the horror of her words. Worse was to come. Wilfrieda's gaze took on a distant look, as if she was no longer in the hospital ward.

"The Russian soldiers laughed at our plight, and some women begged them to stop. I saw an officer pull a pistol out and shoot one woman in the face. A group of soldiers threw a young woman onto the grass and raped her, one after another, then shot her when they had finished."

I squeezed Wilfrieda's hand, tears in my own eyes. I wanted to run from the hospital, from her words, for these were things outside my knowledge. We were both German women, yet her experiences were so different from mine. I felt guilty that she had suffered and I had not, so I stayed and listened.

"They raped a grandmother and killed her immediately, then stripped a girl barely in her teens, raped her repeatedly and nailed her alive to a barn door. Their actions were cruel and barbarous. They raped me and left me alive, but a dozen others were bayoneted or shot in front of me after the soldiers had had their way with them."

111

I lifted Wilfrieda's bandaged hand and kissed it, but she took no notice.

"They drove their tanks through the crowds of people, crushing them and leaving bloody bodies behind. I saw them pick up little children and throw them in the air, spitting them on bayonets. Others they just ripped open and...and left screaming until they died."

Tears ran down my face. "No more, Wilfrieda," I begged. "Please."

"They laughed as they did these things and I thought them very devils from hell, but you know what was worse?"

Wilfrieda's eyes focused on mine, and her grip on my hand tightened.

"You know the worst thing? One of them told me why they did this. Do you want to know why? Shall I tell you?"

I shook my head, trying to pull my hand from her startlingly strong grip. "No. No, please, don't tell me." Suddenly I knew what she would tell me and I did not want to hear it. The war had largely passed me by in beautiful Königsberg and I did not want my safe, clean world tarnished by ugly truth.

"He said it was for revenge. He said Germans had done all this and worse to his people, so we deserved it."

I shook my head, not daring to speak.

"Of course, he was lying," Wilfrieda said. "Germans would never do such things, but I have wondered why he told me that story instead of just killing me." Tears welled in her eyes. "I wish he had killed me."

I could not meet her gaze, nor could I stay any longer and offer words of comfort. I tore myself from her bedside and fled the hospital certain the Russian soldier had lied to her. No German could behave like that.

I returned to the hospital the next day, but I never got the chance to apologise to Wilfrieda for my cowardice or to offer her what comfort I could. She had died of her injuries in the night.

Other stories like hers circulated in the city, and our fear grew...

*　　*　　*

The storm blew itself out in the night, and all that was left was the thunder to the south and flickers of light along the horizon. It looked like another storm coming, but Elisabet knew this one was man-made. It was time to move again. They packed up their belongings and wrestled the pram and their bundles through the drifts of new snow out onto the road, and turned their faces toward Konitz. Another pram wheel collapsed, adding to their burdens. For the first time since they had left Mohrungen, the road was almost deserted. They made their way slowly, six dark forms moving across a great white plain broken only by patches of conifer forest. It was a beautiful sight, but deadly, for the cold slipped effortlessly through their layers of clothing and nipped at fingers and faces. Snow caked on their shoes, weighing down their feet until they seemed to shuffle along encased in ice.

Gradually, as they pushed their way along, the heat of their exertion gave some relief from the cold, though now hunger gripped their bellies. The children cried at first, but soon learned that there was no relief out here in the countryside. Elisabet cajoled, encouraged and bullied them along, her heart aching for her children, but knowing she could not let up for an instant if they were to survive. She fed them the last tiny scraps of food – a piece of stale bread, a sliv-sliver of hard cheese, or a fragment of charred tuber. It was not enough, and she knew her children could not last long in this bitter winter weather.

Despite hunger and cold, the children still sought distraction. Werner and Günter threw snowballs at each other, while Helmut and Kurt roamed the edge of the road investigating the litter of possessions discarded by refugees as their strength failed. Mostly, the objects were worthless and would merely add to their burdens, so they left them behind, but occasionally they found something useful. Kurt found a glove, ice-caked and stiff, but once thawed out and dried it would warm a hand. Then Helmut found a shoe in a snowdrift.

"Here's a shoe...Mutti, come quickly, there's a foot still in it."

Elisabet hurried over. Helmut had pulled on the shoe, and a stiff, trousered leg had lifted free of its icy covering. She bent and brushed more snow away, revealing a coat-covered body. The man was face down by the edge of the road, head turned to one side, staring sightlessly along the line of his outstretched arm.

"Is he alive, Mutti?" Kurt asked.

"Helmut, Kurt, take your brothers to the other side of the road."

"But Mutti..."

"Now."

Elisabet bent to her task once more and brushed more snow aside. The man's arm ended in white frozen fingers interlaced with other, smaller fingers – those of a young woman. She uncovered enough to

be sure, and then cleared the snow from the two fac-
faces.

"Were they married, Mutti?"

Elisabet glanced up at Helmut's pale face. "I
thought I told you to go across the road with your
brothers."

"I did, Mutti. Then I came back. Were they
married?"

"I think so. At least they meant a lot to each other.
He died looking at her and holding her hand."

"What happened?"

"I don't know. Froze to death in the storm
probably."

Helmut looked down at the foot that he had first
seen in the snow drift, and the leather shoe on it. "Are
we going to take his shoes? Or his coat?" He bent
over the frozen bodies. "Or their rings? We could
trade them for food."

"I don't think we should," Elisabet said. "It's too
much like robbing them."

"We stole potatoes and bread and cheese from that
farm."

"The farmer had plenty. He did not suffer from
our theft."

"They're dead, Mutti."

Elisabet stood and looked down at the bodies,
then across at her eldest son. Her moral code told her
to respect other people's property, but her children's
need encouraged her to loot the dead couple. She
considered her options for several minutes.

"Mutti? It's getting cold. What do we do?"

Elisabet sighed. "We leave them as we found them.
We have not become desperate enough to steal from
the dead. I hope we never have to." She crossed the
road with Helmut trailing behind, and embraced her

children. Their teeth were chattering, so she urged them into motion for warmth. A hundred metres fur-further on, she looked back, but the bodies were invisible among the mounds and drifts of snow.

"I should have searched them for identification," she muttered. "Somewhere they have family who will never know what became of them."

Konitz was a town in uproar. Units of the Wehrmacht were pulling out of the town, leaving it undefended, and the townspeople were panicking, loading up their belongings and fleeing in every direction but south and east. Many took to the country roads leading north, and others followed the convoys of trucks and soldiers on foot making for the towns of Schneidemühl and Deutsch Krone.

Elisabet was in a quandary, unsure whether to stick close to the soldiers or to strike out alone across the countryside. There could be a measure of protection offered by the German Army, but they might also offer battle to the Russians and endanger them. Alternatively, fleeing alone might mean they went unnoticed, but if the enemy did happen upon them, they were lost. In the end, partly because her late husband had been in the Wehrmacht, she put her trust in the soldiers and hurried along with scores of others in the wake of the retreating units.

It turned out there were advantages in the first couple of days. The soldiers showed kindness to the refugee women and children, or as much as their officers allowed. They slipped the children hard candies to suck and offered stories if they could keep up. At midday, and at night, the non-commissioned officers gave permission for standard army rations to be issued to the families – hard crackers, preserved meat, erbsenwurst or dried vegetables, and a little ersatz coffee. The soldiers shared their camp fires on the first night, allowing Elisabet and the children the opportunity of a hot meal and dry clothes, as well as a comfortable night. On the second night, however, an Oberstleutnant came down the line, his staff car roaring and slipping on the ice, and angrily ordered the soldiers to cease aiding the refugees. When he had gone, extra rations were issued to the families and supplies of fuel, but then they were reluctantly turned away.

One young Obergefreiter pushed a bag of ration packs into Elisabet's hands. "Don't think too badly of us, Frau. Orders are orders, but we all wish you well. The children are the future of Germany."

"May God look after you, Obergefreiter."

It took them another week to reach the outskirts of Schneidemühl, long after the troops had reached it. The rations lasted the distance, though they were hungry by the time they got there. As they neared the city, the sounds of battle increased, with the thunder of artillery almost constant. In the brief interludes when the great guns fell silent, Elisabet thought she could hear the crackle of rifle fire and the growl of tank engines. It filled her with fear and she hurried the children along, increasingly aware that she was in a race to reach the safety of Schneidemühl before the Russians overtook them.

The city was surrounded by thick forests which gave some protection from the cold, acting as a windbreak for the fierce winter gales. The Küddow River was frozen over when they arrived, but they crossed by the bridge anyway. It was manned by an anti-tank unit and bristling with machineguns and artillery. A Leutnant of Police waved them over impatiently and ordered them to report to the city administration.

As they walked through the city streets, Elisabet became very aware that this was a city preparing for war and had second thoughts about bringing her children into danger. Anxious citizens thronged the streets, mingling with soldiers, and over the confusion and fear came explosions and cannon fire from the southern end of the city. At the city administration building, she registered her family. The official looked disappointed that there were no men in her family and that her eldest boy was only nine years old.

"We need every able bodied man and youth we can get, Frau Daecker. A great battle is about to occur."

"Perhaps we should leave. I don't want to put my children in danger."

"Too late, Frau," the official said with a bitter smile. "The Führer has declared Schneidemühl a Festung, a Fortress City. Nobody leaves now, and it will be defended to the last drop of German blood."

Kapitel Sieben (7)

Elisabet and her children reported, as instructed, to one of the refugee camps set up in a small park on the southern side of the city. She was issued with a tent and rations for a week, told about the sanitary arrangements and water supply, and left to her own devices. They put up their tent on a patch of grass cleared of snow beside a tall leafless birch, then sat in it and looked at their neighbours. The park was crowded – mostly women and children with a scattering of wounded or crippled men – but the atmosphere within the camp was anything but friendly, despite being filled with refugees from the Russian invaders. German settlers mixed with native Poles, Ostpruessen with foreigners on work detail, and the mix of languages and accents raised suspicions and increased distrust. Scuffles broke out and were ruthlessly put down by the Ordnungspolizei and their SS officers. Most culprits were just beaten, but gang leaders were rounded up and hanged without trial, their bodies left hanging from lampposts as a warning. Other men were brought in from the surrounding city and hanged from the lampposts alongside the rioters. These victims were mainly foreign workers, but a few were German youths. The bodies had signs around their necks and Helmut could not be prevented from looking at one of them.

"It says he was executed for looting," Helmut reported.

Elisabet cautioned her children. "Do not even think of stealing anything here, not even a morsel of food. I don't think they would hang a child, but it would be a stupid risk finding out. Understand?'

"Yes, Mutti," the oldest four children said in turn. Joachim just sucked his thumb.

The Russian attack had already started on the German emplacements to the south and east of the city, a steady build up of noise. The battle no longer sounded like thunder, but as a series of blasts that could be felt as the compression waves rippled through the air. Windows blew out and people covered their ears and yet the advancing enemy was still outside the city limits. Presently they started on the city itself. Shells screamed overhead and exploded in masonry-shattering roars in the centre of the city. Rubble rained down into the streets and people died or were injured by explosions or falling debris.

Katyusha rockets howled like a cacophony of demons, delivering sheet after sheet of fire and high explosive to the German positions and beyond, before suddenly falling silent as the German guns found the range. Half an hour would pass and the Katyusha would start up again from a different position, raining down death on military and civilian alike.

All the while, the air was filled with rifle fire and the grinding roar of tanks. Dust and smoke filled the air and the light of the sun became reddened and obscured. At night it was even worse. The electricity supply had been cut and the only illumination came from the screaming rockets, the lurid blast of their payloads and the subsequent fires that consumed the city. Buildings became burnt-out shells and then collapsed into piles of rubble, blocking the streets and killing the people.

The refugees lived as best they could, but their camp in the city park rapidly became uninhabitable, and they fled to the dubious cover of the city streets,

120

Elisabet and her boys included, and lived in terror among the shells and falling masonry. They crept out during lulls in the fighting and scavenged for food and water, for the organised supply of such necessities had quickly disintegrated into chaos. Despite the lack of facilities and the starvation tightening its grip on the populace, units of police still patrolled the rubble-strewn streets, seeking out defaulters and looters. More bodies hung from any lamppost still standing, and when the supply of makeshift gallows ran out, the police would shoot their victims in the back of the head.

*　　*　　*

Day by day, the city of Schneidemühl died, the soldiers retreating slowly toward the city centre and the Russians creeping closer. The Russians did not have it all their own way, though. Time and again, the German units would stage a counterattack and throw back the invaders, retaking ruined streets at the cost of much blood, only to falter and pull back again as the enemy pushed forward in ever-increasing numbers. Acts of incredible bravery were seen on both sides of the conflict, acts of heroism and sacrifice, but it could not last. German supplies of ammunition and men were limited, whereas the Russian tide seemed inexorable. The Russians had to fight for every metre of ground they gained, however.

The Germans had a single Jagdpanther, sole survivor of a Panzer battalion slaughtered in the east by overwhelming force. It now helped defend Schneidemühl. The Jagdpanther is a tank-killer, a heavily armoured turretless tank with sloping sides and an 88 millimetre cannon. It does not move its cannon by rotating its turret like a normal tank – it does not have a turret – but by moving its tracks backward and forward to swing the whole unit toward its prey. A machine gun completes its armaments, ready to take out the infantry that always accompany a tank.

The Jagdpanther sat in wait in the ruins of a farmhouse on the edge of the city, motionless and all but invisible; its commander crouched low behind the parapet on its crown, with his pair of binoculars fixed on the passage between two mounds of rubble. The tip of a tank cannon eased into view between the mounds, hesitantly, and then the rest of the Russian T-34 tank rumbled into the gap.

"Fire," the commander said quietly.

The shot took the enemy tank where the turret meets the base and lifted it off, sending it sailing into the air as the tank burst into flames. A second tank appeared around the flanks of the burning one and shouldered it aside. Its cannon swung back and forth as its gunner searched for his enemy.

The Jagdpanther's second shot missed, showering the new tank with masonry and making it clang like a broken bell. The T-34's cannon swung round and fired, the shot screaming overhead as the Jagdpanther fired again, this time nailing the Russian tank. A third tank appeared then a fourth and a fifth, infantrymen running in their wake, ducking and hiding. The machinegun opened fire, hosing the area down, sending the Russian soldiers diving for cover.

Jagdpanther fired again, blowing the treads off another tank, but the others pinpointed its position and bombarded the ruined farmhouse. A shot hit the tank killer on its sharply sloping sides with a clang that almost deafened its occupants, but the thick armour and the angle deflected the shell and the Jagdpanther survived. Treads moved in opposing directions, swinging the whole vehicle – it tracked the tank that had fired and its cannon belched. The T-34 and its crew died in gouts of flame.

The commander gave new orders and the Jagdpanther moved into reverse, pulling back from its position, leaving four dead tanks behind it. It found a new hiding place and waited for the Russians to advance again.

* * *

The refugee camps were as badly affected as the rest of the city. Artillery and rocket fire cut down civilians by the score, filling the air with shrapnel – shards of red hot steel, fragments of shattered stone, cement and glass. Blood ran in the gutters, mixing with the crushed rock and cement dust. Women screamed and men panicked, running through the streets, seeking safety. Air raid shelters filled to overflowing and men fought for places within the concrete walls, some plucking children from their mothers' arms and throwing them out just so they could take their places. The hospital system collapsed under the weight of numbers of wounded and the morgues burgeoned with bloody corpses. Dead bodies could no longer be treated with any respect and soldiers were laid alongside women and children in the shell-ravaged hospital grounds. Shattered bodies with gaping wounds, flesh ripped from bone, greeted field staff as they laboured to bring new victims for what care could be provided. As often as not, the wounded died in transit and were unceremoniously dumped outside on the ground soaked in icy blood-slush.

Elisabet had led her children early on to the hospital and offered her services. She had served in the hospital at Königsberg and knew something of nursing procedure. Her service was not entirely self-selfless. She believed even the Russians would not knowingly fire on the dying and wounded, and the hospital buildings must therefore be among the safest places in the stricken city for her helpless children. The older boys carried linen or washed down tables and floors in the wards, while the younger followed them around and scurried to keep out of the way of doctors. Elisabet joined other nursing staff, struggling to lift wounded, screaming people onto operating tables in the surgical halls. They ran out of anaesthetics and operated on conscious bodies, ran out of disinfectants and went ahead anyway, wiping the scalpels on a cloth before starting in with a new patient. It was a harrowing experience, and not one Elisabet wanted for her boys, but at least their work was within hospital walls away from the worst of the cold, and the Red Cross symbol on the hospital roof must surely provide a measure of protection from the Russian bombardment. So far, at least, the hospital had not taken a direct hit, though near misses had blown out windows and speckled the walls with debris. The only alternative to work in the hospital was to sit in their tent in the camp or roam the shattered streets and wait for a Katyusha rocket or explosive shell to rip the life from them. It was no alternative, really, and Elisabet could only hope the experience would not prove too traumatic. They were at least doing something useful.

It could not last, and when Elisabet, hurrying to the denuded stores to search for unused towels, looked from the hospital windows, she could see Russian troops advancing through the city. Tanks rumbled into the refugee park in the city centre, crushing tents and anyone slow to flee, and soldiers spread out, bayoneting and shooting anyone they en-encountered. Buildings crumbled and disintegrated while the remnants of German troops fought a last-ditch battle in the heart of Schneidemühl.

An SS-Sturmbannführer, his black uniform dirty and torn, blood staining his hair and one arm hanging limp by his side, moved through the hospital wards and hallways, directing the staff to leave.

"You have done all you can. Go now to the shelters at the rear of the hospital. Save yourselves."

"What of the patients?" asked one of the doctors. "We cannot just leave them."

"Take them if they can walk, otherwise you will have to leave them," the SS officer said. "We cannot defend the hospital, but you may live a little longer in the bunkers."

"We must stay with our patients," a nurse protested.

"If you stay, the Russians will kill you and your patients."

"They...they wouldn't do that...would they?"

"Very likely. Herr Doktor, at least make sure all the nurses and woman volunteers are evacuated to the shelters. If left, their fate will be worse than that of the wounded."

Elisabet gathered her children and together with a mixed crowd of doctors, nurses and volunteers, they helped a dozen or so ambulatory patients along the corridors and down the stairs to the ground floor. Patients in beds, too injured to be moved, watched the evacuation, for the most part in silence though some cursed and others swore or pleaded with their comrades to take them too. Their pleas tore at the hearts of their listeners, as they knew very well the fate of the wounded left behind.

The bunker was underground, separated from the main hospital building by a small courtyard with great timber double-doors thrown wide and steps leading down into a large chamber. Light came from kerosene lanterns as the electrical power had been cut, and Elisabet herded her children down into the gloomy shelter, pushing past people milling around the entrance. Several SS officers were already sitting near the back wall, talking and passing around a bottle of brandy. Voices rose in argument and one laughed raucously. Elisabet could tell they were drunk, and moved her boys away as far as she could in the crush of people. She could not see the wounded SS-Sturmbannführer who had told them to evacuate the wards.

The bunker doors closed with a dull thud, blocking the daylight. Everyone fell silent as the explosions and screams from outside were cut off, and then, with a collective sigh, people settled themselves down to wait. The SS officers at the back continued to drink and started singing. The words were slurred and violent in nature, and one doctor took it upon himself to push through the crowd and complain. He addressed the senior officer.

"Please, Obersturmführer, there are women and children present. Your singing upsets them."

The officer stared at the doctor. "What did you say?"

"The words of your song offend the women and frighten the children. Could you please stop?"

The Obersturmführer snorted and lifted the bottle again. "Go away, Herr Doktor. We will sing what we please, for when the Russians come, we will all die."

"Nevertheless, I must ask you..."

The officer pulled a luger from a holster on his hip and fired point-blank into the doctor's chest, the report loud in the confined space. Several people screamed and the crowd surged away from the back wall and the SS officers, now all on their feet. The stricken doctor made a faint mewling noise and blood oozed from his mouth for a few moments before he died.

The Obersturmführer nudged the doctor with his boot. "Regrettable," he said, "But the fool brought it on himself." He looked up at the horrified faces of the people and smiled, slipping his luger back in its holster. "I am the senior officer here and you would do well to obey me instantly. This man sought to undermine my authority and paid the price. Now, prepare yourselves for what is to come. When the Russians open the doors, they will kill everyone here, so do your duty – die for the Führer and the Fatherland. There is no better destiny for all of us." He suddenly came to attention and threw out his right arm. "Heil Hitler."

His fellow officers followed suit, their shouted words reverberating off the concrete walls. A few of the wounded soldiers and nurses did likewise, but most turned away, shielding children or sinking to their knees in despair. Elisabet comforted her crying children, and steeled herself for what was to come. She had heard dreadful stories of Russian soldiers and knew that they dealt out death and senseless violence toward helpless civilians.

"What's happening, Mutti?" Günter sobbed.

"Are we going to die?" Kurt asked.

"The Russians are coming," Elisabet said. "We must all be very strong and look out for one another."

"If a Russian comes in here, I'll kill him," Helmut declared.

"When the Russians come in, you'll do no such thing, Helmut. You'll keep your head down and remain seated. Do not meet their eyes and if they want you to speak, you answer them politely. Do you understand?" She looked around at her children. "All of you?"

"Yes, Mutti."

"It is very important you give them no excuse for violence, no reason to be angry with you. Show them you are harmless and unimportant. Can you do that for me, boys? Please? I want you all to be safe and unharmed for I love you all very much."

"We love you too, Mutti," the boys chorused, and the smaller boys threw themselves at their mother, hugging her and crying.

For a time, the bunker was relatively quiet and people's hopes rose that somehow they might be overlooked. Some even went so far as to express the hope that the German forces had thrown back the Russians and rescue was on its way. This vain hope was shattered by a pounding on the wooden bunker doors and a guttural voice calling out in a foreign language. A woman screamed, her cry cut off abruptly.

"Does anyone speak Russian?" asked a doctor.

The SS Obersturmführer shouldered his way to the front. He turned and faced the crowd with his luger in his hand. "You will not answer him. It is treason to parlay with the enemy."

The voice spoke again, longer and with a hint of anger.

"He is telling us to come out," said a Polish nurse. "If we do not, they will blow up the doors."

128

The crowd surged back, leaving a space around the SS officer. He turned to face the wooden doors and raised his luger. "Let them do so. We will sell our lives dearly."

Elisabet gathered the boys around her and crouched low, shielding them with her body. A few minutes passed and all they could hear were a few muffled noises from outside. Then the Russian voice spoke again.

"Last chance," said the Polish nurse. "We should..."

The doors erupted inward in a flame-threaded blast that shattered them into fragments and sent sharp splinters of wood scything through the huddled people. The SS officer was ripped to pieces and his bloody body flung backward into the mass of screaming people.

Elisabet felt her eardrums thumped by the detonation and her children screamed in sudden anguish. A sliver of wood tore through the edge of her collar and clattered against the concrete wall. She reached up shakily with one hand, sure that she would find bloody ruin, but felt only the torn fabric of her coat.

Smoke and dust filled the air, and as the ringing in her ears subsided, Elisabet heard the screams and cries of wounded people rise in volume. She looked over her shoulder at the carnage and the doors hanging off their hinges, backlit forms moving against the grey daylight outside.

The screaming dropped in volume, and Elisabet realised many more people had died in the minute or so since the blast. Others lapsed into unconsciousness, and she could now hear voices talking. Some she understood, others not, and she wondered what she should do. If the Russians told her to do something and she disobeyed simply because she did not understand, it might spell death for her family.

"Herauskommen!"

The voice was guttural and the accent strange, but she understood the words. They were being ordered out of the bunker.

"Herausgekommen oder werden sie getötet."

That was unequivocal. *Come out or be killed.* Elisabet stood and held onto her children, Joachim in her arms, and started moving toward the shattered doors. Other women and a few children got to their feet and started forward too.

"Do not go out." One of the other SS officers stood by the rear wall with a pistol in his hand. "We must present a united front."

"We are women and children, not soldiers," Elisabet said. "If we do not go out, the Russians will kill us all."

"If you try to go out, I will kill you," said an Unterscharführer.

Elisabet positioned herself between the SS sergeant and her children. "Will your last act be to kill innocent Germans?" she asked. When the man did not answer, she turned and ushered her children away, her body tense as she waited for the shot that would leave her children orphans. It did not come, and they mounted the debris-strewn steps of the bunker and out into the cold daylight, in company with a small crowd of survivors, many of them wounded.

A tank faced them, its cannon depressed to the maximum extent and its rear treads up on blocks, so the barrel pointed directly at the yawning bunker.

130

Infantrymen stood all around the little courtyard, ri-rifles at the ready, their faces apparently filled with a mixture of emotions – fear, anger, relief – and over it all a veneer of anticipation.

"Kommen sie hier," rapped the German-speaking Russian. He gestured to one side of the courtyard. "Stehen sie dort."

Elisabet and the other women and children moved to the side as ordered, and the wounded soldiers and men were separated and taken away.

"Gibt es niemand anderer in dort?"

"Yes," replied the nurse who had first translated the Russian commands. "There are several SS men in there still."

"Sagen sie ihnen herauszukommen."

The nurse called out. "The Russians say you must come out. I think they will...will kill you if you do not."

"Tell him to go fornicate with his mother," called the SS Unterscharführer.

The nurse turned to the Russian with a stricken expression. "He says..."

"I understand very well what he says." The man shrugged. "It is all one to me." He signalled the tank commander and stepped aside. The cannon belched fire and the bunker erupted in flame and smoke. Debris rained down and several Russian soldiers were struck by falling masonry. They cursed and dodged, and others laughed. Then they turned their attention to the women.

A sergeant, flat-faced and weather-beaten, strutted forward and examined the refugee women and nurses. He grabbed faces in his grubby hands and turned them this way and that before grunting and hauling a nurse out. The woman cried out in protest and fought against his grip, but the Russian slapped her to the ground and ripped away her skirts. He threw himself on top of the struggling woman and raped her violently, subduing her with his fists.

This was the signal for the rest of the soldiers. They ran into the group, laughing, and grabbed women, pulling them aside with expressions of lust. Their faces assumed a bestial look as they threw women to the ground and assaulted them, sometimes stabbing them or battering them with a flurry of fists or feet if they did not cooperate.

Elisabet saw a man coming toward her, his eyes filled with cruel anticipation, and she knew there was no escape. The only thing she could do was ensure her survival for the sake of her children – and protect her children from the coming horror as best she could.

"Helmut, take the children aside and face the wall. Quickly now. Obey me."

The boy was pale, and shaking with anger and fear, but he obeyed his mother, pulling his brothers away, turning their faces to the brick wall of the hospital. Joachim screamed, Werner and Günter cried out for their Mutti, and Kurt sobbed, but they all turned away, clutching the cold brick wall for support. Helmut did not turn away, and he trembled with impotent anger at what the man did to his mother, there in the frozen, rubble-strewn courtyard of Schneidemühl Hospital.

Elisabet knew that cooperation was her only chance, though nausea gripped her at the thought of what she would have to endure. After a quick glance to check if her children had obeyed, she waited for the Russian and quickly asked, "Do you have children? I ask because the father of my children is dead. I am all they have."

The man took no notice and pulled her away from the other rapes taking place around them. He pushed Elisabet against a wall and fumbled with her clothing before committing an assault that, if less violent than those of her fellow refugees, still violated her spirit and body and left her feeling dirty and used.

The man pulled away and allowed Elisabet to adjust her clothing. He fumbled under his tunic and brought out a dirty bayonet, staring at her for long minutes, and then at her terrified and shaking children further along the wall. At last, he sighed and leaned in close to her, his breath stinking.

"You kill family," he said in broken German. "Soldiers rape wife Svetlana and kill daughter Rosa when burn village. Now I revenge. I rape, but not kill you or childs. I civilised, not like German." He shrugged. "Nor like some comrades."

The Russian turned and moved away, threading his way through the courtyard, stepping over his rutting comrades and their screaming blood-stained victims. Elisabet staggered over to her children and swept Joachim into her arms. Werner, Kurt and Günter clung to her skirts while Helmut stared up at her, horror on his young face.

"Did he hurt you, Mutti?"

Elisabet looked down at the pale face of her eldest son and had a thought that swept her out of that courtyard of horrors, *'How like his father he looks.'*

* * *

His name was Hermann, as tall and strong and handsome as my brother Hans, but otherwise quite unlike him. Whereas my brother was fit and extroverted, willing to take the world on head to head,

133

Hermann was quiet and intelligent, thinking before he spoke, and preferred to argue a point rather than re-resort to his fists. I met him on the farm when I was seventeen, during my *Landfrauenjahr*. His parents in Frankfurt an der Oder had sent him to the country to learn something of the peasant life as they thought him too bookish, too interested in learning. Farm life was not something that appealed to him, but despite his introverted nature he found an interest.

Without wishing to be thought vain, I know men like looking at me, and in truth, I rather enjoy it. I am of middling height, neither slim nor plump, my features pleasant without being beautiful (though men have assured me of this), and with long blonde hair tied into pigtails in those days. My best feature was my smile, and I think it was this that first attracted Hermann. He was a lonely and shy young man when he first arrived at the farm, and the owner and his wife were too busy to afford him a proper welcome. I was busy too, but never too busy to be rude, so I smiled and captured his heart.

He gave me a flower – not a rose or a bloom bought from a shop in the town but a simple wild flower plucked from a field. A blue cornflower, I think it was, though he blushed as red as the poppies in the same field when he gave it to me. I thanked him, and offered him a smile in return. He stammered something and fled, but was back the next day and pressed a scrap of paper in my hand. On it were scrawled some lines about the sun shining and a man and woman standing on a wide beach by blue waves and looking in each other's eyes. It had a pleasing cadence and I asked him if he had written the poem.

I could see the struggle within him written on his face, but honesty won out and he told me the lines were from a poem called *Morgen!* By a Scottish-German poet whose name I forget. He admitted that his own efforts at stringing words together were less memorable, so he borrowed from published poets. I told him that while I appreciated the trouble he had been to, I would prefer his own words over those of someone else.

That was the start of our friendship, and it grew from there. I dare say that if we had been in Königsberg, and my parents had had anything to do with it, nothing would have happened. My parents were loving but strict, and I was enjoying my first taste of adult life outside their control. Perhaps I could be forgiven the occasional stumble.

Hermann gave me the cornflower in September, when the wheat in the fields was golden and about to be harvested. He kissed me in October, when the chill winds off the Baltic flushed our cheeks as red as the apples in the orchard, and he warmed my heart in November when he told me he loved me.

In early December, 1934, just before my eighteenth birthday, an official from the Reichsbank came to see the owner of the farm and brought two policemen with him. The farmer drove his wife and children upstairs and Hermann and me outside, with dire warnings about what would happen if he caught us listening at the window. We could not have cared less about his troubles, and as it was a cold blustery day of watery sunshine with a hint of snow in the air, we sheltered in the barn.

The barn was a magical place, decked with golden straw and a high wooden roof that vaulted above us like the nave of a cathedral. The farmer kept his milk and beef cattle in the barn during cold weather and their bodies helped keep the place warm, though they also permeated the air with a rich animal aroma. Hermann complained of this more than I, for I had been raised on a farm and the odour of animals and their dung is a natural part of farm life. The cattle shifted and lowed in their stalls, regarding us with large liquid eyes as we laughingly climbed the ladder to the loft. Sacks of grain were stowed up here, and bales of straw, and we made a nest where we could look out of the small grimed window to the pastures. Motes danced and wavered in the weak sunshine that lit our rustling haven. Other animals shared our dusty kingdom – mice, and probably rats – but we paid them no mind and they left us alone.

We lay in the straw and talked, and laughed, and what with being a young man and young woman, in private and in love, one thing led to another. He kissed me and told me he loved me, and feeling my heart surge within me, I gave him what he most desired. Afterward, he held me close and we talked again, this time of the future and what it held for us.

Little did we know, for in the New Year his parents sent for him and he left me three days before I found out that our union in the straw loft had set me on the path to motherhood. He said he would write, and he did. I replied and told him of my condition but I never heard from him again. Knowing Hermann, I do not believe he would shirk his responsibilities, or deny his love, so it must be that his parents found out and forbade any further contact with me.

In due course, my first-born son came into the world, and I named him Helmut. He has been a joy to me, though he is very different from his father. My parents were none too pleased that I was an unwed mother, but they supported me in my decision to keep my child, and I have never regretted it. My chil-children are my life, and every one of them is as dear to me as life itself. I would die for them – or undergo any travail if it would mean their survival and well-being. Any decent mother would, I suppose.

*   *   *

"Did he hurt you, Mutti?" Helmut asked again.

"No, mein Lieblingsjunge."

Elisabet hid her hurt, both physical and emotional from her children, and looked around the courtyard. The Russian soldiers were still engaged in their orgy of rape and killing, but no one was actually guarding the few weeping women huddled against the hospital walls. She edged away, holding tight to her boys, and reached the corner of the building, slipping around it and away into the streets. Their route took them past the place they had slept the previous night, and found their two-wheeled pram upturned amid the rubble. They took it with them.

Russian soldiers swarmed everywhere, and fighting still continued to the north and west, as evidenced by the explosions and machinegun fire in those directions. Evidently, the German Army still engaged the enemy, but to move in that direction would be to invite danger. Instead, she turned to the south, into the face of the Russian advance. Many men looked at the woman and children running from ruined building to heap of rubble, ducking behind sheltering wrecks of tanks and trucks, walking with downcast eyes past files of soldiers, but none interfered with their flight, being driven by their officers to continue the fight. Elisabet and her boys hurried on toward the southern outskirts of the city.

Kapitel Acht (8)

Elisabet and her children made it out of Schneidemühl without further molestation. The Russian soldiers, hurrying into the city, urged on by their officers and commissars, looked at them in surprise, but made no move to halt or hurt them. It was almost as if they did not recognise the woman and children as refugees or enemies when moving toward them. Flight engendered a violent reaction from the troops, but meeting them face to face seemed to disengage their brutality. It probably would not last, Elisabet knew, but as soon as she was out of sight of the soldiers, she meant to turn their course toward the west once more. She also needed time to get to grips with the brutality of her rape, but she could not afford to even think about her experience until she had made her family safe.

They crossed the stream of the local Russian army units as the troops swung north toward the Baltic, and passed into thick forest. Sheltering by night in the lee of rocky outcrops or hiding by day in thickets on the banks of frozen streams for a few days, they were driven by hunger out into farmland once more. The remnants of the rations issued to them in Schneidemühl ran out on the first day, and they were reduced to foraging from ruined farms and ramshackle peasant huts for half-rotten frozen turnips, a handful of mouldy grain or scraps of leathery animal hide that they sucked and chewed. All they had left after their flight through the Russian army were the clothes they wore and a few matches wrapped in a twist of cloth. The pram, with its precious burden of blankets and spare clothing had been left behind on the second day when it fell to pieces. They donned the clothing and wrapped the thin blankets around their shoulders and trudged onward. Survival had suddenly become much harder.

Fire was essential if they were to survive the freezing nights, but for the first few days, as they picked their way cautiously through the enemy supply lines, they were too frightened to announce their presence with a fire. Even with dry fuel, a tell-tale curl of smoke on a clear day or the ruddy wink of flame in the darkness could bring death swiftly down upon them. So they stuck it out as long as they could, until Günter sickened and had to be carried along with baby Joachim. The other boys were not much better. They could still stumble onward or wade through the drifted snow, their thin limbs shivering in the bitter cold, faces and fingers raw, but their strength had almost gone and this day or the next, one or more of them would simply lie down and die.

They found a woodcutter's hut on the edge of a forest near the village of Usch. The shack was tumbled down, with gaps between the boards and the roof drooping drunkenly at one corner, but it provided a measure of protection from the biting wind, and a plentiful supply of cut, dry wood. Elisabet led them into the hut and gently laid Günter in the most protected part. She swept the snow aside, down to frozen bare earth and removed her coat to lay it down as a protection from the cold. The chill immediately bit deep into her starved body and she knew she must find some other solution quickly.

In the meantime, she and the older boys scraped snow and brush together to form a low wall encircling the hut's old hearth. There was sufficient kindling and a handful of dry straw – enough to lay a fire – and ample logs to keep it going if it should light. They had

139

only half a dozen matches left and once they were gone, the cold would kill them unless they could find more. It took two of their precious matches to light the fire, but once lit it grew in strength and the stone chimney base to the hearth reflected warmth out into the little hut. Elisabet went outside to check the smoke streaming from the broken chimney, and saw that it rapidly spread out through the filter of the forest branches. They might be seen but they would have to risk it – they had to have a fire if they were to survive.

There was a rusted out pot in the shack, but by tipping it on one side it was possible to melt some snow over the fire and heat water. Donning her coat once more, Elisabet left the children by the fire and ventured out into the farmland to look for a willow tree. She found one, bare and stark by a frozen stream and stripped it of an armful of twigs. Back in the hut, her shivering slowly abating by the heat of the fire, she peeled the bark from the twigs with her fingernails and steeped them in the hot water. The resultant liquid was brown and bitter, flecked with dirt and rust, but it would act as a mild painkiller and febrifuge. It was not much, but it was the best she could do to comfort Günter. She poured some into a battered tin mug which was the only other utensil in the hut and, holding her little boy in her arms, feed him the warm tonic. He gagged and wailed his distress before swallowing a few small mouthfuls and slipping into a restless sleep.

The problem of hunger remained, and the forest in winter was not going to supply enough food. Their only chance was to brave the open countryside and possible Russian patrols and scavenge for food near the village. Kurt was left in charge of the younger children, with strict injunctions not to leave the secu-security of the hut, and also to put wood on the fire as needed. Then she took Helmut and ventured outside.

Elisabet took the same path across the fields that she had carved in the deep snow when she went looking for willow bark, and from there she cut across to a dirt road that headed toward the village of Usch. Helmut followed in her footsteps, his passage made easier by his mother. He radiated pride at being chosen to accompany her, and an eagerness to prove his worth.

The village consisted of no more than a score or so of huts, many in ruins, and inhabited by a handful of stone-faced suspicious peasants. They remained ensconced in their huts, smoke curling from their chimneys, and stared out through frost-begrimed windows at the strangers.

"Gut-tägig!" she called out. "My son and I are hungry and have travelled far. Do you have any food you can spare?"

Nobody responded. The villagers continued to stare out at them but made no move to greet them or respond to their request. After a few minutes, Elisabet led Helmut away, through the collection of tumbled down cottages to the countryside beyond. The rutted road in this direction had packed snow in two thin strips either side of the centreline, an indication of the passage of carts, and they could conserve their strength by crunching along the hardened frost-covered surface.

"There's nothing out here, Mutti," Helmut complained. "We should go back to the village and see what we can find. I bet I could get into some of those huts."

141

Elisabet pointed at the cart tracks. "These carts must be going somewhere. Maybe there's a farm or something. A farm will have more food than a hut – and maybe enough that the owner will feel charitable."

A half mile further on, they came across a great churned trail spearing across the open fields from the southeast, crossing the road and on toward the northwest. Snow and frozen earth was mixed and thrown aside as the mighty treads of tanks flattened everything in their path, and around and about were the tracks of hundreds of men. They had come across the route of one of the Russian army units.

Elisabet looked around at an almost featureless countryside and the cart track leading on endlessly, and then looked along the path of destruction toward the northwest. A wisp of smoke stained the air beyond the crest of a low hill, a column that rose straight up to a slate-grey sky in the still air. She turned aside, stumbling over the cut up ground and frozen clods of earth, and followed the tank trail toward the smoke.

Helmut looked around him with great interest, measuring his small feet against the booted imprints of the Russian soldiers, marvelling at the deep grinding tracks of the tank treads, and staring in fascination at the splintered trunks of a small stand of trees where the armoured vehicles had rolled right over them rather than altering course by a mere ten metres to avoid them. He found where soldiers had stopped to relieve themselves, and made sounds of disgust first, and later unbuttoned his own trousers to add his contribution. A gleam in the ripped up grass caught his eye and he followed the metallic glint to where a bayonet lay on the ground, spotted and stained, but still deadly. Some soldier, hurrying with his unit, had evidently dropped it and continued on, unaware. Helmut picked it up, wide-eyed, and ran to catch up with his mother.

Elisabet approached the brow of the hill cautiously, bending low and peeking over the crest to scan the land beneath her. She saw a ruined farmhouse, a shattered tank, and bodies abandoned in the snow, but no sign of life. The crushed earth of the Russian tank advance continued past the farm, arrowing into the distance. Faintly, far to the north and west came the grumble of artillery fire where the tank unit must have caught up with the retreating Germans.

"I think it is safe enough," Elisabet said. "But if I tell you to run, run as fast as you can, back to your brothers. Verstest du?"

Helmut nodded. "Yes, Mutti," he muttered, but his eyes were fixed on the tank, its turret ripped half off and its cannon pointing down at the ground.

They approached the scene of destruction and found bodies in the snow – Russian infantrymen, she presumed. Most had been stripped of their coats, trousers, helmets and rifles, though a few ripped and bloodied garments identified them. They had been left open-eyed and bloody, half-naked and defenceless to contemplate in death the grey sky or frozen earth of a foreign land. Elisabet shielded Helmut as best she could from the sight, but he squirmed in her grip and pulled away, determined to see. He went a little pale at the sight of the bodies, some of the dead soldiers seemingly in their teens, but he took a deep breath and doggedly followed his mother.

The gutted tank stood off to one side, a shell from a Panzerfaust having evidently hit it at the join

143

between turret and body. A corpse hung out of the hatch and the thin column of smoke still rising from the tank indicated that fire had blazed through the crew compartment. A stink of fuel and charred meat hung in the air, making them both gag. They retreated, not willing to investigate more closely.

Close to the crumbling walls of the farmhouse, they found Wehrmacht soldiers – a Feldwebel and five Schützen manning a machinegun nest – their dead bodies sprawled over the rubble or face down in the snow. Their boots had gone; also their greatcoats and their rifles, presumably looted by the Russian soldiers, but their tunics remained, with their insignia of rank. Elisabet set Helmut the task of searching the back of the farmhouse for anything useful, while she scavenged what she could from the bodies.

"Forgive me," she murmured to each body, "But my children are in need and these things are of no use to you now."

Elisabet stripped the belts from each corpse and, in the case of one man who had been shot cleanly through the head rather than having his body riddled with bullets, she wrestled the tunic off his back and his shirt too. The garments were too large for her children, but they might serve some purpose. They were barely spotted with blood. She hated exposing the man's torso to the elements, leaving him naked, so she scooped snow over him, hiding his pale body beneath a white shroud.

"Mutti, come look!"

Elisabet heard excitement, but no fear in her son's voice, but she still ran to the rear of the building. Helmut gripped the Russian bayonet in his hand and stared toward a featureless grey mound draped over a low stone wall. For a moment, she could not identify

144

the object, and then she saw a boot and a white up-upturned hand, fingers like pale sausages, and knew it for another German soldier.

With rising excitement, Elisabet saw that this man had remained untouched by the Russian looters. He still wore his greatcoat and boots. She motioned Helmut away and examined the man. A bullet had taken him through the side of the neck and, because he had fallen over the low wall with his head dangling, the spurting blood had only stained the collar of the coat. Moving limbs that resisted her efforts, Elisabet eased the heavy wool coat off the dead soldier. She also unlaced his boots and removed them, and it was only then she saw the bulging pack at his feet.

Elisabet hauled the pack out and with fumbling fingers undid the straps. She stared at the contents for a few moments, not believing what she was seeing. The pack was stuffed with army rations and, as she dug down into it, even had a few precious packets of matches and a small medical kit. A grin spread over her face.

"We're going to be all right, Helmut."

She distributed the rations between them, stuffing pockets, and reducing the weight of the pack sufficiently that a nine year old boy could carry it without discomfort. The greatcoat was spread out and she piled all the other items into it, folding the fabric over and binding it with the belts. This she lifted onto her shoulders and they started on their long and slow journey back to the woodcutter's hut. They arrived after dark, stumbling over the last few hundred metres, to find the hut in darkness and all four children huddled together in a corner, sobbing their hearts out.

"We thought...we thought you weren't coming back," wailed Kurt. "We thought you'd left us."

Elisabet fell to her knees on the cold ground and swept them into her arms. "I'd never do that, my darling boys. Don't you know I love you all more than anything else in the world?"

The fire had gone out, but Helmut quickly laid and lit another. Günter was still sick, and now Werner was becoming listless, complaining of pains, so Elisabet brewed up some more of her willow bark tonic, and as a reward for drinking it down, gave them all hard sweets from the ration packs. The items in the medical kit included a small vial of painkillers, so she fed one each to Günter and Werner immediately. They only had one rusted pan, so could not make up a hot meal from the rations, but were able to prepare weak ersatz coffee which warmed them while they gorged on cold sausage and biscuits.

There was enough food in the pack to last the six of them a week or more if they did not make every day a feast day, so Elisabet decided they would rest up a while, regaining some of their strength, and giving Werner and Günter time to recuperate. It also gave Elisabet time to reflect on her ordeal. She would sit up at night, after the boys had fallen asleep, nursing a cup of coffee and re-live the assault, wondering if there was anything she could have done differently that might have spared her the experience.

Should I have refused to co-operate?

"Then he would have killed you," she whispered. "Your boys would be orphans, and in all likelihood dead back in Schneidemühl."

I don't know that.

"Yes, you do. There was no other action you could take."

146

But to let him do that...that thing, to me. I let him do it. I did not resist. What does that make me?

"It makes you a good mother. You sacrificed yourself for your children. What? You want to blame yourself?" Unaware, Elisabet's voice rose above a whisper as anger gripped her.

No, but...

"But nothing. This sort of thing happens all the time, especially in war, and who is to blame? Every time? The man. Do you think a woman invites rape? No!"

Joachim woke and cried out at her angry voice. Elisabet soothed him and stroked his head until he fell asleep again. She continued to whisper to herself.

"What do you think rape is about?" she asked herself. "The sex? Nonsense, rape is an act of violence, an assault. It is about the power a man can exercise over a woman. The Russian did it because he had the power and no conscience. He told you himself – it was for revenge on some other man who also had the power and no conscience. You are not to blame for anything that happened to you in Schneidemühl."

Elisabet digested her thoughts, sipping on her cooling coffee. She got up and tucked the children into their makeshift bed – the army greatcoat spread over a thick layer of dry bracken fern. The garments she had taken from the dead soldiers had been laboriously unstitched and now became irregularly shaped coverings. Little hands poked out from under the coverings, so she tucked them back under and smoothed their sleeping brows, envying them their untroubled sleep.

What if there's a baby?

147

Elisabet shrugged and seated herself by the fire again. "No sense in tackling that problem before it presents itself. You've got a week or so before you'll know."

And if there is? What do I do then?

"You've had babies before."

Yes, but from an act of love, not as a result of rape.

"A baby is a baby. It's not the child's fault how it gets here. What else can you do?"

Get rid of it?

"That is an option. Decide, Elisabet. If you find you are going to have a baby, what will you do?"

Elisabet fell asleep in front of the fire considering her answer, and woke briefly in the pre-morning darkness, her unconscious mind having made its decision.

If there is a child, it is my child, not his.

A week passed and the children gained in strength. Whether it was the foul-tasting willow bark tea, the pills from the medical kit or just natural healing, Günter and Werner got better, and through judicious doctoring of the others, they remained as healthy as it was possible to be in the circumstances. Elisabet decided it was time to leave. The army rations were running low, and they needed to continue their trek to the west. Somewhere, surely, the Wehrmacht would have stopped the Russian advance and they could reach safety in Germany itself. She told her children of her decision to leave the next day.

"Where will we go, Mutti?" Kurt asked. "Back home to Königsberg?"

"No, we're going to visit your Uncle Hans' family who live just outside Dresden. You'll love it there. Dresden is a beautiful city and they live on a small farm. There'll be food and warmth, and animals to

148

play with, just like on your uncle Erich's farm near Elbing. We just need to keep going a little longer."

They bundled up their meagre possessions into the army pack and the greatcoat, and said goodbye to their little hut. Elisabet led her family through the little village of Usch, where the inhabitants were as friendly as last time, peering out from behind curtains or watching them pass in silence. The rutted road led onward, past the churned up swathe of the tank advance and on toward the town of Scharnikau on the banks of the frozen Netze River. The distance was not great, but Elisabet shunned contact with the local Poles for fear they would notify the Russians, and went to ground in a barn or under a culvert if she as much as heard the growl of an approaching vehicle. Rather than risk discovery, she led her children across country, avoiding the roads and keeping to the snow-covered fields.

The weather improved, the cloud cover breaking up and weak sunshine turning the bleak countryside into a dazzling swathe of snow-blanketed fields and forest. An unfortunate side effect was to melt the snow surface only to have it refreeze at night. The crusted surface would hold one's weight for an instant before precipitating one thigh deep in a drift. The steady step-crunch-sink rhythm of walking exhausted them, and after a day of floundering, Elisabet knew she had to chance the road again.

They reached Scharnikau, and found Soviet commissars organising the townspeople, sorting out any Pole suspected of having collaborated with the Germans. These unfortunates were summarily tried, shot, and their bodies dumped on the ice of Netze River. Strangely, any German nationals who had lived there were not shot but were rounded up and incarcerated in the old police barracks. Elisabet quick-quickly moved her family through the town, slipping through the net and out onto the road paralleling the river. It led to the city of Landsberg an der Warthe and ran through a river valley bounded by low, forested hills.

Russian troops filled the roads at intervals, passing in a seemingly endless stream of vehicles and foot soldiers. Each time, Elisabet, alerted by the growl of tank engines and trucks, hid in the patches of scrub alongside the road, hunkering down in the snow. When they passed, they would emerge stiff and shivering, the younger children crying, and resume their journey. After the third such incident, Elisabet started to look for an alternate route, one that would remove them from the immediate danger of discovery. She raised her eyes from the valley road once more and scrutinised the pristine slopes leading up to the vast, dark expanse of fir trees on the hilltops that was the Netze forest. Within its high cathedral of trunks and branches there would be less snow and they could make better time, be hidden from Russian eyes.

The sloping farmland leading up to the trees was devoid of cover, and if they attempted it in daylight they were sure to be seen. It was possible that even if they were seen, they would be left unmolested, but they had already seen random acts of brutality by the Russian conquerors, and Elisabet did not want to chance death or capture for her family. She waited until nightfall, sitting cold and hungry in a little frozen watercourse beside the road. While they waited for the short winter's day to pass, huddled together and dozing, a tiny sound caught Helmut's attention and he tugged on his mother's sleeve, pointing and cocking his head questioningly. Elisabet stirred and let her gaze pan across the open snow and bare-limbed bushes, seeking out the source of the faint noise.

It came again, the faintest of crunching as the surface layer of the refrozen snow gave way, the click of a claw on a stone – and a brief flash of russet brown beneath a bush. They held their breath, eyes wide, as a fox stepped out from cover, its onyx eyes staring at the huddled creatures in the watercourse. It remained stock still, its muscles bunched for flight, and then, as no threat emerged, it continued on its way, muzzle high as it snuffed the cold air for any hint of danger or food. The fox was gone within seconds and Elisabet and Helmut sighed, relaxing, and looked at one another.

"Beautiful, wasn't it?"

"Can you eat foxes?" Helmut asked. "I could have thrown a stone and killed it."

They set off at dusk, scrambling up the gentle slopes as night fell around them, heading for the intense blackness that was the Netze forest on the crest of the hills. It took them an hour, Elisabet and Kurt helping the younger children, while Helmut forged ahead, his bayonet in his hand, ready to defend his family from danger. The edge of the dark forest swallowed them, and Elisabet led them in about a hundred metres before finding a hollow where a fir tree had toppled, creating a space around the naked roots.

Travel was easier through the forest. The thick evergreen branches had kept off much of the snow, so they walked over ground carpeted with fallen needles and broken branches. In the few places where wind or insects had toppled a tall tree, thick undergrowth had sprung up in the light window of

151

the canopy, but such areas were easy to avoid. Roads ran through the Netze forest, and a few small timber-cutting villages nestled there, but Elisabet guided the children away from these, using the last of their rations.

The boys, particularly Helmut and Kurt, played a game as they walked along. They collected small pinecones and, nominating a target such as a tree stump or rock, shied cones at it, claiming points if they were the first to hit it. It soon turned out that although Helmut could throw further and faster, his younger brother Kurt was more accurate. Werner and Günter joined in, but hunger and sickness had sapped their strength and they soon gave up, stumbling along in silence. Little Joachim tried to play also but soon cried to be picked up and carried.

Then, as they slipped past the Polish village of Sowia Góra in the early dawn, they were seen by a Soviet soldier. He raised the alarm at once, firing off a fusilade of shots that ripped through the foliage above their heads. Elisabet snatched up Joachim and ran for the shelter of the forest, yelling for the boys to run ahead. They raced through the undergrowth at the edge of the road and into the forest again, crunching and slipping on the needles covering the ground. Behind them, they could hear shouts, and then the unmistakeable sounds of pursuit.

The boys tired quickly, but Elisabet forced them onward at a fast walk. She tried changing direction, angling to the north, but they came to well-used tracks leading toward another village and Polish peasants who cried out in alarm, so they turned and ran back for cover.

"What do we do, Mutti?" Helmut panted.

"I don't know. Keep running."

152

A hundred metres or so further on, Günter screamed and pointed to one side. "They're coming!"

Shapes moved in the dim light of the forest, ahead and to their right. Elisabet's heart sank as she heard rifles cocked and a guttural voice called out to her to halt. It took a few moments for her to realise the voice had been in German.

"Identifizieren sie sich."

Elisabeth gently lowered Joachim to the ground and raised her hands. "I am Elisabet Daeker, and these are my sons. We are German."

The men stepped out into view, a dozen of them, battered and dirty, wearing the uniforms of the Wehrmacht. The leader, an Unteroffizier, put up his rifle, though his men still pointed their weapons in their direction.

"What are you doing here, Frau?"

"Fleeing the Soviets." Elisabet looked over her shoulder. "We're being followed, hunted, by Russian soldiers. They can only be a few hundred metres behind us."

The Unteroffizier grunted. "So you led them to us?"

"I didn't know you were here."

"No matter. Keep going, Frau, but stay out of Landsberg. Ivan kicked our arses there. Stay away from the city and keep your children safe. We'll hold these bloody Russians off." He grinned savagely at his men. "Time to kick Ivan's arse, eh boys?" The Unteroffizier rapped out commands, pointing left and right, and his men fanned out across the path of the pursuing soldiers.

Elisabet hurried her children onward, crossing a small gully and working her way up the far side, into the cover of the trees again before the first shot split the cold air. She shooed her boys on and turned to look back, taking cover behind a large fir tree.

A column of Soviet soldiers jogged into view, the one who had fired working the bolt of his rifle. The Germans opened fire, cutting two down and sending the others diving for cover. A few of the Russians had submachine guns and raked the German positions from the cover of fallen logs and hollows. The German soldiers fought back, but despite outnumbering the enemy, could not match their fire power. A man fell, then another, and the Wehrmacht unit started to fall back. A Soviet soldier rose to his feet and, despite bullets zipping past him, splintering bark and kicking up the leaf litter at his feet, blazed away with his PPSh submachine gun. Several Germans fell, and the others – no more than five men – retreated downhill, drawing the Russians after them, away from Elisabet and her children. She watched them go, blessing them for their sacrifice, but appalled at how little resistance they had put up against a numerically inferior Russian force.

"How different they were at the start of the war," she whispered.

*   *   *

Listening to the BBC news from London was frowned upon, but it was not yet a treasonous offence. That would change shortly. My parents would sometimes tune into foreign stations in the evenings, listening to music, as well as to the official Party broadcasts and speeches by Hitler. We had heard the news reports from Berlin a day or two before of the attack on German soil of Polish troops, and of our army's swift response. It was exciting to hear how our triumphant soldiers were giving the Poles a lesson in modern warfare and punishing them

154

for their unwarranted aggression. I am no lover of war, but Germany could hardly be blamed for re-responding to the cowardly Polish attack. I know now that this was propaganda, broadcast to give legitimacy to the German attack on Poland, but at the time I accepted it as the truth, like most other loyal Germans.

I heard this news in the city, rather than on my parents' radio, but I was with them when they tuned into the BBC to listen to the news, a few days after Germany struck back at the Polish invaders. They took a small risk inviting me to listen as my husband Rudolph was a Party member. However, he was also a good man, and allowed me to remain on good terms with my parents despite their left-wing tendencies. He did not approve of listening to British propaganda though, so I only went to my parents when he was out of town on business. I took my children with me, Helmut, aged 4, Kurt, two and a half, and little Günter, nine months old. They played with their toys while we adults listened.

The measured tones of the speaker were very different from the impassioned rhetoric pouring out of Radio Berlin, so I listened raptly to the crackly voice of the BBC World Service broadcasting in Polish, not understanding a word.

"...unless the German Government were prepared to give His Majesty's Government in the United Kingdom satisfactory assurances that the German Government had suspended all aggressive action against Poland and were prepared promptly to withdraw their forces from Polish territory, His Majesty's Government in the United Kingdom would, without hesitation, fulfil their obligations to Poland."

"What is he saying, Vati?" I asked. My father was erudite; he understood Polish.

"The British Government accuses Germany of being the aggressor in Poland, and demands that we withdraw all our forces immediately," my father said.

"That can't be right," my mother said. "The Poles attacked us."

"Shh..."

"...not later than 11 a. m., British Summer Time, to-day 3rd September, satisfactory assurances to the above effect have been given by the German Government and have reached His Majesty's Government in London, a state of war will exist between the two countries..."

"Du lieber Gott," my father muttered.

"What?" I asked.

"The British Prime Minister says unless Germany agrees, Britain will go to war."

"What, over Poland?" my mother asked. "That's stupid."

"That's what he said. Wait..."

"...No such undertaking was received by the time stipulated, and, consequently, this country is at war with Germany."

"The damn fool."

I was not sure whether my father meant the British Prime Minister or our Führer. "What?"

"He says Britain and Germany are at war." Father switched off the radio and sat back in his chair, staring across the room.

Mother made appropriate noises of shock and disapproval and went off to make some coffee. I picked up little Günter, who had fallen asleep on the carpet, and rocked him. The older boys played as if

156

nothing had changed in the world – and I suppose it had not from their innocent perspective.

"What does it all mean, Vati?" I asked. "Will it affect us?"

"Here in Ostpreussen? I doubt it. It'll probably be like the Great War, fought in the trenches of Belgium and France. The only thing that worries me is if the war in Poland drags on. Then we'll be fighting on two fronts and that's never good."

It appeared my father worried unnecessarily. The Wehrmacht swept through Poland almost unopposed, and then the Russians joined in, dismembering Poland and dividing it between them. The war was over almost before it began and Ostpreussen was joined by land to Greater Germany. Britain and France (for France had also declared war) sat and sulked as their cause for war had now vanished. My husband assured me that they would soon sue for peace.

All the church bells rang in Königsberg when the realisation sank in that Germany now stretched all the way across to Ostpreussen without Poland interposing itself between these two natural parts of Germany. People rejoiced wildly in the streets and the victorious Wehrmacht paraded along the thoroughfares to the sound of martial music and cheering. As I have said before, I do not like war, but who could not fail to be stirred by the sight of our conquering armies, marching in perfectly straight ranks, their uniforms immaculate, their weapons gleaming, their faces filled with pride.

Rudolph was a Party member and had access to the best positions along the parade route. We – and our two older children – watched amidst the blood red banners and fluttering Hakenkreuz flags. The

157

thunderous tramp of booted feet literally shook the ground beneath us and the shouted cries of 'Heil Hit-Hitler' almost deafened us. I stared at the fresh young faces of the soldiers, filled with zeal and patriotic fervour; at the older, experienced expressions of their officers reflecting supreme confidence in their ability; and wondered how any army on earth could stand before this one. Pride in the Fatherland, in the Reich, in Germany, swelled my heart.

*   *   *

The Russians did not follow them. They heard continued shooting behind them, then it died away and there was no sound of pursuit. Elisabet led her children down the long slope that led, through the thinning trees of the forest, to the broad valley of the Warthe River.

To the northwest of their position lay Landsberg an der Warthe, but she heeded the warning of the soldiers. She had no desire to become more closely acquainted with Soviet soldiers, and would keep to the countryside as much as possible. The problem was the main road and certainly the easiest route lay along the Warthe Valley down to the city of Küstrin on the River Oder. Elisabet did not doubt that if the Russians had already taken Landsberg, then Küstrin would soon follow. It was a route to avoid.

She turned their faces to the south again, toward the towns of Schwerin and Schwiebus. They would go round the Russian army heading for Berlin and move toward Dresden and safety.

Kapitel Neun (9)

Elisabet groaned, nausea rising in her throat, clammy sweat breaking out on her forehead in the warmth of the tiny hut. She had felt this way before – five times – and each time it had signalled a pregnancy. A month had passed since Schneidemühl, and her worst fears had been confirmed – the Russian soldier who raped her had fathered a child.

Beside her, Kurt stirred in his sleep, a whimper escaping his throat. He, of all the children, seemed to be suffering the most. His elder brother Helmut had toughened and taken on the role of the man of the family, adamant, despite being only nine years old – 'nearly ten' he insisted – that he should be at the forefront of any foraging expedition. He had seen horrific things but refused to let them govern his actions. Werner acted the brave little man and despite cold and hunger insisted on resolutely marching along with his little rucksack on his back. Baby Joachim travelled in a makeshift sling for the most part. At two years of age, his limbs were too short and his movements too uncoordinated to cope with winter travel, so of them all, he was in the best physical condition.

Günter had suffered physically. Weakened by privation and cold, he had fallen prey to sickness and his weakness often held the family back. Whenever she could, Elisabet prepared a little herbal decoction, drawing on her knowledge of plant medicine gleaned from her grandmother, or made use of the occasional medical windfall to dose her children. But Kurt worried her most. The eight year old was strong enough physically, but the things he had seen and heard, the experience of struggling to survive through a battle zone had shaken his young mind. There was little she could do for him – for any of them – except to protect them as best she could, provide for them and, of course, love them unconditionally.

She reached out and touched her children gently, one by one, as they slept. Outside, the sky was lightening in the east, pink and gold tinges on patches of low cloud. It promised to be a sunny day, welcomed after long weeks of winter, but the warming weather brought its own problems. Snow still lay in drifts, but as the temperature eased above freezing, the melt water soaked into the earth and turned it to mud. Their passage was hard enough without slogging across muddy fields or picking their way along slippery, rutted country roads.

They were still deep inside Poland despite the time that had passed. The Oder River – the border between Poland and Germany – lay somewhere to the west, but they had been unable to approach it because of the gathering Soviet troops. German resistance had stiffened along the river and lengthening supply lines had slowed the Russian advance. Now, they gathered their strength, hauling up huge convoys of supplies, trainloads of men and fuel, readying themselves for their final attack on the Reich.

Elisabet found her task of getting her family to safety made harder by the Russian presence. The troops were everywhere, and she had to be very careful not to be seen, or if detection was unavoidable, to seem innocuous. A woman with small children appeared harmless, and such patrols as came across them generally left them alone, but there was always the risk that a soldier would decide to satisfy his lust on a helpless woman. The Russian soldiers coming up behind the front line troops were less inclined to casual violence, and while there were cercertainly horrific incidents between civilians and the occupying forces, Elisabet's family managed to escape them.

Early on, she had found a small two-room hut with a tiny kitchen garden attached, and even two scrawny chickens in a pen. The Polish owners were present, though dead, apparently shot either by the retreating Germans or the advancing Russians. The hut had been looted, but not methodically, and many useful items had escaped the plundering. The stove was intact, with a small supply of stacked wood, pots and pans, a double bed though with a ripped mattress, several blankets, stored root vegetables, some weevilly flour, and a handful of candles. The two chickens were half starved, but with a little pampering, Elisabet hoped they would start to produce eggs again as the days lengthened. After the privations of the last two months it would be luxury.

Elisabet eased herself off the lumpy mattress and went outside to wash in the tub of water laboriously filled with water from the stream each day. She cracked the ice and splashed water over her face, driving the vestiges of sleep from her eyes. Drying herself on her sleeve, she looked around at the forest, here a mixture of evergreens and deciduous trees. A few weeks more and there would be fresh food to be found, if you knew where to look. In the meantime, there were the chickens. Elisabet walked over to the small run and lifted the lid on the coop. The chickens squawked sleepily but refused to budge, so she slipped her hand under them and found, as expected, no eggs. It was still far too early in the year.

"I'm afraid there's nothing for it, kleine mädchen – one of you is for the pot."

Elisabet had debated whether to sacrifice one of the hens for the meat, but had put it off in the hopes of having a regular supply of eggs when they started laying again. They lacked protein though, and she knew it would be sensible to eat one of them. The old brown hen was scrawnier, and least likely to lay eggs when the days got longer, so she would be the one to die.

"I'll give you another day or two, brauner," she said.

Elisabet walked back to the hut, wondering what to prepare so as to give all the children something tasty and nutritious for breakfast. She had decided on some herbs from the kitchen garden and diced potato, when she glanced toward the forest again. Her throat constricted and her heart started hammering, for walking along the edge of the trees, maybe a kilometre away but coming in that direction, was a patrol. Already she could distinguish the Russian uniforms. Fighting down panic, she slipped inside the hut and hurried into the bedroom.

"Hurry, meine kleinen lieblinge. Get up, we must leave at once."

Helmut was up in a flash, looking around, while the smaller children woke more slowly, sitting up and rubbing their eyes. Joachim stuck his lip out, making up his mind whether to cry or not. Elisabet forestalled him by picking him up and cuddling him.

"Quickly. Put your shoes on and bring a blanket. We have to leave at once."

"What is it, Mutti?" Helmut asked. "Russians?"

Elisabet nodded. "No need to be scared," she reassured the younger ones, "But we should leave before they get here."

They slipped out of the door, and Elisabet could see the men were much closer, coming straight toward them.

"Follow me. Behind the chicken coop and the outhouse, then across the garden. Head toward the forest, but don't run."

She led the way, walking quickly, Joachim in her arms and the other children trotting after her.

"They've seen us, Mutti," Kurt squeaked, and took to his heels.

Elisabet glanced round and saw that the Russians had indeed seen them. Most were running toward them, but two had stopped and were aiming their rifles at the running boy.

"Lie down, all of you." She thrust Joachim at Helmut and ran after Kurt, calling to him to stop. A bullet thwacked into the turf near her and she redoubled her efforts, hurling herself on top of Kurt and bearing him to the ground. Two more shots zipped overhead like out of season wasps, and she lay still, comforting the crying child.

She heard shouts behind her and saw the first of the men arrive at where she had left her other children. Another man arrived, and threatened the prostrate boys with rifle and bayonet. Elisabet rose to her feet and thrust Kurt behind her. She raised her arms and called out.

"Do not hurt my children, I beg you."

At once, the rifles turned on her. The other men ran up and pulled her and Kurt roughly to where her other boys now stood. One of the men, a corporal, stared at her and snapped out a question. When she did not answer, he leaned closer and shouted out his question again, flecks of spittle speckling her face.

"I do not understand you," she said.

163

"Немец?" He frowned, and searched his memory. "Deutsche?"

Elisabet nodded.

"What here do you? Spies?" The corporal's accent was atrocious and he mangled the grammar, but he could be understood.

"No, no. Just a woman and her children, trying to escape the fighting."

"How here get you?"

"We walked."

"Where from walk you?"

"Mohrungen."

"Where?"

"Mohrungen, near Königsberg."

The corporal spoke to his men and they nodded. One of them swept the scarf from Elisabet's head and admired her blonde hair, running his filthy fingers through it. Another plucked at her skirts and said something that brought a rapacious laugh to the lips of his comrades. The corporal spoke again, sharply, and his men grumbled but withdrew.

"You German soldier here see?"

Elisabet shook her head again.

The corporal struck her, back-handing her casually. "You German soldier here see?" he asked again.

"No, none here. We saw some weeks ago in the Netze forest, but none since."

"What?"

"Netze forest. Long time ago."

"I think lie you."

"No."

"Perhaps I just you shoot, nein? Trouble us all save." He thought for a moment and then shrugged. "I you take see commissar in Świebodzin. Question he you." He grinned, showing rotting and discoloured teeth. "Shoot you maybe, or not. Maybe трахните вас." The corporal jerked his hips suggestively and his men roared with laughter.

Elisabet was marched under close guard to the town, but the soldiers were quite relaxed toward the children, allowing them to run alongside their mother or stray off the path as the fancy took them. A couple of the soldiers even carried Werner and Günter for a bit, and would have carried Joachim, but he screamed and clung to his mother. Elisabet held her youngest child and clung to the few possessions she had managed to keep.

The town swarmed with Russian soldiers, most moving toward the west, but a great many guarding great masses of civilians in the town square and small parks. These refugees sat or stood around on the icy cobbles or frost-burned grass and frozen mud, looking listlessly at the activity all around them. Elisabet expected to be ushered into the midst of one of these groups, but the patrol led her past and into the town hall. Here, a more senior officer took her captor's report and issued further orders.

"Children here stay." The corporal said, pointing to a side room. "Commander Commissar you talk."

"Can't I take my children with me? They're scared." They were, in fact, clinging to her dress and arms and all except Helmut were crying.

The corporal shook his head. "No. What you Germans want, no important longer."

Soldiers came and took the children aside, forcibly ripping them from Elisabet's arms and pushing them into the side room. Their screams became muted as the door slammed in their faces. The corporal pushed Elisabet down a hall and into a small uncarpeted office where a small bespectacled man sat behind a desk, reading reports.

"Pompolit Zhabanov," the corporal said, "The female prisoner found near Zieboc."

The man looked up and nodded at the officer. "Dismissed."

The corporal saluted and left the room, whereupon the senior officer indicated a position immediately in front of the desk. "Stand there," he said in fluent German.

He returned to his paperwork and the minutes crept by. Elisabet could still hear her children's screams and she fidgeted, looking toward the door. The officer looked up and regarded Elisabet balefully.

"I am Assistant Commander for Political Work Yuri Zhabanov, and you, Frau, are a spy. I will have you shot, and your children with you."

"Commander Zhabanov, I beg you to spare my children. They are innocent..."

"They are innocent, but you are guilty?"

"No, Commander. I am no spy. I am a widow trying to take my children to safety."

"Your name?"

"Frau Elisabet Daeker."

"Have you seen any German soldiers near here?"

"I told your officer. Only in the Netze forest, weeks ago. None since then."

"And Soviet soldiers? You have noted where our forces are, how strong they are? Which direction they are moving?"

"I have seen nothing since I came to the hut where your men found us. When we were brought into town I have seen many soldiers, moving to the west, but that is something everyone knows."

"Where are you from?"

"Mohrungen, Commander. Before that, from Königsberg."

"You should have remained there. The fighting is all over now, and the people are living in harmony with their Soviet liberators."

"I know what your harmony means," Elisabet said bitterly. "I talked with survivors from the atrocities at Memel and Nemmersdorf."

"Propaganda," Zhabanov said. "You mustn't believe everything you hear. The average Russian soldier is rough but good-hearted and..."

"He is a beast. I know, Commander, and not just from listening to others. I was in Schneidemühl when the Russians took the city. Every woman was raped and many were killed afterward. Children too, so do not talk to me about how noble your soldiers are." Elisabet's voice shook, and she tried to control her trembling, fearing to break down in front of the Soviet officer.

The Commander was silent for a few minutes. He took his spectacles off and polished them, then put them back on. His voice was mild as he went on. "War brings out the worst in many men, but the behaviour of the Soviet soldier compares favourably with the Germans. Your army – and the SS pigs that followed it – committed many atrocities in Russia."

"So I have been told, Commander, but everyone seeks to put the blame elsewhere. Every man – and woman – should strive to do what is decent and right."

"A noble thought, Frau. When the world is Communist, maybe."

Elisabet refrained from comment.

"What is my fate?" she asked after a brief silence.

"You will be sent back east."

167

"And my children?"

The Commander looked quite shocked. "Frau, I will not separate you from your children. You will go back to Königsberg and, who knows..." He smiled. "Maybe in time you will all learn to be good communists."

"My parents were communists, and my grandparents."

The Commander's eyebrows lifted. "Indeed? Well, there may be a bright future for you, Frau Daeker." He lifted the telephone on his desk and spoke a few words in Russian. The corporal reappeared and led Elisabet back to her children, where the family was tearfully reunited. Then he escorted them outside and through the cordon of soldiers to join the other refugees.

"Stay here," the corporal said, "Until you are called."

It was bitterly cold in the square despite the weak sunshine, for a chill wind blew, biting through ragged clothing and gnawing at exposed skin. The people around Elisabet and her family were all German, farmers and townspeople from Ostpreussen, citizens of Königsberg itself, and settlers from all over Poland. She heard accents that were familiar, and others that had her straining to understand them, but there was a feeling of unity among the people waiting in the frigid square of Schwiebus.

Elisabet made her children as comfortable as she could. They had grabbed a blanket apiece as they fled, but no food. She told each child to wrap himself tightly in his blanket, and then huddled them all together and spread her own blanket around them all. They still shivered, but at least the cold was bearable. When the children asked for food, Elisabet could only tell them to be patient and wait. Eventually, the Rus-Russians would feed them.

Towards evening, a cart rolled up to the barricades and soldiers started throwing bread to the crowd, evidently getting a lot of amusement from seeing men, women and children scrambling to catch a crust, or scrabbling in the muddy street for a loaf. When the cart was empty, little more than half the refugees had bread in their hands, and when it became evident there would be no more, many people shared what they had, despite not having enough to sustain themselves. A man handed Elisabet a large crust, stained with mud and indicated it should be divided amongst the boys. She thanked him and the man blushed and smiled, turning away.

A little later, a number of soldiers, evidently off-duty as they were openly drinking and raucously singing, stood outside the enclosure and pointed, laughing. One of them hitched his trousers and pointed at a young woman.

"Frau, komm," he demanded.

The young woman shrank back, so the soldier pushed through the crowd to her and grabbed her by the arm. A man beside her – father, brother or husband – tried to defend the woman but was clubbed to the ground for his trouble. The woman was dragged off to a nearby building. Other soldiers now selected victims, pawing them openly, and dragging them off. Sobs and screams emanated from the building where the women were being raped, and after a while they returned, stumbling and holding their clothing tight about them.

Elisabet had quickly discerned what was happening, and hunched over, not looking at the soldiers pushing through the crowd. Whether by her

169

efforts or by chance, she was not selected, and by the time night fell, the last of the women had been re-returned.

An officer appeared and one man pushed up to the barricade. He was an aggrieved relative of a raped woman, he said, and he complained loudly, demanding to see the commander.

"This behaviour is disgraceful," he shouted. "You Russians are uncivilised animals."

The officer lost his temper and snatched out a pistol, firing several shots at the man. A woman beside him died instantly, but the man was only wounded. Soldiers dragged him out and beat him to death on the cobbles before dragging his, and the woman's, bodies away.

"Does anybody else have a complaint?" the officer demanded, while he reloaded his pistol. "No? Good. Behave yourselves and you will live. In the morning you start for the east. You will march to Poznan, and from there you will be shipped by train. Many of you will be returning to your homes to rebuild them, others will be relocated to areas where you will be put to work repairing the damage your criminal regime has caused to the innocent people of Poland and Russia."

The night was bitter, and what with the lack of adequate clothing and food, many people were found dead the next morning. Urine and faeces polluted the square also, as their captors would not allow them out of their compound for any reason. The Russians did not seem to care whether the refugees lived or died, or what state they were in, and drove the hundreds of survivors out into the road with kicks and shouts, forming them up into a rough column. Elisabet had managed to keep her children alive for another night,

170

and now looked around her for some means of es-escape. She had no intention of returning to Königs-Königsberg, or remaining under Soviet rule. The West was still her aim.

More bread was issued, sufficient for everyone to have something, and then the column oozed into motion, slipping on the icy cobbles and stumbling on the road to Poznan. Other refugee groups joined them, all guarded by small detachments of soldiers, swelling the column to over a thousand. Sick people, and the wounded, fell or stumbled away from the column, and these unfortunates were hauled aside by the guards. Elisabet did not see what became of them but she had no intention of joining them despite her morning sickness. She fought down her nausea and carried on, carrying their meagre possessions.

The younger, fitter people managed quite well, but the bulk of the refugees were made up of old people or mothers with children in tow. Their strength rapidly gave out, slowing progress to a stumbling crawl. One woman looked at Elisabet staggering under her burden, four children stumbling beside her and Joachim sobbing in her arms, and laughed.

"That little one won't survive, Frau. Better you leave him behind."

Elisabet glared at her but did not reply, husbanding her strength.

The Russian authorities ordered a halt and had more food brought up, distributing hot soup and black bread and allowing the people a short rest. Then the march continued. Russian soldiers walked alongside the shuffling column, rifles slung over their shoulders, smoking and chatting amongst themselves.

"They don't look very fierce now," said an older woman walking beside Elisabet.

"No, nor vigilant," Elisabet agreed. "There might be an opportunity to slip away."

"Escape? Is that wise? They'd be angry and who knows what they might do if they caught you."

"I have my children to think of. I cannot let them stay under Soviet rule."

"My name is Elsa Trommler," the older woman said.

"Elisabet Daeker. My sons Helmut, Kurt, Günter, Werner and Joachim." She said nothing about the other child growing in her belly.

"They are fine young boys, and a credit to you." They walked a little further, and Elsa added. "Where will you go?"

"To Germany first, and as far from the Russians as possible."

"Take me with you?"

Elisabet thought about this for a kilometre or so, while Elsa said nothing further. "Where are you going?" she asked at last.

"I have a brother in Cottbus," Elsa replied. "Or at least, he might have been called up, but his wife lives there."

"You think you'll be safe from the Russians there?"

Elsa stared at Elisabet for a moment. "Cottbus is in Germany, over the Oder. I can't imagine the Russians will successfully invade Germany itself."

"You can't imagine that?" Elisabet muttered. "I can." Louder, she added, "All right, why not? If you will help me with the children."

"I'd be happy to. I really can't see how I could escape alone, but as a group it will be much simpler. Do you all want to come to Cottbus with me? I'm sure my brother would be delighted to help you until you can return home."

172

"Thank you," Elisabet said politely. "Let's see if we can escape first."

An opportunity came that evening, and proved easier than they thought. The Russians marched everybody off the road and into a large field for the night, posting guards. Fires were started, both for warmth and also to cook pots of vegetable soup. Elisabet made sure her children ate well, scrounging a bit more bread and soup off one of the more humane guards.

The presence of woods bordering the field meant they could use a bit of cover for basic purposes of hygiene. The Russian commander designated male and female latrines at opposite sides of the camp and allowed women with or without small children easy access, while men and older boys were carefully guarded when they made use of the primitive facilities. Helmut and Kurt accompanied Elsa, while Elisabet took the three younger children and walked casually into the woods. One or two of the guards made suggestive remarks but when ignored, shrugged and lit cigarettes while the women walked toward the latrines.

There were a few women using the thinly screened patch of woods that constituted the facilities, but Elisabet and Elsa walked past casually, the children in tow, deeper into the woods. One or two of the women coming out of the latrines looked at them but nobody else took any notice, and soon the night swallowed them up. A few hundred metres farther on, Elisabet stopped.

"We need to decide where we are going, and what's the best way of getting there."

"Cottbus, I thought," Elsa said. "Then you can decide where next."

"Yes, but do we just keep floundering through the woods or get back to the road? We'd move more quickly on the road. The guards may miss us and start a search. I'd like to be well away by then."

"The road then."

They retraced their steps until almost in sight of the camp and, using a maze of other footprints criss-crossing the snow, cut through the woods at an angle toward the road. It was dark and deserted by the time they got there, and the night was silent behind them.

"I left our belongings back there but they haven't missed us yet, so I'm not going back for it," Elisabet murmured.

She pushed her little group westward along the road, heading back to Schwiebus, and relying on any approaching group using headlights to warn of their approach. There was little traffic on the road, and they only had to take cover twice. Each time, a small convoy of trucks swept up behind them, and the beams briefly lit them up, but the moving shadows hid them effectively and they were not discovered. By dawn, they were close to the city again.

"Grünberg in Schlesien," Elsa said, pointing down a road that led south. "I used to go there sometimes."

"It looks like a well-used road," Elisabet observed. "It might be dangerous using it."

"True, but there's a smaller road a few kilometres down there that swings away to the river. There are lovely picnic spots among the pastures and forest. We used to go there as children."

Elisabet nodded. "That sounds better. I doubt many people will be going for picnics in the middle of a war." She looked up at the lightening sky. "We should find shelter soon."

They found a windfall in the forest a little way off the road and crawled into the dark, tangled mass of dead branches. It was cold, but the shattered timber broke up the chill breeze and by huddling together, women and children slept fitfully.

Elisabet woke in late afternoon, to find Elsa and her older boys gone. She started to crawl out of the windfall, her heart hammering, dread warring with common sense, and then remembered she could not leave the younger children unattended. If they woke and found her gone, they would be terrified. Gently, she shook them awake and told them to follow her.

Panic rose in her breast as Elisabet looked around the deserted forest. She almost called out, but bit it back when she saw the footprints, three sets, leading away from the windfall. They followed, and broke into a run when, half an hour later, she saw the figures of her boys coming toward her, Elsa a little further back.

"Where have you been, you naughty boys? Sneaking off like that."

"She told us to go with her," Helmut said sulkily.

"We were playing, Mutti," Kurt added. "Outside the shelter. Frau Elsa said we'd be back before you woke up. We're sorry."

"Yes, my fault," Elsa said as she approached. "I thought we'd see if we could find something to eat. I didn't think you'd mind."

"You should have told me. I've been so worried something had happened to them...to you all."

"We found some food, though, didn't we, Frau Elsa?" Kurt said. "Can we eat it now? I'm very hungry."

Günter and Werner started clamouring for food, and Joachim tugged at his mother's dress. Elsa undid the shawl from around her waist and spilled a dozen frost-burned mushrooms onto the leaf litter.

"They're old and tough, and have probably been there since the autumn," Elsa said.

Elisabet stopped her children from picking them up and poked one with her finger. "They're mushrooms, but are they edible?"

"I think so," Elsa said.

"Some are poisonous. Do you know how to tell the difference?"

Elsa shook her head. "Some have red caps, I know, but many others look just like ordinary mushrooms."

"I've hunted for mushrooms before, but these are old and I can't be sure. I don't think we should eat them," Elisabet said.

"She already did," Helmut said.

"What? You didn't?"

"Just a bit," Elsa said. "I thought that a small bit wouldn't kill me if it was poisonous, though it might make me sick. Anyway, it hasn't, so that's all right."

"Elsa, that's a stupid risk to take, and for such a little bit of food. How do you feel?"

"Fine. Hungry and cold, of course, but no stomach pains or nausea."

"And how long ago did you eat it?"

Elsa shrugged. "Half an hour? An hour?"

"I'm sorry, Elsa, I don't want to appear heartless, but I think we should wait a bit longer before I let my boys eat them."

On Elsa's advice, they turned and followed her trail back to open farmland. "The river's in this direction anyway. Two or three days should get us there."

"I thought the Oder was further away."

176

"It swings east between Frankfurt and Cottbus. We'll meet it on that eastward course, and hopefully it'll be easier to cross."

By evening, when her boys' complaints battered at her resolve, Elisabet relented. Elsa was showing no ill effects from eating the mushrooms, so they all chewed on the tough, leathery fragments while they walked. There was almost no sustenance in them, but it felt good to be chewing, and at least there was something in their stomachs.

The country roads leading down to the river were almost deserted. A few small villages lay across their path, but Elsa, who knew the area, led them around the tiny hamlets. They scavenged as they went, finding scraps thrown out to the pigs, stealing a few handfuls of oats and once, finding a half sack of wizened apples in a barn. Cold and hunger were ever-present companions, but they struggled on, and after a few days, found themselves on the banks of the Oder River.

"Is that Germany over there?" Helmut asked, looking at the far bank.

"No, still Poland," Elsa said. "Remember, the river is flowing east to west here. If we can find a way across, we can keep going west and find the Neisse River. Across that is Germany and safety."

Kapitel Zehn (10)

The Oder River had ice along the banks, some of it thick enough to walk on, but water flowed in the middle channel and the ice grew thin and brittle near the water. Elisabet wanted to continue westward while they looked for a place to cross, but Elsa pointed out that other streams and rivers joined the Oder and made it a much more formidable barrier downriver.

"We should go east. There are small towns that way and there may be a ferry or a bridge left intact."

"The Russians aren't going to just let us cross," Elisabet pointed out. "And we don't have any money for a ferry."

Elsa smiled. "We'll think of something."

They turned to the east, moving now in the daytime to avoid missing any way across the river. Elsa thought the town of Crossen an der Oder lay in this direction, and that it had a bridge.

"It's our way across," Elsa said.

"Providing the Wehrmacht hasn't blown it up or the Russians captured it."

The country along this stretch of the eastern bank of the Oder had been, until 1939, in Poland, but in the last six years many Germans had settled there, farming the rich alluvial soil along the river valley. They found farmers here who were charitable to the flood of refugees fleeing the advance of the Red Army.

The Russian onslaught had been uneven, with different Army Groups encountering varied resistance from the retreating Wehrmacht, and also different terrains. They had reached the Oder and crossed it many kilometres to the north, and even places as close as Schwiebus were in Soviet hands – yet here, near Crossen, the farms were undisturbed. The farmers were getting nervous at the proximity of the enemy, but still placed immense faith in the Führer, in the power of the German Army, and were convinced that matters would soon be put right by a counter-offensive that would sweep the Russians away.

A farmer who gave them board and lodging on their second night travelling east summed up the attitude of the locals. "I can appreciate your dilemma, Frau Daeker, Frau Trommler, really I can. As a loyal German it is my duty to stand firm and not give an inch to the Ivans, but if I had small children – like you – I would want to take them to a safe haven in the Reich."

"But how can you stand against the Russians, Herr Eichel?" Elisabet asked. "Forgive me, I do not mean to disparage your patriotism and determination, but I have seen these monsters, been held captive by them, and I know their strength."

Eichel pointed to the mantelpiece in his small parlour, where a silver-framed photograph of the Führer stood beside a similarly framed document. "See that? I became a National Socialist in 1933, just after they came to power. I swore an oath to the Führer and I cannot go back on it now that times are hard. He has promised us ultimate victory, and of course, he must know more than a simple farmer – or two Hausfrau from the east, nein?"

He would not be swayed from his path, but neither did he take offence at their seeming lack of commitment to the Reich. When they left in the morning, he gave each child a small bag of sweets and an apple, and pressed a bag of bread, cheese and cold meat into Elisabet's hands. "God go with you all. If you should choose to go to the Crossen bridge, I think you will find a small army unit in charge. Per-Perhaps they will let you cross."

They thanked Herr Eichel warmly and left. The road down to Crossen was packed with refugees again as word of the only existing bridge over the Oder lured people fleeing the Russian advance. Crossen itself was largely undamaged by the war – so far – but signs of imminent destruction were everywhere. A Panzerfaust unit had dug in beside the road north and a detachment of Waffen SS had taken control of the town, instructing every able-bodied man to help prepare barricades. The refugees were not immune from this conscription, and every man who could hold a pick or shovel, or even carry timber or bricks, was rounded up as they entered the town, and put to work. Boys, too, were taken, though so far only boys whose papers showed them to be twelve years or older. Elisabet produced her sons' identification papers and they let Helmut through, though a glance must have told the soldiers he was too young.

"Keep your papers handy, Frau," said one soldier as he handed them back. "They're not letting anyone across the bridge that can't prove they're German and should be here."

A few paces on, once the soldiers' attention was elsewhere, Elsa drew Elisabet aside. "I...I can't cross. You'll have to go on without me."

"What on earth do you mean? Of course you're crossing with us."

"I can't."

Elisabet stared and saw that the older woman was almost in tears. She drew her apart from the children and asked, "Why not?"

"I don't have papers."

180

"You've lost them? Well, that's a problem but not necessarily insurmountable. If you give them full details of who you are and where you come from..."

"That's not the problem."

"Then what is the problem?"

"I can't tell you. Look, it's better if I just leave you here. You go on with your boys and get them to safety." Elsa turned to go, but Elisabet caught at her arm.

"Elsa, no. You're running from the Russians as much as we are. It doesn't make sense you wouldn't want to cross into Germany. Tell me what the problem is and maybe we can solve it together."

"You can't. Nobody can. I..."

"You've committed some crime? The polizei have your details?"

"I have committed no crime...except perhaps in the eyes of the Nazis."

"Then what, for God's sake, Elsa?"

"I'm Jewish." Elsa looked around nervously to see if she had been overheard. "Are you going to turn me in?"

Elisabet suppressed a laugh. "Is that all?"

"You think it is funny?"

"No. No, of course not. I'm sorry, Elsa. I don't mean to make light of...of your heritage, but you being Jewish doesn't matter to me in the slightest."

"It seems to matter to just about everyone else. Even people who knew me before the Nazis came to power started avoiding me. Why should you be different?"

"Because I could easily have been where you are now."

"What do you mean?"

181

Elisabet looked toward where Kurt watched his brothers playing together. "I knew a Jew once."

*   *   *

We met quite by chance, Joseph and me. My son Helmut was only six months old and it was a sunny but chilly day in late March 1936. I lived with my parents, who had been very understanding and supportive of me after I had given birth to a child out of wedlock. Their house in the old part of Königsberg was pleasant and well furnished, and I lacked for nothing, but I still remembered our days on the farm and tried to take walks in the fresh air whenever I could. It had been cold that year, and my opportunities to take the air were few and far between, especially with a small infant to look after.

That day in late March came after several days of cold blustery weather, and the sun shining weakly from an azure sky, the first buds lacing the trees in the park with a delicate filigree of green lace, and the starlings strutting on the lawns searching for early worms. I took Helmut out in his pram, warmly wrapped of course, and walked down past the Schloss to the long lake called the Schlossteich and its famous Promenade.

The Schlossteich is a truly beautiful place – a narrow lake a kilometre in length with a thin strip of vegetation close to the water, a walking path, and trees partially hiding the buildings that pressed close. There are several cafés along the Promenade, and it is a favourite haunt of students. Many people were out taking advantage of the fine weather and I strolled along pushing Helmut in his pram. I sat for a while on a stone seat by Der Bogenschütze and watched the ducks on the water, contending with a thin rim of ice around the edges. Later in the year, rowboats would

182

creak and splash past, filled with young men showing off to their girls, but now the only sounds were the chatter of people taking the air and the quacking of ducks squabbling over a crust of bread.

I walked further, seeking a measure of solitude, and came to the long, thin walking bridge that crossed the lake. As I turned onto it, one of the front wheels of the pram hit the kerbing and lurched. A wheel came loose and wobbled away down the bank and fell onto the rim of ice, while I struggled to prevent the pram tipping over. Helmut awoke and screamed for attention, so I picked him up and the pram half fell. I grabbed it, but with Helmut in my arms, could not control it. I stood there, unable to put my baby down but unwilling to let go of the pram and have it tip over.

"May I be of assistance, Frau?"

I looked over my shoulder and saw a tall slim young man with dark hair and delightfully brown eyes – yes, I noticed that immediately.

"Thank you," I replied. "Could you please take the pram and lean it against the railing? The wheel has come off."

While the young man performed this small task, I rocked Helmut in my arms and spoke to him reassuringly, quieting him down. After a few minutes, he gurgled and closed his eyes sleepily. I looked up to see the beautiful brown eyes of the young man looking at me. I smiled, and he returned it. His gaze dropped to my right hand briefly.

"Perhaps you would allow me to retrieve the wheel?"

"Thank you, though I'm not sure what good that would do. If my brother was here, he would be able to mend it. Hans is very handy with his...er, hands."

183

The young man smiled again and scrambled down the bank to the edge of the ice. He used a stick to hook the wheel toward him and then picked it up.

"It is undamaged," he said. "Whatever went wrong must be a fault of the axle." He scrambled up the bank again and squatted beside the pram. "Ah, yes, here. The split pin has snapped and fallen out. You will need a new one."

"My father owns a store. Maybe he has one, but how am I to get home in the meantime?"

The young man thought for a moment. "The logical thing would be to find a substitute for the split pin, but..." he looked around "...nothing suggests itself. So, may I be permitted to carry the pram home for you?"

"I cannot ask that of you," I said. "I do not know you."

He sketched a mock bow. "I am Joseph Herzfeld, student of philosophy here at the University."

"Good day, Herr Herzfeld. I am Elisabet Machel."

"Now that we are properly introduced, may I have the honour of accompanying you home, Frau Machel...or is it Fraulein?"

I blushed, for while there are a number of unwed mothers in the Reich these days, one should not be reminded of one's status in public. Then I thought to myself that my child was conceived in love and I had done nothing I was ashamed of. I lifted my head and looked him in the eye.

"Fraulein Machel, but if you desire to address me in public, then perhaps you will call me Elisabet."

"Delighted...Elisabet. And please, I am Joseph."

He picked up the pram and, with me walking beside him, carrying Helmut in my arms, we walked slowly back down the Promenade and into the streets

184

of Königsberg. We stopped at intervals, for the weight of the pram was tiring for Joseph, and sat on one of the many benches that dotted the tree-lined streets. It was on one of these stops, near the Schloss, that we were accosted by two members of the Ordnungspolizei.

"Papers, please."

I looked up to see two uniformed members of the police standing in front of us, hands outstretched. I dug into my purse and handed over my little folded booklet, while Joseph – looking rather pale, I thought – pulled his out of his jacket pocket. The officer examined mine and handed it back, but the other officer stared at the booklet in his hand and then at Joseph.

"Juden?"

"Yes, Unterwachtmeister."

Joseph stood up and I stared at him. The officer had called him a Jew.

"What are you doing here, Jew?"

"Taking the air, sir."

"You are a student at the university?"

"Yes sir."

"Taking one of the places that rightfully belongs to a German student, no doubt."

"I am German sir. My family has lived here for two hundred years."

"Don't get smart, Jew." The officer looked down at me. "Why are you with this German woman?"

I spoke up at once, determined that he should not suffer for his kind actions. "He is helping me get my child and broken pram home, officer. Is there a problem?"

"He is not accosting you? Not forcing his attentions on you?"

"By no means. He has been nothing but polite and helpful. A model citizen."

"You knew he was a Jew?"

"Of course."

The policeman grunted and handed the papers back to Joseph. "Behave yourself, Jew. If we hear anything to the contrary, we will be paying you a visit. And as for you, Frau Machel, I advise you to choose your companions more carefully in future. Such associations, even innocent ones, are frowned upon." The policemen walked away and Joseph sat down again, breathing hard.

"Thank you, Elisabet. I thought...well, anything could have happened."

"Are you really a Jew?"

He paused, looking at me. "Yes. Does it matter?"

"No."

"Then you are different from most Germans."

"My parents brought me up to believe all men have within them the essence of goodness, and they should be judged by their actions, not their beliefs. I know many of our friends believe the same."

"Then you have enlightened parents, and they have brought up a beautiful and wise daughter."

I blushed for the second time that morning.

*   *   *

They all crossed the bridge at Crossen. Elisabet presented her papers and those of her children to the SS guard, and told him that her sister-in-law, Elsa Trommler, had lost hers during their escape through Russian lines.

"I have known her for twenty years, ever since my older brother first courted her. I can vouch for her identity."

186

The guard frowned and consulted his clipboard where he was noting down all the names of the people crossing the bridge. He opened his mouth to speak but Elisabet never learned whether her lie had worked, for a loud explosion and a chatter of gunfire to the north of the town elicited cries of alarm from the queue of refugees. The guard swore and looked away, motioning them to proceed, as other refugees pressed up to the barrier, waving their papers. They hurried over the stone bridge, hundreds of refugees now swamping the checkpoint and running after them, their possessions in carts or suitcases.

"Where now?"

"West again, over the Bober River."

Refugees streamed along the road all around them, and the sound of artillery shells and gunfire spurred them onward. They passed a small lake and saw the road forked ahead of them, one road leading to a narrow bridge clogged with people. Elsa pointed down at the small Bober River, almost completely iced over, and led them down. The ice creaked and groaned beneath them as they bypassed islands of open water, scrambling over humped ice floes and up onto the far bank.

"I think we should keep to the fields and woods," Elsa said. "The roads are going to be clogged with people."

"How far to the Neisse?" Elisabet asked.

"Thirty kilometres. Two, three days. We can cross the river by the bridge at Guben. We'll be in Germany before that, somewhere on this side of the river is the district of Lausitz, but don't expect the Russians to respect that border. We'll only be safe over the barrier of the river."

187

The snow in the fields was not deep and, being well fed and rested, they made good time, hugging the edges of the forest and only crossing empty fields or fording frozen streams when they had to. Behind them, the sound of battle raged, and after one particularly loud explosion, died away to sporadic gunfire.

"I think the army has blown up the bridge to stop the Russians."

They slept that night in the forest again, in the shelter of a huge fallen tree. A fire was a risk, but a worthwhile one if the Russians had been delayed. They spread their blankets close to the fire and wrapped themselves up against the cold, quickly falling asleep.

Elisabet and Elsa took the opportunity to check over the children's clothing and shoes, making sure that frostbite and infection had not taken hold unnoticed. One of Helmut's shoes was wearing out in the sole, so Elisabet ripped a strip of cloth from the hem of her dress and wadded it inside the affected shoe. Kurt's footwear had stitching problems, the uppers pulling away from the soles, but there was little she could do for that without a decent needle and tough thread. Günter had the sniffles again, and Werner a persistent cough. There was little the adults could do for these ailments except keep the boys warm. Joachim had a slight fever too, and cried a lot.

"As soon as we get to Germany, I'll find a doctor and get you medicines. Hot food too, I promise."

The wind changed during the night, a frigid blast from the north under leaden skies assailing them as they emerged from the shelter of the forest.

"It's going to snow again," Elisabet said. "Perhaps we should stay under the trees."

188

"If we do that, we could be here for days. We have to get across this open ground before the Russians catch up. Maybe the storm won't be too bad."

By midday, they were nearly five kilometres nearer the river and snow was falling, not heavily yet but increasing. Visibility dropped and the world closed in around them in a cocoon of white swirling flakes, sky and land merging into an enveloping white shroud. The children, particularly the younger ones, were nearing the limits of their strength, and were crying.

"We have to stop," Elisabet said. "Find some shelter."

"I'm sorry," Elsa said. "It's my fault. We should have stayed under the trees."

A hummock loomed, black against the snow, and as they drew closer they saw that it was the burnt out remains of a truck cab, the chassis shattered, the glass in its windows missing. Snow had swept through the gaps during the long winter, but the wind direction now came from behind the gutted wreck and the back wall of the cab offered some protection.

Elsa tied a blanket over one side window and the windscreen, while Elisabet and Helmut shovelled snow from the interior with their bare hands. After half an hour's work, they piled inside, wrapped themselves in their remaining blankets and prepared to wait out the storm. Day cycled through to night and the storm worsened, dropping visibility to almost zero. There was nothing for the eye to hang onto to give perspective, so their world became their crowded cab. They ate scraps of cold food they still had from the generous German farmer and slept, waking to darkness, and sleeping again.

Kurt cried out softly in his sleep, and Elisabet cradled him, kissing the top of his head.

189

My parents were less welcoming to Joseph than I anticipated, though this was, as I later learned, because they saw future troubles for both of us if we pursued our friendship. They thanked him for seeing me home that first day, but thereafter I had to meet him in the city if I wanted to see him. And I did. There was something about his nature, and yes, I admit it, the fact that he was Jewish added a certain allure.

Of course, I had been lectured on Jews when I was in the Bund Deutscher Mädel, and had sat through the propaganda newsreels at the cinema where Jews were portrayed as evil, subhuman monsters living amongst us, lying in wait to desecrate and destroy the Aryan people. I had my doubts, right from the start. If Jews lived among us, how was it that we didn't see the horrible faces from the newsreels on every street corner?

My father told my brother and me about anti-Semitism and the fallacies that lie behind that pernicious dogma, and had then taken us out on the streets of Königsberg and asked us to point out a Jew. It was impossible, as he well knew. He then introduced us to a Jewish friend of his, whom we had known previously only as Uncle Karl. It was a revelation – Jews were no different from other Germans – so what was all the fuss about?

That did not stop my father warning us about indiscreet behaviour. As the Nazi regime gripped Germany in its iron fist, it put in place its terrible race laws, and encouraged the populace to make life miserable for those it did not favour. Even in Königsberg – beautiful, friendly Königsberg – people turned against their fellow Germans. Joseph must

190

have known, even more than me, the danger he was putting himself in. A Jew could be beaten up at any time with impunity, but if he was in the company of a good German girl, he could expect far worse if the Nazi thugs posing as police caught us.

So we met, clandestinely, on walks on the Promenade, at a roadside café, or in the cinema, and we fell in love. I did not always have Helmut with me as my mother was happy to baby-sit, and sometimes we would take a tram out to the city limits and walk into the country, sharing a sandwich and a bottle of beer beneath a tree and talking, always talking. There was so much I wanted to know about him, and he about me, and after a month I dared hope he would ask me to marry him. Yes, I know, a month is not long, but I liked everything about him, not least that he seemed happy to take on the responsibility of another man's child, my little Helmut. I also knew that if he did, and I agreed, we would be embarking on a perilous voyage. Just the previous year, the Nuremberg Rassenschande laws made it a criminal act for a Jew and a German to marry. The penalty would be death for him and incarceration in a concentration camp for me. We would have to flee Germany if we were to marry. The Nazi Reich took no account of being in love.

An early spring day, the middle of April 1936, and Joseph asked me to accompany him once more into the countryside. He seemed pensive, hardly talking on the way out to our favourite spot beneath a spreading oak tree. I spread the blanket and sat down, tucking my skirts around my legs as the air was still a little chilly.

"Something is bothering you, Joseph. What is it?"

191

He sat beside me and took my right hand in his. "You know I love you, Elisabet?"

"Yes." I smiled. "But it's always nice to hear you say it."

Joseph forced a smile. "I love you."

"I love you too."

"Elisabet, I have to go away."

"What? No! Why? Where?"

"The elders at the synagogue have been encouraging the Jews of Königsberg to seek homes in other countries – ones where anti-Semitism is not so prevalent. My father has written to his cousin in America, and received a favourable reply. He will find a place for us in New York, so my family is leaving."

"When?" I whispered.

"In two days. Elisabet, I want you to come with me. We can go to America together."

"Leave Königsberg?" When faced with the actuality of leaving, I quailed. Königsberg was my home. My parents, my brother, all my relatives lived here. How could I give them up so suddenly?

"I love you, Elisabet," Joseph said earnestly. "Come with me."

"Oh, Joseph, you know I love you, but to leave all my family, just like that..."

He nodded. "It is a big decision, I know, but...you would not be leaving all your family."

"What do you mean?"

"My family would become your family. Once we were married."

There, he had said it. "You want to marry me?"

"Of course! Haven't I...no, I haven't, have I?" He got onto one knee. "Elisabet Machel, will you do me the great honour of becoming my wife?"

192

"Yes!" I sat up and threw my arms about him and kissed him. We fell back down to the blanket and continued kissing and stroking each other's hair, looking deep into each other's eyes and uttering sweet nonsense words. As our passion grew, I decided that nothing would stop our marriage – not the Nazis, not their stupid laws, nor even being separated from my family. We would work something out. I loosened my skirts and gave myself to him, as a promise and a bond between us.

I joyfully told my parents of Joseph's proposal when I got home, but was totally unprepared for their reaction. My mother burst into tears, and my father put his foot down.

"No. you will not marry him. I forbid it."

"Why, Vati? You like Jews and you like Joseph."

"Do you have any idea of how much trouble this would bring down on us all? In the eyes of the government, you would be committing a criminal act, polluting your blood..."

"But you don't believe that..."

"No, of course I don't, but that's not the point. You would disappear into a concentration camp and your beloved Joseph would be shot. Do you want that?"

"No, but..."

"Your brother Hans would lose his spot on the Olympic weight-lifting team. Do you imagine the brother of a girl who blatantly pollutes her blood is going to be allowed to represent the Reich in Berlin this summer? And think of your mother – she will have to bear the stares and jibes of her neighbours, and be ostracised by our friends."

"We'll go away together. Nobody here need know. Joseph and his family are going to America. I'll go with them."

"I forbid it."

"Vati, Mutti, you know I love you both, but you can't stop me. I want to be with Joseph."

"You are not yet twenty-one, Elisabet. As a minor, in my house, you will do as you are told."

"No Vati, in this one thing I will not. I love him."

My father got his way. I was bundled off to the grandparents in the countryside and by the time I returned, Joseph and his family had left for America. I might have run away to join him, but I had no idea where he was. All that I had were memories of a wonderful young man – and another baby.

Yes, my indiscretion on our last day together left me with child and in January of 1937, my second son Kurt was born. I kept his paternity a secret for revealing it would have served no purpose. I loved him as much as his brother Helmut, and set about rearing them both as best I could.

∗   ∗   ∗

The storm continued into the second day, a blizzard of white whipping almost horizontally across the fields and building up into drifts against the burnt out truck cab that was their refuge. They crept outside when their bodies required them to do so, hurrying, and returning shivering to the fold; they ate their meagre rations cold; and they waited, listening to the rush of the wind and the rolling thunder of the storm creeping closer.

"Are those guns, Mutti?" Helmut asked.

"No, my sweet, that's only the storm."

"It sounds like guns."

194

"I think he's right," Elsa whispered. "The wind is coming from the north, but the sound is in the east."

Elisabet wrapped her blanket tighter and leaned out of the cab, brushing away the snow as the flakes swirled in her eyes, blinding her. She listened, and the truth of their situation dawned upon her.

"A battle is in progress. The Russians are pushing our army back, toward us."

"What do we do?"

"I don't know. Stay here? Maybe the battle will just pass us by."

"We could run for it. We must be close to the river."

"In this storm? With young children? Even if we could travel, we'd just be figures in the blizzard. They could shoot us by mistake."

They stayed where they were. The sounds of battle were muted by the blanketing blizzard but grew steadily louder until quite suddenly the landscape was lit by an orange glow and a muffled explosion sent tremors through the ground. Something roared overhead, unseen, and exploded toward the river, and on its heels they heard the clanking grumble of tanks forging through the soft snow. Through the swirling snow they saw grey-coated warriors retreating, falling back, and giving each other covering fire. The soldiers passed on either side of the truck cab, paying it no attention, and then one looked inside.

He was a young man with the eyes of a warrior that has seen horrors. A bloody bandage covered one cheek and ice clung to the stubble on his chin. His fingers poked through woollen gloves, gripping his rifle, the flesh torn and blackening through frostbite. The soldier stared at the huddled figures in the cab for several long moments, and then shook his head slowly and stumbled away.

Hard on his heels came the enemy – first tanks, churning through the drifts with snow sprays whipped away by the keen wind, and then the foot soldiers. They were dressed in white and clutched their rifles with gloved hands. The snow muffled their tread and they whispered through the blizzard like ghosts of fallen warriors bent on revenge.

A Russian ran by, and then stopped, turned toward the cab, his visage obscured by felted material so only his eyes showed. He stared expressionlessly at the two women and five children huddled in blankets and slowly raised his rifle. Another figure drifted through the snow storm and joined him, regarded the refugees, and said something to the soldier with the rifle. They both turned and were swallowed up by the driving snow.

"Did that just happen?" Elisabet murmured.

"Someone is looking out for us," Elsa commented.

Over the course of the day, perhaps twenty soldiers passed close enough to be seen, but no others stopped or gave any hint that they had seen the people in the truck cab. Night fell. They ate the last of their food and slept, waking to a bright, clear morning. The storm had blown itself out in the night and the sun shone on a huge expanse of clean white snow, whipped up into spires and mounds where the wind had found some object in its bitter path. There was no sign of battle and almost nothing that told of the passage of armed men.

Elisabet and Elsa climbed out of the cab and looked around, making sure that they were alone before allowing the children out. After an enforced period of inactivity, the boys went wild for a few minutes, running and jumping, but they quickly ran out of energy and started to complain of hunger and cold again. Elisabet called them to order and started them westward once more, following the route taken by the Russian troops.

They trudged steadily, their route leading them on the gradual slope down to the Neisse River, hidden from where they were by forest. They could see smoke rising in many places and could hear the rumble of a protracted battle somewhere ahead of them, but there was nowhere else they could go. The Russians had overrun the land between the Oder and Neisse, and if they stayed here they would sooner or later be captured and sent east again or worse. It was better to take a chance on getting through to Germany and hoping for the protection of the Wehrmacht making a stand to defend the Reich.

"I must be a fool wanting to get back to Germany," Elsa murmured as they walked. "Life is hard for a Jew there."

"Just as hard under the Soviets," Elisabet said. "Anyway, from now on you're just Elsa Trommler, my sister-in-law who is a good Aryan and who has had the misfortune of losing her papers. I doubt they'll be able to check up with the Königsberg records anytime soon."

The fields ended and they took to the road again, edging south of west toward the town of Guben and the bridge over the river. There was evidence here of the passage of many men and vehicles, and they proceeded cautiously. It was as well they did, for rounding a bend in the road they saw a unit of Russians ahead of them. The soldiers had not seen them, so they ducked back and then crept through the woods beside the road to observe them. If they were

197

going to be here some time, Elsa and Elisabet would have to find a way around them. The men were clear-clearing bodies from the road, throwing some into a ditch beside the road and loading others into a truck.

"Can you see what they're doing?" Elsa asked.

"They're clearing bodies. The ones being put in the truck are in uniform, the ones being thrown in the ditch aren't. I think there's been a battle."

"Then who are the ones not in uniform?"

"Refugees caught up in the fight, I'd say."

They watched and waited, anxious to be getting across the river to safety, but wary of exposing themselves to capture or death. The last of the bodies were loaded onto the truck, and it moved off, accompanied by the detachment of soldiers. Elisabet and Elsa led the boys down to the road again and they advanced cautiously to the scene of the carnage. Artillery and tank shells had shattered the landscape and tanks had rolled right over the refugees, smashing bodies and throwing others aside. The road was splashed with blood and a ditch along the road overflowed with bodies of men, women, children and horses.

"Shut your eyes, boys," Elisabet commanded. "You too, Helmut. This is not something you want to see."

The women led the children past the scene of the massacre and into even worse carnage beyond. The Russians had at least cleared the road of their own casualties, and had made a token effort with the civilians, but here, on this stretch of road, lay the remains of the Wehrmacht force that had opposed the victorious Soviets.

Bodies lay everywhere, some crushed and mangled almost beyond recognition, others lying sprawled, eyes open and staring. Many of the faces were young, men scarcely out of their teens – a unit cobbled to-together hastily from some local Hitlerjugend or Volkssturm and thrown into battle untrained and unprepared.

Elisabet found herself sobbing at the waste of life, the futility of it all, and her hand slipped from Kurt's, moving to her face to wipe away the tears. She stepped around a body, but Kurt, lacking guidance, tripped over the body. His eyes flew open and he stared in horror at the blood-smeared German soldier at his feet.

He screamed, rooted to the spot. Elisabet whipped round, a horrified look on her own face – horror at her own culpability. She snatched Kurt to her and buried his face in her skirts, hugging him desperately and holding him until his screams broke down into hiccuping sobs. Elsa hurried the other children on, past the charnel field and Elisabet led Kurt through, covering his eyes with her scarf.

Beyond lay the road to the town of Guben on the River Neisse. The road was too dangerous to take, so they crept through bare-branched woods, over snow-filled meadows, walking along frozen streambeds, and taking shelter behind stone walls and hedges, edging closer to the river. The bridge at Guben had been blown up by the retreating Wehrmacht, and artillery shells were being exchanged, turning the frozen river into a churning maelstrom of ice and water. They moved south, past the town, avoiding Russian patrols and found themselves on a deserted stretch of river. A jumble of hummocked ice and a narrow expanse of smooth ice were all that separated them from the safety of the German Reich.

Kapitel Elf (11)

"It's not a big river, is it?"

"No, and it should be easy to cross. It's been a cold winter and I think the ice should hold us. We're going to be exposed out there though."

"Perhaps we should wait for nightfall," Elisabet said.

"The longer we wait, the more chance a Soviet patrol will stumble across us," Elsa replied. "Also, I'm getting very hungry and I dare say the children are too."

Elisabet worried about the dash across the ice. Just because they couldn't see Russian soldiers, didn't mean there weren't any. They could be sitting in a nice warm gun emplacement, just waiting for someone to break cover.

"I think I'd be happier waiting for it to get dark. The boys have been hungry before, so they'll manage. This is a risky crossing."

From where they crouched in the cover of a grove of willows, their fine branches clothed in a fine fuzz of new growth, the river stretched ahead of them to a scrub-covered gently-sloping bank on the far side, a few snow mounds and a jumble of fallen brickwork where a small building had succumbed to the vicissitudes of war. The river was no more than fifty metres wide at this place, apparently ice-covered, the smooth surface heaved into blocks toward the middle. Elisabet guessed that the recent thaw had broken the surface into floes which had refrozen in the storm of the last few days. If the fine weather continued, the ice would break up again, making their crossing that much harder.

Elsa continued pressing for an immediate crossing, saying they should take full advantage of the absence of Soviet soldiers. "There are none here now, but if they turn up we won't be able to cross at all."

Elisabet could see the sense of her argument and allowed herself to be persuaded. "All right, we'll try it," she said.

Elisabet led, carrying Joachim. Helmut came next, holding Werner's hand, and then Kurt holding onto Günter. Elsa brought up the rear, ready to assist if a child should stumble or fall.

"Remember, boys, if I tell you to do something, you obey me instantly."

She led the way out of the willows and down the bank onto the ice. It cracked and broke close to the bank, wetting her shoes, but firmed farther out. There was a fine covering of snow over the ice and Elisabet probed ahead of her shuffling feet with a willow stick, hoping for some forewarning if the ice proved to be too thin to carry her weight.

She looked back and saw her children following in her footsteps, small bundles of anxious child, hungry and cold but still determined to reach safety. At the rear, Elsa swivelled as she walked, turning this way and that to scour the bank they had just left, searching for danger. She too, carried a stick, but held it as if to ward off an attacker rather than to test the ice.

They arrived at the blocks in the middle of the river, and Elisabet probed a crack between them with her stick, and then lifted Joachim through, setting him down carefully before climbing over to join him. The boys scrambled through, more agile than their mother. Werner and Günter seemed to be enjoying themselves and were chattering and throwing scoops of snow. Helmut frowned, seemingly conscious of his responsibilities as the eldest, while Kurt just shivered and looked about him. Elsa smiled and chided them gently.

"Play on the other side, boys, not in the middle of the river."

Elisabet called them through the jumble of blocks and they waited on the far side for Elsa, scanning the bank for signs of life before crossing the open space. They heard a sharp crack behind them, the sound a stick might make when broken, or ice as it splits open.

Elsa yelled. "Russians! Get moving." The woman scrambled up the side of a block, for a moment silhouetted against the sky, and the chatter of a machine gun split the winter air.

"Get down," Elisabet yelled.

The clatter of the gun came again and Elsa jumped, sprawled on the ice on the German side, but the bullets kicked up a vicious path toward her, punching outward from a gun emplacement on the German side. Elisabet leapt to her feet and waved her hands above her head, screaming out her outrage.

"Schiessen sie nicht! Wir sind Deutsch."

In front of her and above, where the pile of rubble from the brick ruin met a standing wall, she could see the barrel of a machine gun and the flashes as a hail of metal arced out toward them. The children started crying and Elisabet turned and threw herself on them, bearing them down onto the creaking ice as the bullets slashed overhead. Then the gun fell silent and she raised her head.

"Aufstehen," yelled a male voice from the ruins. "Put your hands on your heads."

"Nicht schiessen," Elisabet called back, and then urged her weeping children to their feet. She looked behind her and stared in horror at Elsa, who lay sprawled on the ice, her blood staining the snow from the stitching of wounds across her body.

"You've killed her, you dummköpfe. Can't you see we're women and children, not soldiers. We're Germans."

Elisabet turned to go to her aid, and a warning shot rang out, showering her with ice slivers.

"Come here, Frau. Your children too. Quickly."

As if to accentuate the command, something screamed overhead, from east to west, earth and smoke fountaining up behind the German position. Another shell followed, and now the German guns opened up, shells falling on the bank behind them, and in the river. The ice shuddered beneath their feet, and Elisabet knew she could either stay to see if her friend still lived, or help her children. She turned back to the west and ran, scooping up Joachim and dragging Werner by the hand.

"Run, boys," she yelled.

Helmut grabbed Günter and pushed Kurt toward the bank, and ran for the cover of the snow-covered boulders and scrub. Artillery shells exploded behind them, though whether they came from Russian or German guns it was impossible to tell. Elisabet encouraged and drove her sons up the bank, to the ruins and past them, not stopping until they slid over the top of the bank and into the fields beyond. The children collapsed, hands over their heads, but Elisabet risked a look back, toward the river. The water boiled, ice chunks bobbing and disintegrating as explosives ripped into it. Elsa's body had disappeared into the chaos as if she had never existed.

Elisabet rested her head on her folded arms and prayed to a god she wasn't sure existed. "She helped us...she saved us...take care of her...please."

After a few minutes, Elisabet rolled over and gathered her children to her, talking to them, soothing them, calming them down. Gradually, their terror subsided into sobs and eventually sniffles.

"I'm hungry, Mutti," Günter whispered.

"Me too," said Kurt.

"And where are we going to find food, dummkopf?" Helmut muttered.

"Be nice to your brother," Elisabet murmured. She looked around. The Russian bombardment had moved, ranging in on the German positions to the rear and the explosions had become less immediate, less threatening. She could see men moving at the far end of the field, men in Wehrmacht grey.

"Come children. We'll ask the soldiers for help."

An Obergefreiter and a handful of Schütze soldiers were sitting around drinking ersatz coffee and munching on hard rations when Elisabet called out to them. At once, two of the Schütze grabbed their rifles and started toward them, while the rest of the soldiers looked on. The two with the rifles ushered them back to their Corporal.

"Good day, Obergefreiter," Elisabet said. "My children and I are tired and hungry. May we beg some food from you?"

The Corporal looked her up and down, his jaws still masticating hard biscuit. He swallowed and sipped his coffee.

"Who are you, and where the hell did you come from?"

"I am Frau Daeker from Königsberg, Obergefreiter. My children and I are fleeing the Russians and have just crossed the Neisse."

204

"In this lot?" He waved his hand in the general direction of where the Russian bombardment was aimed. "I don't believe you. I think you're spies."

One of the men laughed and some of the others smirked but looked away when their Corporal scowled.

Elisabet sighed. "I hoped for a little compassion, if not for me, then for my children. Can't you see they are exhausted and starving? We are as German as you. As was the woman whom your companions killed."

The Corporal muttered to himself. "Well, it's not my job to sort out whether you're telling the truth. Walther, Schirer, escort this woman back to camp and hand them over to SS-Hauptsturmführer Brandt."

The two Privates smiled and gestured toward a path leading back through the fields. One walked ahead, while the other, Schütze Schirer, walked beside Elisabet. He dug in his greatcoat pocket and pulled out some hard sweets which he distributed to the boys.

"You don't want to mind Obergefreiter Meister," Schirer said. "He's a bit of an arsch, but he's fairly harmless."

"What's this SS Captain of yours like?"

"Well, he's not our Captain strictly. He's Waffen SS and a bloody good soldier by all accounts. We're 35th Infanteriedivision – were, anyway. Now we're scattered all to hell and beyond. Never mind, Frau, we're going to hold the bloody Ivans on the Neisse. We bloody well have to, see, because we're fighting for Germany now, on German soil. Nothing's going to shift us, you'll see."

"Thank you, Schütze Schirer, your words bring me comfort." Privately, Elisabet thought he was deluded. If the German Army had not been able to stem the flood of Russians all the way across Ostpreussen and Poland, what hope had they now? She planned on getting her children as far away from the front line as possible before the Russians launched the next phase of their attack.

SS-Hauptsturmführer Brandt was pleasant-faced and urbane in appearance, sitting at a desk in a field tent, working his way through a pile of paperwork when Elisabet and the children were shown in. Schirer passed on the message from his Corporal, saluted, and left. Brandt remained seated and regarded the woman and children in front of him.

"Obergefreiter Meister says you are a Russian spy. What do you say to that?"

"I say he is talking nonsense. I am a loyal German from Königsberg, and these are my children."

"You have papers?"

Elisabet placed them in Brandt's hand and waited while he went through them.

"Most refugees cross by way of bridges – or they did before we blew them up. You chose a curious place to cross, right in the middle of a bombardment."

"Not by choice, Hauptsturmführer. We tried to remain unseen by the Russians, and didn't know there was going to be an attack right there. Your outpost by the ruins shot at us, killed the woman with us – Elsa Trommler. They could see it was women and children crossing the ice."

"It was probably the Russians that fired – that killed her."

"It was a machine gun. A German machine gun."

The Hauptsturmführer regarded her steadily, his fingers tapping the arm of his chair. Then he

206

shrugged. "Accidents happen, Frau Daeker. It is war, after all."

"So it seems."

"You managed to come all the way from Königsberg without being caught by the Russians?"

"I didn't say that," Elisabet retorted. "We were captured at Schneidemühl and escaped, then later, at Schwiebus we were caught again. We slipped away in the night."

"So easy."

"No, not easy, Hauptsturmführer. But conditions were chaotic and the Russians had few men to spare for guarding civilian refugees."

Brandt nodded. "Tell me what units of the Russian army were involved in the attacks at Schneidemühl and Schwiebus."

"I have no idea. I can't recognise army units of the German Army, let alone Russians. There were tanks at Schneidemühl, but only soldiers at Schwiebus. Come, Hauptsturmführer, you cannot honestly think I am a spy."

Brandt smiled icily. "No, I do not think the Russians would be so stupid. Besides, I am sure they are very well aware of what Divisions face them at Guben."

"Then you will let us go?"

"Where would you go?"

"I have family in Dresden."

"Then I am sorry to be the bearer of bad news. Dresden has been obliterated. The British and American bombers chose a target without military value or defences and destroyed an ancient and beautiful city. Many innocent civilians suffered as a result of this criminal action."

"Oh, mein Gott...I must go to them. They lived a little out of the city. Perhaps they are unharmed."

"They may have survived, Frau Daeker, but you will not be allowed into the area. I suggest you find some other place of refuge until the war is won."

"I...I will go west."

"These are your sons?"

Elisabet nodded. "Why?"

"As you may appreciate, we need every man and boy we can find to defend the Fatherland. The big one there..." Brandt indicated Helmut, "...I could find a use for him as a runner, carrying messages."

"He is only nine years old, Hauptsturmführer."

"Nearly ten, Mutti," Helmut protested.

Brandt laughed. "I like your spirit, boy, but your mother is right, you are too young."

"I can fight."

"Of that I have no doubt, but your duty is to your family. Protect them, for Germany will have need of them soon."

"Yes, sir," Helmut said, his face glowing with pride.

"Now, I suggest you move away from Guben immediately. The Russians will attack soon and the last things we need are civilians underfoot when we're fighting. So..." Brandt scribbled on a piece of paper, "...take this to the mess, and this..." Another note, "...to the quartermaster, and they will give you some food and new clothing." He handed the notes to Elisabet. "Stay safe, Frau Daeker, you and your children are the future of the Reich."

"What a nice man," Helmut commented, once they left the command tent.

The Scharführer at the mess fed them without comment, dishing up bowls of a hot, filling stew with

208

potatoes and crusty rye bread, and mugs of steaming ersatz coffee and warm milk. They gorged until they could hold no more, and then, with directions from a number of soldiers, they made their way to the outskirts of Guben and the main storehouse.

The quartermaster's assistant, responding to the note from Hauptsturmführer Brandt, led them to a great hall where clothing and shoes of all sizes were stored, great mounds and piles, in all conditions.

"Help yourselves, Frau," said the assistant. "There are rooms off there you can change in, if you like." He busied himself with inspecting the work of a number of thin, haggard looking men in striped pyjama-like pants and jackets who were sorting through the piles, inspecting seams and discarding clothing that was torn or worn.

Elisabet found stout shoes for her boys and a pair of boots for herself, before selecting pants and jackets for them all, and a long woollen skirt. She quickly dressed herself, glad to be out of her old, filthy clothing, and approached the assistant while the boys finished changing.

"There are lots of clothes here," she said. "Where does it all come from?"

"All over the Reich," the assistant said. "Donated for the use of the troops."

"But so much of it is children's clothing, and women's."

The assistant shrugged. "Then it will be given to needy folk, such as you. Have you finished? I have things to do."

They found themselves outside again, clad in their new, relatively clean and warm clothing. Elisabet turned away from the town and headed south and west into the countryside. There were fewer refugees on the road now, hundreds instead of thousands and, filled with good food, they felt full of a sense of well-being. Elisabet allowed herself a feeling of optimism that maybe the worst of their journey was behind them. After all, it was springtime, and they were back in Germany with the German Army between them and the Russians. They had made it to relative safety if not yet to comfort.

"Mutti, who is Solomon Abramsky?"

Elisabet looked down at Kurt, who had tugged on her arm. "Who?"

"Solomon Abramsky. There's a tag in my jacket with his name on it." Kurt pulled his collar up and sideways, craning his neck to read the little stitched name.

"Let me see." Elisabet stopped and bent the collar back.

"I've got a tag too," Werner said. "Mine says Aaron Cohen."

"And me," Helmut added. "Avram Kanter."

Elisabet was at a loss for a minute and then a horrible thought occurred to her. The jackets her children wore – and indeed, all the clothing in the warehouse – had belonged to Jews. What had become of them? Most of the Jews she had known in Königsberg had been taken away and presumably resettled elsewhere, but she had heard stories – horrifying stories of hundreds of Jews, thousands even, dying in specially prepared camps. She had not fully believed them – until now.

"Who are they, Mutti?"

"The...the man in the storehouse said people had donated them." It tasted like a lie in her mouth, but the truth would have been fouler. She felt like stripping the clothes from their backs but knew she could not do that. Her children needed them. "We must be grateful..." Elisabet brushed away a tear and resolutely urged her children onward, knowing they would soon forget. She doubted she would.

*   *   *

After Joseph left with his family, life became much harder for the Jews of Königsberg. Anti-Semitism, always present in German society, worsened as new Nazi laws discriminated more and more against Jews. Bullies gained licence to exercise their sordid proclivities, and the ordinary man and woman in the street, who might otherwise have remonstrated against this blatant cruelty, now looked the other way. A friend of my father, not a communist – in fact he had voted for Hitler – tried to intervene when an SS thug pushed an old Jewish lady over in the street. People looked away, trying not to notice the woman crying on the road, or else hurried past, but this man, Erwin Hueber, protested. He upbraided the SS man, trying to shame him, but he was arrested for his trouble. We heard he had been shipped off to the concentration camp at Dachau, where he died.

"Brave, but foolish," was my father's comment.

"Foolish?" I said indignantly. "His was a noble act."

"And what of his wife and two daughters? What is to become of them now that he has been arrested?" My father sat me down and talked earnestly to me. "You have had a narrow escape with Joseph Herzfeld, and I'm certain there will be other occasions when you feel compassion for Jews. Think though, before you act. If you are arrested, what will happen to your children?"

I remained silent, contemplating that awful possibility.

"If the Nazis left us alone, then of course we would look after the boys, but it is likely we would all be arrested." He sighed deeply. "It grieves me that Germany is losing its moral compass, and my conscience tells me to stand up to these beasts, but I fear for my family. No one is safe under the Nazis, but we can lessen the danger by being circumspect in our actions."

I understood what my father was saying, but it still made me feel ashamed. I did what I could, but I doubt it did anything to alleviate the suffering. I smiled a lot, trying to make them feel welcome, and if the opportunity arose I slipped sweets to the children who by now had to identify their racial status by wearing the yellow star with the word 'Juden' inscribed in it. Once, I warned a man of the approach of the SS, and several times I crossed the road to engage Jewish women in conversation, pretending to ask them for directions. The thugs and the bullies were less likely to molest them if a good Aryan woman was with them. I was also warned a few times by these gangs, and even threatened with a beating if I did not cease my 'Jew-loving' ways. As I said, I did very little, but I did not want these German Jews to think we were all Nazi sympathisers.

The beatings and bullying became more frequent and more severe. All Jewish people had to wear the yellow star and every Jewish business had to be identified by racial graffiti daubed on its doors and windows. Non-Jewish people were discouraged from using Jewish shops and risked beatings themselves if they persevered. Students were expelled from the university and faculty members were dismissed from their positions. Increasingly, Jews were not only ridiculed and harassed, but found it harder to make a living. Many left Königsberg, but others stayed, feel-feeling that they were German too and had lived there all their lives.

Then, in November 1938, a young Polish Jew killed a German diplomat in Paris. This was a signal for the Nazis to take action and the whole Reich erupted in an orgy of violent destruction and hatred, organised by the Nazis. Jewish businesses and individuals were targeted, and so many windows were smashed, so much glass littered the streets, that the night of violence became known as Kristallnacht, the 'Night of Broken Glass'. Rioters broke into the synagogues, desecrated the insides and set fire to them. The fire-fighters turned out when the Königsberg synagogue burned, but just stood and watched it burn, laughing. Gravestones were broken, and others had swastikas painted on them. I was sickened by the violence, and pleaded with my parents to leave.

"Where would we go, Elisabet?" my father said. "This is happening right across Germany."

"We could leave Germany."

"And go where? We know nobody and could not take our possessions. Besides, all our family is in Ostpreussen."

"So there is nothing we can do?"

"It cannot last. Day by day, decent Germans are being made aware of the excesses of the Nazi Party. Sooner or later, they will rise up and say 'No More'."

It didn't happen.

Jews were now prohibited from using the trams and buses, schools and hospitals, and moves were initiated to exclude them from every aspect of life. As a result, more Jews left Königsberg, and then the government acted to accelerate the process. Jews were

213

rounded up and shipped out of the city by train. They were allowed to take a suitcase and the clothes they stood up in, but no more. Their homes were looted, but Jews largely disappeared from everyday life in Königsberg, and we turned our attention to other things.

I got married! A fine young man, Rudolph Daeker, accepted my ready-made family and quickly added two more boys. Then the war started and my man left to do his duty for Germany. He came home on leave from time to time, and on one occasion, in early 1941, he looked troubled. That first evening, as I ironed his shirts, I asked him what the matter was.

"Where did the Jews go, Elisabet, when they were shipped out of Königsberg and a hundred other towns and cities across the Reich?"

I looked up from my ironing. "I don't know. They said they were being relocated. I suppose they were given useful work to do somewhere. I hadn't really thought about it."

"I found out."

"Oh?" My mind turned to the children, asleep upstairs, and I recalled something funny Helmut had said. "You should have heard..."

"They're being murdered, Elisabet."

I stared at him, my anecdote forgotten. "What?"

"For God's sake don't say anything to anyone. I could probably be shot for spreading rumours." Rudolph sipped his coffee and considered his words carefully. "My unit was sent south, to the Polish town of Oświęcim – Auschwitz is the German name. They have made a huge Konzentrationslager there, a concentration camp. It is filled with Jews. More arrive every day on trains, from all over the Reich and the conquered territories, and they are killed, Elisabet, murdered and incinerated in ovens."

I smiled uncertainly. "Is this some terrible joke?"

"No joke. It's actually happening. I spoke to some guards at the camp and they're actually proud of the numbers they're killing. Jews come in by the trainload; the fit ones are set to work but the unfit, the old and the children, are stripped of their clothing and valuables, and gassed to death. The gold in their teeth is melted down, jewels are collected, their clothes are shipped to warehouses, and the bodies cremated."

"You're making this up, Rudi, though I don't know why you'd say such horrible things. No German could be that terrible, not even SS thugs."

Rudolph shook his head, his eyes sad. "It's true. I could tell you stories of the things I've seen in Poland, things done by SS and Wehrmacht and Police Battalions that would sicken you. I've avoided staining my own hands yet, but what do I do if they order me to do likewise?"

"But why?" I asked. "Why are such things done?"

"Because they are Jews."

"What difference does that make? They're human beings like us, Rudi."

My husband couldn't tell me, and I have never heard a convincing explanation of how a human being could be so inhumane, so bestial, and so demonic, as to do that to innocents.

* * *

Elisabet led her children on the country road through Lieberose and toward Lübben. She had no clear idea where to go now that she knew Dresden had been bombed. Her brother Hans' family might be alive or dead, but for now she would have to try elsewhere. If the Nazi authorities told you not to go

215

somewhere, they meant it. She was not going to risk her children testing the hold they still had over the Reich. Where to then? They were already in Germany and the SS Captain in Guben seemed certain that they would hold the Russians at the Oder-Neisse Rivers. If there was no need to flee further, perhaps she should look around for a place to settle until the war was over. Then they could return to Königsberg. She would ask the officials in Lübben.

Meanwhile, they had full stomachs and clean clothes, even if some hot water and scented soap would not go amiss. What's more, they were in Germany, surrounded by other Germans rather than in an occupied land filled with foreigners. Elisabet looked at her children, noting the toll their flight had taken on them. Helmut had lost his sense of humour, becoming belligerent and dour, Kurt was nervous, jumping at shadows, quieter than he had been. Günter was gaunt, his tiny frame having lost weight over the last couple of months, his body as often as not racked by sickness, and Werner had withdrawn into himself, staying close to his mother rather than playing. Of her five sons, only little Joachim seemed relatively unaffected. He was still playful and interested in the world around him, and Elisabet blessed the fact that his young mind would probably remember nothing of their harsh journey.

The weather ameliorated as they slowly moved west, the spring sunshine melting the snow and turning the ice into slush and the earth into mud. Trees broke into leaf and birds returned – swallows dipping and soaring above them, sparrows and finches in the hedgerows and neglected fields, building nests in a furtherance of life that ignored the death that lay like a winding-sheet over Europe. It

216

was still cold, particularly at night, but the air felt dif-different, scented with growing things, hinting at a promise of renewal.

Early wildflowers bloomed on the road verges and one magical day as they neared Lübben, Elisabet caught sight of something yellow fluttering near a buckthorn hedge.

"Look children, a schmetterling. The first one of Spring."

"What does it mean, Mutti?" Werner asked.

"It means the cold weather is mostly behind us. Also, it reminds me of my childhood. I always competed with my brother Hans to see the first butterfly. Often it would be a yellow one like this."

Elisabet watched as it fluttered over the hedge, finding places to lay its eggs. Then it departed, flying fast over the fields. She sighed with pleasure and led her children on.

There was nothing for them in Lübben. Refugees from Ostpreussen and Poland had been pouring into the area for weeks and the town administration was moving them on as fast as possible. They issued meagre rations and advised her to take her children to one of the cities – Berlin, Dresden or Leipzig, where centres were being set up to care for displaced persons. Elisabet knew that Dresden was now impossible, and Berlin would certainly be a target for Russian troops and allied bombers alike, so that left Leipzig. Unfortunately, that was a large city, like Dresden, and she heard that it had attracted a lot of enemy bombing too, so it was not a place to take her children. She decided she would stick to the smaller roads and the towns.

Units of the German Army and Waffen SS were everywhere, digging in and setting up defensive lines

217

stretching north to south, anticipating the Soviet at-attack. Evidently, the local commanders were not as confident as the commander at Guben that the Russians would be held there. They had crossed at least three such lines on the road from Guben, and at each line they had to show their papers before being waved through by tired and nervous soldiers. The troops were edgy and wore a haunted look like an ill-fitting suit. They kept looking to the east and even the distant rumbles of spring storms would make them clench their jaws and tighten the grip on their weapons.

Now, on the way out of Lübben, they came to another road block, another collection of Panzerfaust and mix of soldiers. They stopped all travellers on the road, examined papers minutely, and regarded the refugees with a mixture of resentment and suspicion. Any men or older boys among the refugees were singled out for special attention by SS units. As they waited in the queue to pass the checkpoint, a man with the right sleeve of his jacket hanging loose was hauled out of the line and the jacket stripped from him to reveal two perfectly good arms.

"You are a traitor!" an SS man yelled. "A foul deserter!"

"Please," the man begged. "My family in Magdeburg were all killed except my mother. I have to go and take care of her. I am all she has."

"And how will your mother feel, knowing she has an oath-breaker for a son? A man who would leave his comrades, trying to save his own cowardly life at the expense of theirs?"

"No. No, it's not like that..."

The SS man thrust his pistol into the man's face and pulled the trigger. The man's head jerked back, spraying blood and brains over the soldiers standing near him. They wiped their faces distastefully and kicked the body on the road.

"So? Any other enemies of the Reich?" The SS man brandished his weapon and strolled along the line, seeking anyone who looked suspicious.

People tried to avoid looking at him, but a youth, hardly more than a boy, lost his nerve and bolted, jumping the fence and running for the trees. A soldier brought him down with a shot from his rifle, knocking him spreadeagled onto the new grass. His companion, another boy, younger still, burst into tears and was hauled out to face his inquisitors.

"How old are you, boy?" rasped the SS man.

"F...fourteen, sir."

"Old enough to hold a gun. Old enough to help defend the Fatherland. Why are you running away?"

"Oh, please sir, my friend..." he pointed at the dead boy in the field. "He said..."

"He said what?"

"That...that the war was lost and we sh...should try and save our lives."

"Your friend got what he deserved. He was a defeatist and a traitor, and so are you for listening to him. What is your name?"

"Theodor Hirsch, sir."

"Hitlerjugend?"

"Yes sir."

"Your troop?"

"Lübben, sir."

"What do you think the Führer would say if he knew you were running away?"

"I don't know, sir."

"And your comrades in the Hitlerjugend, Theodor. What sort of lesson does running away teach them?"

219

"I don't know, sir."

The SS man sighed and put his arm around the boy's shoulders. "Then I will tell you, Theodor, because it is important. Running away, deserting your comrades, tells them that you care more about your own life than that of your Führer, or the Reich, or even the other faithful members of the Hitlerjugend who stayed to fight." He patted the boy and then drew out a notepad and a pen. "See? I am writing – 'My name is Theodor Hirsch and I deserted my comrades.' Now, I'm going to pin that to your jacket so that everyone who looks at you knows what sort of person you are." He gestured at the line of refugees. "All these people see your shame."

Theodor started to cry, his shoulders shaking in great sobs.

A soldier held out his hand to the line of refugees and demanded a pin. A woman in the queue offered one up, her face carefully neutral. The SS man pinned the note to the boy's jacket and smoothed it down so it was legible.

"Do you think this is a suitable punishment, Theodor?"

Theodor was crying hard, his eyes and nose streaming. He wiped his nose on his sleeve and hiccuped. "I don't know, sir. I...I suppose so, sir."

"Good boy. Can you give me a salute?"

Hope struggled onto Theodor's face. He stood up straight and raised his right arm. "H...Heil Hitler."

The SS man gravely returned the salute. He turned to the soldier beside him. "Hang him."

Theodor was hauled away toward a dead tree beside the road, a whimper of despair escaping his lips. "Please, sir, please. I won't do it again. I'll return to my troop and..." His pleading became a scream, and his wail of terror was cut off abruptly.

Elisabet turned her children's eyes away and bowed her own head but the SS man saw the anger in her eyes and walked over to her.

"You disagree with my justice, Frau?"

Elisabet never got the chance to agree or disagree, for at that moment a rumbling roar filled the air and the eastern horizon lit up with flashes. At once, the SS man whirled and ran back to the roadblock, ordering them to raise the barrier.

"Clear these people off the road. Quickly. Let them through."

The refugees rushed through the defensive lines and scattered across fields, down lanes and roads, desperate to escape the coming battle.

Kapitel Zwölf (12)

The Russian advance was swift, far faster than the Wehrmacht expected. Units of the First Belorussian Front crossed the river at Guben, and punched through the fortifications supposed to hold them for weeks. South of the town, the First Ukrainian Front pushed over the Neisse to the River Spree in a single day, tanks and infantry overrunning the German lines. The German forces retreated, fighting fiercely, rallied and fiercely defended a perimeter centred on Lübben, halting the advance. Then the Ukrainian Front burst across the Spree and raced west and north, bypassing the Lübben pocket and advancing on the southern suburbs of Berlin.

Elisabet and her children were a mere thirty kilometres west of Lübben, in the company of a hundred or so other displaced Germans, when the Soviet Army rolled over them like a tidal wave. If she thought what had gone before, in Schneidemühl and Schwiebus, was bad, she was forced to reconsider. The tanks rolled through, obliterating everything in their path – villages, farmhouses, trees, vehicles, soldiers and civilians – and the infantry swept up after them in an orgy of pillage, murder and rape.

The tanks roared across the road, through the ragged column of refugees, scattering them, but the Soviet soldiers following in their wake rounded them up and herded them into a field. Men were driven apart and systematically robbed of watches, wedding rings, jackets, trousers, shoes – anything that looked remotely valuable or useful. If they resisted, they were killed. Women were also robbed of jewellery, but men filled with lust and hatred had another use for them, and the field soon resounded to the screams of the raped. Girls as young as ten or twelve were thrown to the ground and violated; women as old as sixty or more receiving the same treatment. Beautiful women and young ones were especially favoured, with men lining up to take their pleasure, but any female could find herself assaulted.

Elisabet was not yet showing the effect of her previous rape by a Russian soldier, but she knew that even expectant mothers were not exempt from attack. As soon as the women and children were separated, she knew what must follow, so scooped mud from the field and smeared it over her face and clothing, making her look less alluring, more bedraggled and unattractive. When a soldier grabbed her, she did not draw back, but spoke instead.

"I have geschlechtskrankheit – venereal disease."

The soldier looked at the muddy woman in front of him and said something to his fellows in Russian. One of them laughed and mimed what might happen to him if he indulged. The soldier took his hand from Elisabet with an expression of disgust, and then back-handed her, knocking her to the ground, and then spitting on her. He left her there and dragged out another woman from the crowd, sating himself on her helpless body.

Elisabet crawled back to her children and sat with them on the muddy ground, shielding them from the worst of the outrages taking place around them. Helmut quivered with impotent anger, Kurt rolled up into a ball, hugging his knees, and the younger children cried, feeding off the anguish and hurt that washed over them.

The horror lasted a long time, and toward the end, the killing started. A family was attacked right by her and the children. The father had already died with the other men, and a young son had fled back to his mother and sisters where he too was shot. The mother, forced to watch as her son was killed, was herself raped and killed. She cried out in anguish to her daughter Geli, but to no avail, the Russians were merciless. The daughter, a tall, blonde young woman still in her teens, was repeatedly raped, her screams and cries dying away to mute misery and then blessed insensibility.

Fresh Soviet troops arrived and found that all the valuables had been stripped from the men. They vented their anger with beatings and stabbings, and fresh attacks on the many injured women. Elisabet, and a handful of other women who had overheard her successful pleas, renewed their protestations of disease, and it worked for some. Others were raped anyway. Women died, from stabbing and choking and from the sheer number of assaults on weakened bodies.

Soviet officers arrived and fired a few shots in the air, dispatched a few refugees, and ordered their men back on the road. With a show of reluctance and a last spasm of violence, the soldiers moved off, their officers yelling at them to catch up with the tanks. The refugees attended to their wounds, both physical and emotional. Husbands found battered wives and mothers, fathers found violated daughters, weeping or catatonic, and those that had survived relatively unharmed, including Elisabet, tended to the stricken women. They moved away from the road, seeking the shelter of a nearby wooded area, but there was no food, and sooner or later they had to continue on their way.

Elisabet decided to go back to her old ploy of travelling alone with her boys, as a group of refugees was certain to attract more attention. As she got up to leave the informal encampment in the woods, though, she noticed the young blonde woman, sitting alone, and her heart went out to her. Both parents and a younger brother had died at the hands of the Soviets and the girl had been repeatedly raped. Elisabet knew nothing about her but her first name – Geli – or even where she was from, but the girl could hardly function after her horrifying experience.

"Geli?" The girl took no notice. "Geli?" Elisabet repeated. "Do you want to come with us? Away from here?"

Geli's eyes moved and she looked up at Elisabet, but said nothing.

"We're leaving now, but you're welcome to come with us."

The girl did not react, just lowering her head and staring at the ground, her hands picking at the hem of her dress. Elisabet waited, but Geli gave no further sign of having heard her and none that she understood her question. She sighed, and left Geli where she sat, gathering her boys to her and setting off westward through the trees.

"Why did you ask her to come, Mutti?" Helmut asked.

"She has no one and she'll probably die if she stays there. I thought maybe we could help her."

"Why didn't she say anything?" Günter asked.

"Terrible things happened to her. Sometimes people don't want to talk about them."

"What things?" Werner asked.

"Bad things. What the soldiers did to her."

They had only gone a hundred metres or so when they heard footsteps behind them. Geli had followed, not saying anything, but fixing her gaze on Elisabet.

225

"Geli, you decided to come with us." Elisabet smiled and held out her hand to the girl, who ignored it, standing still and staring at the ground again. Only when Elisabet turned away did the girl follow, stopping when she stopped, saying nothing and unresponsive to anything they said.

"I'm glad you came with us, Geli. It will be nice to have someone to talk to."

The woods were awakening after the long winter. Leaf buds pushed out on trees and shrubs, and the animal life made itself known by squeaks and scurrying in the leaf litter, or bird cries and song from the canopy. The air was still cold and sunshine intermittent, with rain showers sweeping across the countryside; but the weather was far different from the winter months just past and the lengthening days promised better times to come. Recent events were not forgotten – Geli's stumbling figure a constant reminder – but the resilient minds of the youngsters enabled them to find contentment in their surroundings.

Flowers bloomed within the woods and on the edges – crab-apple and hawthorn, elderberry and aspen, while bluebells, daffodils and crocuses pushed up through the warming soil to gladden the heart and lift the spirit. The children took back their childhood for a time, running and chasing each other through sun-dappled glades, rolling in the leaf litter and splashing through tiny streams. The war was forgotten, and smiles would have lasted longer on faces, laughter longer in the air, if hunger and sickness had not been constant companions.

Elisabet had been raised in the countryside and knew some sources of food common to any wooded area in Europe. Some flower petals could be eaten, but they provided little sustenance. A few fungi were present but at this time of year were unpalatable and tough survivors from the previous autumn. She found sorrel and nettle, the fresh new growth tender and tasty, and watercress along the banks of the larger streams. They found enough to assuage hunger but not to satisfy empty bellies, and Elisabet knew that sooner rather than later, they would have to brave inhabited lands again. She tried to call up a map of Germany in her mind, and after long consideration, thought that they might be nearing the Elbe River, in that part where it runs southeast to northwest. They were too near Berlin for her liking – the fighting would be fiercest there – so she altered their course southward.

"I think we might risk Herzberg," she confided to Geli. "And after that Torgau. We have to cross the Elbe somewhere and I'm sure there's a bridge there."

Geli said nothing.

"Of course, the Russians will have captured it if it's still intact, but we have to get to the West. We'll find a way across."

Elisabet called a halt at the edge of the woods, looking down across pastures and overgrown fields to the town of Herzberg. It looked quiet enough, and the town did not look to have suffered from bombing or shelling. They moved cautiously down the hedge and fence lines to the country road and headed in the direction of town. A kilometre or so along, they found a muddy rutted road leading to a farmhouse and barn.

"There might be food up there," Helmut said.

"Or Russians," Elisabet said. "Still, it's worth the risk."

She led the way, and as they approached, stepping carefully through the mud, a dog started barking and, a few moments later a middle-aged man came out of the house, armed with a kitchen cleaver. He stood in the doorway, chewing on some food.

"What do you want? There's nothing for you here."

"Please, a little food is all I ask – for my children."

"Are you foreigners? You have a strange accent."

Elisabet forbore from pointing out that he did too. "We're from Königsberg."

The man grunted. "Well, there's nothing for you here. The Russians cleaned me out."

"Nothing? Not even a potato or carrot? A piece of bread? We have eaten nothing but weeds and leaves for days. Please, for my young children if not for me."

The man looked at the youngsters, his gaze lingering on Geli. "Who's she? The girl. One of your children?"

Elisabet hesitated, and then nodded. "The Russians caught us near Lübben and...and hurt her."

"Raped her?" The man stepped closer, his eyes gleaming with interest. "Well, maybe I do have some food – for one of you at least."

Elisabet backed up. "I think we had better try elsewhere. Come children."

"Wait up," the man said. "You obviously can't feed all your children, so leave one of them here – the girl. She'll eat well, and it'll be easier for you with fewer mouths to feed."

"For shame. We are good German women and children. What would your neighbours say if they could hear you?"

The man shrugged. "Your loss, Frau. I have some potatoes and beets I could trade for her."

228

Elisabet turned and ushered her family away, leading Geli by the arm. The man yelled crude suggestions in their wake and then stamped back inside. Out on the road, Elisabet looked around, anxiety suddenly gripping her.

"Where's Helmut? Kurt, where's your brother?"

"He was right here."

"He went back to the barn," Günter said.

"What? Why? Wait here."

Elisabet turned and ran back up the farm track. She was met by the sight of Helmut dashing out of the barn with something wrapped in his coat. He slipped on the mud and his burden scattered. As he picked them up and stuffed them back in his coat, the man erupted from the house, cleaver once more in hand and the dog at his heels. The dog darted out, barking furiously but reluctant to engage the trespasser.

Helmut started off again, splashing through the mud and the man bellowed with rage, hurling the cleaver at the boy. It missed and fell in the mud, and Helmut scooped it up with one hand. He turned and held the cleaver aloft, dancing a little jig.

"Verpissen, dummkopf." Then he turned and ran, splashing past his mother and laughing hysterically.

The coat was full of sugar beets, wrinkled from winter frosts. Helmut handed his brothers the roots and offered them to Geli and his mother. He bit into one and chewed, swallowing and biting again.

"Chewy but sweet," he said, around another mouthful.

"You took a risk," Elisabet said, trying to look stern. Her mouth filled with saliva and she took a bite of the fibrous root. The sugar rushed into her system and she felt lightheaded. She noticed Geli was just standing with the beet in her hand, so she raised the girl's hand to her mouth and encouraged her to eat. After a few moments, she did, but the movements were mechanical, and unless she continued to encourage her, she stopped eating.

The other children ate voraciously, though they tended to chew furiously to extract the pulp and spit the fibrous wad out before taking another bite. They worked their way through all the beets, feeling much better for the food in their bellies. Helmut strutted, feeling very important, and Elisabet kept quiet, even though she wanted to remind him that the beets were stolen and not to feel too proud of his deed. She kept the cleaver safely in her pocket.

Herzberg had fallen to the Russians but as the German Army had not defended it, the damage to property was minimal. The road surfaces had been chewed up by tank tracks and some of the narrower streets suffered by the vehicles bulldozing through. Windows had been shot out by exuberant soldiers, and the populace had not escaped unscathed. A woman told Elisabet that a number of the townspeople had been marched out of the town on the Torgau Road, and nobody knew what their fate was.

Elisabet led her family into town, trying not to draw attention to them. This was not too difficult as other displaced persons were drifting through, begging for food, fuel or clothing. The townspeople paid little attention, keeping to themselves. A number of men and youths, of an age to be in the armed forces, but somehow exempted, looked uncomfortable. They held themselves as if they expected subservience from their neighbours, and indeed, the townspeople avoided them. Elisabet suspected they were Nazi officials or Hitlerjugend, seeking to disguise their recent affiliation now that the enemy had overtaken them. There was nothing in Herzberg for them, Elisabet saw, so she took her children through the town as unobtrusively as possible. Geli followed as always, saying nothing, looking down at her feet, and though some of the youths appraised her as she passed, they made no move to stop her.

The Soviet Army units had used the road to Torgau on the Elbe River, as was evidenced by the poor state of the surface after armoured vehicles had ripped it apart. Russian soldiers had cut a wide swathe of destruction through the countryside, as if angry now that they had not destroyed Herzberg. Farms were smoking ruins and the bodies of men and women littered the verges of the road – some obvious refugees with the pathetic remnants of their belongings scattered, others plainly local civilians – probably the same ones marched out of Herzberg. Men lay sprawled in every position, but the women were all on their backs, their dresses around their waists, their pale bodies pathetically vulnerable. They had been raped repeatedly and then killed. There were no German soldiers, these having withdrawn in the face of the enemy, leaving the civilian population to bear the brunt of Soviet hatred and lust.

Elisabet shielded her children as best she could, leading them quickly by the worst of the corpses, but Geli would not be led. She stared expressionlessly at the bodies and moved on, stumbling over the cut up ground, until she came to the body of a young girl close to her own age. Here, her apathy faltered, her face muscles worked themselves into an expression of horror and a low moan escaped her lips. Abruptly,

Geli threw herself down on the corpse of the girl, screaming piteously and stroking the girl's hair, kissing her dead face.

Elisabet had to leave Helmut in charge of his brothers and hurry back to Geli. She managed to drag her upright and embraced her, pulling her onward when she tried to go back to the dead girl.

"Geli, listen to me. There is nothing you can do for her. Geli, please, for me. You must look after yourself...you're frightening the children...it's all right, no one's going to hurt you again...she's at peace now, nothing more can hurt her."

Nothing she said had any effect on her, so Elisabet resorted to soothing noises, patting her and stroking her, gradually turning her away from the dead girl and leading her, step by step, from the horrifying sight. They rejoined the boys who were pale with shock and terror. Kurt voiced his fear that the Russians would return and such was Helmut's state of mind that he quite forgot to call his brother a dummkopf. The younger children clung to Elisabet's coat and wailed that they wanted to go home.

"Shh, it's all right," Elisabet soothed. "We're leaving here now, and soon the war will be over and all our troubles will be behind us. We'll find somewhere nice to live where we'll be safe and there will be plenty to eat."

They approached Torgau on the River Elbe, moving cautiously because the closer they got, the greater was the number of Russian soldiers. Strangely, though, there was a festive air about them as if some great victory had been achieved. Elisabet employed her former ruse and made herself and Geli unattractive, smearing mud over exposed skin and chewing wild garlic leaves to make their breath stink.

Then she led her family into Torgau, hoping to find a way over the river.

There was a bridge over the Elbe, but it was heavily guarded and the other side swarmed with soldiers wearing a different uniform – not the motley rag-tag brown and green of the Russian infantry, nor Wehrmacht grey, but a khaki colour.

"Who are they?" Elisabet asked of Geli. "British perhaps? Or Americans?"

Geli offered no opinion, and Elisabet wondered whether she should risk drawing attention to her family by asking. In the end, she decided not to. It did not look as if they were going to be able to cross the river here, so the information was hardly likely to be useful. Instead, she would see if she could find some food and maybe shelter for the night.

The inhabitants of Torgau were keeping to their houses where they could, though with mixed success. Roving bands of Russian soldiers wandered through the streets intent on pillage. Houses were invaded, and the townspeople evicted while the soldiers rummaged through the rooms for anything that took their fancy. Food disappeared quickly; alcohol of all sorts and jewellery, but the strangest things attracted some. One soldier struggled along the street with a mattress, and another with a wooden hatstand. Four men manhandled a piano out into the street and then abandoned it. Most looters sought more valuable and manageable booty.

Whenever alcohol was discovered, a cheer went up and the whole band descended on it. Tops were knocked off bottles and the wine and spirits guzzled without any appreciation of taste or quality. Drunkenness became commonplace, and wanton destruction followed in its wake. When the bands of

233

soldiers moved on, the owners would return to a gut-gutted home and piece together their shattered belongings.

Fires broke out, some by accident as the houses were looted, others deliberately. There was no fire service operating, and the Soviet officers were content to let some houses burn. If they looked like becoming out of control, however, they had the army bring water from the river and control the blazes.

Sometimes people would object to being robbed, but if they did, they ran the risk of being attacked by irate soldiers. If they were lucky they were only beaten, but some died and many women were raped. The people of Torgau had to learn the lessons of every town and city overrun by the Soviet Army – the conquerors took what they wanted, did as they pleased, and there was nothing anyone could do about it except submit or get out of the way.

Elisabet was in a bit of a quandary. Her family was vulnerable being traipsed through town as she sought food, but where could she leave them with some degree of safety while she went off by herself? She debated whether nine year old Helmut was sensible enough to be left in charge of Geli and his brothers. In the end, she found what she needed by trailing the path of destruction left by the soldiers. One house was almost completely gutted, and the owners killed on the street. Elisabet mourned their unnecessary deaths but took advantage of them by moving her family into the derelict rooms.

"Stay here, and stay quiet," she instructed her boys. "Helmut, you're in charge. Make sure none of your brothers goes outside, or even goes near a window. We must not be seen by anyone."

"Where are you going, Mutti?" Kurt asked with a quiver in his voice.

"Don't go," Günter wailed.

"You will come back?" Werner asked.

Joachim just sucked his thumb, and Geli sat amongst the rubbish on the floor and stared at the wall.

"I'm only going to be a little while," Elisabet said. "And when I return, I hope I'll have some food."

"It's getting cold," Helmut said.

Elisabet looked around the room and grimaced. "I don't think we can risk a fire, but see if you can find something that will keep the wind out. I won't be long." She kissed them all, even Geli, and left, though the weeping of the younger children tore at her heart.

It was too dangerous staying close to the marauding bands of soldiers, so Elisabet made her way back into town. She reasoned that it was only the common soldiers who were any danger to civilians – whenever officers had come on the scene, rape slackened and pillaging moderated. If she approached a group of officers, with a bit of luck they might answer a question or two. At the worst they would drive her away. She did not think they would rape or kill, but she had to take the risk – in these dangerous times, information was almost as essential as food.

The area around the bridge was still crowded. Speakers had been rigged in the trees on the far side and a lively Russian dance blared tinnily while people danced, leaping and jerking. She saw a small group of officers standing on the near side of the bridge and approached them, head lowered.

"Excuse me, sirs. May I ask a question?" She spoke in Hochdeutsch, hoping that if any of the Russian officers had learnt the language it was at a school.

The men turned and looked her up and down. She could see their immediate interest in her as a woman lessen as they took in her dirty and bedraggled appearance. One of them spoke in Russian and two others laughed before another said, in passable German,

"What want you, Frau?"

"Sirs, I live over the river. I, and my children, came to Torgau two days ago to see my sister. Now I want to return to my husband, but the bridge is closed. May we be allowed over so we can return home?"

The German speaker translated for his fellow officers, listened to their comments, before shaking his head. "Nein, Frau. Verboten."

"Please sir, we have no way of getting food over here and my sister's house has been looted."

One of the men, after the translation, made what was obviously a coarse remark for a couple of others made crude gestures.

"Frau, you cannot cross because we have the border reached. Those there are Yanki, ally... verstehen Sie? Germany kaputt. No cross."

"Somewhere else, perhaps? Some other bridge?"

"Nein, Frau. Verboten. Go to civil authority. Prove who you are. You have papers?"

"The looters took them."

"Then explain civil authorities. Maybe they give new papers, you cross, verstehen Sie?

"Ich verstehe. Danke Sie." Elisabet bobbed her head and walked away. She glanced back and saw the German-speaking officer watching her, so she mingled with the people on the street before heading for the town centre. She was distraught that she had not secured a passage over the Elbe, but there were more pressing concerns. There were restaurants there, and cafes, now all closed and boarded up, or pillaged, but she found her way down narrow alleys to the rear of the eating places and nosed out the dustbins. Other people had beaten her to it, the bins scattered and the contents dumped and sorted through. She looked anyway, but could find nothing more substantial than some carrot peelings and an apple core.

"Better than nothing," she muttered, tucking them away in a coat pocket.

Elisabet tried another alley, then another and found a bin hidden in a dark corner that had been overlooked. Checking that she was not being observed, she dumped the contents and started sifting through it. She was rewarded immediately – half a loaf of mouldy bread, three potatoes with black, stinking cores and best of all, fatty rinds of bacon. The food disappeared into her pockets.

The dead bodies of the house owners had been dragged to the side of the road when Elisabet returned to her family. After checking that no one was watching, she picked her way through the debris into the house and called out softly.

"Helmut? It's me. Where are you?"

Kurt came running, and threw his arms around his mother. "Helmut's gone, and you were gone and I thought..." He was crying, gulping and hiccupping in distress. "I thought you'd left us."

Werner, Günter and Joachim ran out now, sobbing with relief, and even Geli stood in the doorway to the next room. The young girl said nothing, as usual, but some emotion struggled for release, contorting her face.

"Where's he gone?" Elisabet asked. "I told him to stay here and look after you all."

237

"I...I don't kn...know," Kurt hiccupped. "He just said he knew where he could get food, and disappeared. W...will he be all right, Mutti?"

"Yes. Yes, I'm sure. Now show me what you've done while I've been gone."

"Did you find any food, Mutti?" Günter asked.

The boys sucked and chewed on a bacon rind with evident pleasure while Elisabet divided up the meagre rations. There was enough rind for one each, half a rotten potato for each child, a few carrot peelings and a chunk of bread. She carefully scraped off a sliver of apple core each, and put Helmut's share aside for his return. As it happened, he arrived back before they had finished their tiny feast, grinning and bubbling with excitement.

Elisabet grabbed him before he could say anything and stood him in front of her. "Where have you been, du böser Junge? You were supposed to be looking after your brothers, but you ran off. Anything could have happened to them in your absence. It's irresponsible, Helmut, and I'm disappointed in you."

Helmut adopted a sulky expression. "They were safe. I told Kurt what to do."

"That's not the point. I left you in charge, not Kurt."

"Did anything happen while I was gone, Mutti?" He looked around. "No? Then why are you upset?"

Elisabet controlled herself, wondering exactly what she could say that would mean something to her wayward son.

"We are surrounded by the Russians and we are trying to reach safety in the West. If we are to do this, we must all act together, which means if I ask you to do something, I must know that you will do it, or all our efforts are wasted. You are a fine, brave boy,

238

Helmut, and smart, so I know you understand. Will you work with me, my darling? I need your strength and determination."

"All right, Mutti," Helmut muttered. Then he brightened. "Do you want to see what I've got?" He brought out a small bundle from within his coat, and opened it out. Lying on the grubby, stained cloth was a small wheel of cheese, a bar of chocolate, and half a dozen cigarettes.

Elisabet lifted the items one by one, sniffed them, and put them back in Helmut's outstretched hands. "Where did you get them?"

"Russian soldiers. They're looting the houses."

Elisabet nodded. "Yes, but how? Why would they give you these things?"

"They didn't. I traded them for a pair of shoes."

She glanced down automatically, but Helmut still wore his shoes from the Jewish warehouse in Lübben. "Where did you get the shoes?"

"Off the dead man outside. When they killed him, they took his watch and wallet but overlooked his shoes." He grinned. "The shoes were no use to him any longer, Mutti. Should I have just left them for someone else to steal?"

Elisabet sighed and took the items from Helmut. She divided the cheese and chocolate seven ways, and put the cigarettes away for future trading. They ate well that night, feasting on little luxuries, but after the children were asleep, she sat next to Geli and voiced her concerns.

"I cannot fault Helmut's instincts for survival. He is becoming a good provider, but what happens after the war, when we go back to our homes? How will I teach him that theft is no longer acceptable?"

Geli did not answer.

Kapitel Dreizehn (13)

The Russians returned to the gutted house the next morning, surprising Elisabet as she prepared the last of their scraps of food for breakfast. Soldiers rushed in and secured her, Geli and the boys and hauled them outside to face their officer. He was a young mild-faced lieutenant with glasses who looked them up and down for several minutes.

"You are German?" he asked. "Or refugee?"

Elisabet hesitated. The last thing she wanted was to be shipped back east or interned somewhere as a displaced person, but the officer might understand 'German' as being local, in which case she might be classified as a looter. She decided to continue the fiction she had told the officer at the bridge.

"German, from over the river. I, and my family, am visiting my sister here in Torgau."

"This is your sister?" The officer indicated Geli.

"No, Geli is my daughter."

The officer's eyebrows lifted. "You do not look old enough. These children I can believe, but not her. Tell the truth, Frau, or it will go badly for you."

"My step-daughter. My husband's daughter by a previous marriage."

"And where is he?"

"Dead. He was in the army."

"Ah. I would offer my commiserations, Frau, but he deserved death for attacking the peace-loving Soviet people. What are you doing in this house? Is it your sister's?"

Elisabet hesitated again. She was tempted to claim it, but if she was asked for proof, or for the whereabouts of her fictional sister, she would have no ready reply.

"No. She lives out in the country, between Torgau and Herzberg. We were on our way back when you – when the Russian Army overtook us. We had no place to shelter, so we found this empty house."

"A dangerous course of action, Frau. I could have you shot as looters."

"It's you who are doing the looting," Helmut cried before Elisabet could stop him. "This is our country, not yours."

A soldier shook Helmut roughly, but the officer stopped him.

"A brave little man. What is your name?"

Helmut looked at his mother and when she nodded, said, "Helmut Daeker."

"And are you a member of...what do you call it? Hitler Youth?"

"He is too young," Elisabet said quickly. "Besides, all boys are required to join. They have no choice in the matter."

The officer nodded. "Feed the young ones lies at an early age and they will grow up to be dedicated fascists."

"My children are brought up to know the truth, not propaganda."

"Be that as it may, your children will grow up in a communist country and will learn proper values."

Elisabet could not stop herself. "Proper values like rape, murder and theft, you mean?"

The young officer stared at Elisabet. "What do you know of such matters? You have been raped? Your step-daughter perhaps?"

Elisabet could not bring herself to admit it, but the officer took her silence as a confession.

"Where did this happen?"

241

Elisabet suddenly realised she had put herself in a trap. If she said where they had been raped, it would be obvious they did not live on the other side of the river.

"Does it matter? It wasn't your men, if that is what's worrying you."

"What about you?" The officer addressed himself to Geli. "Do you have a complaint against my men?"

"She does not speak," Elisabet said. "The experience has damaged her mind."

"I regret the actions of lawless elements within the Soviet Army," the young bespectacled lieutenant went on. "I assure you they are a tiny minority and their actions are not sanctioned in any way." He paused, as if in thought. "However, some men feel that after the savagery of your army in Russia, it is no more than you deserve."

"Women are innocent of such actions – and I do not believe our army ever committed such acts."

"Of course you would say that." The officer waved his hand dismissively. "Yet you are German and you bear a collective guilt for the war crimes of your leaders. So, there is no more to be said. I accept that you are not looters. What am I going to do with you?"

"You could send us back to our homes over the river."

The officer nodded. "I could, but your home does not lie in that direction does it, Frau Daeker? Your voice has an accent that is at odds with the local dialect. I suspect you have come from the east."

Elisabet kept silent, but her heart sank. Would they be sent back east, or interned?

"Am I right?"

"My family came from Königsberg. We live over the river now."

242

"You will find it difficult to return. The Americans have occupied your home, and they are a strange, violent people. Not that they will be staying long. Already they have come further than their generals desire and will no doubt withdraw and leave that part of Germany to Soviet rule. Until then, you would be better off making your home on this side of the river, under the protection of the Soviet Union."

"You are letting us go?"

The officer nodded. "I see no reason to stop you, but, Frau Daeker, in light of your recent experiences, I would advise you to stay out of the towns until the war is over and the situation settles down."

The Russian soldiers saw them out of the property and on the road into town. In an act of generosity, the soldiers gave the children sweets, and one handed a tin of meat to Helmut with a gruffly muttered word. Elisabet could have sworn she saw a tear in the man's eye and wondered whether he had lost a young son in this long and blood-soaked war. She would never know the stories of more than a handful of the people she would meet, but perhaps that did not matter – what was most important was that her children's stories had a happy ending.

"Where are we going now, Mutti?" Kurt asked.

Elisabet thought about their options. The Torgau Bridge was closed to them, and the ice had melted so they could not ford the river easily. They would have to find another bridge, but should they go north or south? South would bring them to Dresden, but that beautiful city had been bombed to ruins by the British and Americans. If the Nazi authorities were still holding out, they would not let refugees in, and if the Russians had taken over, they would not want added burdens. North then. To Wittenberg and Magdeburg.

They stayed close to the river, using few roads, crossing pastures and fields where the crops had been left to wither and die from lack of people to harvest them. The boys spread out on these occasions, looking for hidden tubers and roots, ears of wheat missed by the birds, or newly sprouting leaves of mustard, turnip and beet. Elisabet made a competition of it, offering up the title of champion provider for the boy who found the most food. Because Helmut was most often the winner, she made subcategories and created titles that each boy could be proud of. Geli wandered along in their wake, still silent, but occasionally showing signs of animation at the sight of a butterfly, the cawing of rooks in the treetops, or the russet flash of a fox streaking for cover.

One day, about a week after leaving Torgau, Elisabet sat with Geli on a low earth bank on the edge of an abandoned field while the children played their daily game of finding food in another derelict farm. She had been conducting her usual one-sided conversation with the girl, telling her stories and musing about what they might find in Wittenberg, when she noticed Geli's hands plucking at the fabric of her dress.

"What is it, Geli? Are you hurt? Show me."

Elisabet moved her hands aside and gently touched Geli's abdomen, probing softly. The girl uttered a moan and tried to move her hands back, but Elisabet persisted. She had worried that the rapes had damaged Geli, but had not liked to invade the girl's privacy. Now she would have to.

"Helmut," she called. "You're in charge. Look after your brothers."

244

"Where are you going?" Helmut raced over and stared as his mother helped Geli along toward the scrub willow along the river bank.

"Women's business. Can you manage for a few minutes?"

"Of course, Mutti." Helmut ran back to his spot in the field, shouting at Günter, who was starting to move toward the women, to keep searching for food.

Elisabet sat Geli down on the stones by the water's edge and talked to her gently, soothing her, and then lifted her dress and palpated her belly, examining her. Geli moaned again and squirmed, but Elisabet examined her as best she could. She had worked in the hospital at Königsberg and knew some of the signs of internal damage. She could see inflammation and swelling and feared the worst. Geli had been damaged by the rapes, but how much was the question. She should have medical attention as soon as possible.

She smoothed the girl's dress down modestly. "You will be all right, Geli. We'll get you fixed up and with luck you won't even be having a baby."

Elisabet touched her own belly through her dress and coat. She could feel the swell of her own pregnancy and knew it would start to show soon.

"But what am I going to do, Geli? I've had babies before, but always in a hospital or with a midwife on hand. I had not thought to have one in the middle of the countryside – in a war – without medical help. And its father is a Russian soldier."

Elisabet closed her eyes and rubbed her temples, feeling very alone, and then a hand crept softly onto her belly. She opened her eyes and looked incredulously at Geli. The girl's eyes were fixed intently on Elisabet's abdomen, and a faint smile creased her otherwise expressionless face.

"Baby," she whispered once, then withdrew her hand and her smile.

Elisabet was overjoyed, all her own troubles forgotten. She immediately plied Geli with questions, made comments, and put the girl's hand back on her abdomen in the hopes of eliciting another smile, but Geli's mind had withdrawn again, behind the ramparts of her defences. Elisabet hugged Geli and helped the girl to her feet.

"Never mind. You've made a start, and when you're ready, I'm here to support you."

They rejoined the boys and shared in the fruits and vegetables of their labour before continuing along the river. After months of travelling through countryside wracked by ruin and war, the land around them was remarkably serene. Few people bothered them and most of the ones they encountered were displaced persons from the east like them, or dispossessed local farmers. Their encounters were brief and usually involved only an exchange of information as nobody had much to sell or trade. They heard rumours that the Wehrmacht was about to launch a counter-offensive that would sweep the Russians out of Germany, or that the Germans would join forces with the British and Americans to combat the Russian communists. Other rumours said that the Führer had fled to a mountain redoubt in Bavaria to carry on the fight, or that he was dead, killed fighting at the head of his troops in defence of Berlin, and still others that said the war was over. None of them seemed particularly believable, particularly as Russian troops could still be seen on the roads and in the towns, and war materials were still pouring out of the east.

"It doesn't matter," Elisabet confided to Geli. "We have to continue on and find safety. That's not going to be anywhere there are Russian soldiers."

The cigarettes that Helmut had acquired in Torgau were traded for food, and a precious box of matches. Although spring was definitely upon them, the nights were still chilly and a small fire made from dry twigs cheered them immensely. Staring at the flickering flames and listening to the crackle and pop of the kindling calmed and comforted them.

They came across a Soviet army encamped by the river and had to turn aside, to the east and north, to avoid them. The weather turned foul, bringing chill winds and rain squalls, soaking them to the skin as they searched for cover. The woods dripped and the mud squelched underfoot and through the worn soles of their shoes. They stumbled upon a railway line and followed it northward. The line split and they followed the older tracks, finding shelter in a disused railway culvert. At some stage, enemy bombs had ripped the train lines apart, leaving splintered sleepers and twisted metal. The Deutsche Reichsbahn had built around the damage rather than trying to repair it, and where the warped iron rails crossed a small culvert, they formed a protected hollow roofed over with timber sleepers and earth. The chamber was small and damp, but at least they could shelter out of the rain. Helmut built a fire with fragments of sleeper, but the wood was damp and the fire sputtered and smoked, achieving little. All they could do was huddle together and shiver, seeking communal warmth. Geli became feverish, and Elisabet found herself caught in a dilemma. The girl's possible internal damage required attention but Elisabet was torn between the choice of surrendering to the Russians to try and find her medical aid, or continuing on in the hope of mak-making it over the river to the other enemy, the Americans. The only other alternative was to stay where they were for a day or two and attempt to build up Geli's strength, but the decision was lifted out of her hands by the weather.

During the night, the storm increased, and the following morning rain set in. Grey curtains drifted across hill and field, woods and pasture. Their clothes were soaking and continuing on in the rain would add cold to their problems. At least in the hollow they were protected from the elements. Food was another concern. They had a few potatoes left from the last abandoned field but no way of cooking them as they could not coax the fire beyond a sullen and fitful glow.

Later that day, somewhere to the east, they heard a train approach from the south, slow, and then recede into the distance. Evidently, it had reached the point where the line split and taken the new line north, past their shelter on the old line.

"Maybe we could jump aboard and get a ride," Kurt said.

"We'd more likely be shot by the guards, dummkopf," Helmut jeered.

"Be nice to your brother," Elisabet said. She thought about their situation and knew that something had to be done soon. They were getting no wetter in their little cubby-hole, but their wet clothes were cold and it would not be long before they all sickened. "Perhaps we should see what type of trains they are. Perhaps they are carrying something we could use if we can figure out how to get it. I'll go and have a look when there's a break in the weather."

"I can go," Helmut said. "I'd be quicker, and you should really stay with the babies."

"I...I am n...not a baby," Günter said, his teeth chattering.

"Nor m...me," Werner added.

Elisabet shook her head. "I don't like the idea of you alone out there."

"I'll take Kurt with me. You'd like to go, wouldn't you, dummkopf?"

Kurt nodded, apparently not offended by the name. "We can do it, Mutti."

Elisabet reluctantly agreed.

* * *

Helmut and Kurt stood outside the shelter as the rain lessened to a light drizzle, getting their bearings. They shivered in their wet clothes but started back along the wrecked railway line, looking for the point at which the new line joined it. It was nearly half a kilometre back, and the exercise had warmed them by the time they found the shiny new rails stretching away to the north, bypassing the cratered wreckage of the old line. They followed it, their worn shoes crunching in the gravel, tripping over the sleepers, and soon found they were climbing a gentle gradient. The rail line followed the flat land as much as possible, but at one point had to climb a low ridge just to the east of where the boys estimated their camp was situated.

"This is where we heard the train slow yesterday," Helmut said.

Kurt looked along the track in either direction. "There's no train now."

"I can see that, dummkopf. We'll just have to wait for one."

249

"We should be getting back. Mutti will wonder where we've got to."

"If we go back now, we've got nothing to tell her. All we've seen is a railway track and we knew there was one of those already. We have to wait for a train and find out what's on it, or whether we could jump aboard."

"How are we going to do that? Trains travel fast."

"They'll have to slow for the hill." Helmut regarded his brother with some disdain. "What's wrong? You want to go back and sit with the babies?"

"No. I just..."

"Come on, we can shelter in those bushes over there while we wait."

They sat on wet grass beneath wet branches and waited for the train, amusing themselves by tossing small bits of gravel at the railway lines ten metres away, enjoying the satisfying 'clink' of the metal when they hit it. Kurt was more accurate than Helmut, though the older brother could throw with greater force. Soon, it began to drizzle and Kurt looked up at the grey sky, screwing up his face in disgust.

"We should go back."

"Why?" Helmut demanded. "I want to be able to tell Mutti something when we return."

"But we'll get wet."

"We're already wet. You go if you want, but I'm staying."

Kurt stayed. They hunched further back in the bushes, trying to avoid the worst of the rain. Their throwing game no longer appealed so they sat and stared at the falling rain, feeling cold and miserable.

"Please can we go back," Kurt said again. "There isn't a train coming."

"Go on then, if you want. I'm staying."

Kurt looked down the track, imagining the long walk back alone through the woods. He wiped his eyes, hoping the rain would hide the tears from his brother, and bowed his head.

Another hour passed, and two things happened – the rain stopped, and a train came. It was a long freight train, moving slowly even before it reached the long climb up the ridge. As it approached, it slowed further to walking speed, wheels squealing and slipping on the rain-greased tracks. It crept alongside the two boys, and they saw the driver and a stoker in the engine, an armed guard just behind, and then a long series of open-topped trucks with canvas coverings and wooden boxcars. The boxcars had latched sliding doors, but the canvas covering the trucks was just loosely tied down.

Helmut waited for the first few trucks to pass and got to his feet. "Come on." He ran out and alongside the moving train, easily matching its speed. He drew level with the rear of a truck where a rusty ladder was affixed to it. Reaching out, he grasped a rung and hauled himself up, before looking back triumphantly to where Kurt was running after him.

"Helmut, come back," Kurt wailed. "Don't leave me."

Helmut made an impatient shushing gesture, pointing forward to the guard, and then climbed the short ladder to the lip of the truck and pushed back the edge of the canvas covering. He stared at the contents for a few moments before recognising the shining black lumps filling the truck.

"Coal," he said, and grinned.

He seized a chunk and flung it outward, watching it bounce on the grass beside the tracks. Another chunk followed, and then more, peppering the grass

251

in an intermittent line of gleaming anthracite. Kurt had stopped and was picking up the coal. Helmut flung another one, and heard an angry shout from up ahead. He stuck his head around the side of the truck and saw the guard standing up, his rifle pointing back down the track. The sound of the shot was a whiplash past him and he glimpsed Kurt standing frozen by the train, staring in terror as the guard lined up another shot. Helmut leaned out and pitched a lump of coal at the guard, his left-handed throw coming nowhere near him, but he distracted him enough that the shot went wild.

"Run, Kurt," he screamed. "Into the bushes."

Helmut jumped from the train, stumbled and rolled, and then scrambled to his feet and staggered into cover. He turned and saw that the guard had also jumped down and was running back toward them, but at that moment, the engine crested the ridge and started down the long slope on the other side. The trucks clanked and groaned as the train picked up speed; the guard gave a frustrated look at the bushes, loosed off another round, and scrambled back on board. Silence fell on the long slope of the railway track. Helmut scrambled back out onto the grass and grinned in triumph before turning to his brother who was running toward him.

"I thought he was going to shoot us," Kurt sobbed.

Helmut stared at his brother and burst out laughing. "Look at you. What do you look like?"

Kurt had been crying, and he had wiped his eyes with hands blackened by coal dust, leaving great grimy streaks on his face. Now he looked ready to burst into tears again.

"It...it's not funny. I thought he was going to shoot us."

"I'm not laughing at that, dummkopf. I'm laughing at the way you look. I wish I had a mirror so I could show you." Helmut suddenly grinned and patted his own black hands on the wet grass, then rubbed his hands on his face, leaving black marks behind. "You look like this."

Kurt's mouth dropped open. He touched his own face and then grinned. "I do look funny."

"We both look funny, now help me pick up this coal and let's get back to the others."

* * *

They called out as they approached the culvert to let the others know of their presence. Elisabet came out and stared at her grubby sons holding a small mountain of coal in Helmut's coat.

"Look what we got, Mutti," Kurt said, pride bursting from his face.

"I heard shots. Was that because of you? You're both all right, aren't you? Unhurt?"

"We're fine, Mutti," Helmut said. "There was a train full of coal so we took some. A guard shot at us but he was a terrible shot."

"You mustn't risk your lives like that," Elisabet said. "I was so worried. What would this family do without its strong young men?" She smiled and hugged both her sons and helped them carry the coal back to their shelter.

The coal enabled them to build a bigger, hotter fire that spread welcome warmth throughout the chamber. They were able to remove their outer clothes and spread them out to dry, and still be warm in just damp underclothes. When the fire burned down to embers, Elisabet baked their potatoes and they enjoyed hot food again. As they ate, Helmut and Kurt took it in turns to tell their tale, interrupting each other, contradicting each other, stretching the truth and laughing. The smaller children watched their older brothers in awe and envy.

Kurt snuggled up to his mother that evening after the little ones had fallen asleep. "Mutti, were we wrong to take the coal? Was it stealing?"

Elisabet saw Helmut watching her and stroked Kurt's hair for a few minutes without speaking, gathering her thoughts.

"Stealing is never right," she said, "But sometimes you have to choose between something that is wrong and something that is very wrong."

"What do you mean?"

"Well, you know that stealing something that belongs to someone else is wrong, but letting your family starve or get very cold, perhaps even get sick, is more wrong. If those are your only choices, then if you don't hurt another person by stealing...well, I'm not going to tell you it's wrong."

"We didn't hurt anyone else, did we Mutti?"

"A few lumps of coal from whole wagonloads are not going to hurt anyone, Kurt, but those same few lumps may have saved all our lives."

"It was Russian coal too," Helmut said.

"Indeed. Probably mined from German soil."

"So the Russians stole it from us..."

"...and we were taking it back," Kurt finished triumphantly.

Kurt said one other thing before they fell asleep in front of a warm fire. "That coal's not going to last long."

The coal did not last long, but their hunger grew faster than the pile of fuel diminished. It was still

254

raining, but Elisabet donned her dried out coat and scarf and went scouring the sodden woods and fields for edible leaves and fungi. It was too early in the season for fruits, but the fresh new growth of nettles and sorrel, young beech leaves, the buds of hawthorn and leaves of early strawberry were all edible. She even found a dead rabbit and scavenged a few scraps of flesh from the half-eaten corpse.

She would have asked Geli to join her, but the young girl had slipped into inactivity again, seldom doing anything but lie there looking into the heart of the fire. She lay under a covering of coats, shivering despite the warmth of the fire. When Elisabet tried to rouse her, there was little response. She was troubled by Geli's lethargy, and more so by the fever that now gripped her. The girl needed medicine, but she did not know where they were going to find any. They were going to have to leave soon and find help in one of the towns. In the meantime, they all needed to get what strength they could from the sparse provisions of the spring countryside.

Helmut had other ideas. "We need to raid the train again."

"We can't eat coal," Kurt objected.

"Yes, but what's in the boxcars?"

"I don't like you going," Elisabet said. "It's dangerous."

"We'll be careful, Mutti."

*　　*　　*

The two boys waited by the railway tracks again. Weak sunshine struggled out from behind the clouds, but it carried little warmth. They discussed their plan of action.

"I'm going to try for a boxcar this time," Helmut declared.

255

"Won't they be locked?"

"There's only a latch. I had a quick look last time but I was most interested in the trucks."

"What if there's nothing in them?" Kurt said.

"You think they're going to send an empty train, dummkopf?"

"No, what I meant was, nothing we can use. It might be full of...of...oh, I don't know...pots and pans or something."

"Then we'll steal one to make nettle soup in."

The train came, slowing for the incline, and with a guard on the front carriage roof as before. Helmut ran out and studied a boxcar for twenty paces or so before leaping onto a narrow board that ran along the base of the sliding door. He grasped the lever that latched the door and heaved on it. It groaned but did not move. Another effort, but still no movement of the lever, so Helmut jumped down, let the next boxcar catch him up, and leapt for the baseboard again.

This latch was easier and moved when Helmut put pressure on it, sliding back with a squeal that he felt sure must alert the guard. He peered forward but could see no sign of him, and then, with a cheerful thumbs-up to his brother running along behind, clambered inside the dark carriage. The freight was piled high, on pallets, and as he ran his hands over them in the dim light, seemed to be paper covered boxes tied with twine. Strange words were printed on the boxes, but in a language he couldn't read. Helmut assumed it was Russian.

The train clanked and rocked, and Helmut knew the engine had reached the crest and was picking up speed. *Time to go*. He grabbed boxes and started throwing them out through the open door – one, two, three – and then, as he heard Kurt crying out his name, ran to the door and jumped out.

The ground came up to meet him faster than he was prepared for and he cried out with pain and rolled over and over, into the bushes. Kurt hurried after him and fell to his knees beside his sprawled body.

"Are you hurt? Helmut, say something, please."

Helmut rolled over and grinned. "I'm all right, dummkopf." His smile slipped as he tried to stand up. "Ow. I've hurt my foot." He gingerly put weight on his right foot and grimaced. "You're going to have to carry me back."

"I can't do that," Kurt wailed. "You're too big."

"I'm joking, dummkopf. See?" Helmut limped a few paces. "It hurts, but I can walk on it. Now let's go see what was in those boxes."

* * *

Elisabet heard them laughing and calling out and came out from the shelter, the younger children in her wake. They crowded round the older boys as they staggered along under the weight of three boxes with scraps of brown paper and twine hanging from them.

"Look what we found," Helmut cried out. "Food and lots of it."

"Chocolate too," Kurt said, his tongue licking away tell-tale traces from around his mouth.

"Russian rations," Helmut concluded.

In the warmth of the shelter, Elisabet opened the boxes and took inventory of the contents. There were tins of meat, fish and vegetables, dry biscuits and rye bread, smoked sausage and ground oats, real coffee and sugar, cigarettes and chocolate – enough for them all. There was even needle and thread and a first aid kit with antiseptic cream, bandages, a hypodermic

257

needle and several glass vials of some pale yellow liq-liquid. Elisabet puzzled over the Cyrillic script on the vial's label for a few moments, and then put it aside. Her children's hunger precluded all other considerations, so she set about preparing them a meal.

Kapitel Vierzehn (14)

Each ration box was designed to keep a Russian soldier alive and content for a week, so even six people feeding on the contents would take a few days to deplete them. It would have been seven people, but Geli wandered in and out of consciousness, tossing off her coverings and shivering violently, sweating profusely, muttering and eating nothing. Elisabet grew more concerned as the hours of the night passed, forcing a little sweetened coffee between the girl's parched lips when she could. She sat up with her patient after the boys had drifted off to sleep and took the opportunity to examine her more fully. Geli's belly was rounded and taut, with reddened skin and hot to the touch. Elisabet recognised the signs of infection but was at a loss to know how to counter it. Her only hope was the vials of yellow liquid – if she could decipher the script on them and they proved to be useful.

She held a vial up to the light of the flames and studied the Cyrillic letters – 'пенициллин' it read. Elisabet was not totally unfamiliar with the Russian alphabet and recognised some of the letters – there was a 'P', a couple of 'N's and 'L's, but even if she could spell out the name she still would not know what it was, or how to use it. She put the vial back in the medical kit, made Geli comfortable, and settled back to think.

*   *   *

Germany turned on its erstwhile ally Russia in June of 1941 and invaded. Anyone who had read 'Mein Kampf' knew that this was going to happen sooner or later, as the Führer had laid out his plans for the destruction of Russia years before. Königsberg was

259

agog with excitement as German tanks rolled over the border, and for many months it seemed that Russia would go the way of Western Europe and the Balkans, falling to the Wehrmacht almost without a fight.

My husband Rudolph had been in a Wehrmacht unit patrolling and policing the conquered territories of Poland since the war began, but now he was shipped off to the Russian front. This meant that he was home less often and, as communication lines became stretched, supplies became harder to get and his pay found its way back to his family at irregular intervals. I had four children by then – Helmut, nearly six; Kurt, four; Günter, two; and little Werner less than a year old.

With four little mouths to feed, I could not rely on an army pay-packet, nor did I want to live off the generosity of my parents or in-laws, so I looked for a job. Yes, I know, I could have sought help from the Party as Rudolph was a member in good standing, but that avenue repelled me. You might wonder why I married a Party member, as I have decided communist sympathies inherited from my father – but who can reason with the heart? I fell in love with Rudolph and political ideologies flew off like the swallows in autumn.

Anyway, back to my job. I accepted family help only in babysitting my children, and reported to the hospital in Königsberg. I had no medical training, but I learnt fast, and after a few obligatory months of menial tasks such as scrubbing sheets, emptying bedpans and rolling bandages, I was elevated to the position of nurses' assistant and helped as the medical staff cut and sutured. I was present at operations, handing the surgeons their instruments, mopping

260

sweat from their faces, or administering prescribed medicines to the convalescing patients.

A great many soldiers started drifting into the hospital, as even a victorious army suffers casualties, and the wounded that could not be treated in field stations were sent back to Königsberg to heal and recuperate. We were understaffed and I often found myself in almost sole charge of a ward of wounded warriors. I did everything from changing sheets to bandaging wounds, from giving sponge baths to feeding them, reading to them and keeping their spirits up. And it was here that I saw doctors injecting pain-killers for the first time. The thought of deliberately piercing the skin with a sharp needle made me shiver when I saw it, but I also saw the good it did and paid attention. Desiring to learn, I asked about it.

"Herr Doktor, what is this drug you inject that deadens pain?"

"Morphine, Nurse Daeker. It is an extract from the poppy plant."

"It doesn't seem to cure infection though."

"No."

The doctor was friendly, so I went further.

"I have noticed that a lot of patients die, even though their surgeries are successful, Doktor. Why is this?"

The doctor looked at me, perhaps trying to determine if I was criticising his surgical methods or subsequent care. Evidently, he was satisfied my enquiry was innocent and said,

"Post-operative infection kills more patients than the injuries themselves. I have seen a strong and otherwise healthy man have a simple cut bandaged and yet die of infection a few days later. The best we

261

can do – the best you can do, Nurse Daeker – is to keep the wound, the bandages, the bed linen, as clean as possible. Preventing infection will save more lives than any skill a surgeon can bring to the operating table."

Despite all our efforts, soldiers died from their wounds and from infections that appeared later. We employed all manner of cleaning agents and antiseptics, and no doubt prevented many infections, but once a wound became poisoned, there was little we could do but wait and see if the patient's body had the strength to throw off the attack.

Then in early 1942, one of our doctors returned from a visit to Switzerland and revealed a new drug that was available in limited quantities. He called it Penicillin, and showed us the small box of tiny glass vials he had brought back. The doctor demonstrated its efficacy on a wounded Wehrmacht leutnant with septicaemia – and the man recovered. Suddenly, a window of life had been opened up for so many men facing death.

Alas, the supply of penicillin was small and the patients overwhelming in number, so apart from the lucky few, people continued to die. Germany did not as yet produce penicillin, or at least only in tiny amounts, and we could only obtain small quantities through neutral nations like Switzerland, but I saw the drug and held it in my hands. I even saw a doctor fill a syringe and inject the contents deep into the muscle of a man's leg. The liquid in the small glass vial was pale yellow...

*   *   *

Elisabet rolled over and pulled out the vial of pale yellow liquid from the medical kit and held it up to

262

the light of the flickering flames, reading the label again.

"пенициллин – penicillin," she murmured, excitement growing within her. "But how is it that common Russian soldiers are issued with such a valuable drug?" She knew that Russians often had equipment that came from Britain and America, so maybe the drug came from there too. She shrugged. It did not matter where it came from – if this really was penicillin, it could save Geli's life.

Elisabet pulled out all the vials and the hypodermic syringe, wondering what the proper dose was, or even whether too much would kill her as readily as too little. There was other writing on the labels, but she could not decipher it. Any dose injected into Geli would be guesswork.

"So be it," she muttered. "There must be a reason for the size of the vials."

The children were asleep and Geli moaned softly in her fevered state, so Elisabet lifted the girl's dress to expose one thigh, washing the dirt from a small area with a damp shirtsleeve. When it was as clean as she could make it, she turned her attention to the hypodermic. She fitted the hollow needle to the syringe, took the cover off it and firmly pierced the cap of one vial with the needle. The yellow liquid filled the syringe and drew in air bubbles after it, so she held the point uppermost as she had seen doctors do it and pressed the plunger until the bubbles disappeared and a fine fountain of liquid sprayed out of the end.

She took a deep breath and plunged the point of the hypodermic deep into the muscle of Geli's thigh, depressing the plunger until all the pale yellow liquid was gone. The girl cried out as the needle went in and

263

again as it came out, but otherwise showed no reac-
reaction.

"Sorry, Geli," Elisabet murmured. "Now we wait.
I'll give you another dose in the morning."

Elisabet examined Geli in the light of the new day,
but could not discern any change in her condition.
The older boys watched while she gave the girl
another injection and made her comfortable.

"Is she going to die, Mutti?" Kurt asked.

Elisabet considered evading the question and
decided the truth was best. "I don't know. The drug is
powerful, but I don't know if she is damaged inside.
If she is, no amount of antibiotic is going to cure
her."

"What will cure her then?"

"A doctor in a hospital might, but we've got no
way of getting her to one."

"Could we bring a doctor here?"

"Probably not. I can't imagine a doctor willing to
come out to tend someone when there must be
hundreds of people needing him in the towns. If the
Russians heard about it, they'd probably shoot Geli,
or just let her die."

"So there's nothing we can do?"

"Keep her warm and dry, keep giving her
penicillin, food if she wakes up, and hope that she's
strong enough to fight off the infection."

"We've got food," Helmut said, "But we need
more coal. I'll go and get some more from the next
train."

Elisabet hated her son putting himself in danger,
but knew that they would all suffer without more fuel.
"Be careful," she warned. "Don't let anyone see you.
And take Kurt."

264

The boys arrived back later that day with another load of coal carried in a coat. In the meantime, Elisabet had moved some timbers and scraped away at the earth with her hands to enlarge their hole, plugging chinks that let out the heat and allowed chill winds to eddy the smoke around them. The smaller boys played, Elisabet always making sure they stayed close by and did not make too much noise.

"We must be quiet like mice," she told them, "Else the Russian bear might find us."

Elisabet gave Geli another injection at noon, and another one near sunset, and as they sat around the fire eating a decent meal from the army rations, Geli's eyes opened. Werner noticed and pointed. Elisabet sat beside her and smoothed the hair back from the girl's face.

"How are you feeling? Hungry?"

Geli did not answer, but the corner of her mouth twitched as if it wanted to smile but had forgotten how.

"How about some soup?" Elisabet talked as she prepared soup made from a broth cube, a little tinned meat, and ground oats. She told her how Helmut and Kurt had found trains carrying coal and army rations and taken some to keep them alive.

Geli drank the soup with a little coaxing but refused, with a show of terror, the hypodermic needle. Elisabet felt that the girl needed more antibiotic but she could not force it on her. Instead, she concentrated on feeding her to regain her strength. April had passed into May while they sheltered in the railway culvert, and the front line of the war was probably far away by now. They could set off again, strengthened and rejuvenated, but first, they would need provisions for the journey, and what

265

better place to find them than in the next train from the east.

Helmut and Kurt set off on their foraging expedition as usual, while Elisabet went over every item of clothing and made repairs as best she could with the needle and thread found in the ration packs. Tears in the cloth of shirts, skirts and trousers were easily fixed, but the shoes were disintegrating, soles coming away from uppers, and the thread was not strong enough to bind leather.

Elisabet watched the children play as she worked, and kept an eye on Geli. The girl sat in a patch of sunlight, staring at the forest. Every now and then, a butterfly would tumble past, or a bird flit through the branches and her eyes would track the movement. Her muscles would tense until the threat had been evaluated and she could relax again. Occasionally, a hint of a smile would tentatively investigate her face. When the distant sound of a train disturbed the peace of the woodland, she swung round to face the sound, her eyes wide.

"It's all right, Geli," Elisabet called softly. "It just means the boys will be bringing more food soon."

Elisabet finished her darning and repairs and tidied everything away, fixing a pot of coffee and sweet biscuits for the children. She had just poured the coffee into a tin mug from the ration boxes and was about to call the children from their play when she heard the gunshot.

Everyone froze, and the children looked to their mother for guidance. Elisabet remembered the shots that had been fired at Helmut and Kurt when they brought back the coal a few days before, and hoped that this was similar – a token warning shot and nothing more. Another shot. She called the children

266

to her. Geli came too, stumbling in her haste, an alarmed look on her face.

A fusillade of shots erupted in the east and Elisabet felt a great cry of anguish building in her. Her older boys were in trouble, but she couldn't desert her younger sons to go help them. The shots became more sporadic, moving to the southeast, to where the old and new lines joined, and Elisabet knew her sons were running for their lives.

"Quickly boys, pick up your things and follow me."

She led the three younger boys and Geli into the woods to the northwest and left them hidden in a thicket. They cried and clung to her, but she sat them down firmly.

"Don't move from here until I return."

Elisabet left at a run, back along the old tracks. She wanted to cry out, to call to her sons, but dared not. If they were hiding or had run another way, it might alert the Russians to her presence. They might give up the pursuit of two small boys, but if they knew there were other people about, they might organise a full scale search. That would put her whole family in danger. She ran, her feet crunching in the gravel along the old train track, heading toward the curve where the new track branched off.

She heard footsteps to her left and a crashing in the bushes and the next moment, Kurt burst into view, took a wild look at her and dived back into hiding.

"Kurt, it's me. It's Mutti."

The boy popped his head out of the bushes and scrambled over to her, hugging her. "Men, Mutti," he cried. "With guns."

"Where's Helmut?"

267

"I don't know. He was right behind me."

Elisabet knew she had to take the risk. "Helmut!"

At once she was answered by a shot, followed by an oath and a peal of hysterical boyish laughter. A few moments later, Helmut appeared, grinning. He looked back the way he had come and then at his mother and brother.

"We'd better go. They're pretty mad."

They ran back down the railway line, putting some space between themselves and pursuit, and then turned off into the woods, crashing through undergrowth until the track was no longer in sight. Elisabet stopped and doubled over, catching her breath. She straightened and looked at her sons – Kurt fighting back tears and Helmut grinning.

"What's so funny?" she asked. "You and your brother might have been hurt."

"I got him with a rock."

"What?"

"When he stopped to fire his rifle just now. I threw a rock at him and hit him in the head. Then I ran."

They listened for sounds of pursuit, but heard nothing.

"Where did the men come from? How many are there?"

"Three, Mutti. They were on the train, waiting. I'd just unlatched a boxcar door and they jumped down. I told Kurt to run and went in a different direction myself." Helmut grinned again. "I knew they couldn't catch me, but I thought they might catch Kurt, so I tried to slow them down with rocks." He looked around him. "Where are the babies?"

"Hidden. Back at the...shh."

Gravel crunched on the old train track and a low murmur of voices penetrated the foliage. Elisabet and the two boys crouched, holding their breath as the men hunting them argued scarcely twenty metres away. After a few minutes, the men started along the track and Elisabet whispered, "We've got to get back to the others before the Russians get there."

They slipped through the woods, angling away from the tracks to put more distance between them and the Russians. Their progress was slow as they could not risk creating any noise, and by the time they reached the area of the culvert, they could hear raised voices. The Russian guards had evidently found their camp and were debating what to do.

"Komm," called out one of the men. "Freund. Komm junge." There was silence as the men listened for any response. When none came, they entered into a brief argument before footsteps crunched back down the gravel, fading away up the track.

"I think they've gone," Helmut said.

"Let's wait a little longer, just to be certain," Elisabet said.

They sat and waited, listening for any sign of the men's return. Birds started singing again, and Elisabet relaxed.

"They've gone. We'd better get back to the others. They'll be worried."

She led her boys out of the bushes and into the little clearing around the culvert, looking around carefully before pointing out where the others were hidden.

"Go and get them, Helmut. We'll just check we haven't left anything behind."

Elisabet and Kurt approached the shelter beneath the railway tracks and were just starting to bend down

269

to enter when a man – a Russian soldier – stepped out of it. He straightened and looked at them, his rifle held casually in one hand and a cigarette in the other.

He said something in Russian and when they did not answer, he frowned. "Deutsch? You have stealing from train."

Elisabet put herself between Kurt and the soldier and told him in a low voice, "Go to your brothers. Stay there." Kurt backed away, staring wide-eyed at the man.

The soldier saw the boy leaving and grinned. "Don't want boy see, eh? Good." He flicked his cigarette away and leaned his rifle against the embankment. "You like stand or lie down, eh?" His expression hardened and he fumbled at his belt. "Frau, komm. Jetzt!"

Elisabet took a couple of steps forward, a smile on her face and as the soldier started to smile in return, his trousers dropping to his ankles, she screamed out "Nein!" and threw herself at the man. Taken by surprise, he stumbled and tripped on his fallen trousers and fell to his knees, Elisabet on top of him. She pummelled at him with her fists and feet, and by chance one of her blows connected with the man's testicles. He screamed and doubled up and Elisabet scrambled to her feet and ran for the trees.

Behind her, she could hear the man wheezing and making an effort to rise. Then she heard the sound of a rifle bolt being worked and ducked behind the first tree she came to, changed direction and scrambled for cover as a bullet ripped through the foliage several metres from her. The man cursed and worked the bolt again. Elisabet risked a look and saw that he stood with his trousers still around his ankles, half doubled over in pain, and trying to steady his rifle.

She ran again, and found Kurt, grabbing him and pulling him along.

The shot had alerted the other Russian soldiers and Elisabet heard them running back down the track, heard their exclamations as they reached their friend, and then laughter mixed with angry pain-filled words.

Helmut found his mother and guided her and Kurt back to the other children. They demanded to know what was going on, their voices rising in excitement, and Elisabet had to quiet them before leading them off, away from their shelter, heading west toward Wittenberg. After half an hour of careful travel, Elisabet judged they were a safe distance from the Russian soldiers and allowed talk. Immediately, the children started to chatter, demanding to know what had happened.

"Mutti was wonderful," Kurt declared. "She pushed the man over so hard his pants fell down, and then she hit him and he yelled for mercy."

Helmut opened his mouth to correct his brother's interpretation of events, but caught his mother's look and thought better of it.

"I'm hungry," Günter said.

Elisabet stopped and examined their supplies. They only had a few things with them as most of the food and all of the coal had been left behind in the shelter. It was inadvisable to go back for them, so they must make the best of their circumstances. Elisabet shared out a packet of sweet biscuits between them. They had fed well for a few days and would no doubt go hungry again before they reached safety, but at least they had regained some of their strength, and Geli her health, thanks to the Russian supplies.

They followed the Elbe River to the town of Wittenberg, arriving three days later, hungry again. Elisabet tried to engage her children in conversation and quizzed them about the places they came to in Germany. Their education had suffered greatly in the last few months, and she thought that any small facts they could glean from their travels might help them.

"What do you know about Wittenberg?" she asked.

The younger children shook their heads, and Kurt knew only that it was on the Elbe River and had some tall buildings.

"You can see that from here, dummkopf," Helmut jeered. "Mutti means things you might have learnt in school."

"So what do you know, smarty?"

"It's where somebody called Luther nailed something to a church door and started a war or something."

"Very good, Helmut. Martin Luther started the Reformation by that action. There's a statue of him in the town square, so maybe we can have a look at it. We might even see the church. Now don't look like that, Werner. This is the history of your country and you should know about it."

They circled the town to enter from the north, because Elisabet thought they might look less like refugees from the east if they arrived from a different direction. By the time they drew near to the built-up areas though, it became apparent that the town was in chaos and locals were treated no differently from refugees by the Soviet authorities.

Wittenberg had been largely protected from bombing throughout the war, but not completely. A large factory on the outskirts, the Arado Flugzeugwerke, or Aircraft Factory, had been severely damaged despite it being staffed by prisoners. Bullets had damaged some of the buildings within the town itself, but the Russian advance had been so swift the town and its population suffered little.

They heard the news as soon as they entered the town, there being any number of people willing to pass on the latest stories, whether they were based on facts or unfounded rumours. Elisabet found it hard to distinguish between the two at first, but gradually the truth became clarified.

The war was over. The Führer had committed suicide and passed over government in the Reich to Grossadmiral Dönitz, who had, a week later, surrendered to the Allied forces. Germany was now ruled by the foreign powers and, Elisabet was told, they had lost no time in extracting what they could from the shell-shocked German population.

"What do you mean?" Elisabet asked one portly middle-aged man whose flesh and clothing could never have withstood a winter flight from Ostpreussen.

The man looked at Elisabet and her children with a moue of distaste, but his gaze lingered longer on Geli. "You're not from around here."

"We came from Königsberg."

"Ah. Well, I am...or was...a town councillor. I was never a Party member, you understand, just a loyal German trying to serve my community. You would think I would be thanked," he grumbled, "But what happens? The Soviets accuse me of being a Nazi, dismiss me from my position and throw me out of my house without so much as a by-your-leave. It won't do, I tell you."

Elisabet led her children away after making vague commiserating comments. She found a group of women with a bunch of young children and greeted them. They stared back, making only rudimentary re-responses.

"Good day Frauen, is there any food or shoes to be had in Wittenberg?"

"What did you say?"

Elisabet frowned but repeated herself politely.

"You see? There's that accent again. She's a blutig foreigner."

"I am not a foreigner. I'm a German like you – from Ostpreussen."

"Well, go back there with your brats. There's not enough food and clothing for Wittenbergers without trying to look after you lot."

"I can't go back; the Russians have overrun my city."

"Look around you," one woman said sourly. "The Russians are here too."

"There's no food?"

"Not for the likes of you. You foreigners think you can just arrive in your thousands on our doorsteps and demand to be fed. Well, it's not going to happen. Clear off."

Elisabet led her children and Geli away, deeper into the town. They arrived in the town square, the town hall now starkly decorated with a great blood-red banner where the hakenkreuz had once hung. Russian soldiers swarmed and Elisabet and Geli shrunk back, but the men paid the women little attention beyond a glance and, for Geli especially, an appreciative smile. Eventually, Elisabet plucked up the courage to address a Soviet officer.

"Excuse me, sir. My children are hungry. Is there any food you can give them?"

The officer frowned and asked a question in Russian. When no answer was forthcoming, he shrugged and moved away. Elisabet tried again, and on the fourth attempt, found someone who could speak some German.

He shook his head. "Not for Germans. We have better things to do. Find your war-mongering countrymen and demand food off them."

"It is the children I ask for, not for myself."

"So I am to feed not the Nazi, but the Nazi's children?"

"I have never been a Nazi," Elisabet declared.

"That's what you all say now. Since I have been in Germany I have never spoken to a Nazi. You all deny being one – even knowing one. You would have me believe there never were any. Well, I do not believe it. As far as I'm concerned, you are all Nazis – man, woman and child – and if you starve to death it saves us the cost of a bullet. Now get out of here before I shoot you myself."

They left, shaken by the enmity of the occupying force. On their way out of the town square, Helmut asked about the statue of Martin Luther, but it was nowhere to be seen. Elisabet thought about asking but did not want to stay in the town centre longer than they had to.

"Perhaps they've taken it somewhere for safekeeping."

The roads out of Wittenberg were clogged with people, but as many were flocking into the town as were leaving it. Elisabet said nothing but listened to the grumbling conversations around her and gained a picture of what had happened locally. The Russians had swept up to the Elbe River before turning north to Berlin, while the Americans had come in from the west, meeting at the River. The city of Magdeburg was divided, the Russians on the east bank and the Americans on the west.

"We still need to make it into American-held territory," Elisabet said. "We have to find an intact bridge where they'll let us cross. Perhaps there'll be one in Magdeburg."

"Magdeburg," Geli whispered.

"What? My God, what did you say, Geli?"

"She said 'Magdeburg', Mutti," Kurt said. "Do you think that's where she's from?"

"Geli, can you say that again?" Elisabet pleaded.

The young girl did not say anything, just appeared to withdraw into herself again.

"Geli, you and your family were in Lübben, heading west with the rest of us. Were you going to Magdeburg? Do you know someone there?"

"Magdeburg," Geli whispered again.

"That settles it. We're going there."

Kapitel Fünfzehn (15)

Magdeburg was a very different proposition from Wittenberg. While the town of Martin Luther had largely been spared the ravages of war, the capital city of the region had come in for great attention from the enemies of the Reich. The British, in particular, had targeted the region and, in a series of raids culminating in an attack in January 1944, almost obliterated the city. People still lived and worked there, by the thousand, but life for the inhabitants had become much harder.

Elisabet and her family arrived in East Magdeburg two weeks after leaving Wittenberg, and faced the same problem they had all the way along the Elbe River from Torgau – finding an intact unguarded bridge. The bridges of Magdeburg were destroyed, rebuilt and damaged in the course of the war, but reconstruction was always rapid because of the need for communication between the two sides of the city. They approached the river diffidently, scouting out the area without seeming too eager to cross, not wanting to attract attention.

It proved easier to cross than they hoped. Both occupying armies were organising a clean-up of their respective holdings, but as the American-held city was much larger than the eastern side, there was a steady flow of workers toward the west. They joined the shuffling column of men and women in the early morning.

There was a checkpoint on the island in the middle of the river, where names were written down. As they waited in the queue, Elisabet studied the soldiers from both armies manning the checkpoint. She was used to the impassive Russian faces, the flat stares and cruel weighing up of every woman, and she hoped for something different from the Americans. In comparison, the western faces were open, reflecting their thoughts and emotions, and hatred was uppermost in those she saw. Lust was evident too, particularly when a young attractive woman presented herself at the barrier. Geli was one of these, but she hid behind her wounded emotions and seemed unaware of her effect on the men.

Elisabet had a similar effect, for her pregnancy was not yet showing and her ragged clothing disguised any hints her body might display. She stepped up to the barrier with her papers in her hand.

"Name?"

"Elisabet Daeker. My children." She handed over the papers in her hand, and the Soviet representative checked the names against a list of names of people wanted by the authorities. The American officer just made a note of the names, yawned and examined his fingernails.

"Who is she? Where are her papers?"

"My step-daughter Geli. She lost her papers, but I have known her for fifteen years."

"Last name?"

"Daeker, like mine. She is the daughter of my husband's first marriage."

The Soviet representative looked Geli up and down. "Where did you lose your papers, Geli Daeker?"

"She cannot answer you," Elisabet said. "But it was at Lübben. We were attacked there by...by Russian soldiers and she was severely traumatised. Her papers were confiscated by the soldiers."

"And were you also traumatised, Frau Daeker?"

Elisabet shrugged, not answering.

278

The Soviet representative grunted and made a notation on his documents. "Home city?"

"Königsberg."

"Destination?"

"Magdeburg."

"Why?"

"Our homes are destroyed, and Geli's aunt lives here."

"Her name."

Elisabet hesitated, thinking of possible names. One sprang to mind. "Elsa Trommler." She hoped her late companion would not mind the use of her name.

"And her address?"

"I don't know."

"Then how will you find her?"

Elisabet shook her head. "I don't know."

The Soviet representative looked at the long queue of people waiting to cross over into West Magdeburg, and shrugged. "On your way then. Your passage is approved."

They crossed the bridge onto the west bank of the Elbe River and as they stepped onto land not ruled by the Russians, they breathed sighs of relief, feeling as if a weight of worry had been lifted from their shoulders. Elisabet remembered what her husband had told her about the forces arrayed against Germany.

"Do not fall into the hands of the Soviets. If the enemy will not allow a free Germany after the war, seek out the British or Americans. They are more civilised."

And here she was at last, in the part of Germany occupied by the Americans. If what Rudolph had said was true, their problems were behind them, though West Magdeburg did not look like a land of freedom and hope. The city spread out before them, but it was a city in ruins – cratered streets and shattered, burnt-out buildings, with the fresh grass and weeds of spring coating the rubble in a faint fuzz of green.

"Where do we go, Mutti?" Helmut asked.

"Follow the others." Elisabet pointed to where the other people who had come off the bridge were heading. Soldiers stood around or lounged in jeeps, staring at the Germans, many of them chewing something. They did not look friendly, so Elisabet picked up Joachim and herded the other children and Geli ahead of her.

Whole city blocks were in ruins, piles of rubble having cascaded down into the streets. The roadways themselves were clear of debris and jeeps and trucks emblazoned with white stars in circles or with a string of numbers and letters roared past, scattering the pedestrians. It did not seem possible that people could live in the shattered remnants of the buildings, but as they passed, faces stared out from gaps in the masonry or peered through the vegetation cloaking craters. Slowly, Elisabet and her family picked their way through devastation to a building that was relatively untouched. An American flag flew from a flagpole on the roof and guards in smart uniforms stood at the entrance stairs. There was a small crowd of Germans outside, and American officers harangued groups of twenty at a time.

"You damn Krauts had better get used to the new order of things around here," a young Lieutenant yelled at a small group of middle-aged men. An older sergeant translated his words into passable German. "We want none of your smart-ass fascist comments. We Americans are the occupying power in this sector and if we say 'jump' your proper response is 'how high?' – got it?"

The Germans looked puzzled, and one of them said, "Herr Leutnant, we only wish to know how we can get food. We can pay." The sergeant translated again.

"Pay? How?"

"We have Reichmarks..."

"Fuck your Kraut money. It's worthless."

"...Also watches, some jewellery..."

"Show me."

The spokesman unbuckled his watch and handed it over. The Lieutenant examined it and slipped it into his pocket.

"What else ya got?"

The other men offered up their watches, which an enlisted man collected, and then, after a display of reluctance, proffered a few gold wedding rings. They all disappeared into the pockets of the American soldiers.

"Anything else?"

"We have given you all we have, Herr Leutnant. We seek food in return."

The officer tossed the spokesman a pack of gum. "Here, share it out amongst you."

"I protest," the spokesman said. "We have given you valuable watches and rings on the understanding we would receive food in exchange. What is this?" he asked, holding up the gum. "This is not food. Give us food or give us back our belongings."

"They are confiscated as being possible Nazi plunder. By rights I should arrest you all, but I'm feeling generous today. Get the hell outa here."

The soldiers drove the protesting men away, with liberal use of rifle butts, and then stood around laughing and smoking, gloating over their booty.

Elisabet led her family around the American soldiers and approached another officer sitting at a table in the bright spring sunshine near the entrance to the American building. This man was older, bespectacled, and had a half-drunk cup of coffee cooling beside him. The aroma was delicious and made Elisabet's mouth water.

"Yes?"

Elisabet could not recognise the officer's rank. "Please, sir," she said in German. "My family need food."

"You'll have to work for it," the American replied in quite passable, if accented, German. He pulled a form towards him and took out his fountain pen. "Your name and city of origin?"

Elisabet told him, and then gave the names of her five sons.

"What about the young woman? Is she family too?"

"My step-daughter Geli."

The man wrote down the names and pushed the form across the desk. "Take this to Captain Wodzicki in Stadtfeld Ost, he'll give you work to do, and at the end of the day, he'll stamp your form. You can then use it to pick up food at designated food stations. You'll have to return here every morning to pick up another form."

Elisabet looked at the form, but could not read the English words. "Thank you, sir. Where is this Stadtfeld Ost?"

The man pointed. "That way. About a mile – that's about a kilometre and a half to you – you can't miss the work gangs."

They set off in the direction of Stadtfeld Ost, threading their way through ruined streets and past ragged people. There were plenty of American soldiers on the streets, tall and fresh-faced for the most part, quite unlike the silent, shocked populace. The soldiers stared at everything but paid more attention to the young women. Elisabet walked alongside Geli, guiding her past the soldiers, and studying the girl's impassive face.

"Do you know where we are, Geli? Magdeburg? Stadtfeld Ost? Do you recognise anything?" She looked around her with a wry smile. "Mind you, I don't know how anyone could recognise this." Geli said nothing. Elisabet sighed and squeezed the girl's arm. "Never mind, maybe it'll come back to you."

They saw work gangs, clearing rubble and sweeping the streets, and other American soldiers standing around watching. Some of them laughed and made jokes, others stared at every German with hate-filled eyes, but Elisabet had to ask for directions whatever her personal inclination, so she chose a group that was laughing.

The American soldier calmly examined the two women. "Captain Wodzicki? Sure, he's here, but I reckon I could show you a better time than him. You especially," he said to Geli.

"Jesus, Lenny," one of the other soldiers said. "Remember what the Colonel said – no fraternisation with the locals. They're all Nazis or Nazi sympathisers."

Lenny grinned, his jaws moving relentlessly as he chewed gum. "It ain't fraternisation if you don't enjoy it."

"Yeah, but you do. Come on, we shouldn't even be talking to them."

Elisabet and Geli had not understood any of the words, but understood only too well the message in eyes and gestures.

"Captain Wodzicki?" Elisabet asked again.

"Over there." Lenny pointed to an officer with a clipboard some distance away and sauntered off with his fellow soldiers.

Laughter and crude comments followed the two women as they gathered the children and approached the captain. Elisabet handed him the form and the captain looked it over, noting the extreme youth of the children.

"They're not going to be able to do much work, are they?" Captain Wodzicki observed in German. "You will have to work harder to make up for them if you expect them to be fed."

"My boys are strong and willing to work – we all are. We need food."

"I'm sure." He pointed. "There are some work gangs. Join them."

The gangs were engaged in clearing some of the buildings and the narrower streets of rubble, dumping the chunks of masonry in one of the many bomb craters, and piling usable bricks and timber to one side. Elisabet reported to a German overseer, wondering why he was trusted when every other German seemed to be viewed as vermin. The overseer assigned them various duties – Elisabet, Geli and Helmut in the lines passing bricks and concrete rubble along, and the smaller children sweeping dust and small stone fragments from the road. Kurt threw himself into his work, but the smaller children lost interest quickly, stopping to play or chase each other with their brooms. The overseer would shout in annoyance whenever this would happen, and Elisabet had to call them to order.

There were many other children in the lines or sweeping the road, several with the unmistakeable hauteur of Hitlerjugend members. Their uniforms had disappeared along with all insignia, but harder to shed was their expression, their suspicion of their neighbours and their ingrained hostility toward the Americans. They worked resentfully, and with dour expressions, and were not above bullying the younger children. One such youth tripped Kurt when he came close and pushed him as he fell.

"Stupid little boy," the youth said.

Before Elisabet could react, Geli was there. She gripped the youth by one arm, saying nothing, but staring into his face with such ferocity that he quailed. Elisabet was there a moment later. She made sure Kurt was unhurt, and then confronted the youth.

"Shame on you," she said. "Have you become nothing but a bully now the Americans are in charge?"

The youth shook himself free of Geli. "I am...was...a squad leader in...in...you know. I have not given up the fight against the invader."

"Yet here you are oppressing your fellow Germans. Did you actually fight the invader?"

"No. Our commander surrendered."

"Then be aware that my son Kurt here and my other son Helmut over there, fought against the Russians on our journey from Königsberg. They even deprived the enemy of vital war supplies. Don't you think that deserves respect instead of derision?"

The youth flushed, and then walked away quickly, joining another line. The overseer called out angrily to Elisabet.

"Get working, Frau, or lose your job. There are plenty of others willing to work."

They went back to work. The drudgery of lifting and passing blocks of masonry, bricks and timber, strained bodies already racked with hunger and weakened by months of cold and exhaustion. Children suffered the most, having few reserves within their tiny, emaciated bodies, but women were not far behind. Body reserves were eaten up, but exercise did not build up muscle tissue as there was very little protein to be had in the rations meted out to a subject population. When the day drew to a close and they staggered to collect their stamped form and shuffle off to exchange it for food, the meagre offerings barely satisfied an immediate hunger.

There was no accommodation provided, so Elisabet and Geli had to wander for some time before they found an unoccupied and uncontested niche in the lee of a ruined wall. The weather remained clement, though the night chill brought them huddling together for warmth. They slept without interruption, exhausted, and dragged themselves back to consciousness with the dawn. Their overseers provided them with a new work form and breakfast of rye bread, and as the long shadows of early morning started to shorten, they were back at work, muscles aching, fingertips bloodied, and minds dreading the prospect of another long day's labour clearing some tiny part of the Reich's ruin.

"The damned Americans made this mess," one woman complained. "You'd think they should clean it up."

"So tell them," said another. "See where it gets you."

Days passed, and the rubble from one site was cleared and the gangs moved on to new areas. It seemed impossible that a city could be filled with so much debris, and that the thousands of people labouring to shift it could have so little effect. The rations given to the labourers were not sufficient for the work demanded of them and people grew sick, or collapsed from exhaustion as they worked. This put a strain on the medical facilities of the ruined city, and as the Americans were loath to spend more on Germans than they had to, increased the food rations slightly.

Food could be obtained outside the rationing system, especially for women and children. The boys and girls on the work teams learned that some American soldiers had big hearts and could be persuaded to part with a chocolate bar or a cigarette. The chocolate would be wolfed down immediately, but the cigarettes would either be smoked to quell pangs of hunger or traded for more substantial food elsewhere. Helmut became quite adept at cadging gifts from servicemen and he taught Kurt how to do it. The younger boys, Günter and Werner, also tried, with some success, but Elisabet tried to dissuade them from a life of begging. It was easier than shifting piles of rubble or sweeping streets for hours, though, so the boys were always sneaking off whenever new soldiers were spotted.

As time went on, the rules against fraternisation were unofficially relaxed and young women found another way to supplement their income. The Ameri-American servicemen were far from home, in need of female company, and with a surfeit of consumer goods at their disposal. Although their officers reprimanded them severely if they caught them, the common soldiers could often be seen talking to a young German woman in a doorway, or in an alley, and luxuries like nylons, lipstick, chocolate or cigarettes would be offered for sexual favours.

Elisabet was showing her pregnancy by this time and few soldiers approached her, but Geli drew her share of attention. One soldier or two or three would approach her and try to draw her away, but Elisabet was vigilant and immediately interfered. Usually, she could dissuade the servicemen from assault simply by explaining that Geli was her daughter, other times by telling of her experiences at the hands of other soldiers, Russians, and hinting that many of them may have had diseases. This usually sufficed to repulse their attention, and it sometimes earned them a shame-faced withdrawal and a small gift by way of apology.

*   *   *

By no means all the children of Magdeburg worked in the many gangs of labourers. Helmut often saw groups of children, ragged and dirty, skulking in the shadows and in the overgrown bomb craters. He wondered about them and pointed them out to Kurt.

"How do they survive? They don't work, so they don't get rations."

"Maybe their parents are well off and they don't have to work," Kurt said.

Helmut scoffed. "Look at them, dummkopf. They're in rags. Their parents are poor and working – if they have any at all."

288

"So their parents are working. What does it matter?"

"They're not working on these gangs. Those children don't appear at the ration stations we've been to."

"So?"

"I'm going to talk to them. See what they do."

Kurt considered this. "Do you think we ought to? Mutti wouldn't like it."

"I'm not going to tell Mutti, and what's this 'we' anyway? I said I'm going, not you."

"Why not me?" Kurt complained. "I raided the train for coal and food with you, didn't I?"

"And I was the one who boarded the train. You just helped carry the stuff."

"I can't help it if I'm smaller than you. I want to come, and I could be useful too."

"How?"

Kurt shrugged. "I don't know, but are you saying I couldn't be useful?"

"No, I suppose not. All right, you can come."

"When? Now?"

"Soon. When we break at midday. And don't say anything to the others."

The midday meal was simple – a thin soup, usually cabbage, sometimes flavoured with pork, and rye bread. It was offered to those on the work gangs from carts that came to each gang, allowing no outsider to benefit from the generosity of the Americans. Work gang members would seek the shade and the children would often play, as much as their strength allowed. Elisabet was used to the children being out of sight during the break and did not worry when Helmut and Kurt slipped away.

There was plenty of cover to hide their escape, and once away from the immediate area, they were just two more children wandering the ruined city. They ran or hid from any American soldiers they saw, and sought out the lonelier places where children hiding from authority might congregate.

"Are you sure this is safe?" Kurt asked nervously. "I mean, we don't know anything about them."

"Of course we don't. That's why we're here."

"What if they don't want us to find them? They might...might hurt us."

"Go back if you're scared."

Kurt fell silent, but followed his brother nonetheless.

They came to an area of the city that had not a single building standing, mounds of rubble and cratered roadways choked with vegetation. Rounding a solitary, precarious brick wall, they stumbled upon a group of about a dozen boys and girls sitting and standing around a dead and bloated dog. Helmut nudged his brother and stepped into view.

"Hello. What are you doing?"

The effect was immediate and unexpected. Some of the children melted into the landscape with the merest rustle of vegetation or scuffle of shifting rubble, while five of the largest boys grabbed sticks or stones – and in one case, an iron bar – and advanced toward the two brothers.

"Who are you and what do you want?" Iron Bar rasped.

Helmut weighed up the boy in front of him. He looked to be about fourteen years old and wore the tattered remnants of a Hitlerjugend armband. "Just interested in what you're doing," he replied. "We saw you when we were on the line gang this morning."

"You're refugees?" Iron Bar made the term sound like an insult.

"From Königsberg," Helmut confirmed. "Does it matter?"

Iron Bar shrugged. "What are your names?"

"Helmut Daeker. This is my brother Kurt."

"I'm Heinrich. My father was a Blockleiter here in Magdeburg. The Americans locked him up when they took over and they'd probably shoot me if they caught me. I'm not going to tell you the names of anyone else until I know whether you're staying – or dying."

While Heinrich had been talking, other boys armed with sticks had crept around behind them, using the rubble as cover, and Helmut now saw that their escape had been cut off. He thought he could probably make a dash for it, but his brother wouldn't stand a chance.

"Why would you want to kill us?" he asked.

"You could be American spies."

Helmut laughed. "That's a pig's arse. My father fought on the Eastern Front and died fighting the enemies of the Reich. There's no way I'd dishonour his memory by helping Russian allies."

"Good answer," Heinrich said. "Tell me something you've done to aid the war effort."

"The war's over."

"Bad answer. The Führer is gathering a new army and will throw the invaders out of Germany very soon."

Helmut decided not to say anything about hearing the Führer had died in Berlin and that the government had surrendered. He glanced at Kurt, hoping he wasn't about to blurt the truth. "What sort of thing? To aid the war effort, I mean?"

291

"We steal from the Americans, weakening them. We also destroy American property when we can."

"Kurt and I stole from the Russians. Coal and food."

"Good answer," Heinrich said again.

"And I hit a Russian soldier in the head with a stone. A platoon of soldiers was hunting us, but we got away."

"And your brother?"

"He helped me with everything. I couldn't have done it without him."

"Another good answer." Heinrich considered for a few minutes, the other boys in his gang waiting patiently for their leader's decision.

"You were not to know the Führer is still leading the fight. That's a secret. The Americans say Germany has surrendered, but that's nonsense. Just enemy propaganda. Your other answers were good, so you'll undergo the test of strength. If you pass, you'll be given the chance to join our Troop. If you fail..." Heinrich grinned and drew his thumbnail across his throat.

Helmut sized up the boy. He was scrawny but tall and had numerous scars that told of a hard life. He had no doubt he was facing a major challenge. "You're bigger than me. That's not fair."

"Life isn't fair, Königsberger. But you're not fighting me...or any of us. I have something much more entertaining in mind."

Heinrich led the boys back to the dead dog and stood looking down at it for a few moments. "Stinks, doesn't it? Kneel down on either side of it, Königsberger, you and your brother." He waited until the two boys had complied. "Now, Erik here is going

to count up to sixty, and you are not to turn away be-
before he does. Got it?"

Helmut nodded, thinking that the test should not
be too difficult. The dog stank, but it was bearable.

"Then breathe out – empty your lungs. Erik, start
your count." Heinrich leaned forward and jabbed the
dead dog's belly with a pointed stick just as the boys
started to breathe in. The swollen belly ruptured,
releasing noxious gases that swept into the boys lungs.
Kurt immediately turned away, retching, vomiting up
his recent meal, heaving violently. Helmut hung on,
gagging and eyes streaming as he forced himself to
keep kneeling, fighting his urge to throw up. He
closed his eyes and concentrated on the sound of Erik
counting, willing the seconds to pass. Somewhere to
one side he heard another boy retching and a bit
further off, muffled laughter. Another breath and he
almost lost control, tasting acid in the back of his
throat, the stink of corruption in his nostrils.

"Enough. Open your eyes and move away,
Königsberger. You did well."

Helmut scrambled away and threw up, emptying
his stomach until he felt spent and light-headed. He
lifted his face and saw his brother off to one side,
vomit down his shirt and his eyes red from crying.
Looking around further, he saw Heinrich and Erik,
grinning, and several other boys and girls, one or two
of whom had evidently been sick when the rotting
body gases had swept over them.

"What do we do with them, Heinrich?" asked one
of the girls. "The bigger one stood his ground but the
little one blubbered like a baby."

"You think you could do better, Ulla? Come and
have a sniff, there's more stink in the old dog yet. No?
Anyone else? I see Rulf and Martin couldn't take it

293

either, and they were further away." Heinrich laughed. "I say they passed. Does anyone dispute my deci- decision?"

Nobody did, and the gang gathered round, staring curiously at Helmut and Kurt.

"All right, you get the chance to join our Troop, but you'll have to prove yourself first."

"Doing what?" Helmut asked. The stink still clung to his nostrils and back of his throat, so he hawked and spat to one side.

"You'll see. Be here at the same time tomorrow. Just you, Helmut. Your brother's a bit soft, but I'm willing to let him go if you vouch for his silence. Do you?"

Helmut nodded. "Yes."

"On your life?"

"Yes."

"Good. Same time tomorrow. Come alone and tell no one. Remember, we can always find you...and your brother."

Kapitel Sechzehn (16)

Elisabet was worried about her children. Something had happened a few days before when Helmut and Kurt skipped the afternoon work detail, appearing just before the end of work to claim their rations for the day. They stank of rotting flesh, the odour clinging to their clothes. Helmut said they had just gone exploring and found a dead dog. However, since then, her eldest boy wandered off most days, strutting back near nightfall, without caring that he had missed out on the issue of food. He did not starve though, as he produced little luxuries like American cigarettes that could be exchanged for a great many other things, including extra food for his family.

Naturally, his mother talked to him, trying to find out where he was getting things like cigarettes and, more importantly, what he had to do to obtain them. Helmut was evasive, and when pressed, said he had a job running errands for an American officer, who paid him in cigarettes, chocolate or a tinned meat called spam. Elisabet questioned Kurt too, about that first day, but he stuck to his story about a dead dog. As he was obviously mystified about the source of Helmut's acquisitions, she issued only a warning.

"I don't want you to tell tales, Kurt, but remember that this city is a dangerous place. Helmut might be in danger, so if you ever want to tell me anything, you would only be protecting your brother."

Shortly after that, her troubles increased. Kurt went off now, and sometimes took Günter or Werner with him. Joachim was too young to go far, and one of his older brothers was always on hand to watch over him, but as often as not, the other would wander off, always in the company of Kurt. Elisabet could find out little when she quizzed them.

"Where do you go when you go off with Kurt?"

"Nowhere special." Werner said.

"And what do you do in these places that are nowhere special?"

"Wander around. Sometimes we find things."

"Such as?"

Werner shrugged, unhappy that his mother was asking all these questions. "Things," he said vaguely. "We found a knife once."

"You didn't bring it back. What did you do with it?"

"We traded it to an American soldier for some chocolate."

"Which you ate? It would be nice if you brought some home for little Joachim."

"Yes, Mutti."

Her question and answer sessions with Günter were equally unrevealing.

"We don't do anything much, Mutti," Günter said. "Sometimes we go down to the American camp and beg for food. Some of the men just tell us to 'get lost' but others throw us sandwiches or sweets."

"You shouldn't be begging for food. I'd much rather you worked for it."

"We can get chocolate from the Americans. Once a man gave us tins of meat and fish."

"He just gave you them?"

"Well, he wanted something in return."

Elisabet stared at her young son, feeling a chill envelop her heart. She was almost afraid to ask. "What did he want?"

"He wanted to take our photograph."

"And...did he? Did you let him?"

296

Günter nodded. "He seemed very interested in our shoes." He grinned. "I showed him my toes through the end..." He lifted his foot and waggled his toes through the open end where the leather had worn away. "...and he took a photograph just of that."

"Günter, listen to me. It's very important that you don't let American men...any men for that matter, touch you or ask you to touch them. If they do ask you, you are to run away immediately and come and tell me. Will you do that?"

"Why, Mutti?"

"Just do as I ask. Will you?"

Günter looked puzzled. "Yes, Mutti."

Kurt assured her that his brothers were in no danger. Sometimes they just collected cigarette ends and shredded the unburnt tobacco into a tin, which they then traded to a black marketeer for chocolate. Elisabet pondered this and decided to give her boys some leeway, but made sure they recognised the dangers involved. She had other worries, besides.

Geli's sole utterance in the weeks that she had travelled with them was 'Magdeburg' and Elisabet knew that the city must mean something to her. She asked her often enough, but she had not repeated the word or expanded upon it. Elisabet sometimes led the young girl off to view some local landmark that was still standing, or at least recognisable amongst the ruins – river views, a town hall, a shattered church, or even ordinary houses that had somehow been spared the ravages of the bombing raids. Nothing seemed to jog Geli's memory, but Elisabet persevered.

"Magdeburg means something to you," she told the young girl. "We'll look until we find what it is."

Weeks slipped by and May became June. Nature was not to be denied despite the best efforts of man, and the surviving trees in the parks and along the riverbanks burst into full leaf and the birds returned to nest and bring up their young. Other animals that infested cities also returned and burgeoned – sparrows, rats, starlings, pigeons. They foraged and squabbled among the ruins and the ragged human population.

The meagre rations dispensed to the populace hovered at subsistence level or below and as hunger and disease bit deeper, people looked to other means to keep body and soul together. The warmer weather helped, the bodies no longer needing to burn so much fuel to keep warm, but the monotonous diet of dry bread, potatoes, oatmeal, milk powder and tiny scraps of meat and fat depressed them and encouraged deficiency diseases. Elisabet found herself longing for a bit of fresh fruit or green vegetable. She mentioned it to her boys when Joachim developed sores on his arms and legs.

"Forget chocolate or cigarettes," she said. "If you want to do something really useful, try and get some fruit from the Americans."

The next day, Kurt and Werner arrived back with a dozen oranges. The younger children had never seen an orange and tried biting into one like an apple, chewing dubiously on the rind, until Elisabet showed them how to peel the fruit and extract the sweet pulp and sticky, delicious juice.

"We didn't get them from the Americans," Kurt said, licking his fingers. "They only give us gum or chocolate, sometimes cigarettes. We had to trade them for oranges on the black market."

"Why haven't we had oranges before, Mutti?" Günter asked. "Can't you get them in Königsberg?"

"We used to eat them," Elisabet said, "But by the time the war came, many things were in short supply. You and your brothers Werner and Joachim never had oranges."

Günter sucked every scrap of pulp from a segment of orange and nibbled thoughtfully on the peel. "Did many things change when the war came?"

"More things than you can imagine."

* * *

Things change so drastically you wonder whether you genuinely remember them or whether they are merely dreams. Königsberg was a beautiful city once, even after the Nazis took control of our beloved Deutschland. The palace, the cathedral, the town hall, railway station, the Schlossteich and its Promenade – even the Jewish synagogue – all are fixed in my mind as pure and beautiful places reflecting seven hundred years of German civilisation. The port, the river, tree-lined streets and bustling city centre – I remember all these things fondly, but I have to consciously overlay them with Nazi panoply if I am to remember them as they really were in my early twenties. The Nazis changed Germany, raising us to heights of patriotic fervour, only to plunge us into ruin and degradation. I remember Königsberg as it once was, as it became, but I have been spared the sight of what it must be like under the Russians. I love the Königsberg of my childhood but I fear it is no longer the city I knew.

I was married early in 1938, meeting a wonderful young man willing to take on a ready-made family. The fact that he belonged to the Nazi party gave me pause, for my family derived from the opposite end of the political spectrum and I had imbibed communist teachings with my mother's milk. Expediency won out – and love – for I had two young children to

299

think of. I put my misgivings away and spent time getting to know the young man. Well, I say 'young man' though he was eleven years older than me, but he made me laugh and forget that I was an unmarried mother. I have never been ashamed of having children out of wedlock, you understand, though others sometimes tried to make me feel worthless. My Rudolph never did.

He was a supervisory gardener in the Königsberg Botanic Gardens. I was there in the late spring of 1937 with my two young sons – Helmut about eighteen months old and rather a handful, and little Kurt still in his pram. The day was sunny though a chill wind blew off the Frisches Haff, so we were all dressed warmly. I stopped to watch the gardeners at work planting out a huge bed in seedlings of multicoloured plants and flowers, staking out pegs and string, though from where I stood I could see no pattern. A man stood off to one side, folded plans in his hand which he consulted from time to time, and called instructions to the planters to move such-and-such a peg thirty centimetres to the right or to tighten or loosen a string. He was a handsome man with a broad smile and hair as neatly trimmed as the lawn on which he stood. Despite the chill breeze, he had taken off his jacket and tie and stood in his shirtsleeves ignoring the cold. His voice was gentle and precise, though his eyes flashed if one of the planters was slow in carrying out his instructions. I edged in his direction, intent only in asking the design.

He nodded in my direction, his eyes moving rapidly over me in the way that men often do. "Good morning, Frau."

"Good day, Herr Gardener," I replied. "What are you planting?"

"A display to coincide with the Party rally in Nürnberg in September." He smiled. "It would be better for the Führer's birthday, but that happens too early in the year for a decent floral tribute."

"What is the form of the display?"

"You will have to come back in September and see for yourself. Ask your husband to bring you. It will be the talk of the city."

"I have no husband."

"Ah...my condolences, Frau."

I saw no reason to dispel his misconception, handsome though he was. If he thought me widowed, it was none of my concern. I thanked him and bid him good day.

I returned to the Botanic Gardens the next day, without my children, having given my mother a treat in caring for them. You will think me dreadfully calculating, but I was still a young woman and enjoyed the attentions of handsome men. I got little enough of that as two young children deterred suitors.

He saw me coming and walked over to meet me, his gaze casting about for the presence of my children or at least a family member looking out for my interests.

"Good day, Frau. I had not thought to see you here again so soon." He gave a mischievous smile. "Couldn't wait for September?"

"I hoped to persuade you to tell me before then, Herr Gardener."

"Ah, now I wonder what would persuade me." He flashed that smile again. "Perhaps while you are marshalling your arguments, you would permit me to buy you an ice-cream at the kiosk?"

We ate our little dishes of creamy vanilla ice-cream at a little table near the kiosk and looked out at the lawns and trees of the Gardens. He ate faster than me and soon threw down his spoon and watched me eat, fixing me with a quizzical gaze.

"So, my dear young Frau, how will you persuade me?"

I was a little shocked by his forward manner, but also excited, though I think I hid it well. "Perhaps you will take pity on me, Herr Gardener, and reveal your secret."

"And what secret might that be?" His eyes twinkled and I could not help myself. I blushed.

"The design, Herr Gardener."

"I will if you will tell me your name."

"Elisabet Machel."

Though seated, he sketched a mock bow. "And I am Rudolph Daeker."

I inclined my head in return. "Herr Daeker."

That smile again. "If we are to share secrets, then you must call me Rudolph ...Elisabet."

"Very well...Rudolph. And you will tell me your secret now?"

"I'll do better than that. I'll show you."

Rudolph led me to the nearby university building and we ascended to the roof. For several minutes I looked out over the city, never having seen it from that vantage before. The Schloss and Schlossteich dominated the east and south, the river and docks to south and west, and the great jumble of streets filled the west and north, laid out like a child's toy. I lowered my eyes to the Gardens and stared at a large round flower bed, filled with string outlines and thin rows of seedlings.

"What am I seeing?" I asked.

Rudolph stood just behind me, his arm outstretched over my shoulder and I followed where his finger pointed. "It is only in outline, but soon we will fill in the spaces with massed plantings, and by September, all will be in readiness."

"Yes, but what is it?"

"See the outline – eyes, cheeks, brow with lock of hair, nose, firm resolute mouth and moustache…"

I laughed out loud. "It is Herr Hitler, outlined in petunias and marigolds. Whose idea was this? Yours, Rudolph?"

He smiled most beautifully, not taking offence at my mirth. "Alas, not mine. The Gauleiter mentioned to me that he thought a large image of the Führer would concentrate people's attention when listening to the broadcasts of the Nürnberg speeches."

"But how will people see it? Will they all have to ascend to the top of this building?"

"The Gauleiter suggested a large stand of seats overlooking the park…and the display."

"You know the Gauleiter?"

"Not socially, of course, but I see him at Party meetings."

I held my voice carefully neutral. "You are a Party member?"

"Yes, I have that honour."

That should have ended our relationship, though it would never do to let him think that was the reason for my never seeing him again. I did not know if he was a Nazi fanatic, but if he became suspicious and asked the Gestapo to investigate my family, it would be the end. The Party abhors any political view not their own and communists rapidly found themselves incarcerated in a re-education camp.

Instead, I thanked him for showing me the design and made my excuses, hurrying downstairs and away to my family. I took my exercise elsewhere after that,

303

but Rudolph was not to be denied. Of course, with his connections and my name, he tracked me down. One day I returned from the shops to find my father waiting for me on the doorstep.

"You have a visitor, Elisabet. Is there something you should be telling me?"

I hurried inside to the living room and was astounded to see Rudolph in an armchair reading a book to a rapt pair of children, while my mother looked on bemused. Kurt took his thumb out of his mouth long enough to smile, and Helmut grinned.

"I like Rudi, Mutti. Can he come and read to us again?"

* * *

Elisabet marvelled at the things available in a Germany ground down by the occupying forces. The population starved, wore ragged clothing, shivered in the cold and few had a roof over their heads, yet luxuries could be had if you had something of value to trade for them. People brought out possessions they had hoarded through the war years – clocks, china, jewellery, musical instruments – and sold or traded them for something that would keep them alive. The fraternisation laws eased and some young women cultivated friendships with servicemen, reaping the benefits of increased food and luxuries by leasing their bodies. Elisabet refused to allow Geli to talk to Americans. The girl was traumatised enough already, without having some lonely and frustrated soldier have his way with her for the price of a pair of nylons.

Then, as the summer solstice approached, a jeep pulled up to the work gang one day and a young lieutenant got out and spoke to the supervisor.

"Frau Daeker, kommen sie hier bitte."

304

Elisabet froze, hearing only those dreaded words uttered by Russian rapists – 'Frau, komm'. Fighting down panic, Elisabet approached the two men. The American spoke again, and the supervisor translated.

"You have a son? Helmut Daeker?"

"Yes. What has happened? Is he all right?"

"He is under arrest for theft. You are required to go with this officer and answer questions."

Dread gripped Elisabet. She had so many calls on her attention she felt herself drowning, and now this. At least Kurt and Werner were off on some outing together. "I must bring my...my daughter Geli. I cannot leave her alone. And my sons Günter and Joachim."

The supervisor translated and the American shook his head.

"The lieutenant says no, but may I suggest Frau Brandt? She is a grandmother and I think will be willing to keep an eye on your children."

The supervisor explained matters and hurried off to find Frau Brandt, while the lieutenant tapped his foot impatiently. The child care was quickly arranged and the jeep roared off, carrying Elisabet to American headquarters.

She was greeted by hostile faces, and was led through to an office at the back. The lieutenant knocked on a door with the name-plate Major Berendson, and entered. Major Berendson looked up from his papers and motioned Elisabet to a chair in front of his desk. The lieutenant went to stand by the door.

"Frau Daeker, you are the mother of Helmut Daeker?" the major asked in fluent German. "Do you have a husband? Perhaps I should be talking to him."

"My husband died nearly three years ago. What is this about?"

"Your son has been arrested for wilful damage to American Army property, and theft. What do you say to that?"

"What can I say? This is not at all the behaviour I would expect from my eldest son. What is the evidence against him?"

"I'll come to that. Why is your son wandering the streets instead of working with you? He is old enough to work."

"He is young and curious. Magdeburg is a strange city and one in ruins. I would imagine he looks around to satisfy his curiosity. It is a lot to ask a child to work as hard as you Americans tell us to work."

"So he steals instead of earning a living?"

Elisabet thought about debating the worth of the work she was given, and its inability to provide a living, but knew that this would only antagonise the American major more. "You have accused my son, major, but where is the proof?"

Berendson consulted some papers on his desk. "Your son was apprehended three blocks from the army store with a small can of gasoline. He stated that he found it lying in the road."

"Isn't that possible?"

"It was American gas, found in the possession of a German boy only a few hundred yards or so from an American depot. I'd say that constitutes proof of his guilt."

"Are you sure it was American? Maybe he got it somewhere else or maybe he really did just find it."

"American gasoline is coloured pink. It came from the depot. Your son is a thief."

"Was the gasoline the only thing taken?"

306

"No, a lot of tinned food, chocolate and cigarettes were taken."

"And were any of these things found with my son?"

"No."

"Why not?"

"You tell me, Frau Daeker."

"How is my son supposed to have entered your depot?"

"There was a diversion, and when the guard left, the lock was removed with a crowbar."

"So other boys were involved? Or men even?"

"It would appear so. What is your point, Frau Daeker? Your son refuses to identify his fellow criminals."

"My point is, Herr Major, that a group of men or boys entered your store and carried off a great many things. It is entirely possible that they dropped something as they ran away and my son picked it up, not knowing its origins."

The Major scowled. "It's possible," he said grudgingly.

"Did anyone see the theft?"

"The returning guard saw a number of boys running from the scene, carrying stolen articles."

"Did he identify Helmut?"

"No, not specifically, but he was picked up close by."

"Doing what?"

"What do you mean, Frau Daeker?"

"Was he running, walking, sitting on the footpath – what?"

Berendson consulted the report again. "He was walking."

307

"Isn't it odd that a boy you say has just helped steal things from your store is found walking close by? Not running, like the other boys your guard saw? They seem to have escaped easily enough. If my son just found it in the road, like he said, then what reason had he to run?"

The major frowned and looked at the lieutenant by the door. He repeated what Elisabet had said in English.

"She makes a good point, sir."

"He had stolen goods on him, damn it."

"Herr Major," Elisabet went on, "It seems to me a mistake has been made, a natural mistake but a mistake nonetheless. I suggest that as this small part of the stolen goods has been recovered by my son, then no further action should be taken against him. Rather, he should be thanked for recovering it."

"Please wait outside, Frau Daeker."

Elisabet stood outside the Major's office listening to a heated argument going on inside in a language she could not understand. After about five minutes the door opened and the lieutenant came out, beckoning to her to follow. He led her first to the secretarial pool where he collected a German-speaking young woman and then out the back of the building to some concrete outhouses that had been converted into cells. The guard opened one cell and hauled Helmut out.

The boy looked defiant until he saw his mother, and then hung his head as if ashamed. "I didn't do anything, Mutti. I just found this can in the road. I hadn't even opened it to see what it was before some soldiers ran up and arrested me. What's going to happen?"

The secretary translated and the lieutenant nodded. "All right, tell him this. You have been lucky this time, but if we catch you with stolen goods again, we'll lock you up and throw away the key. Understand?"

The secretary translated and Helmut burst into tears, burying his face in his mother's side. Elisabet led her son out onto the street and away from American headquarters before she said anything.

"That could so easily have gone differently."

"I thought it went well, Mutti."

Elisabet stopped and looked at her son. His tears had disappeared and he wore a cheeky grin on his grubby face.

"What do you mean?"

"The Americans are dumb. They accept any old story."

"Helmut, I argued your case with the Major. I told him you could not possibly be guilty."

"I know. Thanks, Mutti, but fancy them believing me. I was caught red-handed."

Elisabet stared unbelievingly. "You actually did it? You stole from the American depot?"

"Why not? They're our enemies aren't they? You didn't mind when I stole from the Russians."

"That was different."

"How? Russians and Americans are both the enemy."

"We stole from the Russians to survive. Without the coal and food from those trains we would probably all have died, but the war is over now. We have food, supplied by the Americans..."

"What? Thin soup, dry bread, a scrap of meat? You call that food? Have you seen what the Americans have in their stores?"

Elisabet sighed and hugged her son. "We're trying to survive as a family, and that means you must stay out of American jails. Curb your thefts, please, Helmut. I appreciate the extra food you bring the family, but don't do anything that is dangerous. I couldn't bear it if anything happened to you."

"I'll be careful, Mutti. Anyway, I won't have to do anything for a while now."

"What do you mean?"

"The petrol was only one thing I took from the store. Nobody would believe I found food or cigarettes, so I hid those quickly."

"The Americans will be watching you now."

"I know, but they're quite safe where they are. I'll wait until the Americans get bored of watching me and then retrieve them."

June had ushered in the warmer weather, and thousands of new people flowed into Magdeburg. German soldiers started to return from detainment camps throughout the American and British sectors. These prisoners had been vetted thoroughly for their political views and having been judged no guiltier than any other German, and a lot less culpable than many, were released. They arrived by the hundred and by the thousand, taxing the American administration in Magdeburg. The authorities responded by giving them work on the road gangs, displacing the women like Elisabet and Geli.

Rations were still available, though at a reduced rate, so Elisabet took Geli out to see more of the city and try and discover why the girl had responded positively to the name of Magdeburg. She took to asking people if they knew her or recognised anything about her, but while a few men responded enthusiastically, Elisabet doubted their sincerity and led the girl away. And then, one day, they came to the suburb of Nordwest.

The street was less damaged than many in the vicinity, the plane trees that lined the pock-marked road struggling to clothe their stark bomb-shattered limbs in leaves, while the tiny gardens surrounding the houses still standing were overgrown and wild. There were people in the street, in the gardens and on the front porches of the houses, but there was no energy in them. They stood and stared at the two women as they walked slowly down the street but at one house, Geli showed animation for the first time in weeks. She clutched Elisabet's arm and started to cry.

"What is it, meine süsse?" Elisabet asked. "Do you recognise something?"

Geli stared at a stone house and at the ruins of another one next to it, emotions washing over her face, her lips trembling.

"Did you live here, Geli? Do you know who does?"

After a few moments, Elisabet led the girl through the squeaking gate and up an overgrown path where unkempt roses struggled to bloom and lavender plants reared tiny mauve flower heads through the rampant weeds. The June sun warmed the garden and reflected warmly off the chipped and faded brick walls of the house as they approached the front porch. With a creak, the front door swung open and an old woman stepped out onto the weathered boards of the porch, a suspicious look on her face.

"We have nothing here worth stealing," the old woman said. "Go away before I call my husband."

Elisabet smiled in what she hoped was a reassuring manner. "We have not come to steal anything. I only

311

want to know if you recognise this girl." She drew Geli from behind her.

The old woman screwed up her eyes and looked for a few moments before shaking her head. "Never seen her before. Why? Who is she?"

"Geli is her name. I found her near Lübben. Her parents were dead and she had been assaulted by Russian soldiers. I brought her with me to Magdeburg because she once said the name. She doesn't say anything else."

The old woman's face softened. "Poor girl. These are dreadful times for women, but then, any time is dreadful for women. At least we have Americans in charge here, though sometimes they are scarcely better than the Russian animals." She shook her head and started to turn away. "Wait. Her name is Geli, you say? Geli what? Reiniger?"

"I don't know," Elisabet said. "I've only ever known her as Geli. You are a Reiniger? You might be her relative?"

"Carl and Reinhard Reiniger are my...were my cousins. Carl lived here with his wife Lotte until he was called up. He died in the east somewhere. We...my husband and I, lived next door there..." The old woman pointed at the overgrown ruins of the next-door house. "We moved in after the raid eighteen months ago and looked after Lotte until she died. They have a son somewhere – in the army..." She shrugged. "Who knows, these days? Anyway, Reinhard and his wife Katerine moved east to Lübben with their daughter Geli. This girl could be that Geli, I suppose. She certainly has the look of her, but if she is, how she has changed."

Elisabet pondered the problem. "So she could be that Geli, but how do we prove it? Did Geli Reiniger ever visit here? This Geli seemed to recognise the house."

"Yes, she came here once or twice for Christmas. All the family."

"Do you have photographs?"

"Somewhere. Come in, I will see if I can find them."

Elisabet and Geli followed the old woman into the house, and through a dark hallway into a sunny kitchen at the rear of the house. Elisabet looked out the window at a neat handkerchief-sized lawn, some apple trees and a large square of tilled soil with vegetables in neat rows. An old man was bent over the rows with a hoe. Tall privet hedges strained the breezes, turning the whole garden into a haven of peace and warmth. A droning of bees and the contented clucking of chickens drifted through the open window, making Elisabet think of childhood days on the farm in far-off Ostpreussen. The old woman saw the direction of Elisabet's gaze.

"My husband Wilhelm. I'm Hanna. Hanna Zweig."

"I was actually marvelling at how neat your back garden is compared to the front."

"My husband's idea. We couldn't possibly protect ourselves if looters came looking, so the front of the house looks poor and rundown. Nobody could possibly imagine there's anything worth stealing." The old woman filled a kettle and put it on the stove. "Coffee?"

"Thank you. The photographs?"

"Ah yes, now let me think..." Hanna took a few steps toward the door, stopped in thought and crossed to a china cabinet and pulled out a drawer. She lifted several tablecloths and napkins out and delved deeper, pulling out a battered photograph

313

album. The cloths and napkins were replaced and she flicked some imagined dust from the cabinet before crossing to the kitchen table with the album.

"Let's see..." she turned the pages slowly, peering at page after page of faded monochrome pictures of people standing in self-conscious poses, a faint chemical smell wafting off the photographs lending an atmosphere of age to the snapshots of a former life. "Yes, here we are. That's Reinhard and Katerine Reiniger, and their daughter Angelika, Christmas 1939."

Elisabet stared at the individuals in the photograph, trying to see them as real people rather than two-dimensional images of people who had once lived in this city. The man stood stiff-backed, in an old-fashioned suit, a thickset, moustached face with hooded eyes staring out belligerently at the camera. The woman was frail, no more than chest-high to her husband, in a long plain dress and with a cloche hat that hid her hair except where a few curls escaped from the sides. Both adults wore stony expressions, apparently seeing nothing amusing or entertaining in the grim duty of preserving their likeness for posterity.

Between them posed a girl who was very different from her dour parents. Tall and gangly, a girl of perhaps eleven or twelve with blonde hair in pigtails grinned at the camera – or perhaps at the cameraman behind. She wore a white blouse with a tie and long dark skirt in the fashion of the Bund Deutscher Mädel. Her likeness to Geli was striking, allowing for the six years that had passed and the harrowing experiences that had etched their signature on the young woman's face.

Elisabet held the photograph so Geli could see it. "Do you recognise these people?"

Geli stared at the photograph for several seconds, her eyes flicking back and forth over the grainy images. Her face crumpled and tears carved tracks down her gaunt cheeks.

"Mutti," she whispered. "Vati, Geli."

An expression of horror gripped the young girl's face and she burst into tears, a wail of anguish starting deep in her chest, escalating up through her throat. Startled at the sudden onslaught of grief from a girl who had been virtually mute and unresponsive for weeks, Elisabet was slow to react. The old woman though, Hanna, stepped forward and enveloped Geli in her arms, pressing the girl's face to her shoulder, soothing and stroking her. By degrees, Geli's screams lessened to racking sobs and then to whimpering cries, her hands plucking at the old women's dress. The cries brought the old man in from the garden. He stood in the doorway looking from his wife to Elisabet and then to Geli.

"Geli? Is that Angelika?" Wilhelm asked.

"Shhh, Geli, it's all right," Hanna said. "Yes, it is little Geli returned to us."

"Where is Reinhard? Katerine?"

Hanna shook her head. "This kind lady brought Geli to us."

Elisabet introduced herself. "I didn't know she lived...had visited here. She seemed to recognise the house, so... I found her near Lübben...the...the Russians..."

"Enough said, Frau Daeker. Those animals have a lot to answer for." Wilhelm looked at his wife hugging Geli and nodded. "Thank you for bringing her back

315

to us. You may be certain she will be looked after as if she was our daughter."

"I had not thought to leave her," Elisabet said. "She has been a part of my life for so long, but I suppose..."

"Where better than with her relatives?" Hanna asked. "We have no surviving children of our own and if, as you say, her own parents... She would be loved and cared for here."

"We have food and shelter to offer too," Wilhelm said. "Better than she has had on her journey from Lübben. You too, I daresay." The old man looked at his wife with an enquiring expression. Hanna smiled and nodded.

"Stay here too," Wilhelm said. "From the looks of you, you could do with some proper food and er, in your er..."

"As you are expecting, my husband is trying to say," Hanna chuckled. "Are you far along?"

"About four and a half months," Elisabet said. "But I am so thin now, I must look more. I thank you for your generous offer, but I have five small sons I must get back to – the eldest is nine, the youngest only two. They will be wondering where we...where I am."

"Bring them too," Hanna said. "It will be a bit cramped, but the boys can help Wilhelm in the garden and you and Geli can help around the house. It will be nice to have some female companionship. The boys would probably like to sleep in proper beds again."

"You are very kind," Elisabet said. "Perhaps for a little while?"

"As long as you like, my dear."

Kapitel Siebzehn (17)

"Where's Geli?"

The boys crowded around their mother in the little shelter they had constructed from scraps of timber and canvas in the lee of a ruined wall. She hugged them all in turn and set about preparing dinner for them all. Kurt had acquired a few potatoes, while Günter and Werner had collected enough cigarette ends to trade for a little sugar, so they had sweetened coffee as a treat.

"Where's Geli?" Helmut asked again.

"That's what I want to talk to you about. I found her family, or at least some of it. An old couple called Zweig are cousins of Geli's parents. They recognised her and even Geli recognised photographs of herself and her parents."

"So she's staying with them?"

"Yes, but they've invited us to stay too. They have a nice house, undamaged by bombing, and a garden with apple trees, a vegetable patch and...and chickens."

Kurt cried out joyfully. "I can have another chicken like my little Chickie."

"Told you we'd find you one," Helmut said.

"When are we going?" Werner asked.

Elisabet looked outside at the gathering dusk. "Tomorrow morning, I think. It will take us an hour or so to get there."

"How long would we be staying?" Helmut asked.

"They've said we can stay as long as we want to. Maybe until things settle down and we can return to Königsberg."

"I think we should move on, go further west," Helmut said.

"Mutti, we don't have to, do we?" Günter said. "I like the city, 'specially as there's no Russians here."

"Me too," Kurt said. "It'll be good if we can stay in a house."

"I think it would be good to stay for a while too," Elisabet said. "We need to get over the effects of our travel and bad diet. You like it here well enough, don't you Helmut? Why do you think we should move on?"

"I saw some Russian soldiers today – officers."

"Russians? In West Magdeburg? You must be mistaken. This is part of the American zone."

"So they say," Helmut said. "Anyway, they were going into the American headquarters so I waited around and listened to the soldiers talking. I can understand some English now and I heard enough to worry me."

"What?"

"The Americans are going to give Magdeburg to the Russians."

Elisabet looked at her eldest son, noting how much he seemed to have grown up over the last few months. He was still a little boy, but now overlain with a hard veneer of adulthood – not surprising given the experiences they had all undergone. He looked serious now, but surely he must have misheard the American soldiers. Why would they hand over some of their territory to the Russians? Certainly they were allies, but from what she had heard, there was no love lost between the two nations.

"Why would they do that?"

Helmut shrugged. "I don't like Russians."

Elisabet shuddered and drew her shawl about her more snugly. "Perhaps it won't come to that. There's no reason for it." She thought for a moment. "I'll see

318

what I can find out tomorrow morning, and then we'll go to the house."

The next day, they ate the last of their rations from the previous day, together with scraps of food traded for loose tobacco collected by the younger children. Elisabet impressed on the boys the need to remain close to their shelter so that when she returned they could set out for the Zweig house, and then she left for the American headquarters without a firm plan in mind.

She considered her options as she walked, but could not imagine the Americans telling her anything unless it suited their purpose. Her knowledge of English was slight, and not many Americans spoke German with any degree of proficiency, so it was going to be difficult holding any worthwhile conversation. Perhaps she could find out by asking other Germans. If Russians really had been here the day before, other people would have seen them and maybe know something.

The American headquarters was like a kicked-over beehive. Men were almost running to carry papers and furniture to trucks parked in front of the building. The flag with its stars and stripes still flew from the flagpole though, so perhaps they were not leaving. A number of city folk stood around watching, and Elisabet joined the crowd, listening to murmured conversations. Nobody seemed to know anything, though rumours abounded, some of which did, indeed, involve the Russians.

"I heard there is going to be another war," said one man. "The West against the Soviets."

"If that's so," said another, "Then the Reich will fight alongside the Americans."

319

"How?" asked a third, bitterness colouring his voice. "Our soldiers have been locked in concentration camps."

"They're releasing them though. I saw some just the other day."

"I saw them too, and a fine sight they were – missing limbs, bandaged wounds, emaciated bodies and with ragged clothing. They're not going to be fighting anyone soon."

"So the Americans will fight alone?"

"I don't think there's going to be any fighting. The Americans and the Soviets are allies. All that's going to happen is we Germans getting our arses kicked again."

Elisabet moved away, seeking someone who might know anything more definite.

"What is happening?" asked an old woman.

"The Americans are moving out," said a man with one arm. "They are handing over government to the Reich again."

"So who will be in charge?"

"As before. There are enough National Socialists left to take charge."

Elisabet did not believe this scenario either, so she moved on, looking for someone who would really know the truth. She spotted one man through the crowd, a man in khaki sporting the insignia of a major. Pushing through the crowd to where American soldiers formed a cordon, she called out.

"Major Berendson."

Berendson turned and scanned the crowd. He recognised Elisabet and told the guards to let her through. "What are you doing here, Frau Daeker? Is your son in trouble again?"

"No, Major. I heard rumours, and now I see that something is happening. Can you..."

"What rumours?"

"That America is leaving and the Soviets are coming."

Berendson regarded Elisabet coolly. "I really can't comment on that."

"Why would such a thing happen?"

The major looked around the scene of activity in front of the American headquarters, and at the gathering crowd of Germans. "If something like that ever happened," he said, "It would be because Roosevelt and Stalin had agreed on their spheres of influence before the war ended. If the Soviets hold territory that should belong to America, then they would have to withdraw and let us take over. Or vice versa," he added.

"I see." Elisabet knew the talk of Soviet withdrawal was just a fiction told to illustrate a point, but played along with the major. "If America was to take over Soviet held territory, when might such a thing happen?"

"Soon."

"A week? A month?"

"You ask a lot of questions, Frau Daeker, and I'm not at liberty to answer you. I understand you had some unfortunate dealings with the Soviet authorities in the past and are reluctant to renew your acquaintance. If I were you, I'd take my family and move away quickly and quietly."

"How far?"

"A long way."

"Thank you, Major Berendson."

Elisabet returned to the crowd and ignored questions thrown at her by people who had seen her talking to the American officer. She said only that the officer had wanted to talk to her young son, and this seemed to satisfy their curiosity.

Rumours had spread and the streets were crowded with people out and about, creating disturbances, anxious about the future. Elisabet hurried back to the shelter where her sons were waiting, their rucksacks packed and ready.

"We have to leave immediately," Elisabet told them.

"The Russians are coming?" Helmut asked.

"Are we still going to the house with the chickens?" Werner asked.

"Yes, and yes," Elisabet replied. "But we aren't staying. We'll collect Geli and perhaps the old man and woman and head west together."

Hanna and Wilhelm Zweig refused to leave, however.

"This is our home," they explained. "We've lived in Magdeburg all our lives and we don't want to leave now."

"But the Russians are coming."

"I doubt that," Wilhelm said. "You must have misunderstood the American. They won't give up territory they've conquered. Americans may be crass and uncultured, but we can live with them. You'll see, things will settle down quickly and life will go on as before."

"Let us take Geli with us, at least."

"No, no, no," Hanna protested. "She has been through enough. She will be safe here. You too, if we can persuade you to stay."

Elisabet shook her head. "Thank you, but I want to get my boys as far west as possible, as quickly as possible."

"Eat with us before you go. I have made a chicken stew knowing you would be coming."

They stayed and ate as Elisabet knew it might be their last decent meal for a while. There was no telling how far west the Russians would advance and they had to travel swiftly. She made sure all the boys cleaned up their plates and ate everything that was offered them. Elisabet felt bad that they were eating so much as hard times were coming for the old couple and Geli. That was hard too, leaving Geli, but even though the city would soon be under Soviet control, the old woman was probably right – she would be safer with her family than on the road again, living rough. The girl needed time to heal emotionally.

They said their goodbyes, and Geli clung to Elisabet, weeping softly. She parted from her though, when Hanna put her arm around the young woman. Wilhelm gave them a bag of fresh vegetables and a box of matches, while Helmut took something from Werner's little rucksack and slipped it quietly to the old man. Elisabet could not see what it was and did not like to ask.

Out on the road again, Elisabet led them as fast as they could manage toward the outskirts of the city. They made good time, though evidently a number of people had given some credence to the rumours, for there was a steady stream of people fleeing in the same direction. A few motor cars swept past, driven by people still well off and who could afford petrol. There were horse-drawn carts too, and people pushing wheel barrows and prams or pulling trolleys. Others were on foot, carrying suitcases, rucksacks on their backs, or clutching bundles of possessions wrapped in sheets or blankets. Elisabet looked at her

323

children, noting how unencumbered they were except for their bulging rucksacks.

"What's in them?" she asked Helmut. "I didn't think we had much. I hope you haven't cluttered them with unnecessary things."

"Just food and a few other things, Mutti," Helmut said.

"I saw you give the old man something."

"A little gift because he was kind. He is looking after Geli too."

"What did you give him?"

"Five packs of cigarettes."

"What?" Elisabet stopped and stared at her eldest son. The other children stopped too and looked at their mother, worried that something was wrong.

"That's...that's a huge gift. You could buy kilos of meat for that."

Helmut shrugged. "I have more."

"This is what you stole from the American store?"

"Not steal exactly, Mutti. The Americans are rich and we are poor. It seems only fair they should help us."

"What else have you got?"

"A couple of cartons of cigarettes, a dozen cans of meat, a bottle of brandy."

"Mein Gott," Elisabet muttered. She looked around to make sure they were not observed. "Those are riches indeed. Keep them well hidden."

Getting clear of Magdeburg and its outlying suburbs took them the rest of that day and two others. The first night, they camped in a derelict house, scrounging in the overgrown garden for edibles. They found some carrots gone to seed and a few sprouting potatoes, but combined with two tins of meat they provided a nourishing and tasty meal.

324

The second night found them in a bomb crater, where a slab of concrete from the exploded building head fallen horizontally across the rubble, forming a shelter with a sloping roof. The dry dust underneath showed signs of recent habitation, but nobody was there to claim it. They built a small fire and roasted some of the vegetables from the derelict garden, and another two tins of meat. They were thirsty, but Helmut and Kurt found a puddle of relatively clean water left over from a rain shower and scooped it into old tin cans to bring back to the family.

On the third day they cleared the city and sheltered in a copse of trees a little way off the road that led to Braunschweig. Elisabet had heard that Hannover and Braunschweig were in British hands, though she knew that could change. If portions of American-held Germany were being handed over to the Soviets, then maybe the British would also give up their conquests. At the moment, though, she could not think of a better destination.

They heard the roaring of engines in the night and saw the roads lit by headlights and wondered if it was the Russian advance. The morning light confirmed it, as fresh columns of Soviet trucks rattled along the roads, heading west. Refugees from Magdeburg still cluttered the roads but everywhere they saw the devastation of ruined carts and abandoned automobiles where the Russian convoys had run them off the road. They found bodies too, men and women, and fresh evidence of rape, so Elisabet led her family back into the countryside, taking a more south-westerly route.

That night they found a barn to shelter in. The farmer, though almost destitute from the depredations of the American troops that had stripped his farm of its livestock and grain, offered them what hospitality he could and Elisabet repaid his kindness with a pack of cigarettes. Then he produced clothing that had belonged to his sons, and Elisabet selected old but warm shirts, jerseys and pants for her boys to replace the threadbare clothing and worn shoes that had kept out the worst of the winter weather. The bottle of brandy paid for those.

"Go south," was the farmer's advice. "The Russians will be occupying the cities and towns, so you need to stick to the countryside."

"I was thinking that," Elisabet said. "There's forest near here, isn't there?"

The farmer nodded. "The Harz – mountains and forest. They can be inhospitable though, if you're a city person."

"I was raised on a farm in Ostpreussen. I know my way around woods, particularly this time of year."

They continued southwest across farmland and through stretches of woodland. When they came to roads, they sheltered behind hedges and stone walls until there was nobody in sight, and then hurried across to shelter on the other side. Despite the presence of Soviet troops, the local farming population, and hundreds of refugees still drifting westward, few people saw them and none came close enough to accost them. They sheltered in barns or in densely-leaved copses, and the weather remained clement, if still cool at night. Sometimes they risked a fire, other times they made do without and ate their food cold or raw.

At night, when the darkness of an unfamiliar place would close around them, they would sing, if they were in an area where they thought no one would overhear them. Elisabet led them in every song they could remember, whether nursery rhymes, folk songs, Christmas carols and church hymns. The only thing they drew the line at were the marching songs or the rousing Hitlerjugend verses they were used to hearing at every festival or march down the streets of Königsberg.

On their journey to the Harz, Helmut took it upon himself to scout ahead, seeking out easy routes for his young brothers and always looking for the chance to liberate useful items from the countryside. He found a wire fence and removed a section, coiling it up and secreting it in his rucksack against some unspecified future need, some wooden palings and acquired them to use as fuel.

Kurt, too, became more independent, taking his cue from his older brother, though he never liked to be far from his family. His progress through the countryside was quieter, more circumspect, preferring to observe from cover before committing himself to action. He saw wildlife this way, and sometimes entertained his young brothers, Joachim especially, with stories of what he had seen.

"I saw a squirrel; head down on an oak tree trunk, staring at the bush I was hiding in, so I thought he must have seen me. Then he came down to the ground and searched through the fallen leaves until he found an acorn. He just sat there and ate it."

"I would have chucked a rock at it," Helmut claimed. "Then we could have cooked and eaten it."

"It was too nice," Kurt said. "It had a lovely ginger tail."

"I think that's a good story," Werner said. "Tell us another one."

The younger children stayed close to their mother, though their temperaments and attitudes were very

327

different. Werner marched along with his little ruck-rucksack on his back, and if they found a pinecone or a coloured stone, he would insist that someone add it to his load. Then in the evenings he would take them out and make up stories about them, augmenting Kurt's tales.

Günter was quieter, perhaps because he suffered from ill health. Chills settled on his chest at the slightest pretext and he often snuffled from a head cold. Elisabet doctored him as best she could from the herbs and remedies at her disposal – willow bark tea, flavoured with a little sugar if they had it, a soothing draught of elderberry flower or peppermint tasting pennyroyal, refreshing wild raspberry leaves steeped in water.

Joachim was irrepressible, a lively two year old who always found some pretext for playing if he had the strength – chasing butterflies, turning over stones and laughing delightedly at the things that scurried out from underneath them, or watching open-mouthed as swallows skimmed the still waters of a pond looking for insects. Other times he carried a stick and poked everything with it, looking for a reaction, or collected small stones and played with them in the evenings, moving them about in patterns as he listened to his older brothers tell stories.

Elisabet walked quietly among them, watching for danger, guiding the younger boys and telling them stories to keep their spirits up. The woods and fields were full of food if you knew where to look, and she would find sorrel, nettle and watercress leaves, and flowers of syringa, elderberry and wild rose. Once they came across a field of sunflowers, old and broken, a remnant from a crop neglected in the sweep of war. They harvested handfuls of old seed and spent hours shelling them at night, hungrily eating the oily kernels. Another time they found a ruined cottage, with nasturtiums rampant over the piles of stone. Elisabet showed them how the flowers had a delicate taste, sweet from the nectar but with a mild peppery aftertaste. The round leaves and juicy stems made a delicious salad, pungent and strong, while the freshly formed seeds were so hot they brought tears to their eyes.

Once or twice they stopped at an out-of-the-way farm and were rewarded with a little food and a warm barn to sleep in. The farmers would tell Elisabet the latest news and warn her of conditions in the towns.

"Don't go near the towns unless you have to. The Russians are arresting anyone who is not a local, rounding up the refugees and deporting them back to the east."

And so they came by degrees to the foothills of the Harz Mountains. They passed near the town of Quedlinburg at night, slipping over busy roads and skirting houses and farms in the dark of the moon and by the time the first slivers of the new moon were showing on the eleventh or twelfth of July, they had reached the relative safety of the forests. There were still many people about, both locals and drifts of refugees, or displaced persons as they now were called, but fewer as they went deeper into the Harz. Most people kept to the roads and the towns scavenging for food scraps and ran the risk of being herded into concentration camps or starved by the Soviet authorities. Elisabet was determined to avoid this fate, and was confident that she could lead her family through the mountains to safety, wherever that might lie.

She followed the Bode River upstream, paralleling its tumbling course, keeping close to the water and its life where they could, bypassing the gorges and rejoining the river further up, camping on the flatter reaches. A bridge let them cross to the northern side. They found tiny crayfish in the still pools or under rocks and added them to their menu. Their stores of stolen food had long since been eaten and though they had traded cigarettes for food along the way, they still had a full carton left. There were few people in the wilds of the Harz to trade with though, so they were thrown on their own resources, having to find food and shelter.

It rained for three whole days, and though the canopy of the forest ameliorated the downpour, and they huddled under a fallen tree, sufficient water leaked through the foliage to saturate them and their clothing. By the time the clouds cleared and the warmth of the summer sun broke through, they were shivering and hungry. Elisabet led them to the rain-swollen river and found a patch of boulders beyond the reach of the swirling muddy waters. They stripped off their wet clothing; the boys down to bare skin though their teeth were chattering, and spread their garments on the sun-stroked stones to dry. The surrounding forest blocked the breeze, so the boulders heated up and the cold that gripped their thin limbs slowly eased.

With the easement of their cold, hunger became dominant, so Elisabet left the boys dozing in the sunlight and went searching the riparian forest for sustenance. She moved quietly, enjoying the sounds of the birds, the soft twitterings of finches, the occasional caw of rooks and the distant staccato drumming of a woodpecker.

"At least he is finding something to eat," she murmured.

She found a steep-banked stream bed leading into the river, a tiny freshet of crystal clear water cascading over its moss-lined gullet, and followed it up, pushing aside the burgeoning plants. In sun-spangled arenas where the intermittent canopy let through beams of golden light, she found wild strawberries, tiny rubies gleaming among the green leaves. She bit into one, closing her eyes and letting the rich flavour transport her back in memory to her childhood, where she had partaken of similar treasures in the woods around Königsberg. After a few moments she opened her eyes and shook herself, and set about gathering every fruit she could find, placing them carefully in her shawl.

She moved on into more open areas where she found blackberries, though only a few of the swelling fruit were ripe. Elisabet picked what she could find, scratching her bare skin in the process. A grassy field in the midst of the forest where a woodcutter long ago had felled trees for building and fuel, yielded mushrooms and a large round puffball. She broke the puffball open and was rewarded with an interior of solid white flesh, the brown spores not having yet formed. An aroma of mushroom drifted up from it and she wished she had a skillet and butter to cook it. Her mouth watered with the memory of similar feasts.

On the way back to the river she stumbled upon a stand of sweet-smelling plants with finely divided leaves and umbels of pale yellow-green flowers. Elisabet looked at it carefully – she knew there was a

331

similar plant that was poisonous – examining the stems for any hint of the purple streaks or spots that were found on the hemlock plant. There were none, so she crushed a leaf and sniffed. Hemlock has a rank, unpleasant odour whereas this plant's leaves yielded only the sweet aroma of angelica. She broke off some of the younger leaves with their long stems and added them to her cache of food. The leaves had a liquorice flavour that would please the children and the stems were reminiscent of celery.

She heard the boys before she broke through the vegetation onto the riverbank. Helmut, Kurt and Werner were throwing rocks into the water, screaming with excitement, while Günter dozed, huddled up near a large rock, on which Joachim sat, watching his older brothers. When Elisabet stepped out onto the boulders with her shawl of food, Helmut looked over and yelled to her, beckoning.

"Come quickly, Mutti. There's a fish."

Elisabet placed her shawl down carefully and ran over to where the boys were still lobbing rocks into the water. The floodwaters had washed a small fish, perhaps the length of her forearm, into a pool and it was flicking this way and that, looking for an escape while missiles rained down on it. Taking in the situation, Elisabet directed Kurt to block the only exit to the pool with a few large rocks and then got the boys to link hands with her and wade into the pool, slowly driving it into the shallows. After two or three abortive attempts, it flashed the wrong way and found itself flapping furiously, half out of the water. Elisabet leaped forward, and rather than trying to grasp the slippery silvery body, flipped the fish into the air so it landed on dry land. Helmut yelled and smashed a rock down on its head; it gave a spasm and lay still.

The boys erupted into cries of joy and victory and crowded round to look at their prize. Even Günter roused himself to come and look, though he coughed and shivered so much, Elisabet wrapped him back up in his dry clothes and laid him down. Joachim had found her shawl and his lips were already stained with wild strawberry juice.

"We need a fire, Helmut. Kurt, Werner, find some dry twigs from the forest. Let's have a fish supper."

Kapitel Achtzehn (18)

Günter was sick again. Of all her five children, her middle child had always been the most delicate. If a cold was going round at school or a childhood illness struck among their friends and relatives, all the children caught it, but only Günter was sick enough to require bed rest and medicine. The older boys shook off illness as a dog shakes off water, and Werner fought against it, refusing to give in. They all had scratches and bruises, and for the last month or so had suffered from insect bites. Elisabet put it down to the warmer weather bringing out biting insects, though they targeted areas covered by clothing. Fleas were likely, and lice, so they often scratched as they walked, and searched for the insects in the evening, crushing them between fingernails when they found them.

Now, in the Harz Mountains, Günter lay in his bed and hacked and coughed, developed a fever and cried with the pain. He had always been like that, but now he was worse. They were all in a weakened state after months of stress and deprivation, on the borderline of starvation and suffering from cold and damp. It was no wonder that Günter was ill again, but Elisabet was limited in what she could do.

She made willow bark tea, making it more palatable with an infusion of liquorice-tasting angelica leaves, but though that eased his fever temporarily and lessened some of his pain, it did not cure him. His cough remained, deep chest-shuddering coughs that left him red faced and gasping for breath, and Elisabet thought he had bronchitis. What she was most afraid of was it turning to pneumonia. He needed proper medicine, and a town was the only place to find that. Elisabet would either have to take them all down into the town, or leave them here and make a quick foray herself. She hated the thought of leaving them alone, but Günter could not walk and she could not hope to carry him all that way.

"Helmut, I am leaving you in charge, and either you or Kurt is to stay with Günter at all times. If you go off to gather wood or get water, Werner is to go with you. Never go anywhere alone, and never leave Günter alone. Joachim is to remain here always. Is that clear?"

"Go wiff you, Mutti?" Joachim asked. He burst into tears when his mother told him he had to stay.

"The town of Blankenburg is north of here, I'd estimate ten or fifteen kilometres. That should only take me three hours there, three back and a couple of hours to find medicine. That means I should be back before dark." Elisabet took Helmut aside and told him there was a possibility she might be delayed. "I can't move as fast as I once could," she said, laying a hand on her swelling belly. "If I'm gone longer, you'll look after your brothers?"

"I promise, Mutti."

Elisabet left mid-morning, cheerily waving goodbye though inside she was crying at the thought of having to leave her babies. Joachim was the biggest wrench as he had cried so piteously when she left, but he was small and would slow her down drastically. Her forced march out of the hills proved harder than she anticipated. She had slimmed right down with the constant motion of their flight across country and near-starvation diet, and her limbs shook in response to her efforts. Her pregnancy slowed her also, and she had to take rests when she felt light-headed. The distance to the town was greater than she thought, and the cut-over scrub in the foothills denser than she had foreseen.

It was mid-afternoon before she came in sight of Blankenburg and she realised she could not hope to get back before the next day. Elisabet almost cried out in her grief and worry for all her children, but for sick Günter in particular. Having come so far, though, she had no choice but to continue. The survival of her children depended on her.

∗   ∗   ∗

My father had displayed his liberal background when I had announced myself pregnant with Helmut, and later with Kurt, so I thought he would be pleased at the prospect of his wayward daughter finally getting married. Rudolph, after sounding me out on the subject, had wanted to formally ask my father for my hand in marriage, but I persuaded him to wait until after I had broached the idea to my father.

My father's reaction was not what I expected.

"Have you taken leave of your senses, Elisabet?"

"What do you mean, Vati?" I said, quite bewildered. "You've met him. He has a good job and he is prepared to take on my children as well. The boys love him and..."

"He is a Party member."

"Yes, but what...?"

"You know what they stand for."

I thought for a moment about what my father must be feeling. He was a communist – as was I for that matter – and knew that our beliefs were diametrically opposed. Nazis were cruel, bigoted and fanatical for the most part. Still, I also knew Rudolph Daeker was a good man.

"He is a Party member, Vati, I know, but he is not a Nazi."

336

"That is nonsense. Party members are Nazis, you cannot separate the two."

"Nevertheless," I said. I thought a bit more, quashing my emotions. "Vati, he joined ten years ago when it was all new and exciting, before he really knew what it was all about. He says he joined up with his friends at the university in patriotic fervour. You know how Herr Hitler held out the possibility of Germany becoming great again. It appealed to many people. Since then, some of his friends have risen in the Party ranks – the Gauleiter is one of them – and he is a member now because he cannot resign."

"You can always renounce something you don't believe in," my father grumbled. "Does he have no conscience?"

"That is not fair. You know what happens to people who resign from the Party. He would disappear into Dachau and probably die there. As for having no conscience, he is a Supervisory Gardener in the Botanic Gardens and he uses his position and contacts to help people get work." I lowered my voice and glanced round automatically, though we were alone in our living room. Already, Germans had learnt to guard their speech. "He has even helped Jews."

"Does he know who Kurt's father is?"

"No. I don't think it's relevant."

My father folded up his newspaper and sat lost in thought. The only sign of inner agitation was the tapping of his foot on the carpeted floor. At last, he looked at me.

"Do you love him, Elisabet?"

"Yes."

"And you are sure of his love?"

"Yes."

He sighed. "Then I suppose I must give my permission, though you are over twenty-one and do not strictly need it." He held up a hand to contain my sudden joy. "Let me speak to your mother before you announce it to the world."

We married in April, almost a year to the day from when I first saw him designing the floral tribute to the Führer. As a Party member in good standing, there were several uniformed officials in the wedding party, resplendent in brown and black with gleaming insignia, and even the Gauleiter put in a brief appearance to wish us well. My father's family attended, and managed to hide their apprehension and consternation well, and the day passed without incident.

I became Frau Daeker, and my new husband took me on a honeymoon to Berlin. We took the train, passing through checkpoints in the Polnischer Korridor. Rudi told me that one day soon, Ostpreussen would be physically reunited with Grossdeutschland, and in that he was right, though it took a war to achieve it. In our great capital city, we toured the historic streets and restaurants, took in the museums and parks, marvelled at the Reichstag still in ruins after the fire years before, the glorious Unter den Linden leading to the magnificent Brandenburger Tor, and the colossal Siegessäule or Victory Column in the Königsplatz – and started my third child.

Günter came early, in the dead of winter, and his birth was not an easy one. He was a sickly child, but I loved him immediately, and my Rudi doted on him, though he required a lot of attention and medical care in his first year of life. Nor did my husband neglect his older adopted children, for he made them toys, read to them, played with them, and was as good a

338

father as one could wish for. Two years after we got married, I was with child again, but Rudi was not at Werner's birth, for war had broken out the year before and he was serving with a Wehrmacht unit in Poland.

This was the only instance in which Rudi used his influence selfishly, and even then it benefitted his wife and children more. He could not escape conscription as Germany swung onto a war footing, but being a Party member, he could influence where he was sent. The war in Poland was over in weeks and the attention turned to Western Europe. Troops were moved from Poland to France, but Rudi remained in one of the units based in Königsberg. His duties carried him throughout Poland, more in a policing role than a soldierly one, and he was seldom in any real danger. He was due home for Christmas, but Werner could not wait. When Rudi came home he found his latest little soldier and announced himself content.

Four children I had, four boys, and all so very different – Helmut headstrong and boisterous, Kurt sensitive and loving, Günter quiet and sickly, Werner serious and determined. I loved them all equally, in different ways, and like any mother suffered with them for every single cut, scrape, bruise or illness that came their way. I suffered most with Günter, but I did not begrudge it.

*   *   *

Blankenburg was a large town, set around and on low forested hills. The streets and buildings were largely undamaged by the passage of the war, though recent occupation by Soviet forces was in evidence. Squads patrolled the streets, though few people were bothered by their presence. Elisabet bent her head, avoided eye contact, and hurried into the town, scan-scanning name plates on the houses for evidence of a doctor. In the end, in the early evening, she had to ask, and was directed to a neat house with a linden tree shading the front door.

She knocked on the oaken door and after a few moments, the door swung open a few centimetres and an old woman peered out through the crack.

"Yes? What do you want?"

"Please. May I see the doctor?"

"The surgery is on Unterstrasse. Go there at nine tomorrow morning." The old woman started to close the door.

"Please, it is urgent. I cannot wait until tomorrow."

The old woman peered at Elisabet, her lips compressed and her eyes narrow and glittering with hostility. "What is so urgent you must disturb Herr Doktor at his home?"

"My child is very sick."

The old woman peered past Elisabet, looking down the steps to the street. "Where is he?"

"As I said, he is very sick."

"What is it, Greta?" called a voice from deep in the house.

"Nothing, Herr Doktor," said the old woman. "I'm telling someone to go to the surgery in the morning."

"Doctor, please see me tonight," Elisabet called out. "My son is very sick."

Greta closed the door firmly in Elisabet's face, cutting off her words. Behind the thick door, she could hear muted voices, so she waited and after a minute the door opened again, wider, and a portly man in neatly pressed trousers, white shirt, tie and waistcoat looked out at her. His gaze travelled over

Elisabet, faintly frowning as he took in her condition, and back to her face.

"You need to see a doctor, Frau?"

"Please. My son is very sick."

"Too sick to move?"

"Yes. We also live...far away. In the hills."

"From your accent, you are not local. Not from Blankenburg."

"No, Herr Doktor."

The doctor smiled. "You had better come in then. My housekeeper Greta is very protective of my privacy, but I think I can make an exception for you." He led Elisabet through the house to a room in the back set up as a small surgery. "I have my rooms in the Unterstrasse, but some of my patients come here after regular hours."

"Thank you for seeing me, Doktor...er?"

"Osterhagen. Doktor Theodor Osterhagen. And you are?"

"Elisabet Daeker."

"I see you are with child, Frau Daeker. May I examine you?"

"It was my sick child I came about."

"I understand, but it will do him no good if his mother sickens in the meantime. It will only take a few minutes."

Doktor Osterhagen called in his housekeeper while he examined Elisabet, probing gently with his fingertips and asking many questions.

"About five months, Frau Daeker?"

"A little more."

"You need to eat more. The baby will strip the fat and muscle from you unless you have a good diet."

"Easier said than done, Doktor. These are hard times."

"You have been on the road a long time?"

"Six months."

"Your husband is with you?"

"He died on the front two years ago."

Osterhagen nodded sagely and told Elisabet to fasten her clothing. Then he told Greta to leave and indicated a chair. "I don't need to ask where the baby came from. I have seen too many instances of our conquerors' arrogance and hate. If you had come to me sooner, I might have been able to help you."

Elisabet nodded. "I understand, but the child is innocent and I will give it a mother's love."

"You are a brave woman, Frau Daeker. Now, you have a sick boy?"

"Yes, my middle child Günter. He has bronchitis and I'm worried it might turn into pneumonia."

"You sound sure of your diagnosis. You have some medical training perhaps?"

"Nothing formal, Herr Doktor, but I have worked in hospitals."

"It would be better if I could examine the child myself, but I accept you cannot easily bring him in. Tell me his symptoms."

"The thing you notice most is his deep racking coughs and the thick mucus which is expelled. He has a fever, is listless, wheezes, and has a sore throat and runny nose."

Osterhagen nodded. "Chest pain? Shortness of breath?"

"Only after a coughing fit."

"It does indeed sound like bronchitis."

"Can you give me something for it?"

"Aspirin for the fever and pain, something to soothe his throat – honey, lemon and ginger perhaps.

342

Apart from that, keep him warm and rested and give him plenty to drink."

"Do you have penicillin? I can pay."

Osterhagen stared and then chuckled. "Where would I get that? This was never a rich practice and since the Russians arrived it has become even harder to get essential medical supplies, let alone new-fangled drugs."

"Sulpha drugs?"

"The same."

"Then I suppose I must do the best for him with my meagre resources."

"I can let you have aspirin. What else do you need?"

Elisabet laughed wryly. "What don't I need? You mentioned honey, lemon and ginger. A blanket to keep him warm, something to keep the rain off him, proper food, matches..." She shook her head. "The list is endless."

"I don't mean to sound venal, but you said you could pay?"

"I have cigarettes."

"Really? Russian ones, I suppose."

"American."

"Excellent. You have more than one or two, I hope." Osterhagen coughed and looked away. "I'm sorry. I don't want to appear avaricious, but American cigarettes are like gold. I can buy things the surgery needs with a pack or two..."

"Tell me what you can supply, Herr Doktor, and tell me how much you charge, and I'll see whether I can pay."

Osterhagen thought for a few moments. "Twenty aspirin, one lemon, a small jar of honey, a loaf of bread, a small cheese, two...no, three kilos of

343

potatoes, and a blanket." He considered their worth and what he thought the woman might be able to af- afford. "The cost is a pack of cigarettes."

"Accepted," Elisabet said, striving to keep the relief off her face. "Do you have anything to keep him away from the damp ground? Something waterproof?"

"I have a waxed canvas groundsheet. One more pack. I even have a small tent I used to use before the war when I hiked in the Harz. It would sleep two adults, three if you did not mind a squeeze. That is worth...another two packs?"

"Four in all? I accept. Do you have any shoes? Needle and thread? Clothing?"

"It sounds like you need everything, Frau Daeker. Sit here. I will have Greta prepare you a simple meal while I collect the things together."

Greta grumbled but put together a simple but nutritious hot meal of sausage, potatoes and sauerkraut, together with a mug of sweet ersatz coffee. Elisabet felt a bit guilty eating the delicious fare while her children went hungry, but reasoned that she needed to keep strong for them. When she finished, the doctor still had not returned, so she got up and wandered round the room, looking at the titles of the books in the bookcase, examining the charts on his walls.

Osterhagen returned at last, bearing a sizeable knapsack. He hoisted it onto the table and removed its contents. "All the food we agreed upon and I've added a kilo of sausages, a box of matches and a candle. A small bottle of aspirin, two lemons, needle and thread, an old pair of Greta's shoes which may fit you and one of her jerseys. The tent and groundsheet, one blanket. If you want, I'll add the knapsack itself

344

and another blanket for another pack of cigarettes – five packs in all. Deal?"

"Deal." Elisabet concealed her bag and carefully separated out five packs of the cigarettes from the carton. She handed them to Osterhagen with a warm 'thank you'. "Oh, one other thing, Herr Doktor. I don't suppose you have a spare cooking pot and perhaps a cup?"

The doctor produced the extra blanket, a camping pan and two tin mugs, waving away Elisabet's offer of further payment. "Also a newspaper." He smiled. "There is no good news, I'm afraid, but paper has many uses."

"You are generous, Herr Doktor. My thanks...and those of my children."

"You have paid for the items, Frau Daeker, and besides, I have no real use for my old camping things." Osterhagen looked through the window at the gathering dusk. "Can you make it back to your children before nightfall? You are welcome to stay in my living room overnight and leave in the morning."

"Once more, you are generous, Herr Doktor, but if I hurry, I can reach the foothills by nightfall. Then I am that much closer to my children."

"Your other children are healthy?"

"For the most part, though we suffer the usual afflictions of rough living. Coughs and colds, and rashes."

"What types of rashes?"

Elisabet shrugged. "From dirty clothes, insects."

"Fleas?"

"From time to time. Lice also."

"I'll give you a bar of soap too. Try and find new clothes."

345

Elisabet set off through the darkening streets with her knapsack on her back. The weight of it tired her rapidly, but the thought of her children quickened her pace and she made it to the outskirts of the town, where the houses were further apart and the darkness nearly complete, before a guttural voice stopped her.

"Wohin gehen sie, Frau? Where are you going?"

Elisabet's heart leapt as she detected a Russian accent. She stopped as a torch beam stabbed out and half blinded her.

"I...I am going home."

"Where do you live? Don't you know there is a curfew?"

She could see the shapes of at least three men, dressed in Soviet uniform and bearing rifles. Their voices were cautious, but as yet they displayed neither anger nor suspicion.

"I am sorry, sir. I did not know there was a curfew. I am just passing through."

"Show me your papers."

Elisabet passed them across and the torch beam dipped as the soldier scanned them. "You are a long way from home," he said. "Why are you here?"

"I have family in...in Hannover."

"Hannover is in British sector. You will not be able to go there. Königsberg is in Soviet sector. You belong there."

"Yes sir. Thank you sir."

The soldier handed back her papers, and the torch beam slid over her body and knapsack. "What in bag?"

"A tent, blankets, a little food."

"Show me."

Elisabet squatted beside her knapsack and undid the straps. She took out the tent and one blanket, and

346

then dug the bread out, hoping he would not dig deeper. One of the soldiers lifted the loaf and sniffed it before ripping off a chunk with his teeth, chewing noisily.

"Good, but I prefer rye." He dropped it onto the blanket. "All right. Stand up, Frau."

The soldiers regarded Elisabet with interest by the light of the torch and made comments as if she was not there, or could not understand them.

"She is thin but still pretty."

"Da, but would you want her? Give me a woman with flesh on her bones."

"What about you, Dmitri? You want her?"

"Thinking about it."

The man called Dmitri grinned and ran his hands over Elisabet's dress. "Shit, she's pregnant."

"That shouldn't stop you," another man laughed. The torch beam settled on Elisabet's belly.

"Are you pregnant, Frau?"

"Yes."

"Your husband?"

Elisabet said nothing.

"No? Who then – a lover? No? A Russian?"

Elisabet looked away and the men laughed.

"Bravo," Dmitri cried. "We conquer German men with our guns and German women with our pricks." The soldiers clapped each other on the back, laughing. "Go then, Frau, and look after your evidence of Soviet-German solidarity."

The Russian soldiers left her, and Elisabet hurriedly repacked her knapsack and almost ran until she was clear of the town and into the forest. When she could no longer see the path, she stepped off it into an alder thicket, spread the groundsheet, wrapped herself in a blanket, and fell asleep. She slept

347

as though dead, exhausted both by exertion and expe-experience, waking at first light.

She ate a mouthful of bread and dipped her finger in the honey jar, sucking until every trace of sweetness had gone. The sugar energised her and she shouldered her knapsack and set off up into the hills, guided by the distant peaks. Before long, weariness set in. The slope was steeper than she remembered, the undergrowth denser, the knapsack heavier than she could easily manage, and she worried incessantly that her children were in trouble.

"I'm coming, meine lieben kleinen," she murmured.

The forest looked different approaching it from this direction, but she pushed on, keeping her course by the direction of the sun as it moved across the morning sky. She knew that if she kept going she would find the Bode River, and then she could just follow it until she reached the camp.

It was midday before she heard the sound of rushing water and burst through the intervening tangle of trees onto the boulder-strewn river bed. She thought the surrounding landscape was familiar, so turned upstream and worked her way along the bank, looking for traces of her family's passage. Hours passed, and Elisabet became more worried, afraid now that she had entered the river bed above the camp and was now moving away from it. Then she heard boyish laughter and her heart leapt within her. She quickened her pace.

Four boys were sitting in a circle on the leafy loam of the forest floor within sight of the river, playing with something that lay between them. Every so often one would poke with a short stick and there would be another peal of laughter. Elisabet saw Günter was

348

missing, and looked around in growing alarm until she saw him propped against a beech tree bole, his pale face turned toward his brothers.

"Boys," Elisabet murmured.

Heads turned and all four boys leapt to their feet and ran to her, hugging and uttering cries of joy. Günter smiled and raised one hand weakly, while Joachim burst into tears.

Suddenly, Helmut cried, "He'll get away," and ran back to where they had been sitting.

Elisabet saw that a hedgehog had uncurled itself and was shuffling towards the cover of the bushes. Helmut, and then Werner, headed it off with sticks and it curled up again.

"You can eat them, can't you, Mutti?" Helmut asked.

Elisabet did not answer, but ran over to her sick child and shucked off the knapsack, dropping to her knees beside him. She ran her gaze over his pale face and haggard look, her hand caressing his fevered forehead.

"I have something that will help you," she murmured. She unpacked the knapsack and started issuing rapid orders to Helmut to build a fire, to Kurt to fetch water from the river, to Werner to spread the groundsheet so Günter could sit on it, and even Joachim to help unfold a blanket.

An hour passed and Günter slept, dosed with aspirin, throat eased with honey and lemon drink, while the other boys tucked into a decent meal of sausages spitted on sticks, boiled potatoes, and bread and cheese.

"In answer to your question, Helmut," Elisabet said. "Yes, you can eat hedgehog, but we'll have to catch another one. Yours has escaped."

Kapitel Neunzehn (19)

They had stayed in their camp by the Bode River, caring for Günter and easing him back toward health. He had responded to the aspirin, warmth, rest and soothing drinks and after a week was up to moving on. By then they had exhausted the natural food of the area, and Elisabet was still keen to move them westward, out of the Soviet zone. They had come to a little lake and worked their way around the steep northern shore, scrambling over loose stones and clinging to stunted shrubs until they attained a sunny slope and a small level space a few metres from the edge of the forest.

A series of explosions woke them. For several minutes they lay crammed in their little tent, sharing warmth and the comfort of proximity with much-loved family members, before Kurt asked the question in all their minds.

"Has the war come again?"

"I don't think so," Elisabet said. "The explosions are sporadic and I don't hear any gunfire."

"What then?" Helmut asked.

"Thunder?" Günter croaked.

"Not that." Elisabet exited the tent and stood outside in the scrub and looked down the long slope toward the tiny lake formed by a recent rock slide across the river.

The greenish waters of the lake surface erupted upward in a spray of white foam, and a muffled 'crump' reached her ears. She stared down at the water from her vantage point a hundred metres above, wondering what was happening. Waves spread outward, sloshing on the shore, and she heard laughter and shouts below her. Cautioning the children to remain by the tent, she eased herself down the slope. Helmut went with her, and ignored her pleas to go back.

"Kurt can look after the babies. I'm coming with you."

Elisabet shrugged, though secretly she was glad of the company. Together, they crept down the hill until they were ensconced in the woods a mere twenty metres above the boulder-strewn lake edge. They peered through the vegetation, taking care not to sway the branches or loosen stones underfoot. Another few metres further down and they could see what was happening.

Moving along the water's edge were several men, talking in Russian. As they watched, one of them took a rounded object from his belt and lobbed it into the water. It fell with a splash twenty metres out and for a few moments nothing happened. Then the lake surface lifted in a welter of white water and a muffled thud shivered the leaves in the bushes. As the water subsided, pale things drifted in the water and the men waded out to pick them up, holding them aloft and shouting delightedly.

"Fish," Helmut said in surprise.

"Stunned or killed by the grenade, I should think."

The men left, laden with fish, and when silence reigned again along the shore, they descended to the water's edge, to where little waves slapped the boulders, and found that the Russians' success had outstripped their ability to carry away the fruits of their labours. Bobbing in the muddy water were another dozen fish, including two or three sizeable trout. Helmut waded out and used a stick to draw the fish in closer.

Elisabet gutted the fish with the edge of an old tin can and washed them in the clear lake water, before threading them together through gaping mouth and gills with plaited grass stalks. Helmut proudly carried them up to the waiting children and boasted of his hunting prowess. His brothers eyed the catch enviously and vowed that they too would become successful hunters. Elisabet smiled and said nothing, but then moved their camp along the dammed river for at least a kilometre, past the limits of the temporary lake, to where a small stream tumbled down the steep sides of the Schieferberg and debouched into the placid waters of this section of the river. They set up camp under the cover of the trees and foraged for food along the water's edge.

They cooked the fish whole, charring the skin in the embers of the fire and picking carefully at the steaming white meat with their fingers, threading out and discarding the bones. The sweet flesh contrasted nicely with the sharp tang of sorrel and the bite of watercress, and they all pronounced themselves content.

The river got smaller as they ascended further into the Harz and soon became little more than a rushing mountain stream. The bed became choked with boulders and vegetation, and when it burst through a culvert under a road, Elisabet decided they must use the new route provided.

The population of the Harz could hardly let themselves be affected by the presence of their Soviet overlords, as they still faced the daily problems of earning a living. The mountain roads had few people on them, and Elisabet instructed her children to remain close together and say nothing whenever they met others. Elisabet herself would nod a greeting or maybe exchange a comment about the weather, re-remaining vague about their origin and destination. Once they met a hunter taking meat down to the town of Blankenburg and exchanged some cigarettes for a chunk of wild boar.

A Soviet presence was absent in the little town of Elbingerode, and they managed to exchange a little more of their dwindling supply of tobacco for bread, sausage and cheese. They took the road west out of town with no interference or even interest from the locals. The Harz people were used to displaced persons from the east moving through their lands, and as long as they kept moving and did not become a burden on the community, they could not care less. It was in Elbingerode that Elisabet first heard where the boundary of the Soviet zone was now situated.

The road west divided, one branch heading north to Wernigerode, the other, less used, south and west toward Schierke. They took the latter, and after passing through this tiny hamlet, found themselves ascending an increasingly potholed and overgrown road onto the high ridges, switching back and forth as they climbed. A vista of mountain ranges covered with forest spread out before them with hardly a sign of human habitation. Behind them and to the north stood the high peaks of Brocken, Königsberg and Heinrichshöhe. Elisabet pointed them out.

Kurt looked up at the high mountains with a puzzled expression. "Is it really called Königsberg, Mutti?"

"Yes. It's really big and looks like a king might live there doesn't it?"

"Why is our town called Königsberg then?" Werner asked.

"There was a fort there named in honour of King Ottokar of Bohemia. The city grew up around the fort and was given the same name."

"How do you know so much, Mutti?" Kurt asked.

"I listened to my father and my teachers. They told me many things." Elisabet stood her children on a high point and pointed west into the setting sun, toward the Oberharz.

"There, meine kleinen Lieblinge. There is the West. That is where we must go."

The path down the mountain ridge into the vegetation-choked valley was arduous, but after a day or two they entered older forest where the canopy dimmed the light on the forest floor and precluded the undergrowth. They rested here a while, setting up camp and foraging for food. July had passed into August, and Elisabet's pregnancy was now well advanced. She found it harder to exert herself, but still managed to secure food for her family by using the knowledge she had of forests. The Harz Mountains in late summer provided wild fruits in abundance – nuts, mushrooms and, along the edges of breaks in the canopy, wild parsnip, cress, wild garlic, hogweed, lily bulbs and bracken rhizomes. These rhizomes needed special attention, and Elisabet spent hours grubbing up the plants and then grinding the underground stems and washing free the starch. A boggy area produced a few cranberries and a cluster of old cattail plants provided them with several kilos of nutritious rhizomes – stringy but tasty. A hazel tree yielded a fine crop of fallen nuts, and they gorged themselves on the oily kernels, feeling energy flow back into their starved bodies.

Protein was necessary too, and here the older boys excelled. Helmut was already a good shot with thrown rocks and Kurt was rapidly improving. While their mother and younger brothers scoured the forest for edible plants, the two older boys stocked up with rounded river pebbles and crept through the forest in search of small game. Hardly a day went by without one of them bringing down a squirrel or songbird, the wounded animal rapidly despatched with rock or stick. Sometimes they found a grass snake, which when cooked tasted something like chicken, and once they stumbled on an injured kite. It hissed at them and hopped away, its wing hanging useless. Helmut pursued it and with some difficulty beat the life out of it with a stick. Plucked and gutted, the raptor was roasted on the fire, but its flesh was rank and almost inedible.

Wild boar inhabited the forests of the Harz, and the boys occasionally caught a glimpse of dark forms plunging away from them through the undergrowth, sometimes with tiny streaked piglets at their heels, squealing in alarm. Helmut thirsted to catch a piglet and roast it.

"They're too fast," Kurt said.

"So we have to ambush one."

"How?"

Helmut shrugged. "I'm working on that. Are you with me?"

He cut himself a long straight sapling, whittling away the end to a point with the ragged edge of a tin can. Kurt watched him, frowning.

"How are you going to get close enough to spear one?"

"Wild boar like acorns. Remember we saw that herd rooting around under the big oak a few days ago? Well, they haven't eaten all the fallen acorns, so I think they'll be back. We just have to wait."

355

The next day, the boys found themselves a dense alder thicket near the oak and settled down to wait. As daylight started to fade from the forest, they stretched cramped limbs and dejectedly trod the path for home. The same thing happened the next two days, and Kurt started to worry that they were wasting their time.

"We could be hunting squirrels," he said. "Mutti's already wondering why we don't bring anything home."

"You go if you want. I can be a hero by myself. I don't need you."

Kurt stayed, yearning for hero status. Another day passed uneventfully, but as the forest passed into shadow that evening, they heard several somethings approaching through the leaf litter, hooves treading softly, punctuated by muffled grunts and squeaks.

"They're here," Helmut breathed. "Be quiet and wait for my signal."

A boar broke cover and stood at the edge of the clearing snuffing the air, ears pricked forward. After a few minutes it moved forward, its muscles bunched for instant flight, but in the absence of any obvious danger, relaxed and grunted. Several other adults emerged from the trees and half a dozen brown and cream-streaked piglets ran about at their feet. They all started feeding, grunting and snuffling and moving slowly over the forest floor.

Helmut had collected handfuls of acorns and spread them near the alder thicket, and the abundance attracted a sow with piglets. She snorted at the faint odour of humans on the acorns but saw no danger and moved closer. When a piglet moved to within a few metres of his hiding place, Helmut rose to his feet with an excited cry and flung his spear. It passed over the piglet, bouncing and sliding in front of one of the adults.

The pigs erupted into a storm of activity, the air rent with alarmed squeals as they, and the piglets, took to their heels in every direction. Only the boar held his ground, ripping at the ground with his sharp hooves before launching himself at the boys in the alder thicket.

"Run!" Helmut screamed. Without waiting to see if his brother had obeyed, he raced for a smaller oak and scrambled up into its branches. He looked down, his limbs shaking with fright, and could not see Kurt, though he heard the boar's enraged squeals.

"Kurt! Kurt, are you all right?"

"Y...yes, I think so."

Helmut could hear tears in his brother's voice and sympathised. He knew he was not far from bawling himself. "Are you in a tree? Out of reach?"

"Yes, but...he's only just below me and he's angry."

"Hang on. He'll get tired and go away."

"I hope so, because my arms are getting very tired."

"Can't you sit astride a branch?"

"No."

Helmut racked his brains for a solution. If anything happened to his brother, Mutti would never forgive him – he'd never forgive himself, for that matter.

"There must be something," he muttered. Helmut looked down and saw no sign of the boar, but could still hear grunts and the occasional angry squeal off to his right. He thought of his spear and wondered if he could find it and drive the pig away.

"What's it doing?" he called.

"Standing staring up at me. Helmut, my arms are aching. I'm going to have to let go soon and then...and then..."

"Just hang on a bit longer." Helmut made up his mind and quietly climbed down to the forest floor on the left side of the oak. He peered around the bole of the tree and saw the boar underneath an old beech tree. Scarcely more than a metre or so up, his brother clung to a branch with his feet wedged in cracks in the bark. As he watched, a foot slipped and swung, almost brushing the boar's upturned snout before scrabbling at the bark again for purchase. Tearing his gaze away, Helmut looked for, and spotted his spear a few metres away in the opposite direction. He crept away, treading carefully so as not to make any noise, until he could grasp his puny weapon.

Back at the oak, he saw that Kurt's feet had swung free again and now his whole weight bore down on his hands, slowly prying them loose from the branch. If Helmut was to save his brother, it would have to be now. He stepped out and cast his spear as hard as he could at the boar. Unweighted, the sharpened wooden stake flew in a flat trajectory and merely tapped the animal across its hindquarters. It swung round, startled, and squealed with rage.

Helmut did not hesitate. He scooped up a fallen branch and threw it. The wood fell short, but the boar sidestepped, drawing back, and at that moment Kurt's hands lost their grip. He screamed piercingly and fell, thumping into the leaf litter just behind the boar. The boy's sudden cry and precipitate arrival was too much for the pig and it turned and raced for the cover of the forest, leaving two relieved boys in its wake.

Kurt got to his feet and brushed his pants off. He looked apprehensively toward the forest. "Do you think he'll come back?"

Helmut shook his head and grinned. "Not after the scare you gave him. You crashing to the ground just behind him was just too much."

"But if you hadn't thrown your spear..."

"Well, then, we both chased him off. Now, not a word to Mutti about this."

"Why not? We were brave."

"Yes, heroes even, but she'd be worried and might stop us coming out alone. You wouldn't want that."

Dusk was falling by the time they neared the camp by the stream, and both boys were tired and hungry. Meat or fish would have been nice, but vegetables and nuts would do, just so long as there was enough of it. They splashed across the stream fifty metres from camp and stopped dead, their hearts in their mouths. A murmur of voices pierced the darkness in front of them – men's voices.

"Russians?" Kurt squeaked. "What do we do?"

"Shh."

It was too late. The voices fell silent, and into the quiet, their mother's voice came to them.

"Helmut? Kurt? Is that you? Come into camp. Don't be afraid."

The two boys advanced, cautiously, ready to run if need be, or defend their mother. Helmut gripped his spear, and Kurt clutched a stone from the stream bed. As they stepped into the little clearing, eyes intent on the shapes of their family and two men standing with them, they were grabbed from behind. Helmut's spear was twisted from his grasp and thrown aside, Kurt's stone fell impotently to the ground as he gasped with pain.

"That's an unfriendly act, boy," a deep voice rumbled. "Seeing as how we come in friendship."

"Who are you?" Helmut asked. "Russian?"

"As German as you, boy. Don't go calling us Russians."

"My name's Helmut, not boy." He struggled against the grip of the man holding him. "And if you're friends, why have you attacked us?"

"Brave little man, isn't he?" remarked the deep-voiced man. "A few more like him and we might have driven back Ivan. Let's have some light here."

A cigarette lighter flared, illuminating faces in flickering shadows. The expressions were grim, and Kurt cried out.

"Mutti? Where's Mutti?"

"I'm here, Kurt. It's all right; we're all here, unhurt. These men are friends."

"That's right. Listen to your mother, boys. Stop playing with that lighter and light the goddamn fire, Wolfe, we need some proper light."

There was a short delay of moving shadows and scraping boots, a muffled curse or two, and the camp fire slowly waxed, forcing back the encircling darkness.

Helmut saw shapes emerge from the shadows, four men and two women, together with his mother and brothers. He was relieved that his family were unharmed, but suspicious of the strangers. His journey from the east had made him wary of chance encounters, and at least one of the men was armed. The one called Wolfe had a machine gun of sorts slung over one shoulder.

"So, Frau – some introductions," the deep-voiced man said. "I'm Martin, as I've already said. I'm ex-Waffen SS. This skinny man is Wolfe, Wehrmacht;

the one with a passing resemblance to our late unla-unlamented Führer is Victor, Party official; one-armed Rolf over there, also Wehrmacht; and the ladies are Nina and Gisela."

"Secretaries," Nina said with a smile.

Elisabet held out her hands and Helmut and Kurt ran to her. Joachim clung to her dress, crying softly, while Günter and Werner peered from behind her.

"I am Elisabet Daeker. My sons."

"Why are you here?" Helmut asked. "We have no food. Only what we can find in the forest."

"We haven't come to take your food, or anything else for that matter," Martin said. "Rather, we've come to give you some advice."

"You knew we were here?" Elisabet asked.

"Not exactly," Wolfe said. "Though we saw tracks a couple of days ago."

"And heard the children playing," Gisela added. She smiled, her thin, severe face lighting up. "We wanted to approach you, but didn't want to frighten you."

"Yet now you have," Elisabet pointed out.

Martin nodded. "I'm sorry for that, Frau Daeker. You know we are in the Soviet zone of occupation? I fear their rule is not going to be pleasant, but it's bearable out here in the wilds of the Harz..."

"As long as it's summer," Victor said.

"And the Russians leave us alone," Rolf added.

"So we've decided to seek a better future in the American or British zones," Martin finished.

"Why does that involve us?" Elisabet asked.

"The Russians are sending patrols through the Harz with orders to kill or capture any displaced persons..."

"And a displaced person is anyone who does not live in one of the towns or hamlets," Nina said.

"If they catch us, they'll shoot us..."

"Or worse," Gisela added.

"We came to warn you and to offer you a way out," Martin said.

"That is what we were doing," Elisabet said. "We've been moving slowly, but we're heading west."

"Well, you've run out of time, Frau Daeker. There's a Soviet squad heading this way."

"We cannot flee in the dark, I have young children."

"Then at first light."

"Why are you doing this? You could have fled on your own."

"We're all Germans, and while the war may be over, our enemies are all about us," Martin said. "If we don't stick together, we're lost."

They shared the food they had and the men offered some tinned meat for the communal pot. After dinner, when the children retired to the tent to sleep, or in Helmut's case to lie awake listening, the men and women talked in quiet tones, sharing their tales of escape and privation. The women asked about Elisabet's condition and she hesitated before replying evasively.

"You are a brave woman," Nina admitted. "It is hard enough to survive without five children and a baby on the way."

"Plenty of women having babies now," Victor said. "Russian fathers."

Gisela nodded. "I saw women raped by Russian pigs, but thank God I was spared," she added.

Nina opened her mouth to say something but appeared to change her mind.

"If it was me raped and I had a child, I'd kill myself for shame," Victor said. "Better dead than bring another Russian bastard into the world."

Nina glared at the ex-Party official. "You understand nothing," she spat.

"It's easy for a man to say, Victor," Gisela said. "You think a woman has a choice?"

"Apologise, Victor," Martin said. "How is it the woman's fault if she is raped? It is the Russian soldier's fault, so blame him."

Victor mumbled a few words that could be construed as an apology, then got up and walked off to sleep under a tree a short distance away.

Nina came to sit alongside Elisabet and talked quietly to her so the others could not hear. "Do not think too harshly of him. He is a fool, and he does not understand women. He spent the war in an office and has not seen much of the real world."

Elisabet said nothing.

"My boss worked with army supply and I followed him to the front and back. I was visiting my parents in Leipzig when the Russians came. My parents died and I was...I was raped. Several times." Nina sat and looked at the fire in silence for several minutes. "I thought about killing myself, but in the end I decided to live. Victor knows my story, so perhaps he thought..." She shrugged. "I don't know what he thought. Why am I making excuses for him?"

"What of the others?"

"Martin is SS. He doesn't talk about it but I think he has nightmares about what he saw and did in Russia. The Soviets would shoot him if they caught him. As for Wolfe and Rolf – they are simple soldiers who fought until their commanders surrendered.

363

They were put in an internment camp but escaped and want to make it to the West."

"And Gisela?"

"A secretary, like me, but to the Gauleiter of Magdeburg-Anhalt. The Russians will not treat her kindly if they catch her."

"And do you think things will be better in the West? You have faith in the Americans and British?"

"Who can say, but they can scarcely be worse."

"The Americans were in Magdeburg when we were there."

"So what were they like?"

"Better than the Russians but they are still men and men..." she fell silent.

"What about the British?" Nina asked.

"I have no reason to think well of the British," Elisabet said. "It was they that bombed Königsberg, and Dresden where my brother's family lived."

"Did they survive?"

"I don't know."

"What will you do in the West? Where will you go?"

"Find somewhere safe to bring up my children." Elisabet rested her hands on her rounded belly. "All of my children. Maybe when things have quietened down and the Russians withdrawn back to their own borders, we can go back to Königsberg."

"I pray that will happen," Nina said, "But I doubt it."

They left at first light, packing up their camp and heading north along the stream valley toward its source. Martin said he knew of a gap in the forested ridges, a meadow where the rocky spine of the Harz gave way to easy travel. The border between the Soviet zone and the Western allies lay somewhere there. He wasn't sure they would recognise it, but maybe there would be guards.

"It could be dangerous," Martin said, "But it must be crossed if we are to have the chance of a decent life."

The source of the stream was in a dribble of water seeping from the rocks and they took to the scrub forest, working their way over rock-strewn ridges and back down into vegetation-choked gullies, the land slowly flattening out. They entered a zone of spruce and fir trees, walking over crunching needles and feeling the summer wind blow through the rough-barked columns of the forest.

"Shouldn't we be heading west?" Elisabet asked. "Going north doesn't help us."

Martin gestured at the high mountains all around. "It will be difficult crossing those, so we follow the valley floor. It should open out soon and we can see where we are."

Another half day brought them to within sight of the foothills and farmland. They stood in the shelter of the spruce forest edge and stared down, looking for something that might tell them where the Soviet occupation zone border lay. They could see no guards, nor any sign of activity.

"We must scout it out," Martin declared. "Women and children stay here, the men come with me."

"I'm not staying here," Nina said. Gisela agreed.

"We've come this far with you. We're not staying back now."

"We can't stay here," Elisabet said. "There's little food in this part of the forest. We might as well all come down a bit further."

"As you will," Martin said. "I'm only trying to keep you safe."

They moved down, into the open, passing through patches of scrub, open woodland, and into neglected farms. There were few people moving around, mostly farmers trying to wrestle their abandoned fields back to some semblance of productivity, but apart from a curious glance or two, they ignored the group of people from the forest. They found a dirt road leading northwest and followed it. It led them into farmland that appeared cared for, pastures with cattle grazing, and fields with lines of crop plants. Victor looked hungrily at the cattle and fingered his machine gun, murmuring something to Rolf.

"Not yet," Martin said. "Let's find out where we are first."

"What about the fields?" Wolfe asked. "Those look like potatoes or beets. They'd never miss a few of them."

"All right, but..." Martin broke off and stared up the road. A growl of motors emanated from a small dust cloud rapidly approaching. Within seconds, they could see two small vehicles. "Damn, a Russian patrol."

"We've got to hide," Wolfe said.

"There's nowhere," Martin growled. He pointed to the fields. "Into the crop. Look as if you're supposed to be there, weeding or something."

They scattered, and Elisabet led her boys a bit deeper into the field, instructing her boys to crouch low. The smaller ones were almost hidden by the plants, but it was still obvious people were there.

"Bend over. Pretend to be doing something, and ignore the vehicles. Maybe they'll just drive straight past."

They almost did. Two jeeps laden with men appeared out of the dust, and a small open truck

366

behind. Faces turned to look at the men and women in the field, and the vehicles slowed. Someone called out something and when there was no reply, a commanding voice called out in German.

"Are you supposed to be here? Identify yourselves."

Nobody said anything and the jeeps stopped.

"Produce your identity papers. Now."

Victor swore and swung his machine gun, opening fire on the speaker, who ducked behind the jeep. Men piled out of the vehicles and returned fire, cutting Victor down and whipping the leaves of the plants to shreds as the Germans threw themselves to the ground.

"Cease fire."

Men came running into the field, rifles at the ready and quickly surrounded the survivors. One man ran over to where Elisabet cowered with her boys and stood staring down at them. Elisabet looked up to see a sandy-haired young man in khaki, with a flat-bowled helmet standing over her. The man turned and called back to the others in a language Elisabet did not recognise, but knew was not Russian.

"Hey, sarge, we got some bleedin' young kiddiewinks over 'ere."

Kapitel Zwanzig (20)

The survivors were rounded up and given a swift interrogation by the German-speaking soldier. He quickly ascertained that the women were civilians but that Martin, who had been wounded, and Rolf – unharmed except for minor cuts – were ex-military. Wolfe and Victor had died in the storm of fire from the British rifles. That was a point quickly picked up on by Elisabet.

"You British? We in British place?"

"Aye, that's right, Frau."

The sergeant ordered their prisoners onto the truck, together with the two dead bodies wrapped in tarpaulins, and the convoy headed back the way they had come, to Bad Harzburg. British soldiers kept their rifles trained on them all the way back to the town and the military headquarters there. Here, the men were taken away for medical treatment, and the women locked up until they could be properly interrogated.

When it was Elisabet's turn, she was led off alone. Her children tried to follow but they were turned back. Helmut struck out at his captors, but the younger children burst into tears. A German-speaker told them there was nothing to worry about, but did not succeed in placating them.

Elisabet was shown into a room where an officer sat behind a desk and a soldier at another desk tapped away on a typewriter. This one glanced up before carrying on with his work. The officer stood, however, and indicated a chair. He said something and the soldier who had collected her translated. The translator spoke stilted text-book German but Elisabet had no difficulty understanding him.

"Please be seated, Frau."

"Danke."

"Your children will be upset by your absence, but I must ask you some questions. The easier you make my task, the sooner you can rejoin them. Do you understand?" The soldier translated.

"Yes."

The officer sat down and made some notes on a pad. "What is your full name?"

"Elisabet Margarete Daeker."

"Married?"

"Widowed."

"Husband's name?"

"Rudolph."

"Where did he die?"

"Stalingrad."

"You have five children. What are their names and ages?"

"Helmut, nine; Kurt, eight; Günter, six; Werner, four; Joachim, two."

"City or town of origin?"

"Königsberg."

"And where's that?"

"Ostpreussen." The translator called it East Prussia.

"Why did you come to Bad Harzburg?"

"To escape the Russians."

The officer tapped the pencil on his front teeth. "Frau Daeker, I'm about to ask you something that you may think you can deny. However, if you do so, and we find out you are lying – which we will – you will be sent back to the Soviet sector. Do you understand?"

"Yes."

"Were you, or any member of your family, a member of the National Socialist German Worker's Party, commonly known as the Nazi Party?"

Elisabet hesitated, feeling trapped. The British were clearly in league with the Soviets on this issue, and she could not risk her children being sent back east.

"Frau Daeker. I must have an answer."

"I am sorry, Herr Offizier, I was trying to think whether any of my uncles or aunts may have joined."

"Immediate family only please – parents, husband, brothers or sisters."

"Then no. My parents voted against Hitler."

The officer sighed and made a notation. "My dear Frau Daeker, that's what they all say. To listen to you Germans, nobody ever liked him, voted for him, or even supported him. I don't know how such a universally detested man clung to power for twelve years." He nodded to the translator. "Take Frau Daeker back to her cell."

"What will you do with us, Herr Offizier? Whatever you might think of me, my children are innocent."

"You and your children will be taken to Wolfenbüttel. The authorities there will decide what happens to you."

Her children were overjoyed to see her and pestered her for information. All she could tell them was that they were heading for Wolfenbüttel. Kurt had a more pressing question though.

"When can we get something to eat? I'm starving."

Elisabet spoke through the bars to the soldier on guard who said he would find out. A few minutes later, a junior officer came down to the cells and escorted them to the officer's mess, where they were treated to a large but plain meal of sausage, boiled potatoes, and boiled vegetables, with plenty of sweet milky tea with which to wash it down.

The officer watched them scratch constantly during the meal and noted the threadbare condition of their clothes. When they finished the meal he took them to the ablutions block and let them scrub themselves clean in hot soapy water. Nothing could be done about their clothes, though, so they donned their dirty rags afterward and were soon scratching again.

A truck came the next day to take them and about twenty other displaced persons to Wolfenbüttel. A couple of armed British soldiers rode in the back with them, but they were there less as guards than as helpers. Their attitude to the refugees was one of reserved friendship, though they were not above chatting with the young frauleins and offering them cigarettes. There was a lot of traffic on the road and they were held up several times by convoys. The trip to Wolfenbüttel took nearly three hours.

They were fed again when they arrived, though with simple fare of soup and rye bread, and then interrogated again. Elisabet was interviewed by a German-speaking officer who produced sweets for the children and had them play in an anteroom while their mother answered questions. The questions were very similar to the previous lot, and the officer appeared to be checking her answers against a typed sheet.

"Frau Daeker, you stated previously that no one in your immediate family belonged to the Nazi Party. Do you stand by that statement?"

The barest hesitation. "Yes."

"You also said your parents voted against Hitler. What was their political affiliation?"

"They were communist."

"Indeed? And you?"

"I don't understand the question."

"It would not be surprising if the children followed their parents' beliefs. Are you communist also?"

"When I was a young woman."

The British officer smiled and stroked his moustache. "You are still a young woman, Frau Daeker." He sat and looked at her for a minute or two in silence. "Are you still a communist?"

"I have said I was when I was younger. It is possible my name is still on the membership rolls."

"Why did you not stay in Königsberg? The Russians are communist. You'd be safe there, wouldn't you?"

Elisabet closed her eyes for a moment, marshalling her thoughts. Then she met the officer's gaze. "My parents and I held to a pure form of Communism – Marxist, you might say, not the Stalinist revision that rules modern Russia. If I had stayed, my family would have been imprisoned or shot, together with any other German, Communist or not, that they captured. I chose to flee to the West, in hope of better treatment than I would find at the hands of the Soviets. Was I mistaken, Herr Offizier?"

The British officer coughed and looked away. "We are only looking for Nazis and those that aided the war effort."

"And you imagine I, or my children, fall into that category?"

"We must be certain. I'm sure you can understand that." He changed tack. "When is your child due?"

372

"I'm not sure. End of October, beginning of November."

"A doctor will examine you before you are relocated."

"Relocated? What does that mean? What will happen to us?"

"We will find you accommodation, and issue you with ration cards. It will be subsistence level only. If you wish to better your circumstances, you will have to work."

"I'm not exactly in any condition to work," Elisabet pointed out.

The officer shrugged. "I don't make the rules."

"Where is this accommodation?"

"That's not up to me. Possibly Wolfenbüttel, Braunschweig, or in some other town close by. You arrived in this area, so you'll remain here for the foreseeable future."

Elisabet attended a clinic in Wolfenbüttel, where they became concerned that she had put a strain on her body during her pregnancy, the growing child stripping her body of its sustenance. They issued her with extra ration cards. The placement officials then assigned her a small apartment and a few days later, she and her family found themselves in another truck with a handful of other families, leaving the town. They were alarmed to find themselves heading east.

"Are we being sent back to the Soviet zone?" one of the refugee men asked. "I will not go. I will kill myself first." The man started to shout and kick the sides of the truck until it stopped and the single guard riding in the cab came round to see what the matter was. He held his rifle at the ready, and barked at them to shut up.

373

"I will not let you hand me over to the Soviets," the man yelled. "Shoot me before you do that."

"Don't think I won't," the soldier threatened.

"Where go us, soldaten?" Elisabet asked, using almost the limit of her newly acquired English. "Soviet?"

"Schöppenstedt. Not Soviet. British."

"Promise? Not Soviet?"

"Promise. Half an hour. British zone."

The man allowed himself to be mollified and the truck resumed its journey. In less than the promised time, they entered a small town bearing the name of Schöppenstedt and were dropped off in the town centre. The town itself had not suffered much during the war. Lacking army depots, factories or important rail yards, it had escaped the bombing, and British forces had captured the town with few shots being fired. The townspeople likewise, had suffered little. Known Nazis were arrested or if they were just suspected of having National Socialist leanings, they were fired from their jobs pending investigation. For ordinary Germans, life continued, though now with different masters. The townspeople, interested in everything new, gathered in the town centre and stood around watching as each refugee family was given a piece of paper with an address on it and a sketch map of how to get there. Ration cards were issued too, and then the group of displaced persons broke up and headed for their new homes. Elisabet led her family along the streets, looking for the address on her piece of paper, feeling the unfriendliness of the watching locals. The children felt it also, saw the unwelcoming stares, heard the muttered comments.

"Why don't they like us, Mutti?" Kurt asked.

374

"It's because we're vertriebene," Helmut told him. "People pushed out of our homes by the Russians. They're afraid we're going to take food from them."

"Where did you hear that term, Helmut? It's not one I've used."

"Victor told me."

"Well, he's wrong. We weren't pushed out by the Russians, we fled from them. There's a difference. If you must give people like us a name, it should be flüchtlinge."

"Either way, they don't like us."

"It's all right," Elisabet said. "They don't know us yet. When they do, they'll be nice."

"And if they don't, they'll be sorry," Helmut muttered.

Their new home was very close to the town square, the church and the school, and had two ground floor rooms in a house, reached by a gate and a little alleyway. A tiny sink and wood stove in one room served as a kitchen, and the toilet facilities were primitive – a series of holes in a board over a pit in the back garden. There was running water, but no way to heat it except in pans over the wood stove. The painted walls of the apartment were peeling and the curtains were either missing or torn. They had been told the place was furnished, and it was, after a fashion. There were no beds, just grubby mattresses, and the solitary table had only four rickety chairs with it. An armchair and a standard lamp without a plug or a bulb completed the furnishings. Elisabet looked around the tiny rooms and smiled. It was better than any place they had lived in for many months.

"At least it's dry, and we'll be able to heat it easily. We just need to tidy it up a bit."

As the British Officer had said in Wolfenbüttel, the rations doled out to German civilians were basic, little more than subsistence level – a few slices of rye bread, a cup of oatmeal, a scrap of bacon or sausage, a little butter, a taste of milk, a few grams of ersatz coffee, a spoon or two of beet sugar, and a few potatoes each day. These had to be queued for daily, adding to the stresses of day-to-day living. They needed other things besides food. Their apartment needed cleaning to make it liveable, some basic furnishing to make it comfortable and insulation if it was to withstand the coming winter. September weather was clement still, though the first bite of the turning season greeted them in the mornings, a chill that made them reluctant to leave their beds, but eager for a cup of hot coffee to start the day. Fuel for cooking and heating was in short supply, so one of the tasks each day was to forage for sticks or scraps of planking in and around the town. Some people stripped the trees bare, drying the green wood before burning it; others hunted along the railway lines, searching for lumps of coal that had fallen from freight trains.

New clothes were needed too. The ones they had worn in their travels had thinned and eroded until they scarcely kept out the cooling breezes and harboured all sorts of vermin. Fleas and lice abounded and bit freely, despite their best efforts at grooming each other. Elisabet washed their clothes regularly but lacked a regular supply of hot water and soap. Everyone shivered, wrapped in thin blankets, while their clothes were washed and dried, but the continued presence of old clothing meant the washed clothing was readily reinfested. Joachim and Günter suffered constantly from the presence of vermin, and

Kurt's health also declined. These three all had rashes over their bodies that itched, and the younger boys felt the cold more. Headaches and joint pain made them cry, and all that Elisabet could do for them was dose them with willow bark tea and let them rest in a darkened room.

"We have to get medicine," Elisabet told her boys.

"And clothes," Helmut said.

"More food," Kurt whispered.

"Shoes," Werner said.

Joachim just clung to his mother, and Günter cried.

"I've tried to get work," Elisabet said, "But no one wants to hire me. I'm willing to work at almost anything, but there are hundreds of people looking for work."

"Can we trade?" Helmut asked. "We've still got some cigarettes, haven't we?"

"Four packs, but that won't be enough. I can trade for some clothes or a little food, but probably not both."

"Get clothes," Helmut said. "It's easier to steal food."

"I don't want you stealing any more. Besides, would you steal from your fellow Germans?"

"If they're Germans, why don't they help us?"

"Nobody has very much, but the townspeople at least have some belongings they can sell. We have nothing."

Helmut did not answer but he did not look convinced either.

"We could try the farms," Elisabet went on. "Harvests are being brought in and there may be work available."

Elisabet traded their last cigarettes for soap and clean underwear, a few shirts and two pairs of shoes, as well as two loaves of bread. She scrubbed their old clothing vigorously with the soap and hung them out to dry, throwing away anything she could replace. As a result, they were warmer but still itched as the vermin that infested the apartment merely shifted from dirty clothing to clean. Günter and Joachim started running a fever, and Kurt developed a cough.

"I've found work bagging potatoes," Elisabet said one day. "It won't last long, but it's better than nothing."

"And I found a pair of shoes," Helmut said. He held them up for inspection. "I found them by the side of the road."

Elisabet said nothing, not wanting to push her son into an admission of guilt. It was unlikely he had found them, but his own shoes were in tatters and he would need decent footwear with winter coming on.

Dozens of people descended onto one of the farms just out of Schöppenstedt, where work was being offered for bagging potatoes. Payment was per bag filled, so fit men took the prime positions just behind the cultivator that turned the soil and brought the potatoes to the surface, while the women and children spread out behind them. It was difficult for Elisabet to bend and the late stage of her pregnancy exhausted her, but she kept it up as long as she could. Helmut and Werner worked with her, the other children sitting under the trees at the edge of the field, wrapped in blankets. They guarded the sacks their mother and brothers filled as they were too sick to help pick up potatoes.

The sacks filled slowly, but during one of her enforced rest breaks, Elisabet noticed another woman

378

doing something curious. Every now and then, the woman would pick up a potato and place it in her sack, and then press another one into the soil, placing a stone on top. Straightening, the woman saw Elisabet watching her. She winked and carried on down the row, while Elisabet considered her actions. When a field had been harvested, the farmer usually allowed gleaners into the field to search for parts of the crop that had been missed. If this woman knew there was a potato under every stone, she would be certain to glean a good amount later. Elisabet worried about the honesty of the practice, but decided her children came before the small amount of extra profit the farmer would lose. She decided to follow the woman's example.

The day ended, and Elisabet was paid the small amount of money owing for their labour, but instead of going home immediately, she went back to the field with a sack and showed her two sons the double heel indentation she had made an intervals along the furrows. She dug into the loose soil and pulled out two or three large potatoes, adding them to the sack.

"We're allowed to keep any we find after the field has been harvested," she said.

"But how did you know they would be there?"

"I put them there myself."

Helmut grinned. "So, under every double heel print?"

They filled a sack with potatoes and wrestled it home with some difficulty. Similar actions yielded more over the next few days as they made the round of neighbouring farms, contesting with refugees and townspeople alike for the privilege of bringing in the harvest. Potatoes, beets and carrots were easiest to hide and find later, but they also managed to secrete apples and plums in the long grass bordering the or-orchards. Their foraging filled their stomachs, but they longed for something tastier. Meat was highly prized and usually unobtainable for poorer people. Fat was also sought after, and the meagre butter and bacon rations did little to assuage their hunger.

The harvests ended and Elisabet found herself out of work again. Helmut and Werner went off on foraging trips of their own, sometimes returning with scraps from rubbish bins, other times with more substantial fare. The boys did not have it all their own way, of course, for there were many other boys, and a few girls, out looking for anything not nailed down. Fights broke out, and sometimes the boys would return home battered and bruised but clutching a hard-won trophy in triumph, or else filled with chagrin at a lost opportunity, having come off second best. One thing Helmut did find that was potentially useful was a pair of pram wheels and an axle. He worked with scrap timber and rusty, bent nails to make a workable cart.

"It'll help when we next have to carry potatoes," he said.

Elisabet found part-time work in the sugar factory. Sugar beets were crushed and boiled to extract the sugar, and she could sometimes steal a handful of sugar or some of the dried beet pulp to augment their diet and give them extra energy. The dried pulp was usually used as animal feed once the sugar had been extracted, but the boys enjoyed the taste and the residual sweetness.

Kurt, Günter and Joachim were sick every day now with chills, fever, joint and abdominal pain. Headaches were common and the rash persisted on their bodies despite increased cleanliness. It had even spread to their limbs now and was darker. Elisabet doctored them as best she could without proper med-medicines, preparing herbal teas and soothing ointments from animal fat. She thought of taking them to the British authorities, but hesitated when she heard tales in the town of sick people being returned to their home city for treatment. A return to the Russian sector would be like a death sentence. The only other option was to purchase drugs either from a pharmacist or on the black market, but for that they would need something marketable as trade. They looked around for opportunities.

A local fishmonger was heard to say he needed grass and clover. Helmut and Werner collected sackfuls of clover from the countryside and offered it to him. They received two good-sized fish in payment. As they were leaving the shop, Helmut could not contain his curiosity.

"Please, Herr Fellen, why do you want clover?"

"I have rabbits."

"Pet rabbits?" Werner asked.

The fishmonger laughed. "No, I breed them for meat."

"Could we have meat instead of fish?"

"Clover is worth fish. Rabbit meat fetches a much higher price."

They ate the fish rather than trading it, as the commodity was of low value compared to medicines, but a welcome source of protein.

There was a forested region a few kilometres north of the town, in a region called the Elm Hills. They would have to walk, but Elisabet knew she would not be able to make many more forays finding food. It was worth the effort to see if there were any useful things in this particular patch of forest.

She set off one day, taking Werner and two empty knapsacks. Helmut was left behind to look after his younger siblings, much to his disgust, as he saw himself as the main provider for his family. His mother had to point out to him that the care of his sick brothers was a great responsibility, and Werner was just not old enough to be left in charge. She left instructions for feeding and medication, and told him to call a next-door neighbour – Frau Henkel – if he felt really worried.

The Elm Hills were only about five or six kilometres away, so Elisabet knew they could be there and back in a couple of hours, leaving plenty of time to scavenge for food. They had a bottle of water with them, some bread and a little cheese, and an apple each. Elisabet kept little Werner's spirits up by playing games as they walked along the road.

"Let's look for things that start with every letter of the alphabet. Can you see anything that starts with an A?"

"Apfel," Werner replied promptly.

"Where?"

"In your knapsack, Mutti. I saw you put it in."

Elisabet laughed. "Very clever. How about a B?"

Werner looked around. "Um...there on the flower, ein biene."

"That's a big furry bee, ein hummel."

"It's still a kind of bee isn't it?"

"All right. C then."

Werner wanted to use the hummel again when they got to H, but Elisabet said he could not use the same thing twice. He grinned and pointed to the bowl of the blue sky above.

"Himmel then."

It took them a while, and a little stretching of the rules, but they worked their way through the alphabet. Elisabet told stories and encouraged her little son to tell her a story, which he did – a confused mish-mash of things that had happened to them over the last few months, but as if it had happened to another little boy. Elisabet listened attentively, and praised his effort, telling him he would grow up to be a storyteller like 'die Gebrüder Grimm'.

They reached the Elm Hills and found a broad expanse of beech forest. Elisabet led Werner off the road and under the spreading trees. The shade under the larger trees was quite dense, preventing other plants from growing, but where gaps appeared in the canopy, a plethora of other plants struggled for a share of the light. They scuffed their way through the leaf litter, Elisabet alternately looking up at the foliage and down at the ground.

"What are you looking for, Mutti?"

"There are many things to find in a beech forest, but it's a little late for some of them." She reached up and plucked some leaves from a hanging branch, discarding the ones chewed by caterpillars, and nibbled on one of the undamaged ones.

"A bit chewy now, but in spring they taste like mild cabbage. Remember, we ate some near Wittenberg."

Werner tried the leaf his mother handed him, but screwed up his face and spat it out.

Elisabet spotted something yellow in the leaf litter and crossed to it, bending and picking up a meaty yellow funnel-shaped fungus. She sniffed it and smiled, before breaking it open and tasting a small amount.

"Pfifferling," she said, handing a piece to Werner. "Look and learn. Sniff it first – smells a bit like fruit. See the yellow colour is just on the surface – it is white inside. Now nibble on a small piece. What do you think?"

"It tastes like pepper."

"That's right – Pfifferling. Look around and see if you can find more, but don't eat any. Just collect it and bring it to me. There is another fungus that looks like it but is not good to eat. I can tell the difference though."

While Werner looked for more golden chanterelle fungi, Elisabet squatted and cast about in the leaf litter. She held up a small spiky beech burr and opened it up revealing tiny triangular beech nuts. Using her fingernails, she peeled the outside off and chewed on the kernel. It was slightly bitter to the taste but quite oily, and she knew it was worth collecting if present in large enough amounts. She started gathering the burrs together.

Werner returned with half his knapsack full of buttery yellow fungi, and Elisabet sorted through them, discarding a few, but making sure her son understood the differences between the edible varieties and the poisonous ones.

"Experience is very important. I learned all this when I was a girl in the forests around Königsberg. At any time, if you are collecting wild food, and you are not sure about whether something is poisonous or not, don't eat it. It's better to be hungry than to get sick."

Elisabet showed Werner what she was collecting and let him chew on a fat beech nut kernel. He screwed up his face, and spat it out. Elisabet sighed.

"Never mind. If we can get enough, we can get some oil from them which we can sell, and we might even be able to make some cakes from what is left."

"Yuck."

"We can get rid of the bitter taste. Now help me gather as many as we can find. I want to fill my knapsack if I can."

They had a break from their labours at midday, and sat with their backs to the trunk of a large beech and ate their bread and cheese and crunched on the sweet apples, consuming everything except the stalk and pips. While they ate, they kept quiet and watched the wildlife of the forest. A tiny brown bird flitted and clung to the trunks of trees, flicking its tail feathers this way and that, pecking at something in the bark before whirring off into the depths of the forest. Larger birds kept to the foliaged branches, calling, and occasionally descending to the forest floor for a quick visit, while a woodpecker tapped out its Morse message on a distant tree. Squirrels ran along the branches or scampered from tree to tree, delighting Werner. They sat up, scrutinising the interlopers in their forest with bright beady eyes before flicking a tawny bushy tail and disappearing back into the trees.

Butterflies were there too, but not the bright yellow schmetterling of open country and hedgerows that was Elisabet's favourite. A red admiral sat head-down on a sun-splashed tree trunk, opening its dark brown wings to display a flash of crimson. Peacock butterflies flitted past, the large ring-spots on their open wings glowing in the dappled light. In the sunnier glades where low plants flourished, orange and brown-stippled fritillaries fluttered, and once, a brilliantly luminous orange large copper butterfly cruised past them intent on a destination far removed from their station under the beech tree.

Elisabet and Werner resumed their labours and found a fall of hazelnuts to add to their beech mast and Pfifferling. The work was slow, sorting out the little beech burs and opening them, or searching for scattered beech nuts in the leaf litter. They discarded any nuts with holes, or with flattened shells, wanting only wholesome ones. As the sun started lowering into the western sky, Elisabet straightened and they headed back through the forest to the road, and thence back to Schöppenstedt, shelling and nibbling on hazelnuts as they went.

They were tired and looking forward to a rest and a nice hot cup of coffee by the time they reached their home, but waiting on the corner of their road was Helmut, hopping from foot to foot with anxiety. Elisabet started forward, fear gripping her heart.

"Mutti, it's Günter," Helmut said in a rush. "He's really sick."

Kapitel Einundzwanzig (21)

Elisabet rushed inside and to the room where her three sick children shared a mattress. Kurt was sitting cross-legged, stroking Günter, who thrashed around, sweating profusely and mumbling incoherently. The older boy looked up when his mother entered the room and burst into tears.

"Is he going to die, Mutti?"

"Of course not." Elisabet knelt beside the mattress and ran her hands over Günter. She was chilled to the heart to feel his raging fever, for she knew this was a serious turn of events. She looked over at her youngest, Joachim, who was fast asleep, oblivious of the crisis taking place beside him. That, at least, was a burden relieved. Kurt also looked a bit feverish.

"How do you feel, Kurt?" Elisabet asked.

"It hurts, Mutti," Kurt muttered.

Werner hovered at the door to the room, afraid to come in, but Helmut stood beside his mother.

"I gave Kurt some willow bark tonic earlier, but Günter and Joachim wouldn't take any."

Elisabet shook her head. "Things have moved beyond mere tonics. I must take him to a doctor."

"The British?" Helmut asked. "Won't they just hand us over to the Soviets? That's what people in the town say will happen."

Elisabet considered her rapidly narrowing options. "The pharmacist first then. Günter must have medical treatment. Bring your cart, Helmut, and help me load your brother onto it."

She went alone. Helmut wanted to accompany her, but she insisted he stay behind and care for his brothers. Elisabet trundled the shaky cart into the town centre and beyond to the Hinterstrasse. The apotheker, the pharmacist, lived there in an apartment above his tiny shop, dispensing such pills and potions as he could scrounge from the medical authorities now that normal lines of supply had collapsed, or make up from raw materials and herbs.

The pharmacist was short and tubby, his eyes mellow and sad in his florid face. He answered the door to Elisabet's frenzied hammering after a few minutes, and glanced beyond her to the bundle wrapped up in the rough cart.

"What is so urgent, Frau?"

"My son, Herr Apotheker. He is very sick and I don't know what to do."

"Bring him in."

The pharmacist took them through to a back room, and laid the sick child on the table. He peeled back the covering blanket and frowned. Günter's shirt followed and the pharmacist made a tut-tutting noise. He leaned over the boy's body and poked it with his fingertip.

"How long has the rash been there, Frau?" he asked.

"A month or two. Never this bad. We all had it, but we haven't felt really sick until recently."

"There are insect bites." The pharmacist pointed.

Elisabet nodded. "Fleas and lice. We wash, Herr Apotheker, but until recently we were without soap and hot water. We still lack clean clothing."

"So I see." The pharmacist examined the extent of Günter's rash, turned back his eyelids, and opened the boy's mouth. "Has he complained of any pain? Shortness of breath?"

"Headaches and joint pain. His back too. No shortness of breath."

"Coughing? Blood in his sputum?"

"Coughing only."

"He has a high temperature, Frau, and I cannot render an accurate diagnosis. You must take him to a doctor, to the British Army Clinic."

"I...I cannot, Herr Apotheker. We came from Königsberg. If we are ill, they will send us back."

"I believe that to be an unfounded rumour, Frau. But even if it is true, you risk your son's life by delaying. You must take him there."

"Can't you give him something?"

The pharmacist tut-tutted again. "I have nothing that would heal this one. No, Frau, you must put yourself and your son in the hands of the British occupiers."

"There is no other course?"

"Not if you want your son to live. I believe he has typhus."

"Oh my god, no. You must be mistaken. It is just a...a fever. He will get better soon with some medicine. I only have willow bark tonic. He just needs something stronger."

"Go to the Clinic immediately, Frau," the pharmacist insisted.

Elisabet took Günter to the Clinic, but not without considerable trepidation. The British had taken over the Town Hall and transformed a community hall into an examination room with a doctor and two nurses to handle the small health issues of the town. She was prepared for an inquisition when she turned up with her unconscious son, and was surprised when a nurse whisked them into a side room and made a preliminary examination.

The nurse pursed her lips and muttered, "The doctor will have to look at this one." She looked up at

389

Elisabet severely. "Warten Sie hier. Ich werde dem Arzt bringen."

The doctor was a young man with army khaki and a captain's pips beneath his white coat. He tapped and prodded, listened to the boy's breathing with his stethoscope, and took Günter's temperature by slipping a thermometer into the boy's armpit.

"Typhus," he said matter-of-factly. "Look at the state of his clothing. He must be infested with lice." The doctor instructed the nurse to order a car and driver immediately. "We must get him to hospital at once. Schöppenstedt is in the Wolfenbüttel district, but they won't have the facilities to handle this. It'll have to be Braunschweig. Ring the hospital there and tell them to expect him. When he has gone, have this bed thoroughly disinfected." He turned to Elisabet and ran his gaze over her dishevelled state. "You look pretty bad yourself," he said kindly. "Would you like me to examine you too?"

"I do not feel sick, but thank you for your concern."

The doctor nodded, but seemed in no hurry to leave. "Nevertheless, a woman in your condition cannot be too careful. When is your baby due?"

"I don't know exactly. End of this month, beginning of November maybe."

"You're seeing a doctor?"

"No."

"You should see one. Would you like me to arrange it?" He smiled encouragingly.

Elisabet shook her head, but she found herself thinking of another doctor in kinder times who had also expressed an interest in her, though in a very different way.

* * *

The war went well for Germany for several years. News came in of great victories in France, in Scandinavia, and in North Africa. If Britain remained undefeated in the West, she was undoubtedly cowed into submission and could pose no immediate threat to the victorious Fatherland. Now attention had turned to the East, where Russia would soon be bludgeoned to her knees by the ever-triumphant Wehrmacht. They were heady times for all loyal Germans, whether they openly supported the Nazi Party or not.

Elisabet had four children to raise and a husband who was absent for long periods of time with his company, scouring the Polish countryside for dissidents and rebels. Her two eldest children had started school, and the youngest, Werner, was a toddler. Günter was a sickly child and as often as not needed to stay indoors, so Elisabet felt herself tied to the home. She took every opportunity that presented itself for getting out into the city, whenever she could prevail on her parents or other relatives to look after her young ones.

In late 1941, the Spanish allies of Germany sent their 'Blue Division – División Española de Voluntarios' – to participate in the eastern war, and for a short while the city was filled with exuberant dark-haired Spaniards. These soldiers, though dressed in Wehrmacht uniforms with the '*España*' insignia of their Division, brought a certain informality that rapidly endeared them to the citizens of Königsberg. My husband Rudi saw them in action once and was both scathing and praising of them.

"They are undisciplined, slapdash and slovenly soldiers who often sleep on guard duty or get drunk instead of cleaning their rifles – but in battle they are lions. They never give an inch. Our boys are happy to fight alongside them for they know their flank is safe."

The Blue Division was gone all too soon, heading east, but that was not the last the city saw of them. Pitched battles were fought as Russian resistance stiffened, and a steady flow of wounded filled the hospital wards. Spanish doctors, seconded to the Blue Division, attended their own wounded and also Wehrmacht regulars.

In early 1942, Rudi went back to his Company and left me alone again. Wishing to do my bit for the Fatherland, I volunteered to help out at the hospital, and was assigned to the team of one of these Spanish volunteers, a dashing young doctor with the magnificent name of Ricardo Gualterio Del Monte. Doktor Del Monte was a fine physician with a wonderful bedside manner, always ready to encourage a wounded soldier or sick civilian. He was also very popular with the nursing staff, being handsome and outgoing, but he kept to himself when not on duty.

I would sometimes see him walking the streets of the city, and he would always offer me the courtesy of an inclination of his head or a kind word, but it was not until he came across me on the Promenade of the Schlossteich, pushing Werner in his pram, that he actually talked to me.

"Guten tag, Frau Daeker. It is a lovely day, isn't it?"

"Indeed, Herr Doktor. How are you enjoying our fair city?"

He sketched a thin bow and a broader smile. "You Königsbergers have made me feel very welcome."

"It must be very different from your homeland."

"Have you ever been to Spain, Frau Daeker?"

"Elisabet, please – and no, I have never been outside Germany."

"It is very different...Elisabet. And please, you must call me Ricardo."

I had not known then how homesick Ricardo felt, or how melancholy he became at the thought of his hot homeland, but he told me about his home and his family on other occasions. We were very proper at work, calling each other 'Doktor' and 'Frau Daeker', but off duty we came to know each other well.

I suppose I pushed the boundaries of what was appropriate for a married woman but I enjoyed his company and I always made sure we met in a public place so there would be no hint of scandal. It was exciting too, and Ricardo was attentive and unfailingly polite. He never presumed upon our friendship, sharing a coffee at a sidewalk cafe, a stroll in a park, or sitting in the sun on a street bench talking about this and that. I don't know what he saw in me – a married woman with children – unless it was a safe outlet for his loneliness. He was engaged to be married, to a sweetheart back in Spain, and he wanted to remain faithful to her. I wanted to remain faithful to my Rudi also, so did not take him home to meet my parents, and stayed away from the streets where my relatives lived, for it would be hard to explain to them my attraction to this handsome young man.

It was all very innocent – no, that is not strictly true – but it was innocent on his part. I found his company exciting and daring, and on more than one occasion I found myself staring at his handsome face, listening to his cultured voice, and wondering – until one warm spring day when, on one of our walks along the Promenade, he passed me a letter.

"What's this?"

"Please, Elisabet, just read it."

I glanced at it, but could not understand a word. "I'm sorry," I said. "I can't read Spanish."

"Of course not. Silly of me." Ricardo took it back and looked at it pensively before reading it out to me in a low voice, translating into German. It was from someone called Gabriela. She may have loved Ricardo once, but absence had not made the heart grow fonder and she now informed her erstwhile fiancé that he had lost her affections. She had met someone else...

"Ricardo, I am so sorry."

He folded the letter and tucked it into his jacket pocket. "It is nothing."

Pity wounded his Spanish pride and he made light of his hurt, but I could tell he suffered inside. I wanted to take him in my arms and soothe him, stroke him and tell him it was all right, that not every woman was so cold – but of course I could not. How would that look? What would he think?

"I have put in for a transfer," he said, staring off into the distance. "I have decided I will serve my country at the front line."

I felt my throat tighten. My heart ached both for his hurt and my loss. "Do not punish yourself, Ricardo."

He shook his head, not saying anything.

"Do not punish me, Ricardo," I whispered.

He turned then and stared at me. "You, Elisabet?" His forehead wrinkled in puzzlement, the meaning behind my words sinking in. "I could never punish you."

"Then...then stay."

His dark eyes regarded me and he leaned closer. "What are you saying?"

I looked into his eyes and turned my face up to his, moving into his arms. "You know what I am saying."

We kissed.

* * *

"Frau Daeker?"

Elisabet saw the British army doctor staring at her and collected her wayward thoughts. "It is kind of you, Herr Doktor. Maybe when I have made sure my children are safe."

"Of course." The doctor smiled again and left the room.

The nurse ordered the car and within half an hour it had driven off at speed toward Braunschweig. Elisabet was not allowed to go with her son, but now had to answer many questions which tended to confirm her fears of being handed over to the Soviets. The nurse asked where they were from, how they had managed on the trip, where they lived now, what their diet was and whether other family members were sick. In the end, the stress of the situation and worry over Günter's health led Elisabet to break down and sob out her fears.

"My goodness, no," the nurse exclaimed. "Whatever gave you such an odd notion? The only people who are ever returned to the Soviets are Nazi criminals."

Elisabet was not sure whether to believe the nurse, but after being given a cup of ersatz coffee, slowly came round to the notion that her arrest and deportation was not imminent.

"When can I see my son?"

"Tomorrow," the nurse said. "Go to the Braunschweig Hospital."

"How do I get there?"

395

"I don't know. Do you know anyone with a vehicle?"

Elisabet shook her head. "I suppose I could walk. I've done a lot of that."

The nurse looked shocked. "Not in your condition. You come to the clinic if you can't find anything else. We might be able to help."

"What about my other sons? They are too young to leave at home alone." Elisabet elaborated as to their ages.

"Can you get someone to look after them?"

"Perhaps."

Elisabet returned home and outlined the situation to her children. "It seems we will not be sent back east, but the British have taken Günter to Braunschweig Hospital. I will go there tomorrow."

"We can come too, can't we?" Werner asked.

"It would be better if you stayed at home. I'll ask Frau Henkel next door to keep an eye on you while I'm away."

"We don't need anyone," Helmut said. "We're not babies – not all of us anyway."

"You'll be in charge," Elisabet told her eldest son, "But I want Frau Henkel to know I'm away. If you should need her for any reason, tell her immediately."

"How long are you going to be away?" Kurt asked. He valiantly tried to suppress his coughing.

"I don't know. Braunschweig is only twenty kilometres away, but it will depend on whether I can get a ride with someone there and back. The nurse at the clinic said I should go there and they might be able to take me, but getting back might be more of a problem. I suppose I can always walk back if need be."

"Just tomorrow then?"

"I hope so. Maybe they'll let me bring Günter back too."

Elisabet prepared a meal using the produce from the forest. While Werner regaled his brothers with stories of squirrels and butterflies, of birds and beech nuts, she sautéed some of the golden chanterelles in a little butter. They did not have meat on the menu that day, so she fried some potatoes and added a small salad of dandelion leaves and wild rauke. The remaining chanterelles she set aside to be dried. They could be added to soups or stews when she had more varied ingredients to hand.

The boys tentatively nibbled on the golden fungus and were pleasantly surprised by the taste. Helmut even went so far as to offer the opinion they could get money for these by offering them to restaurants.

"Are there more in the Elm Hills?" he asked.

"I'm sure there must be."

"I'll come with you next time," Helmut declared. "I'll bring the cart and we can fill it up with yellow fungus."

"Pfifferling," Werner corrected.

They finished their meal with hazelnuts, and Elisabet showed them how to shell the beech nuts. The boys tried a few of the kernels, but complained they were bitter.

"They have oil in them," Elisabet said. "I want to see if I can work out a way to crush the nuts and extract it. What's left can be soaked in water to remove all the bitter stuff – tannin I think they call it. Then we can add flour and make delicious and nutritious bread."

Joachim's fever worsened that evening, so she dosed him up with willow bark tonic and made sure he had plenty of fluids. Kurt was not nearly as bad, though he had a nasty cough and was generally list-listless. The thought crossed her mind that Joachim might also have typhus, but she was unsure about Kurt. Helmut and Werner displayed no symptoms, though they also had insect bites on their bodies – as she did herself – so perhaps her other children only had a summer cold or something. Perhaps they had avoided catching typhus. She thought it was transmitted by lice but was not sure. Someone had mentioned mice, and as far as she knew, there were no mice in the walls of their apartment. She pondered whether she should have all her children checked at the clinic. If the nurse was right, then they were in no danger of being sent back to the Soviet zone – but what if she was wrong? Or what if she was right, but a whole family fell ill? Even if it was not typhus, would the British want to be rid of the extra health problem?

In the morning, Joachim was much sicker, and Elisabet decided she had to take him with her to the clinic. Even if it meant being sent back, the health of her children was paramount. It was a risk she would have to take. She had a talk to Frau Henkel and made sure she was happy to be called on if the boys needed her.

"I've left them food, and they are sensible children, so they shouldn't bother you."

"When will you be back, Frau Daeker?"

"I hope tonight, or tomorrow morning."

Elisabet made Joachim comfortable in the little cart and wheeled him down to the clinic. She had to wait for a while as the nurse she had seen the previous day was busy with other patients, but around mid-morning she turned up in the waiting room.

"Good day, Frau Daeker. What brings you here today?"

Elisabet felt a bit taken aback. "I...you said if I could not get to Braunschweig Hospital, to come here and you'd see if you could help."

"Ah, so I did. We're a bit busy today and unfortunately there are no serious cases...I'm not sure I should say that...well, anyway, we don't have any serious cases that need transport. You could wait around if you like, or try again tomorrow."

"But I have to see my boy in Braunschweig today." Elisabet stared at the British nurse in disbelief. "If you cannot help me, I must walk there."

Elisabet heaved herself off the wooden bench and bent to pick up the swaddled form of Joachim. The young child let out a plaintive cry and erupted into a series of barking coughs.

The nurse immediately stepped forward and parted the blanket around the crying boy. Her eyebrows knitted together in a frown as she took in Joachim's condition.

"How long has this child been like this?" the nurse snapped.

"He worsened last night, but he's been sick for some time."

The nurse plucked Joachim from his mother's arms and rushed off with him. She called for the doctor, who emerged from behind some curtains and immediately started talking to the nurse in English. Elisabet hurried up to them. She could not understand what they were saying, but caught the word 'typhus' and felt her heart clench. She tugged at the doctor's arm.

"What are you saying? What is wrong? Is it...is it typhus?"

The doctor said nothing and ushered them all into an examination room, where he removed Joachim's clothes and studied the little boy's wasted rash-covered body.

"This child almost certainly has typhus, and is much sicker than the one you brought in yesterday, Frau Daeker. How long has he been like this?"

"Like this? A few days."

"How long has he had the rash? Been scratching? Days, weeks, months – what?"

"Weeks...a month or two. Since Lübben. We were given clothes..."

"Probably infested with lice. I imagine this child contracted the disease first and spread it to your other child. Do you have other children? Are they sick too? Are you?"

"No, Herr Doktor...or rather, yes. I have other children – three in fact – but only one is sick. I am not sick."

"I will need to examine them, and you, but that will have to wait. The most important thing is to have this child taken to Braunschweig Hospital immediately. We must isolate these cases or they'll spread like wildfire."

"I'll have a driver come round immediately," the nurse said.

"I want to go too," Elisabet said. "Günter – my third child – is already there."

The doctor hesitated for several moments, and then nodded. "You must tell me your address in Schöppenstedt. I shall have to have your family examined."

The trip to Braunschweig was rapid. Elisabet found herself thinking how much her boys would enjoy a car trip as the countryside flashed by. The driver drove skilfully, using his horn to clear a path through pedestrians and the limited amount of traffic on the roads, finally pulling up at the hospital.

Joachim was whisked away and Elisabet put in a small room to wait for a doctor. He arrived after some time and assured her that her boys were being taken care of. His attitude was one of self-importance and condescension.

"Can I see them?"

"Soon, Frau Daeker, but I need to talk to you about something else." The doctor motioned her to take her seat again, and he sat down beside her. "Frau Daeker, your sons were...I'm sorry, I can't remember how to put this delicately in German...they were filthy. I would say these children have not seen soap in a long time. Now, this may be cultural, but it cannot be tolerated. Diseases are made worse by unhygienic conditions, and frankly, you do your children no favours by keeping them..."

"Herr Doktor, you will do me the courtesy of listening to me." Elisabet's eyes flashed as she cut the doctor off in mid-sentence. "I don't know how things are in England, but here in Germany we believe in cleanliness. I have always kept my home and my family spotless, and if you find us less than that now, it is because of your country's bombing and destructive warfare against women and children rather than any lack of German standards of hygiene."

"My dear Frau..."

"I am not your dear Frau, Herr Doktor, and I haven't finished. My sons and I are not responsible for this war or for anything that has happened in it. We were thrown out of our homes in Königsberg in the face of Soviet murder and outrage, forced to flee for our lives without our belongings, without food and with only the clothes on our backs. We were

401

forced to don any scrap of clothing we could find, forage for food in forest, farm and town, walk across hundreds of kilometres, through a brutal winter, to find a home where I could raise my children. I have no husband to support me, but I have five children and another on the way, courtesy of your Soviet allies, so I don't need your platitudes and criticisms, well meant though they might be."

The doctor flushed red and opened his mouth, but Elisabet raised her hand and continued.

"You British have given us a tiny two room apartment in Schöppenstedt and provided us with subsistence-level rations to replace what we had before. We are suitably grateful for the largesse of the occupying power, but we still lack basic furniture, heating, clothing, and decent food. We also lack soap, and often hot water, so while we might wash ourselves in water, we must don our threadbare, louse-ridden clothes again afterward. I do my best to work in the fields, to beg or borrow food for hungry mouths, or gather nuts and fruits in the forest to keep my children fed, and my children work with me, but we are dispossessed, Herr Doktor, foreigners in our own country, left without money and in rags through no fault of our own – and you tell me that I have chosen this life for my children, that I do not care for them properly, that I do not love my children. For shame, Herr Doktor."

The doctor opened and shut his mouth several times, and looked away. He cleared his throat and started to speak, thought better of it, and then started again.

"I...I'm sorry, Frau Daeker, I did not mean to cause offence. I know that the actions of we British are not always perceived well, but we..." He sighed and ran his fingers through his hair. "We have limited means, but you have my word we will do something to help you."

"May I see my children now?"

"Er, there is a problem..." The doctor blushed and looked away again. "We have had to wash and fumigate your children and well, we had to burn their clothing. If we let you in to see them in your present er, condition, we run the risk of reinfecting them."

Elisabet plucked at her dress. "I do not have any other clothes."

"No, but maybe we can find you some. If we can, will you consent to bathing and being fumigated?"

"Herr Doktor, what did I just say about cleanliness? Of course I am willing to bathe and change my clothes. I look forward to it."

"Excellent." The doctor ventured a smile, saw Elisabet's expression, and decided to put it away for some other occasion. "If you will, er, excuse me, I'll set things in motion." He leapt to his feet and hurried from the room.

Time passed. A nurse delivered a parcel of used but clean clothing that seemed of a size to fit her, and then another one came to lead her to a bathroom where a tub of steaming water had been drawn. Elisabet firmly closed the door and wedged a chair under the handle before stripping off and lowering herself gingerly into the hot water. Soap had been provided – it even had a faint perfume – and she lathered herself up and rinsed off several times, washing away the accumulated grime of months on the road. She washed her hair, tugging at the tangles, and combed it roughly with her fingers after towelling it damp. The steamed-up mirror allowed a hazy image

403

after rubbing with one hand, and she could see that she needed her hair trimmed.

Elisabet drew on the clean clothes with a contented sigh. Her skin was blotched from insect bites and still itched, but the garments were clean and nothing crawled on her as she checked herself in the mirror. She left her dirty clothes in a heap in a corner of the bathroom, not caring what happened to them. They would probably be burned. Replacing the chair against the wall, she opened the door and walked along the corridor to the nurse's station.

"May I see my children now?"

The nurse sent for the self-important doctor, who nodded in satisfaction at the clean woman standing in front of him. "One more thing remains, Frau Daeker. You must be fumigated in case any lice crossed over from your old clothing to the new." When Elisabet looked doubtful, the doctor explained. "DDT is a substance that kills insects but is harmless to people. It is a very valuable tool in the fight against typhus. You might not realise it, but typhus has killed millions of people down through the centuries. Napoleon lost more of his army to typhus than to the Russians, but if he'd had DDT, the whole course of history might have been changed."

The nurse took Elisabet into another room and brought out a brass cylinder with a plunger handle at one end and a nozzle at the other. The nozzle was poked down the neck of Elisabet's clothing, up her skirts, and into her sleeves and the plunger depressed, releasing clouds of smoke-sized DDT particles to billow through her clothing. It was even pumped into her hair. Elisabet sneezed and wrinkled her nose at the unpleasant odour of the chemical, but did not complain. It was a necessary hurdle to cross if she was to be reunited with Günter and Joachim.

Her boys shared a room isolated from the main wards of the hospital. Both were conscious and Günter was obviously revelling in the clean sheets and pyjamas in which he was clad. Günter bounced out of bed when his mother walked into the room, but Joachim was too weak to follow suit. He stretched out his arms and burst into tears. Elisabet scooped up Günter and carried him to Joachim's bed where she embraced both her boys and showered kisses on them.

The nurse insisted Günter get back into his own bed and reprimanded him. "It is far too soon to be getting out of bed. You only had the antibiotic yesterday. I imagine it will be days before the doctor allows you up." The nurse went on to explain to Elisabet that though her boys had been fumigated and dosed with antibiotic, it might be days before the doctors could be certain that they were cured of typhus.

Toward evening, the hospital authorities laid on a car to take Elisabet home, though the act of kindness astonished her. The driver took her to the Army Clinic in Schöppenstedt, where she found her other children waiting for her. She was not allowed to embrace them, but could talk to them through a door with a grill set into it.

"Just a precaution, Frau Daeker," explained the army doctor. "We're rounding up some disinfecting equipment and clean clothes. As soon as that's done you can go in with them."

"How are you boys? Have you been good? Caused no trouble?"

405

"We couldn't help it, Mutti," Helmut said. "The army raided us and brought us here. I think they're going to destroy our apartment, pfifferling and all."

"You smell funny," Werner said.

"And where are Günter and Joachim?" Kurt added, before coughing.

"They are safe in Braunschweig, and getting better. How are you feeling, Kurt?"

"I feel sick, Mutti."

"They are going to dust you all with DDT and give you clean clothes. It will kill the lice and make you feel better. That's what they did to me. It doesn't hurt or anything, though it might make you sneeze."

"Then what happens to us?"

"I expect we'll just go home until Günter and Joachim are all better. Then they'll come home too."

"But we won't have a home," Helmut said. "The British said they were going to destroy it."

"Are you sure that's what they said?"

Helmut shrugged. "I can't understand English properly, but I think so."

Some soldiers and nurses came then and took the boys away to be washed, fumigated and clothed in clean garments. While that was going on, Elisabet went in search of the doctor once more.

"Have you had our apartment destroyed, Herr Doktor?" Elisabet asked.

"Good god, no. why would we do that?"

"My son said he heard the soldiers say that."

"He must have misheard, Frau Daeker. Your house is being thoroughly fumigated and I'm afraid your furnishings will be destroyed, but you'll be able to move back in a day or so."

"Then we are not to be detained or...or sent anywhere."

"I can't think of any reason for that to happen," the doctor said with a smile. "A week or two, and if your children in Braunschweig Hospital respond to the treatment, they should be home too. Of course, their release is not up to me. That'll be up to Doctor Kampf, the Public Health Officer. We have to be absolutely certain we've got rid of the typhus. That could kill hundreds if it spread."

"But my children are safe?"

"Yes, they are responding well to antibiotics, so they should make a full recovery."

Kapitel Zweiundzwanzig (22)

The British Army doctor was right in that the boys in Braunschweig Hospital recovered quickly, and would have been released by mid-October; save that Kurt now fell ill. The fumigation, coupled with clean clothes, had made them all feel better. Fleas and lice disappeared and there were no more bites on any of them, but the rash on Kurt's body worsened and he developed a fever. Typhus was diagnosed, and he was rushed into Braunschweig Hospital. Elisabet and the other boys – Helmut and Werner – were re-tested, but showed no symptoms. Just to be safe, though, their apartment was fumigated again. Kurt was dosed with antibiotics and started to recover, but the convalescence of all the children was slow. Their poor diet put added stress on their weakened bodies, and as the British Hospital lacked the facilities needed, the boys were moved to the American Hospital in Braunschweig. The better food made all the difference, and their health rapidly improved.

And then, to add more stress to the family, Elisabet suddenly experienced the onset of labour pains. She recognised them for what they were and took herself off to the clinic, together with her two healthy children. Again, a car made a rapid trip to Braunschweig. The hospital at Wolfenbüttel could have easily coped with a birth, as indeed could the Schöppenstedt Clinic, but taking her to the Women's Hospital in Braunschweig would mean she had easy access to her recovering children.

The birth of Elisabet's sixth child was not an easy one. The last year had been harrowing, and her health had suffered in her battle to bring her children safely to the West. Her body was thin, without reserves, without inner strength, and the ordeal exhausted her. The child came into the world on the twenty-fifth day of October, 1945 – a few weeks early – and marked, for Elisabet, a symbolic end to a dreadful year in which her whole life had been shattered and reconstituted. It marked too, a beginning, as her sixth child was a girl.

"Fine and healthy," the doctor said after examining mother and child. "Have you thought of any names?"

Elisabet had not considered names, not even that the baby might be other than another son. She was reluctant to name the child after one of her relatives, given her violent conception, but the memory of that horror, now thankfully dulled by swathes of experience, brought to mind something what the Russian rapist had told her in Schneidemühl.

"Soldiers rape wife Svetlana and kill daughter Rosa when burn village."

Elisabet had an idea but debated within herself if it was a proper thing to do. There had been so much hatred and hurt in Germany for so long, but the birth of a child was the complete opposite – a good thing with which to start a new life.

"I thought of calling her Rosa," she told the doctor.

"Nice name." The doctor continued on his rounds, and Elisabet set about bonding with her daughter. She would be both mother and father to this innocent child, and she vowed that an act of violence and hate would produce a life of peace and love.

By the time the family returned to their apartment in Schöppenstedt, November had brought rain and chilly winds. The British authorities had made up for the destruction of their furniture and bedding by finding rough but serviceable replacements. They now had beds, tables and chairs – nothing luxurious, but infinitely better than the things they had before.

Food was as ever a problem as the rations remained at subsistence level, and with a new baby, Elisabet could not go out to the forests in search of edibles. Mice had found their store of beech nuts and hazelnuts and reduced them to a pile of husks. Helmut and Werner managed to find another bag of clover and grass for the fishmonger's rabbits, but with winter approaching, there would be little enough left. The children scoured the orchards and fields for anything missed by hundreds of other gleaners and scraped together a few extra meals.

Heating was another problem. The apartment was cold and heat leaked out through cracks around the windows and holes in the ceilings. They plugged them as best they could with dried grass and rags, but it was still cold. The woods of the Elm Hills were littered with old beech wood, but Elisabet was reluctant to let her children walk the lonely kilometres to scavenge for fallen branches. They shivered, wrapped up in all their clothes and blankets until Helmut and Kurt took matters into their own hands.

* * *

"What we need is another Russian coal train," Helmut said.

"There are trains," Kurt said. "Down at the train yards."

"I know, but they are British trains. Are they even carrying coal?"

"British people must get cold too," Kurt reasoned.

They decided to investigate and set off for the southern end of town where the railway line linking Schöningen and Wolfenbüttel split into several lines. Freight trains were often shunted onto a spur line for a day or two, depending on the demands for goods in the other centres.

The spur lines were surrounded by a tall wooden and wire mesh fence, but the boys found gaps that they could look through. There was a freight train on the spur that day, but only of eight or ten carriages, two of which were canvas-covered open trucks. A guard was on duty, a German railway guard, whom the boys had seen before. He was dressed in the uniform of a Deutsche Reichsbahn official, but he did not carry a rifle. Stretched beyond their capacity, the British authorities had brought back hundreds of minor officials to handle mundane tasks and were in the process of interrogating senior officials for Nazi sympathies before allowing them into positions of authority again. This guard was an old man and known in town for his mellow attitude.

"It's Heinz," Kurt said. "Should we ask him if there is any coal here?"

"Do you think he's going to tell us if there is, dummkopf? No, we'll have to sneak in and have a look for ourselves."

They walked around the train yard, looking for a way in, and eventually found some loose boards. Helmut tugged at one and pulled it away enough to create a narrow opening. He stuck his head through and had a good look round.

"Nobody in sight. Come on."

Helmut wriggled through and Kurt followed. They found themselves near an abandoned line, where rusting rails ran into head-high weeds, now turning brittle and brown in the autumn chill. Coarse gravel crunched underfoot as they worked their way back to the freight trucks and crouched in the weeds staring out at them.

411

"What do you think is in them?" Kurt asked.

"How should I know? We'll have to take a look. The open trucks are our best bet."

"There might be food in the carriages," Kurt said. "There was in the Russian trains."

"We'll look later."

Helmut ran over to one of the open trucks and went to the back, looking for the attached iron ladder he had found on the Russian trucks. It was not there, nor did it look as if one had ever been there.

"What now?" Kurt whispered. "Do we try the carriages?"

Helmut looked up at the sides of the truck. "I think I could climb up there." He ran his hands along a narrow horizontal flange and studied possible handholds above it. "Give me a leg up."

With a good deal of grunting and pushing, Kurt heaved his brother high enough for him to get his feet on the flange. Helmut straightened and clung to the side for a few seconds before working his way up another half metre by thrusting the toes of his shoes into a crevice and clinging to rusted rivets. The canvas cover was not tied down tightly, and Helmut managed to work his head and shoulders under it. He said something unintelligible.

"What did you say?" Kurt asked. He looked around nervously for the guard.

Helmut withdrew from the canvas cover and looked down at his brother with a grin. "Coal, and lots of it. I'll throw you down some."

He pushed his way back in and, after a few moments, a lump of coal fell to the ground, followed by several more chunks. Kurt grabbed them and started stuffing his pockets, but soon filled them. He took off his jacket and started heaping the shiny black fuel onto the fabric. The lumps continued to rain down until Kurt knocked on the side of the truck.

"We've got enough."

Helmut jumped down and started collecting coal into his own jacket. They shivered in their shirtsleeves in the cool November air, so worked fast. When they could carry no more, they started lugging their burdens back through the weeds to the fence. Kurt went through first and Helmut had handed one bundle through to him when a heavy hand fell on his shoulder.

"What have we here, a pair of little thieves?"

Helmut dropped his bundle and twisted round to look up at the guard. "Herr Heinz," he squeaked. "We're not really thieves."

Heinz did not relinquish his grip. "So what would you call it when someone takes something that doesn't belong to him? I think the authorities will be glad to get their hands on you."

"It's only a bit of coal," Helmut protested. "Our whole family is cold and our Mutti has just had a baby."

"What are your names?"

"Er..." Helmut hesitated, chary of identifying himself. "Heinrich and...and Konrad, Herr Heinz."

"Your family name?"

"Er...Missel."

"I'm going to have to report this theft, you know."

"Please, sir, we only took it to get warm."

The guard looked at the boy beside him and at the scared expression on the face of the smaller one peering through the fence. "You," he said, addressing himself to Kurt. "Why didn't you run away?"

"He...he's my brother, sir."

"Loyalty is a commendable virtue, boy, but remember that you are German, and German's are not thieves."

"Yes, sir."

"This time, I will look the other way, but don't let me catch you here again. I have your names and if I see you again, I'll report you."

"Thank you, Herr Heinz."

"Go on. Take your coal and get out of here."

The guard lightly cuffed Helmut on the side of his head and walked away. Helmut thrust his jacket through the gap in the fence and climbed through. The two boys picked up their bundles and ran off.

Dusk was falling as they made their way through the town and many people watched them stagger through the streets with their heavy loads. One man stopped them and demanded to know what they were carrying and where they were going.

"It's ours," Helmut said.

The man grunted and grabbed at Kurt's bundle. A piece of coal fell out and the man raised his eyebrows in surprise as he picked it up.

"What's this? Coal? I'll trade you for it all."

Helmut considered the offer. "What have you got? Food?"

The man shook his head. "I've got this." He took out a pocket watch on a chain and opened it up. "Belonged to my father. It still keeps good time."

"We've got no use for a watch," Helmut said.

"I could just take your coal."

"You could, I suppose, but we'd cry for help and...and there are lots of people who might help us." The man hesitated, so Helmut continued on quickly. "There's plenty more coal where this came from. You could just help yourself to as much as you want."

414

"Where is it?"

Helmut told him about the loose boards in the fence around the train yards, the weeds and the coal trucks, but said nothing about the guard.

The man studied Helmut's face in the failing light, seeking signs of deceit. After a while, he nodded. "All right. Be off with you, and don't tell anyone else."

Helmut and Kurt reached home without further mishap and the family enjoyed a warm evening and comfortable night. They heard shots during the night, though they did not stir outside seeking explanations. These were available the next morning as the news swept through the town. Many men had descended on the train yard in the night, ripped away a section of the fence, and removed every last lump of coal from the trucks. The shots had come from British soldiers responding to an alarm from the guard on duty. They had failed to stop the thieves, who got clean away with several tonnes of the precious fuel. Security tightened around the train yard, and when the boys decided to try for coal again, found they could not even get close to the train.

*　　*　　*

The winter of 1945-46 was a hard one, frosts and snow coming early and relinquishing their icy grip late in the New Year. Their apartment was cold, and they needed heat, so Elisabet was forced to let her children wander far and wide looking for food and fuel. Werner guided Helmut and Kurt to the beech forest and loaded up their cart with dry branches. The wood burned well, giving off a lot of heat, and by making repeated trips even managed to obtain enough fuel to trade for food. They were not the only ones using the forest, of course, and every week they had to forge further in to find the wood they needed.

415

Rosa was a quiet baby, and Elisabet delighted in her care. She looked for useful things to do within the apartment, and included Joachim, who was too young to go out foraging, and Günter who, though cured of typhus, was still a sickly child, in these activities. They all became quite proficient at plaiting dried grass and weaving it into little place mats or rings for serviettes. It occupied their minds and hands on the short winter days and long nights, and she even traded them to neighbours for some soap, or a little sugar or coffee.

The older boys had found small amounts of beech nuts and hazelnuts, missed by the squirrels, in the Elm, and she soaked out the tannins and ground them up to make nutty-flavoured flour she could use to eke out their rations. Often, the older boys would come in from a day in the cold to find a warm fire and freshly baked bread or little cakes to reward them. Helmut sometimes killed a squirrel with a well-aimed stone, and they ate a little extra meat.

In the late spring, when the days were warming and longer, Kurt found a chicken run within a barn on the far edge of town, and a loose board in the fence lining an alley behind the barn. He investigated and sat curled up behind bales of hay watching the chickens for hours at a time. The chickens had just started laying again after the winter. He found the nests they made here and there in the barn, and stole an egg or two, careful never to take so many that the owner would become suspicious. Elisabet took the egg each time with thanks, and never asked questions about its origin, except the first time, when she took her son aside and sat him down.

"You're not going to tell me you just found this egg, are you?"

"No, Mutti. I went..."

"I'm not going to ask you where it came from, Kurt, but I want you to think about this question I'm going to ask you, and give me an honest answer. Will you do that?"

"Yes, Mutti."

"Will the owner of this egg suffer in any way because it has gone?"

Kurt screwed up his face in puzzlement. "Umm...I don't..."

"Were there more eggs at this place?"

Kurt's expression brightened. "Yes, Mutti."

"Will the owner notice one has gone?"

"Oh no, Mutti. I'm sure he won't."

"You do realise stealing is wrong, don't you?"

"Er...yes."

"But letting your family go hungry is more wrong," Elisabet said. "I'll say no more about it, and if an egg turns up every now and then, I won't be angry." She hugged and kissed her son, and he went off smiling.

The egg added a delicious flavour and texture to the next cake, and Kurt brought back another egg whenever he could sneak one away. As the egg supply became regular, Elisabet would sometimes take two or three and trade them for a special treat for the boys, a cake of chocolate or some hard jellied sweets.

Summer arrived, and the weather turned rainy. The rain turned soil to mud, and as they were now continually damp, it remained a depressing time despite the warmth. Helmut continued his forays into the town, scavenging anything that was not nailed down, and sometimes Werner would accompany him. Kurt continued to purloin eggs until one day he turned up looking furtive and concealing something in his jacket pocket.

"What you got there?" Günter asked.

417

Kurt grinned and brought out a tiny yellow bundle cupped in his hand. "It's a baby Chickie."

Helmut poked a finger at it. "It's not very big. Won't make much of a meal. You should have brought another egg."

"It's not for eating," Kurt said, sounding shocked. "It's my Chickie and it's going to lay eggs when it's all grown up."

"We're not keeping it, are we, Mutti?" Helmut asked. "That's just crazy."

"Oh, please, Mutti, I can keep it, can't I?" Kurt pleaded.

"Please." Werner and Günter added their pleas, and Joachim laughed delightedly.

"Want chickie," he said.

"I don't see why not," Elisabet said. "But Kurt, you will have to look after it, and find it food."

The chicken became part of their household. It lived in an apple box lined with an old shirt, and ate bread crumbs and the handfuls of chicken mash that Kurt now removed from the barn along with the eggs. It was this additional theft that brought his depredations to the notice of the farmer. The chickens laid eggs throughout the barn, making nests in the loose straw, and the farmer was largely unaware if a few went missing. However, the chicken mash and grain were stored in bins and one time Kurt was careless and left the lid up. The farmer knew a thief was at work and bought a dog. The next time Kurt raided the barn, the dog uttered a volley of barks and flew at him, and Kurt had to make a hurried exit, tearing his pants on the way out. He returned the next day for a cautious reconnoitre and found the fence repaired and no way in. His foraging had come to an end, and to make it worse, little Chickie grew up into a rooster, so there were no eggs from that source. Chickie remained Kurt's pet for about six months, and had just started foraging on its own in the garden when one day it disappeared. Whether it went looking for others of its kind, or whether somebody popped it in a pot, no one knew. Kurt cried for days, and could only be consoled by the thought that somewhere, little Chickie ruled over a flock of chickens of his own.

"Dummkopf," was Helmut's response.

"Be nice to your brother," Elisabet murmured.

The school reopened, and the older boys now found themselves having to sit in crowded classrooms learning boring lessons from recently reinstated teachers. The first response of the occupying powers had been to prohibit Germans from holding any position of responsibility, but as post-war society wound down into chaos, they saw the need of bringing in responsible people who knew the language and the culture. Every applicant had to fill out a long and complicated 'fragebogen' or questionnaire that examined every aspect of that person's life and belief. Any hint of having belonged to the Nazi Party or even having worked alongside party members was enough to prevent a person being employed.

After a while, as it became apparent that few people had been able to avoid knowing and working with Nazis, the regulations were relaxed somewhat, and life started on the long road back to normal. The boys found themselves being taught by teachers who strove to hide their National Socialist roots.

At home, Elisabet had just three year old Joachim and baby Rosa to look after. The baby slept much of the time, so Elisabet found herself spending more time with her youngest son than she had had the opportunity in the past. She would play with him, or at other times sit and watch him play on his own, thinking back over his short life and the many things that had happened in it.

∗   ∗   ∗

Ricardo left Königsberg, as he said he would, but not before gifting me with my youngest son. You may wonder how a married woman could so forget her duty to her husband as to have a child with another man. I have wondered so, but in truth a man and a woman may grow apart in the best of times, let alone in a savage and divisive war. In love, one can forgive one's partner anything, but in a society that puts husband against wife, parent against child and neighbour against neighbour, the little things become magnified, and trust is put aside.

I have said how I was raised to believe in the Communist ideal and how my husband Rudi was a Nazi Party member. This did not seem to matter at first, for we loved each other and did not seek to convert the other to our cause. Rudi was not a typical Nazi and did not practice the hate that was encouraged within the Party, at least not at home. Rudi had used his party membership to secure a relatively safe position in a unit that remained out of the front lines. He would return at intervals from his duty with his Wehrmacht unit, bearing tales of what he had seen and done behind the lines in Poland. Jews were rounded up and relocated; dissidents were shot, and the Polish population oppressed. It made me ashamed to be associated with such actions, and by degrees, I became ashamed of my husband's part in the war effort.

Perhaps that is why I was attracted to a healer – someone who gave life rather than took it, who improved people's lot in life. I had even seen Ricardo operate on a Russian prisoner of war and save his life, though I do not know what happened to the man afterward. In any event, I felt increasingly distant from my husband, and gave into my desires when my Spanish doctor evinced such need. It was a foolhardy act, and I paid for it, though good often comes from evil. If I had not erred, I would not have had my darling Joachim.

Ricardo left Königsberg in May 1942, and Rudi came home on leave in the middle of August. He was happy to be home and I put my best face on it for the sake of the children who were delighted to see him. Inside, I dreaded telling him I was expecting another man's child. Even if I had wanted to hide my indiscretion, I could not. Rudi was as capable of counting back as anyone, and he knew he could not be the father. I waited until the children were asleep and told him. I expected anger and prepared myself for it, but not for such deep hurt and sorrow. His expression, when I told him, was one of hopeless resignation, like a prisoner informed of his imminent execution.

"Who is the father?"

"A doctor at the hospital."

"His name?"

"It doesn't matter. He's no longer there. He volunteered for the front."

Rudi thought about this for a while. "At least he is a patriotic German," he said at last. "I suppose I must be grateful for that."

I should have left it at that, but I didn't. "Spanish actually."

"A foreigner? A man who takes advantage of the women left behind?"

"Yes," I whispered.

"Did you love him? Do you love him?"

"Perhaps at the time," I said. "He did not love me, but he was a lonely man far from his home, whose heart was broken, and I was sorry for him."

"Do you feel sorry for many men? Has this happened before? Or since?"

I shook my head. "No Rudi. Never. Apart from this one time, I have been faithful."

He smiled wanly. "One is either faithful or not faithful. Having been unfaithful once you cannot claim to have been a faithful wife."

Tears streaked my cheeks, for despite our differences, Rudi was a good man and a good father. He had done nothing to deserve this, but having done it, I could not undo it. We could only make the best of it and move forward. I said so.

He said nothing.

"I am sorry, Rudi. I would take it back if I could. I have wronged you, but...but I still love you. Please forgive me."

He got up then, and I involuntarily flinched, believing his anger would now spill over, but apart from a brief look of reproach for believing that of him, he would not look at me. Without saying another word, he left the house and I did not see him for three days.

When he returned, he said little beyond taking a tearful farewell of his children. He included Helmut and Kurt, for he had always treated them as equal to his own natural children.

"You are leaving already?" I asked. "When will you return?"

He faced me, and searched my face as if imprinting it on his memory. "I have been granted a transfer," he said. "They are sending me to the front."

"Rudi, no. Don't put yourself in harm's way."

"If your Spanish doctor can do it, then so can I. I would not have you think less of me."

I was crying by now. "There is no need, Rudi. I made a mistake, but you are my husband. I need you."

Rudi smiled tiredly. "I'm not being sent anywhere very dangerous. I'm to be attached to General Paulus' Sixth Army. We are heading for Stalingrad."

He left, and I never saw my husband again. The German army captured Stalingrad, but in the bloodiest battle of the war, the Russians surrounded the city and recaptured it, forcing death or captivity on the German soldiers. My fifth son Joachim was born in January 1943, and such were the communications on the front, that it was not until a month or two later that I heard Rudi had gone missing in action at the end of the previous year. I was on my own with five sons to raise.

Kapitel Dreiundzwanzig (23)

Germany was a land in flux, a land crushed first beneath the jackboot of National Socialism and then hammered into the dust by the relentless efforts of its enemies. Now it struggled against the policies of four occupying powers that ripped the Reich asunder and forced millions of people to become refugees in their own country. Elisabet and her family had travelled hundreds of kilometres from Königsberg, now deep inside the Soviet zone and renamed Kaliningrad. Many of their neighbours in Schöppenstedt had fled the Russian advance too, finding sanctuary in the relative peace and prosperity of British occupied Germany. All things are relative though, and though the British were milder masters, life for Germans was still hard. Other displaced persons came later, drifting from one place to another, unwelcome in the lands that they had once called home, having to look for somewhere else to lay their heads.

One such person was Gotthard Scherer, a Yugoslav-born German fleeing the new Communist regime that had flooded like a red wave over his homeland. He came from the south in troubled times, travelling alone, and working his way from town to town, using his skill with wood to eke out a living. He was a simple man, taciturn, most at home with a block of wood and his tools, but he had a loving heart and enjoyed the company of children. Whenever he came into a new town, he would find a sheltered spot and pull out his tools and start whittling and carving. Children would gather, and then adults, watching him work. Some wooden toys he would give away, but others he would sell, and when he did so, he intimated that he was handy in other ways. He had a

424

knack for fixing broken things, and even if he was unsuccessful with some items, he repaired enough to buy his food and shelter.

By the time Gotthard arrived in Schöppenstedt in 1947, he was tired of wandering from town to town, and looking for a place to settle down. The town appealed to him, as did the populace. Having an easygoing personality, he got on with most people and soon secured a job as a general handyman at the school, where he became a popular figure with many of the school children. Not every child, however. There are always people who resent outsiders, and most towns and cities in the occupied zones were crowded with outsiders – displaced persons, 'foreigners'. The adults were prejudiced and their children learnt from them. Gotthard became a target for a few of the older boys, being taunted for his odd accent and made fun of for his simple ways.

One day, after he had finished his duties at the school, he ambled out onto the streets in the early evening, taking in the mild summer air. His route took him close to where the Daeker family lived, though at that time he was only vaguely acquainted with the younger Daeker boys. A gang of older boys followed him, hanging back whenever other pedestrians approached, and drawing closer on empty stretches of road. As he turned the corner into the street where the Daekers lived, a boy ran up and pushed him hard. Gotthard stumbled on the kerb and fell to his knees.

"That's right, Ausländer," the boy crowed. "On your knees in front of decent Germans."

The other boys gathered round, pushing and punching, calling him names. He struggled to his feet and faced his tormentors. Beyond the four large boys he could see smaller children gathering, and spoke placatingly, trying to calm the situation.

"I am an expatriate German, boys. I was only born in Jugoslawien, that's all."

The boys laughed and started chanting out names. "Ausländer, foreigner, Jugoslawisch, stummes schwein..."

"Leave him alone!" A small boy burst upon the scene and pushed one of the older boys away. "You don't know what you're talking about."

"What have we here? Another blutiger Ausländer," jeered the boy who had pushed Gotthard. "What you gonna do, little Ostdeutscher? Fight all of us? I know you, Daeker. Helmut, isn't it?"

"If I have to," Helmut replied. "But I'm not alone either."

"That's right," another one squeaked from behind the older boys.

They turned to see two pale young boys looking determined. Half hidden behind them, a smaller boy stood with his fists bunched.

"My brothers Kurt, Günter and Werner," Helmut said.

"You think I care? They're just babies."

"You should care."

"Go away, Nazis," Günter said.

"What did you just call us?"

"Nazis," Helmut said. "That's what Nazis do – gang up on people and bully them. We've had enough of them."

The boy looked slightly uneasy. "You're talking nonsense."

"Am I? I know you, Axel Kreb. Your father used to be a Party member here in Schöppenstedt, didn't he? People talk, you know. I wonder what people

426

would say if they knew you were becoming a Nazi like him."

"You're full of scheisse, Daeker." Axel shrugged and turned away, posturing for the sake of his friends. "Come on, let's leave these dumme Ausländers. They're not worth the trouble." He swaggered off, and his cronies went with him.

Gotthard smiled at Helmut. "Danke dir, junger Daeker."

"You're welcome, Herr Scherer. There are some real clodhoppers – bauerntölpel – in this town."

Gotthard took out a handkerchief and dabbed at the palm of his hand where he had scraped it on the road. Helmut noticed the wound for the first time.

"Come home with us, Herr Scherer. You can wash your injury in our kitchen. We live just up the road."

Gotthard was willing enough to get washed up, so accompanied the four boys back to their apartment. Helmut made the introductions, avoiding any mention of confrontation or altercation.

"Mutti, this is Herr Scherer. He works at the school and he fell over in the street and cut himself. I told him he could wash his injury here. I hope that was all right."

"Of course it is." Elisabet smiled and wiped her hands on her apron. "Good day, Herr Scherer. Please come in. I'm afraid you have caught me in the middle of some baking, but you are welcome to get cleaned up. Werner, find a clean towel for Herr Scherer. Gunter, fetch the soap."

While Gotthard cleaned his hand, and the smaller boys fussed around him, Elisabet boiled water for a pot of coffee, and buttered some nut bread she had just made.

427

"Will you join us for a cup of coffee, Herr Scherer?"

"Please," Kurt urged.

"You are very kind, Frau Daeker, but please, will you call me Gotthard? Whenever anyone says 'Herr Scherer', I have to stop myself looking around for my father." Gotthard chuckled. "He was very strict and to tell the truth, I was a little afraid of him."

"Of course...Gotthard, but it would be strange for me to use your first name, if you continued to be so formal. My boys all know you, so perhaps you had better call me Elisabet."

Gotthard smiled and looked around. "I know your older boys from the school, Elisabet, but not this little one."

"This is Joachim. Say hello, Joachim." Joachim hid behind his mother and pressed his face into her skirts. "I have a daughter also, a baby, asleep in the other room."

Gotthard smiled at the shy little boy, and drank his coffee. He made complimentary comments about the nut bread. "I can taste hazelnut...and something else?"

"Beech nut," Elisabet said. "We collect it from the Elm forest."

They made idle conversation while the boys stood around and listened to the adults talking. When he had finished his bread and coffee, Gotthard stood and thanked Elisabet for her hospitality.

"Perhaps you would allow me to repay your kindness."

"Really, there is no need. It was a pleasure."

Gotthard looked at the kitchen window, where rags stuffed into a crack in the wooden frame served to keep a draught out. "Will you allow me to mend your window frame? I enjoy working with wood."

Elisabet hesitated, and Helmut immediately said, "He is very good, Mutti. I have seen him fix many things at school."

"I don't doubt your ability, Gotthard, but really, there is no need. I'm sure you have other work that needs your attention." Elisabet blushed and looked away. "Paying work, I mean. I cannot..."

"It would make me happy to be of service, Elisabet." Now Gotthard hesitated, opened his mouth, closed it again, and then blurted, "All I ask is the p...pleasure of your company."

"Then I would be delighted," Elisabet said. "Thank you."

Gotthard returned the next day after school with his bag of tools and set to work removing the glass and the split window frame, fashioning a new one from a length of timber he had brought with him. He refitted the glass, puttied it into position, and when it was dry a day or two later, painted it. The repaired window frame now stood out against its weathered and faded neighbours, so Gotthard now set about sanding, filling and painting the other surrounds.

He whistled while he worked and the children, particularly the younger ones, stood around and watched, chattering away as if the man was one of their friends. After a bit, he set them to work, rubbing the old paint away with a wire brush and sandpaper. Elisabet pottered in her kitchen or sat in the evening sunshine with some knitting or darning and enjoyed the feeling of domesticity. She invited him to stay for the evening meal that first evening, and after a bit, as his repairs expanded to the wainscoting and walls, to minor plumbing and electrical maintenance, he stayed more often and brought over some of his rations to augment theirs.

429

Gotthard fitted in with the Daeker family, and having no family of his own, unofficially adopted them. His job at the school did not pay much, but he was able to augment his income as a handyman around town. The townsfolk were slow to accept a stranger into their midst, as was evidenced by the harassment he faced at the hands of Axel Kreb and the like, but he finally gained acceptance when he performed a valuable service for the town fathers.

Schöppenstedt had two main claims to fame. One was the museum dedicated to Till Eulenspiegel, a mythic character who had become part of German folklore. Supposedly born near the town, he was seen as a joker or a trickster who delighted in playing tricks on people, exposing their greed, folly and hypocrisy. The other claim to fame was St. Stephen's Church which was built in the twelfth century and had a famous leaning tower. Inside were carved stone pillars depicting figures from pagan mythology. The church was the means by which Gotthard gained the approval of the town.

One spring day in 1947, a rainstorm provided the final straw for an aging piece of timber in the church roof. Weakened by decay and beetle, it sagged, dragging with it a tile, allowing water to pour into the ceiling. The damage was slight, but the hole needed to be repaired as quickly as possible to prevent further destruction. Unfortunately, the previous builder had been a Nazi and was currently under investigation by the British Occupying Force, so the principal of the school had the bright idea of bringing in Gotthard Scherer as a temporary arrangement. The town council agreed.

His skill was evident, and he effected such subtle repairs that it was hard to tell where the old timber

430

ended and the new began. The church warden praised him and suggested Gotthard be kept on as a perma-permanent builder. The town council agreed once more, and offered him the job, but Gotthard declined as gracefully as his shy nature would allow.

"I'm a simple man," he said, "And I enjoy working with children. I'd rather keep my job with the school, though I'm happy to help out when I'm needed."

Gotthard's standing in the town thereafter improved, and he received many other offers of employment. He still found time to visit the Daeker family though, and delighted in spending time with the children, carving toys out of scrap wood or playing games with them. Often, he would take them out, a little band of boys, and they would explore the town and the surrounding countryside, sometimes returning with something useful, other times with just smiles on their faces and a cheery farewell for the man who had come into their lives.

His interest in her children pleased Elisabet, but it also gave her cause for concern – not because she was afraid for their safety in his presence, but because it made her insecure. For nearly twelve years she had been the strength upon which her children relied, the one person in a shifting world who was always there for them, supplying their needs, caring for them, giving love equally. Her late husband Rudi had loved the children too, both his own and the two older boys he had adopted, but he was away often and it was Elisabet who reared them. For nearly twelve years she had been central to all their lives, but now there were signs that they were growing up and straining the bonds that bound them to her, particularly the older ones. Helmut had matured since they left Königsberg; he was now nearly twelve, becoming strong and

431

determined, and he spent more time with Gotthard than with her. She feared the other boys would follow his lead.

"I cannot just ask him to stop seeing my boys," she told Rosa one day when the older boys were at school and Joachim was playing outside. "He is a friend...indeed, more than a friend, and it would be wrong to send him away just because my sons like him so much. I fear, though, that if he stays, he will weaken the bonds that bind my family together. Perhaps they will even look to him rather than to me. Would that be wrong? What am I to do, Rosa?"

Rosa looked up from the building blocks strewn across the floor upon hearing her name. When it was not repeated, she went back to trying to balance one on top of another.

Elisabet idly watched her daughter play, but her mind was concentrated on her problem. She thought back over her life and knew that her strong independent streak had encouraged her to become self-reliant – that, and her determination to live life on her own terms. Even her marriage to Rudi had not altered that. He had been a National Socialist, but she had openly remained a Communist – as if she had been daring him to make an issue of it. She had remained true to herself and had not surrendered to any man.

"No, that's not quite true," she murmured. "I loved Hermann...what was his last name?" Elisabet thought for a moment, and then shook her head. "It doesn't matter. I loved him at the time, but he left me. I loved Joseph too, but I wouldn't follow him to America; and Rudi, I must have loved him enough to marry him and bear his children..." She remembered Königsberg days and the bitter regimentation of the

Third Reich and the Party members that Rudi had associated with. "I fell out of love...else why Ricardo? Poor Rudi, the shock was too much for you, wasn't it? You were a decent man and a good father but, in the end, I needed more. And as for you, poor little Rosa, your father doesn't count at all, I'm afraid. I've loved four men, given myself to four men, but on my terms. I never relinquished control of my life to any of them."

A strong odour assailed Elisabet's nostrils. She picked Rosa up and kissed her before carrying her into the next room and changing her soiled nappy. The cloth went into a bucket with water and a splash of bleach, and she balanced the little girl on one hip while she made herself a cup of coffee. Rationing had eased slightly in the last eighteen months but real coffee was still unobtainable. The boys collected acorns from the forest, and Elisabet roasted them and ground them up to make an acceptable coffee substitute, particularly with the addition of a little wild chicory root. She set Rosa down and went to the back door and looked out into the little enclosed patch of garden where Joachim was happily digging in the dirt with an old spoon.

"Are you all right, Joachim? Do you want a drink of water?"

The little boy looked up. "No thank you, Mutti." He went back to his game.

Elisabet sat down again and sipped her acorn coffee. Privation and rationing had stripped her of her need for milk and sugar and she enjoyed the plain taste of the unadulterated brew.

"So what do I do about Gotthard?" she asked Rosa.

The little girl gurgled and said something that might have been interpreted as 'da da'.

Elisabet smiled. "No, my sweet one, he is not your dada." She sipped again, an idea congealing in her mind. "But he does like all my babies as if they were his own. Would that be the answer? If Gotthard was here all the time, my children would be here too."

The more she thought about it, the better she liked the idea. Gotthard was a hard worker, good with his hands, if perhaps quiet and reserved. He would provide for her family without fear of taking over, would provide the father figure her growing boys needed without imposing his own ideas on them. They would still be raised her way.

"But I don't love him," she told Rosa. "Do you think that matters?"

Elisabet considered the love of the men in her life and what it meant. Love was all very well, but it did not keep its promises. Her father had loved her, but he had still died and left her. Hermann had loved her and left her, as had Joseph and Ricardo. Rudi had loved her too, and she had loved him, but it had not been enough. All those men were in her past. They had all been loved and had loved in return, but promises of undying affection had withered with time and changed circumstance. Perhaps love was not necessary.

"There was no love involved in making you, sweet Rosa, yet here you are and I love you enough for two. In fact, I love all my children enough for two parents – I am Mutti and Vati to you all. I don't need anyone else, Rosa...really." Elisabet thought for a few minutes before sighing gently. "But, on the other hand, it would be nice to be with a good man."

434

The children came home from school and an hour later, Gotthard turned up. He greeted the boys, lightly punching the arms of Helmut and Kurt, hugging Günter and Werner, and tossing little Joachim into the air, precipitating squeals of glee from the boy. Rosa received a small present, another building block carefully shaped and smoothed with the edges and corners carefully rounded. She gurgled and uttered nonsense syllables.

When the children had eaten and been read bedtime stories, the smaller ones were tucked in, and the older ones allowed to stay up reading or playing quiet games. Elisabet and Gotthard took cups of coffee and sat on the backdoor step in the dark, enjoying the cool of the summer's evening. They sat in companionable silence and looked at the darkening sky and the glow of the street lights.

"You like my boys, don't you?" Elisabet asked, her voice little more than a murmur.

"Of course I do. And your little girl too."

"What of the bigger girl? Do you like her?"

"Eh? What bigger girl?"

"Me, Gotthard. Do you like me?"

"Er, yes, of...of course."

"How much?"

"H...how...what do you mean, Elisabet?"

"I can see how you are with my children. You act with them as if you were their father."

"They are good children. You have raised them well."

"Thank you, but they need a father." When Gotthard kept silent, she pressed onward. "They need someone like you."

Gotthard buried his face in his mug of coffee, holding it in both hands. When he spoke, his voice

435

was muffled and uncertain. "I...I will, of course, con-continue to be as a...a father to them, if you wish."

"Not as a father, Gotthard, but a father."

"What do you mean?"

"I want you to be their father."

"But only your husband can be their...you want me to marry you?"

"Don't you want to?"

"I...er, hadn't thought...er, yes. I suppose so."

"You don't sound very sure."

"I hadn't expected..." Gotthard put down his mug and turned to face Elisabet, his face in shadow and unreadable. "It is customary for the man to ask the woman."

"In normal times, yes. These are not normal times."

"Even so."

"Well?"

Gotthard cleared his throat. "Elisabet Daeker, will you marry me?"

"Yes, Gotthard Scherer, I will."

They were married in September of 1947 and Gotthard moved into their tiny, and now severely overcrowded apartment, but as Gotthard only had a single man's room at the school, staying there was not an option. Then an opportunity presented itself, but it was one that ripped the family apart.

The British Occupying Force made an offer to struggling families in their zone. Under an official program, German boys could be fostered out to homes in England for short periods to ease the burden on their families. Elisabet hated the idea of any of her boys moving away and said so in no uncertain terms.

436

"How can I send my boys away? What sort of a mother would I be?"

"A good mother. You want what is best for your children, don't you? This is a great opportunity."

"They are too young to be leaving home."

"It need only be for a short while. They will return."

Gradually, Gotthard talked her round, pointing out that the overcrowding would be just as likely to drive them away, and that the offer from the British was too good for the boys to pass up. They would be fed, clothed and educated in England, and would escape the hardship that presently gripped a divided Germany struggling to reconstitute itself. It would not be forever, he said.

Elisabet still hated the idea, but Gotthard persuaded her. And so, in early 1948, twelve year old Helmut, eleven year old Kurt, and ten year old Günter, were accepted into the program and set off for England. When it came right down to the day, Günter decided he did not want to go, but the arrangements had been made and he could not back out.

"I don't want to go," Günter sobbed.

"I don't really want to either," Helmut said. "But we have to. It won't be forever, and who knows, we might enjoy it."

"That's right," Gotthard said. "Think of it as an adventure."

"Like stealing coal," Kurt said with a brave grin. "But this time you can come along too, Günter. We'll look after you."

Günter blew his nose and wiped his eyes. "I'd like that."

437

Everybody still cried at the bus stop, and after many protestations of love and regret, three brave little boys were farewelled, tears streaming down their faces. Werner, Joachim and Rosa waved goodbye, calling out last messages as the bus pulled away, carrying their older brothers to a foreign land and uncertain future. Elisabet held herself together for the sake of her boys, but as the bus passed out of sight, she fell to her knees on the grass beside the road and cried out in anguish.

"My boys. My lovely boys have gone. When will I see them again?"

Kapitel Vierundzwanzig (24)

Gotthard was right saying it would be an adventure. The three Daeker boys were put in a boys' home near Leeds in Yorkshire and were enrolled in a nearby school. They learned English among all their other subjects and suffered the cruelty that young boys everywhere were capable of inflicting when their schoolmates discovered where they were from. Shunned for their nationality, they clung to who they were and to each other, finding solace together. It was not a happy time for Helmut, Kurt and Günter, but they stuck it out, determined to be strong for each other and for the sake of their family back home in Schöppenstedt. They imagined the shame that would reflect on them if they admitted failure in England.

It was not all hardship and homesickness though. A circus came to town, and the boys from the home were allowed to go. The three Daeker boys sat together, separate from the others and watched the clowns and the trained dogs, the elephants and the trapeze artists. It was a welcome treat after the hardship and deprivation of recent years, and if post-war Britain was an austere and alien place, it was still far better than a country struggling to raise its head from among the ruins of its cities.

The boys laughed and applauded the antics of the performers, chattering away in German, and many heads turned in their direction, with some disapproving stares and a few pointed comments made. They paid little attention, sharing the crisps and candy floss they had bought on the way in. After the show, they filed out with all the rest of the audience and were accosted by a middle-aged couple with a fair-haired teenage girl in tow.

439

"Guten tag," the man said. "We couldn't help noticing you are German."

"So? What's it to you?" Helmut automatically put himself in front of his brothers, ready to protect them.

"We were German once, though our families have been here for hundreds of years. Our names are Victor and Magda Schroeder. This is our daughter Anna. Have you been in England long?"

Helmut shrugged, but politeness won out over a reluctance to talk to strangers. "A few months, Herr Schroeder."

"Is your family over here? Your parents?"

"We're at the Hopeton Boys' Home. Why do you want to know?"

"It can be a daunting prospect coming to a new country at the best if times, and this is not one of those times. Regrettably, England is not very welcoming to Germans at the moment. We just wanted to tell you, you do have friends here."

Helmut looked the couple over carefully. "Thank you, but we must be getting back. They will wonder where we got to." He started to walk away, guiding his brothers.

"Can we come and see you at the Home?" Magda Schroeder said.

"If you want," Kurt replied.

Helmut cuffed him lightly. "Dummkopf."

"What's your name?" Victor called. "Who should we ask for?"

"Daeker," Kurt called, and then hurried to catch up with his brothers.

The three boys lost themselves in the circus crowd, moving slowly toward the entrance and then out onto the streets of Leeds. They walked in silence for the most part, the two younger boys lost in memories of the things they had just seen, the older boy weighing up the more recent events and what they meant.

"Why did you tell him that?" Helmut asked.

Kurt looked up, his mind full of clowns and dancing dogs. "Tell who what?"

"That Herr Schroeder. You told him our name and that they could come and see us. I don't want them to."

"Why not?" Günter asked.

"And you told him where we live," Kurt added.

Helmut grunted. "I don't trust him. Why did he want to know?"

"Perhaps he just liked us," Günter said.

"Then you're a dummkopf too. He doesn't know us, so how can he like or dislike us?"

"I liked him," Kurt declared. "Frau Schroeder too. Even Anna looked nice though she didn't say anything."

"You just like anyone who smiles at you," Helmut said. "Who knows what he really wants? Hopefully, we've seen the last of them, but if they do come round to the Home and ask to see one or other of us, you just make sure we're all there together."

"Why?" Günter asked.

"So I can protect you."

"From what?"

"I don't know, do I? Could be anything. Maybe...maybe he wants to take you away and make you work in a coal mine or...or something worse. You can't trust these verdammt Englanders."

"But he's German."

Helmut shrugged. "Living over here with the English. Doesn't that make you even a little bit suspicious?"

441

"But we live over here too," Kurt said.

"Ach, you're just babies," Helmut muttered. "What would you know?"

The Schroeders did come to the Hopeton Boys' Home a few days later and asked for the Daeker boys. The matron in charge, after extracting information on their identities and where they lived, allowed them to meet the boys in one of the rooms.

"Hello, boys. Remember us from the circus? Victor and Magda Schroeder. Matron says you are Helmut...is that right? And Kurt? And Günter?"

"Hello Herr Schroeder. Hello Frau Schroeder," chorused Kurt and Günter.

Helmut scowled and jerked his head. "Why are you here?" he asked bluntly.

"To see you," Victor said.

"To make friends," Magda added. "Children can be lonely when they come to a new country, especially when the rest of their family is back in Germany."

"We manage," Helmut said.

Victor smiled. "I'm sure you do, but you can never have too many friends, can you?"

That visit was the first of many. After a bit, the Home allowed the Schroeders to take the Daeker boys out to the park to walk in the fresh air and have an ice-cream at one of the tea kiosks, or if the weather was foul, as it often was, even in summer, to go to the cinema. They had a little bother at the first cinema they went to, as the national anthem played and Helmut steadfastly refused to stand for the king.

"He's not my king. I'm German and proud of it."

The other patrons protested vociferously and the manager came bustling up to see what the trouble was. When he heard, he asked the Schroeders to leave his cinema, and they all had to. Magda and Victor made the best of it, explaining to Helmut that stand-standing for the anthem was only politeness to their English hosts.

"An acquaintance of mine felt the same way as you when he first came to England," Victor said. "He was thrown out of many cinemas until he came up with a solution. Do you want to know what it was?"

Helmut shrugged.

"He waited until the lights dimmed and then stood up, just standing casually. When the anthem played and everybody else got up, he could tell himself that he hadn't stood up for the king, but because he wanted to. When everybody sat down, he remained standing for a few moments and then sat down too."

"Sounds like cheating."

"Perhaps, but everybody was happy and he got to see the film. There's nothing to be gained by getting people angry."

The next week, at a different cinema, as the lights dimmed, Victor stood up and, with Helmut beside him, pretended to examine the scrolled decorations around the ceiling of the theatre. The anthem played, and everyone around them stood, but nobody said anything and a few moments after everybody else sat down, Victor and Helmut joined them.

"See?" Victor murmured. "You did not stand for the king, yet nobody noticed."

"But you don't do this, except with me," Helmut said. "Why not?"

"I see it as a mark of respect for the country that has invited my family to live here. I'm still German in my soul, though outwardly I'm an Englishmen. It's politeness, nothing more."

Helmut considered this and for a few more weeks, stood up before the anthem, though Victor did not join him. Then, one day, he shrugged and stood up with everybody else.

"You're right," Helmut told Victor. "It means nothing."

Over a period of months, the Schroeders came to take the boys out more often and started taking them to the little shop that Victor owned – he was a tailor of some skill – and to their home. Victor even took them to performances of the band he conducted in his spare time. The Schroeders endeavoured to make all the boys welcome, but Helmut wanted to do things, to see things, rather than sit around with another family. Günter missed his own home, and though he was unfailingly polite, the kindnesses the Schroeders showed him only made him miss home all the more. Only Kurt responded with enthusiasm. He waited impatiently for every visit, could hardly contain himself on the drive over to the Schroeders house, and hung on every word the adults uttered, content to sit around and listen to their conversations. Anna was a source of interest too, and he liked to watch her read, or listen to phonograph records with her, or just follow her around, asking questions. She thoroughly reflected the local culture and under her guidance, Kurt started to appreciate things English.

"You're becoming a proper little Englander, aren't you?" Helmut said after one visit.

"Thank you."

"It wasn't meant as a compliment, dummkopf."

Kurt looked hurt. "What's wrong with it?"

"You're a German, not an Englander. You'll be going home soon, so there's no point getting too interested in this place...or the Schroeders for that matter."

"I like them," Günter said, "But I want to go home."

"I like home," Kurt said cautiously, "But I like it here too, and the Schroeders are very nice to me."

Helmut wrote home, asking if they could return, even though it would mean a bit more crowding in their apartment. The reply was slow in coming, and when it did, there was a surprise in it. First of all, he had another baby sister and second, the whole family had moved to the little town of Watzum, near Schöppenstedt.

"Hello Helmut," Gotthard said in his letter, "You will be happy to hear you have a baby sister called Angelika, born at the end of September last. Your mother says she is named for somebody called 'Geli' you all knew and says you will remember her. She is a darling little baby and I'm sure you will love her as much as we all do, when you meet her. A funny story is attached to her birth. Werner and Joachim sat on the doorstep outside while your sister was being born, staring up at the sky as if looking for something. When I came out to fetch them in to see little Angelika, I asked them what they were looking for. 'We're waiting for the stork to bring the baby,' Werner said.

"We had an opportunity to move out of the poky little apartment in Schöppenstedt and into a more spacious one in Watzum, just south a kilometre or two. A doctor in the town wanted to move into Schöppenstedt, so her house became vacant. Not that we have the whole house, of course, only the upper floor. The Elber family lives on the ground floor, with their two daughters Elsa and Charlotte, and Werner, Joachim and Rosa enjoy playing with them. Angelika is a bit young as yet. There is a garden of sorts

445

running down to a lane and the wall of the church-churchyard with a big cemetery beyond it. We have a well to supply water in the grounds of the house, but your Mutti is worried that water percolates past dead bodies in the graveyard, so we must all make the trip down to another well half a kilometre away to collect water daily.

"There is a row of huge linden trees along the lane behind the house and one of the Elber girls – Elsa is her name – climbed up in one of them and couldn't get back down. They had to call the Feuerwehr to come and get her down. The Elbers keep pigs also. It's a bit smelly at times, but they give us meat when they slaughter one of the animals. They do it on the street outside, collecting up the blood for blutwurst and making sausages of the meat. Your Mutti adds what herbs and spices she can find and the sausages are delicious."

A little later, Gotthard wrote again, directly addressing Helmut's plea.

"You are, of course, welcome to come home any time you want. Let me know and I'll send money for the fares. You won't be returning to Schöppenstedt, or even Watzum, though, as we have all moved to Wuppertal near the River Rhein. If you have an atlas at the school, you can look it up. It is close to the big cities of Essen, Duisburg, Düsseldorf and Köln. It is a lovely place with lots of parks and trees, though it was heavily bombed. The good news is that we have a proper house to live in, with a vegetable garden, and there is plenty of building work to be had. If you decide to come home, give me some warning and I can probably get you a job. Take care, Helmut, and give my love to Kurt and Günter too. We all miss you and look forward to seeing you. Gotthard."

Helmut showed the letter to his siblings and told them he was heading home as soon as Gotthard sent him the money. He asked his brothers to accompany him.

"It's been nice enough here," he said, "But it's time we went home."

"I am home," Kurt muttered.

Günter was ambivalent – he liked it in England, but he did want to go home and see his family, particularly his brother Werner. He would have gone with Helmut if Kurt had not asked him to stay.

"I don't want to go back to Germany – at least, not yet. Won't you stay with me a while, Günter? The Schroeders are really very nice, you know. They like you too."

Günter looked from Helmut to Kurt, wanting to please both his older brothers. Helmut shook his head and shrugged so Günter said, "All right, Kurt, maybe for another few weeks."

Kapitel Fünfundzwanzig (25)

Helmut returned home the next month, travelling by train to the coast at Harwich in Essex, then by ferry to the Hoek van Holland, and train again to Wuppertal. Günter followed a few months later, having given in repeatedly to Kurt's pleadings to stay a bit longer. He had fallen in love with England, like his brother Kurt, and lost no opportunity of telling people. He especially admired the police.

"They don't carry guns," he said. "Yet they still catch bad people. It's wonderful."

Kurt stayed on in England, however, living with the Schroeders until 1952. He was now fifteen years old, and had imbibed English customs and language so well, he often thought of himself as English. The Schroeders were musically minded and Kurt had even sung as a choir boy in York Minster. The tenor of his infrequent letters home disturbed Elisabet, so she wrote asking him to leave England and rejoin his family. He vacillated; torn between two families he loved, and toward the end of 1952, gave in to his mother's pleas.

It was an emotional parting from the Schroeders, who regarded Kurt as a son, and scarcely six months passed before Magda Schroeder turned up on the Scherer family doorstep in Wuppertal, demanding to see 'her Kurt'. Naturally, Elisabet was upset at her demands, and then devastated when Kurt expressed a desire to go back to England with his foster mother. Elisabet refused to let him and played her trump card, saying that Kurt was under-age and could not leave without her consent. Magda returned to England, but the drama did not end there, for she kept up a correspondence with her foster-son and in 1955,

448

when Kurt turned eighteen, he told his disbelieving family that he was going back to England to be with his other family – the Schroeders. Once there, he changed his name to Schroeder and lost all contact with his natural family.

Helmut had taken the building job with his stepfather Gotthard, and learned a trade. When he came of age, he went travelling through Germany, seeing his birth country and supporting himself by working at whatever came to hand. The experiences of his boyhood trek across a land torn apart by war instilled in him a restlessness and desire for new things. He loved excitement and held down a string of jobs that offered danger or something different from the normal run of life. Although he roamed throughout Germany, he could not enter the Soviet zone, or return to the city of his birth. Königsberg had become part of Russia and was renamed Kaliningrad. He never managed to get back there.

Günter and Werner, the natural sons of Rudi Daeker, were inseparable, and decided that they too wanted to see the world. They looked further afield than Germany though, and took advantage of the assisted passage program to Australia. For two years they roamed around the huge southern continent, working in the cities, the towns and on the sprawling cattle stations, the tropical plantations, and on the fishing boats, enjoying themselves immensely. They sent back glowing reports of the country and Elisabet started to think seriously about a new start for her family. Helmut decided to see for himself and left for Australia, joining his younger brothers.

Little Joachim meanwhile, was growing up to be an inquisitive and intelligent young man. His older brothers were off adventuring and he only had sisters

449

at home, so he went exploring the countryside on a bicycle, cycling to many of the neighbouring cities and along the Rhein. The flat farmland of Lohausen near Düsseldorf attracted him and here he probably passed a young English boy also out exploring the countryside on his bicycle. Though they did not meet then, and neither of them knew it at the time, the English boy would later work for Joachim on the other side of the world.

When Joachim turned nineteen, in 1962, he became eligible for military service in West Germany. Not being attracted to this way of life, he looked around for an alternative, and as his family was moving to Australia, thought that he would join them. It was only for a couple of years, he told himself, and then he could return to Germany.

Elisabet ruled the little family in Wuppertal, and Gotthard was content to let her do so. She made enquiries, re-read the letters from her sons, and found out all she could about the sun-burnt land Down Under, so different from the land she had lived in all her life. She weighed up the advantages and disadvantages and came to a momentous decision. The family took ship to Australia – Elisabet and Gotthard, their daughters Rosa and Angelika, and their son Joachim. They did not forget Kurt, even though he appeared to have forgotten them. They sent word that they were off to Australia and invited him to join them. He declined, saying that England supplied all his needs, and also expressed surprise that, if they were leaving for the ends of the earth, they were not going to New Zealand, as that Dominion was far more British in its outlook than Australia.

The family made Adelaide in South Australia their home and it is here that Elisabet's story came to an end a few years later. She left a husband, five sons and two daughters secure in the knowledge that she had protected and guided them through a horrific period of Germany's history and delivered them safe into a land of opportunity. The children married and raised families of their own, all of them in Australia except Kurt. He was adopted by the Schroeders, then married and moved to Portugal later in life, and now corresponds with the rest of his family.

Information on the fate of other family members – ones left behind in Königsberg –came later, after the fall of Communism. Elisabet's brother Hans, who had been wounded, took up arms with the Volkssturm and died in the battle for Königsberg. His body was buried in a mass grave. For sixty years his fate was unknown, and his wife in Dresden refused to remarry, convinced that he would return one day. Then the Russian authorities released his Erkennungsmarke or Identity Tags, and the truth came out. Elisabet's father was bedridden by the time the Soviets took the city. He greeted the Russian soldiers with comradely greetings but they laughed and ripped his mattress to shreds with their bayonets, releasing clouds of down feathers. The old man suffocated.

Joachim and his wife made a journey back to Germany in May 2012. They visited Schöppenstedt and Watzum, and in the school at Watzum found an old lady who, by some strange coincidence, was Elsa Elber, the girl who had lived in the same house as Joachim all those years before. They spoke for a long time, exchanging reminiscences and catching up on the course of their lives.

Elisabet's life was a full one, living through an historic time. She gave love freely to those in need and sacrificed everything for her children. Through it all, she maintained a firm belief in who she was and what she wanted out of life. Her early years were shaped by the political beliefs of her parents in East Prussia and being raised in the beautiful city of Königsberg on the Baltic. The city has fallen into Russian hands, bears a different name, and has had much of its beauty destroyed, but Elisabet and her boys could still say with pride...

"We came from Königsberg."

Leben macht weiter...
Life continues...

About the Author

Max Overton has travelled extensively and lived in many places around the world – including Malaysia, India, Germany, England, Jamaica, New Zealand, USA and Australia. Trained in the biological sciences in New Zealand and Australia, he has worked within the scientific field for many years, but now concentrates on writing. While predominantly a writer of historical fiction (Scarab: Books 1 – 6 of the Amarnan Kings; the Scythian Trilogy; the Demon Series; Ascension), he also writes in other genres (A Cry of Shadows, the Glass House trilogy, Haunted Trail, Sequestered) and draws on true life (Adventures of a Small Game Hunter in Jamaica, We Came From Königsberg). Max also maintains an interest in butterflies, photography, the paranormal and other aspects of Fortean Studies.

Most of his other published books are available at Writers Exchange Ebooks,
http://www.writers-exchange.com/Max-Overton.html
And all his books may be viewed on his website:
http://www.maxovertonauthor.com/
Max's book covers are all designed and created by Julie Napier, and other examples of her art and photography may be viewed at www.julienapier.com

If you want to read more about other books by this author, they are listed on the following pages...

The Amarnan Kings Book 1: Scarab - Akhenaten

A chance discovery in Syria reveals answers to the mystery of the ancient Egyptian sun-king, the heretic Akhenaten and his beautiful wife Nefertiti. Inscriptions in the tomb of his sister Beketaten, otherwise known as Scarab, tell a story of life and death, intrigue and warfare, in and around the golden court of the kings of the glorious 18th dynasty.

The narrative of a young girl growing up at the centre of momentous events - the abolition of the gods, foreign invasion and the fall of a once-great family - reveals who Tutankhamen's parents really were, what happened to Nefertiti, and other events lost to history in the great destruction that followed the fall of the Aten heresy.

Max Overton follows his award-winning trilogy of ancient Greece (Lion of Scythia, The Golden King, Funeral in Babylon) with the first book in another series set in Egypt of the 14th century B.C.E. Meticulously researched, the book unfolds a tapestry of these royal figures lost in the mists of antiquity.

Ebook:
http://www.writers-exchange.com/Scarab.html

Print: https://www.createspace.com/900002544

The Amarnan Kings Book 2:
Scarab – Smenkhkare

Scarab – Smenkhkare follows on from the first book in this series as King Akhenaten, distraught at the rebellion and exile of his beloved wife Nefertiti, withdraws from public life, content to leave the affairs of Egypt in the hands of his younger half-brother Smenkhkare. When Smenkhkare disappears on a hunting expedition, his sister Beketaten, known as Scarab, is forced to flee for her life.

Finding refuge among her mother's people, the Khabiru, Scarab has resigned herself to a life in exile, when she hears that her brother Smenkhkare is still alive. He is raising an army in Nubia to overthrow Ay and reclaim his throne. Scarab hurries south to join him as he confronts Ay and General Horemheb outside the gates of Thebes.

Max Overton's series on the Amarnan kings sheds new light on the end of the 18th dynasty of pharaohs. Details of these troubled times have been lost as later kings expunged all records of the Heretic king Akhenaten and his successors. Max Overton has researched the era thoroughly, piecing together a mosaic of the reigns of the five kings, threaded through by the memories of princess Beketaten – Scarab.

Ebook:
http://www.writers-exchange.com/Scarab2.html

Print: https://www.createspace.com/3983488

The Amarnan Kings Book 3:
Scarab - Tutankhamen

Scarab and her brother Smenkhkare are in exile in Nubia, but are gathering an army to wrest control of Egypt from the boy king Tutankhamen and his controlling uncle, Ay. Meanwhile, the kingdoms are beset by internal troubles and the Amorites are pressing hard against the northern borders. Generals Horemheb and Paramessu must fight a war on two fronts while deciding where their loyalties lie – with the former king Smenkhkare or with the new young king in Thebes.

Smenkhkare and Scarab march on Thebes with their native army to meet the legions of Tutankhamen on the plains outside the city gates. The fate of Egypt and the 18th dynasty hang in the balance as two brothers battle for supremacy and the throne of the Two Kingdoms.

Ebook:
http://www.writers-exchange.com/Scarab3.html

Print: https://www.createspace.com/3983501

The Amarnan Kings Book 4: Scarab - Ay

Tutankhamen is dead and his grieving widow tries to rule alone, but her grandfather Ay has not destroyed the former kings just so he can be pushed aside. Presenting the Queen and General Horemheb with a fait accompli, the old Vizier assumes the throne of Egypt and rules with a hand of hardened bronze. His adopted son, Nakhtmin, will rule after him, and stamp out the last remnants of loyalty to the former kings.

Scarab was sister to three kings and will not give in to the usurper and his son. She battles against Ay and his legions under the command of General Horemheb, and aided by desert tribesmen and the gods of Egypt themselves, finally confronts them in the rich lands of the Nile delta to decide the future of Egypt.

Ebook:
http://www.writers-exchange.com/Scarab4.html

Print: https://www.createspace.com/3983517

The Amarnan Kings Book 5: Scarab - Horemheb

General Horemheb has taken control after the death of Ay and Nakhtmin, and forcing Scarab to marry him, ascends the throne of Egypt. The Two Kingdoms settle into an uneasy peace as Horemheb proceeds to stamp out all traces of the former kings. He also persecutes the Khabiru tribesmen who were reluctant to help him seize power. Scarab escapes into the desert, where she is content to wait until Egypt needs her.

A holy man emerges from the desert, and demands that Horemheb release the Khabiru so they may worship his god. Scarab recognises the holy man and supports him in his efforts to free his people. The gods of Egypt and of the Khabiru are invoked and disaster sweeps down on the Two Kingdoms as the Khabiru flee with Scarab and the holy man. Horemheb and his army pursue them to the shores of the Great Sea, where a natural event or maybe the hand of God alters the course of Egyptian history.

Ebook:
http://www.writers-exchange.com/Scarab5.html

Print: https://www.createspace.com/3983534

The Amarnan Kings Series Book 6:
Scarab - Descendant

Three thousand years after the reigns of the Amarnan Kings, the archaeologists who discovered the inscriptions in Syria, journey to Egypt to find the tomb of Smenkhkare and his sister Scarab, and the fabulous treasure they think is there. Unscrupulous men, and religious fanatics, also seek the tomb, either to plunder it or to destroy it. Can the gods of Egypt protect their own, or must they rely on modern day men and women of science?

Ebook:
http://www.writers-exchange.com/Scarab6.html

Print: https://www.createspace.com/4277389

Scythian Trilogy Book 1: Lion of Scythia

Alexander the Great has conquered the Persian Empire and is marching eastward to India. In his wake he leaves small groups of soldiers to govern great tracts of land and diverse peoples. Nikometros is a young cavalry captain left behind in the lands of the fierce nomadic Scythian horsemen. Captured after an ambush, he must fight for his life and the lives of his surviving men. He seeks an opportunity to escape but owes a debt of loyalty to the chief, and a developing love for the young priestess.

Ebook: http://www.writers-exchange.com/Lion-of-Scythia.html

Print: https://www.createspace.com/4109734

Scythian Trilogy Book 2: The Golden King

The chief of the tribe is dead, killed by his son's treachery; and the priestess, the lover of the young cavalry officer, Nikometros, is carried off into the mountains. Nikometros and his friends set off in pursuit.

Death rides with them and by the time they return, the tribes are at war. Nikometros is faced with the choice of attempting to become chief himself or leaving the people he has come to love and respect, returning to his duty as an army officer in the Empire of Alexander.

Ebook: http://www.writers-exchange.com/The-Golden-King.html

Print: https://www.createspace.com/4198204

Scythian Trilogy Book 3: Funeral in Babylon

Alexander the Great has returned from India and set up his court in Babylon. Nikometros and a band of loyal Scythians journey deep into the heart of Persia to join the Royal court. Nikometros finds himself embroiled in the intrigues and wars of kings, generals, and merchant adventurers as he strives to provide a safe haven for his lover and friends. The fate of an Empire hangs in the balance, and Death walks beside Nikometros as events precipitate a Funeral in Babylon.

Ebook:
http://www.writers-exchange.com/Funeral-in-Babylon.html

Print: https://www.createspace.com/4232367

Sequestered
By Max Overton and Jim Darley

Storing carbon dioxide underground as a means of removing a greenhouse gas responsible for global warming has made James Matternicht a fabulously wealthy man. For 15 years, the Carbon Capture and Sequestration Facility at Rushing River in Oregon's hinterland has been operating without a problem – or so it seems.

Annaliese Winton is a reporter, and when mysterious documents arrive on her desk that purport to show the Facility is leaking, she investigates. Together with a government geologist, Matt Morrison, she uncovers a morass of corruption and deceit that now threatens the safety of her community and the whole northwest coast of America.

Liquid carbon dioxide, stored at the critical point under great pressure, is a tremendously dangerous substance, and millions of tonnes of it are sequestered in the rock strata below Rushing River. All it takes is a crack in the overlying rock and the whole pressurized mass could erupt with disastrous consequences. And that crack has always been there...

Ebook:
http://www.writers-exchange.com/Sequestered.html

Print: https://www.createspace.com/3987028

Made in the USA
Charleston, SC
22 December 2013